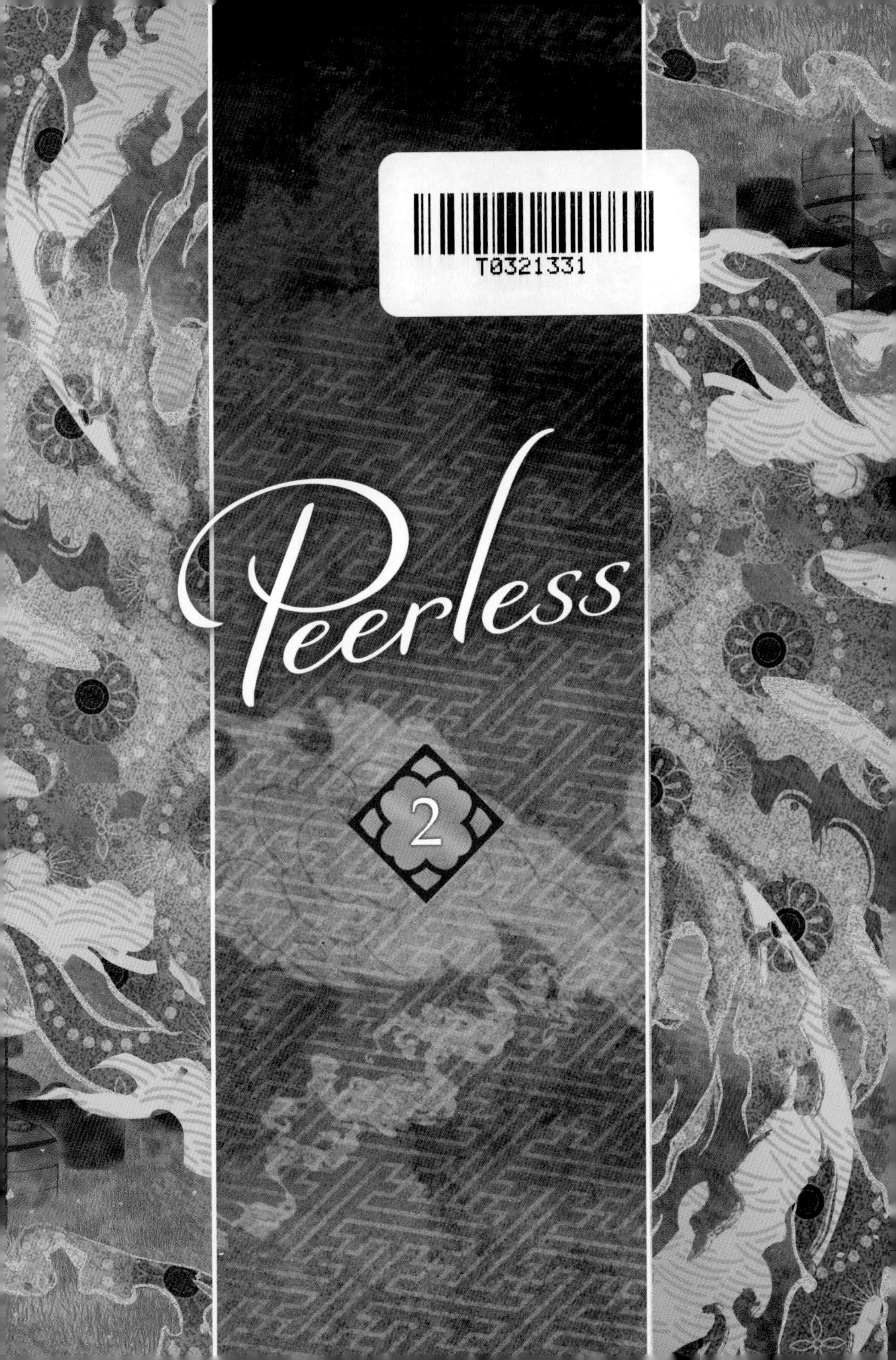
Peerless
2

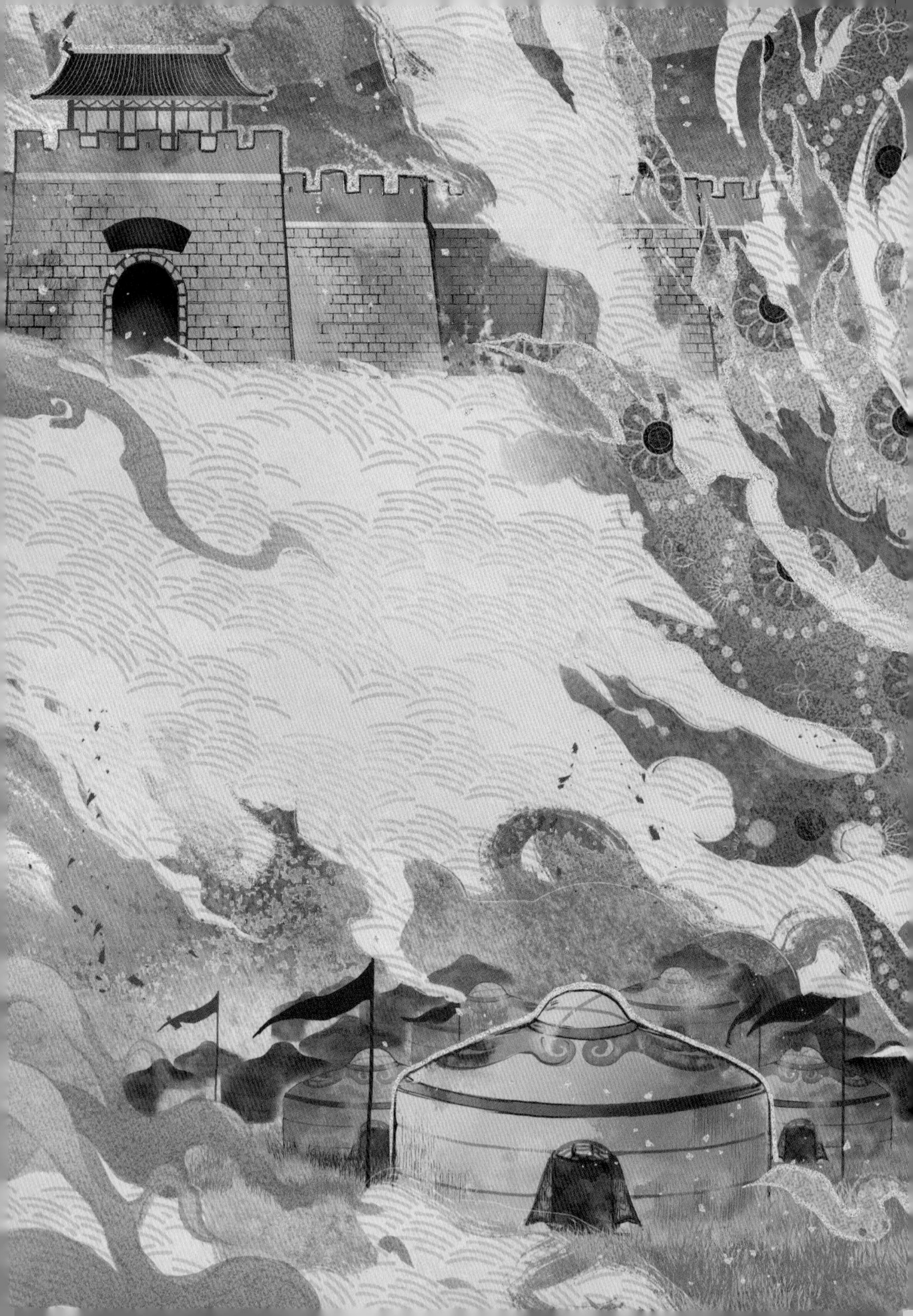

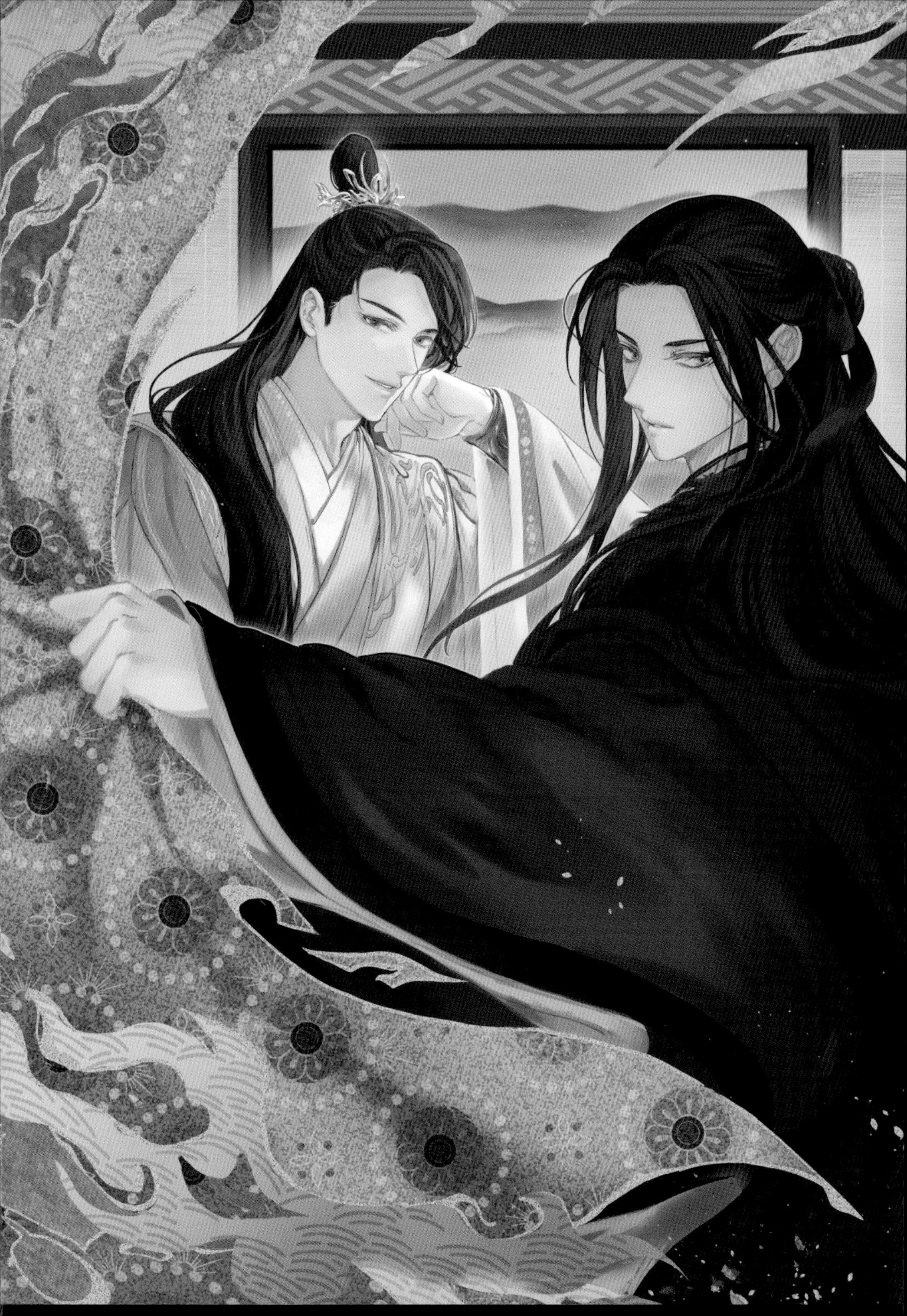

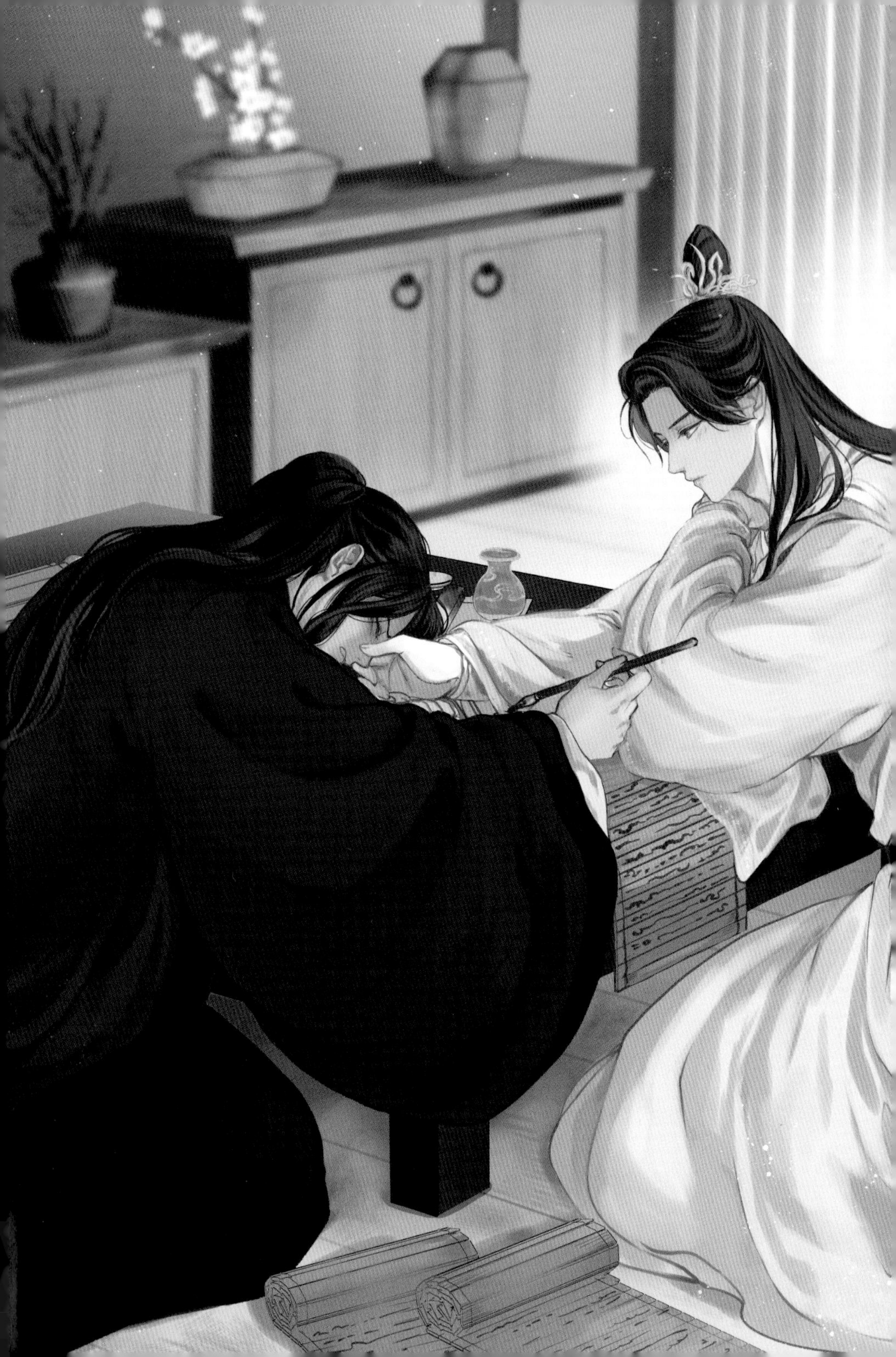

Peerless

2

WRITTEN BY
Meng Xi Shi

TRANSLATED BY
Faelicy

COVER AND ILLUSTRATIONS BY
Me.Mimo

Seven Seas

Seven Seas Entertainment

Peerless: Wu Shuang (Novel) Vol. 2
Published originally under the title of 《无双》 (Peerless)
Author©梦溪石 (Meng Xi Shi)
English edition rights under license granted by 北京晋江原创网络科技有限公司
(Beijing Jinjiang Original Network Technology Co., Ltd.)
English edition copyright © 2024 Seven Seas Entertainment, LLC
Arranged through JS Agency Co., Ltd
All rights reserved

Cover and Interior Illustrations by Me.Mimo

Seven Seas press and purchase enquiries can be sent
to Marketing Manager Lauren Hill at press@gomanga.com.
Information regarding the distribution and purchase of digital editions is available
from Digital Manager CK Russell at digital@gomanga.com.

Follow Seven Seas Entertainment online at
sevenseasentertainment.com.

TRANSLATION: Faelicy
ADAPTATION: Imogen Vale
COVER DESIGN: M. A. Lewife
INTERIOR DESIGN: Clay Gardner
INTERIOR LAYOUT: Karis Page
COPY EDITOR: Jehanne Bell
PROOFREADER: Kate Kishi, Hnä
EDITOR: Kelly Quinn Chiu
PREPRESS TECHNICIAN: Melanie Ujimori, Jules Valera
MANAGING EDITOR: Alyssa Scavetta
EDITOR-IN-CHIEF: Julie Davis
PUBLISHER: Lianne Sentar
VICE PRESIDENT: Adam Arnold
PRESIDENT: Jason DeAngelis

ISBN: 979-8-89160-263-2
Printed in Canada
First Printing: October 2024
10 9 8 7 6 5 4 3 2 1

Peerless

40

B Y THE TIME Cui Buqu had recovered his strength, five days had passed.

Within that span, the new envoy sent by the Khotanese king arrived in Liugong City. He brought a generous gift: another extraordinary jade. Khotan was abundant in high-quality jade; though the new gift wasn't an unrivaled treasure like the Jade of Heaven Lake, it was still a beautiful piece. This jade had been carved into a pendant with exceptional qualities. Keeping it on one's person, it was said, could calm the spirit, and it released a unique fragrance when worn, like a perfumed sachet.

Yuchi Jinwu had perished outside Liugong City; his death was not the fault of Khotan. But if the Khotanese king still wished to forge an alliance with the Sui dynasty, he had to make a great show of sincerity. Fearing the first jade was lost forever, he'd sent a second envoy carrying this new gift to demonstrate his earnest desire for friendship.

Feng Xiao sent Pei Jingzhe with the Jiejian Bureau eagle riders to escort the envoy to the capital. Su Xing, who remained in their custody, was to be remanded to the Jiejian Bureau for interrogation. Feng Xiao entrusted them with a memorial describing the details of the case, including, of course, the contributions of the Zuoyue Bureau.

As for Qin Miaoyu, whether intentionally or otherwise, Feng Xiao neglected to mention her. She was like a mirage, a brief yet lovely vision that, like a fleeting dream of spring, vanished without a trace.

Feng Xiao said no more, and Cui Buqu didn't ask. The case of the Khotanese envoy had been cracked, and the contributions of the Zuoyue Bureau documented. For him, this was sufficient. He had matters of greater importance to attend to. It was fine to keep some secrets from one another, to avoid asking unnecessary questions—knowing too much was never a good thing.

After all, their identities were both rather special.

The moment he was no longer dizzy, Cui Buqu refused to take his medicine, which was more bitter than goldthread. He instructed Qiao Xian to prepare for their journey west. When it came to choosing a travel companion for Cui Buqu, however, Qiao Xian and Zhangsun Bodhi had a difference of opinion.

Zhangsun Bodhi considered himself the more skilled martial artist, and thus believed Cui Buqu would be safer if he came along.

But Qiao Xian considered herself just as adaptable in the face of the unknown as Zhangsun. More importantly, Zhangsun Bodhi was one of the two deputy chiefs of the Zuoyue Bureau. If he went with Cui Buqu, only a single deputy would remain in the capital, one with no knowledge of martial arts. Qiao Xian thought Zhangsun should return to headquarters to oversee things.

Watching them argue, Feng Xiao smiled lazily. "With me there, what difference would Zhangsun's presence make?"

Only then did Qiao Xian remember Feng Xiao was accompanying them as well.

This man was indeed a formidable martial artist, but Qiao Xian had never seen him as one of their own. Subconsciously, she worried Feng Xiao might purposely drag them down.

Finally Cui Buqu announced his decision. "Zhangsun will head back to the capital. Qiao Xian alone is enough."

"But..." began Qiao Xian.

"If Deputy Chief Feng is unable to guarantee my safety, the Jiejian Bureau might as well find themselves a new leader."

"Ququ, when you put it like that, I feel so stressed!" Feng Xiao sat with his chin propped in his hands, his posture careless and graceful. He showed no hint of stress.

Since it was Cui Buqu who'd made the call, Zhangsun had no objections.

Cui Buqu's mouth quirked in a half smile. "I'll be relying on your protection, Deputy Chief Feng. Though we solved the murder of the Khotanese envoy, the jade was still damaged. If the emperor decides to pursue the matter, I fear you'll find yourself in a difficult position. I suggest you earn yourself some credit on this journey or your thousand-mile trip will have been in vain."

"In that case, wouldn't it be better if I waited for you to finish and killed you on the way back, snatching all the credit for myself?"

Qiao Xian glared at him in alarm, but Cui Buqu wasn't concerned in the slightest. Anyone who said such a thing would never do it. "There's one more thing. As the four of us are traveling together, we'll need disguises and new identities."

Even if people these days were more open-minded than in the past, two men and two women running off to the Western Regions together would still raise some eyebrows. Feng Xiao's languid expression didn't change a mote. "Why don't we find a merchant group to travel with?"

"It's not easy to find a group of trustworthy merchants," said Cui Buqu. "Most only stop briefly in the city of Qiemo before continuing their journey west along other routes. We'll disguise ourselves as two married couples. Kucha isn't far from Apa Khagan's encampment; our story can be that we're visiting relatives in Kucha and conducting some minor business along the way."

Feng Xiao arched a brow. "Couples? Who's with whom?"

"Qiao Xian with me, and you with Jinlian," said Cui Buqu. "Our households have been friends for generations, and we make our living trading textiles. There's a family in Liugong City with the surname Ye. Years ago, their daughter married a businessman from Kucha, and they had a son. Now that the son is grown, he's bringing his own wife to Kucha to visit his paternal aunt at the behest of his parents."

Feng Xiao hadn't expected Cui Buqu to have made such thorough preparations; he'd already found this family and created identities to match. "Why would anyone bring their wife out so far?"

Cui Buqu smiled. "Because coincidentally, his wife happens to also be from Kucha. The same year she came to the land of the Hans with her father, she married into the Ye clan. So not only is he visiting his aunt, he's also bringing his wife to see her family."

"I object to playing half of a couple," said Feng Xiao. "Can you imagine someone as outstanding as myself—a man capable of toppling nations with my magnificence—marrying an older woman?"

"Not a problem," said Cui Buqu. "Qiao Xian is a master of disguise. Your appearance is too eye-catching anyway. We wouldn't want to draw the attention of bandits; you ought to be made up to look more ordinary."

Feng Xiao brought a hand to his own face. Cui Buqu expected him to protest, but instead he said, "Ququ, do you also find my face eye-catching? Tell me the truth: did you fall for me at first sight?"

"I did."

Feng Xiao scrutinized him as if he suspected an imposter. After a moment, he said suspiciously, "Why didn't you argue?"

Cui Buqu was unruffled. "Anyone who claims to be unmoved by Deputy Chief Feng's face is an obvious liar. However—"

"Now, now," said Feng Xiao. "No need to continue. I'm sure nothing good will follow."

Cui Buqu smiled. "However, after spending a day with you, any normal person would be forced to give up their fantasies, no?"

Feng Xiao was speechless.

He spent the entire day ruminating over Cui Buqu's words. On the way back to his residence, he couldn't resist asking Pei Jingzhe, "What do you think? Was he praising or insulting me?"

The corner of Pei Jingzhe's mouth twitched. "From a certain point of view, it could be considered praise."

Feng Xiao hummed in affirmation. "I knew it. He's trying to cover up his faltering heart." He chuckled. "The chief of the Zuoyue Bureau, a rare genius, has fallen for me. Surely anyone in my shoes would be delighted. In deference to his feelings, my venerable self shall deign to travel with him!"

Pei Jingzhe wished very much to remind him, *Sir, did you forget the last part of what he said? The first part was hypothetical—the last bit was the main point!*

What Cui Buqu had been implying was this: no normal person would fall in love with Feng Xiao.

But Feng Xiao had already selectively forgotten both the last half of the statement and Pei Jingzhe's reaction. He hummed a little tune as he sauntered toward his quarters—tonight, he was sure to have a lovely dream.

Cui Buqu didn't know what wonderful dream Feng Xiao had. But he did observe the next day that Feng Xiao's face was bright and dewy, his complexion practically glowing. Jinlian was no blushing maiden, and she'd looked at Feng Xiao plenty the day before. Yet upon seeing him in the light of a new day, she was overwhelmed. It was as if someone had shoved a bouquet of flowers in full bloom right before her eyes, their splendor and radiance stamped into memory for the rest of her life.

Göktürks had strong features, and they valued strength of the body as well. Their men were broad and strapping—none were like Feng Xiao, so stunningly beautiful. Feng Xiao's beauty was all the more exceptional because it wasn't the delicate kind. His lovely face concealed a power capable of ending anyone's life. Even at her age, Jinlian Khatun couldn't stop her heart from fluttering.

Cui Buqu shot Feng Xiao a glance. Why did he feel this oleander spirit had grown more provocative overnight? Now he was flirting in broad daylight!

Catching him looking, Feng Xiao returned his gaze with a brilliant smile. *Because you admire me so,* he thought, *I'll let you take a few more glances.*

For his part, Cui Buqu found the exchange entirely baffling. What was this man thinking?

Feng Xiao had been blessed by the heavens from birth. His appearance was dazzling, his martial arts incredible. His intelligence outshone the vast majority, and he naturally viewed everyone else as beneath him. Over the twenty-plus years of his life, countless men and women had fallen for him—even a royal princess among them—yet he considered none deserving of his attention. Those he saw as intellectual equals and worthy opponents were fewer still. If Fo'er, the foremost martial expert of the Göktürk Khaganate, learned Feng Xiao only considered him halfway to an opponent, he'd probably fall down dead from rage.

Cui Buqu was the exception. The pair of them had gone head-to-head several times, and though Feng Xiao had never suffered unduly, neither did he gain much advantage. He'd even been roped into this journey to the Khaganate with Cui Buqu. Such a thankless errand hadn't featured in any of Feng Xiao's plans, but here his perfectionist tendencies had fully manifested. He'd been involved in this matter from the start and was unwilling to abandon it halfway. Plus, if he used this opportunity to observe the arrangements the Zuoyue Bureau had made within the Western Regions, perhaps he could turn the situation to his advantage.

Time and again, he found himself making exceptions for Cui Buqu—this alone was proof of the man's singular status. In Feng Xiao's eyes, though Cui Buqu could not be considered a friend, he could be counted as a worthy opponent. The man lacked even the strength to truss a chicken; he was plagued by illness and spent half his time at death's door. Yet this contrast made his perseverance and resourcefulness shine all the brighter.

Feng Xiao had to admit he was growing more and more interested in Cui Buqu. He was looking for more chances to challenge him, and this trip to the Western Regions ought to provide plenty of opportunities.

At Cui Buqu's insistence, Qiao Xian disguised Feng Xiao. Unfortunately, Feng Xiao had been born with a pair of exquisite eyes. No matter how she adjusted his appearance, it was impossible to conceal them. She could only direct her efforts elsewhere, darkening his skin and dressing him in a set of rough-spun clothes.

But Feng Xiao's expression turned stormy when Qiao Xian tried to rub dust and grass into his hair. He rejected her firmly.

"That's enough." Turning the porcelain of his skin into sun-beaten tan was already pushing the limits of what he could endure.

Qiao Xian was dissatisfied. "What kind of merchant family could produce someone with hair like yours? A family busy trying to make ends meet wouldn't pay that much attention to their appearance!"

Cui Buqu had changed his clothes, but his face was delicate and refined; he looked no more like a merchant than Feng Xiao. Qian Xiao had made several adjustments, and now he appeared appropriately crude and sleazy. He knew Feng Xiao's neurotic obsession with cleanliness had flared up again, so he took a slow sip of tea before saying, "I have a proposal. A way you won't need to dirty your hair or darken your skin."

Feng Xiao raised a brow and waited. He knew with absolute certainty that Cui Buqu's idea wouldn't be to his liking.

Sure enough, Cui Buqu said, "Disguise him as a woman. Let's have a beautiful young lady."

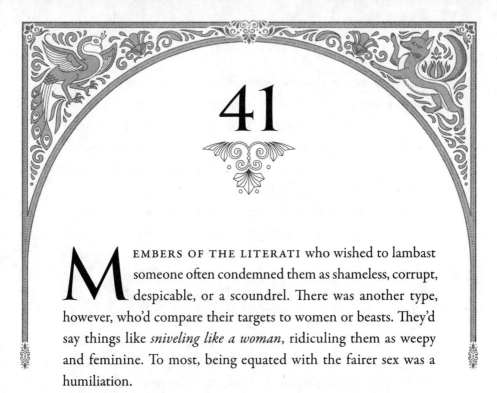

41

MEMBERS OF THE LITERATI who wished to lambast someone often condemned them as shameless, corrupt, despicable, or a scoundrel. There was another type, however, who'd compare their targets to women or beasts. They'd say things like *sniveling like a woman*, ridiculing them as weepy and feminine. To most, being equated with the fairer sex was a humiliation.

Feng Xiao disdained such vulgar views. Once someone rose to his or Cui Buqu's station, everyone else in the world, whether man or woman, could be generally divided into two categories: friend or enemy, useful or useless. Those who were quick and adaptable, like Qin Miaoyu, might receive leniency. Su Xing, on the other hand, received nothing of the sort. When Feng Xiao made a judgment of character, gender never entered the equation.

But now he faced a tiny dilemma.

Was the cleanliness of his clothes and hair more important? Or his dignity as a man?

A real man knew where to bend. Just as he'd called Cui Buqu *Daddy* on that cliff without hesitation, Feng Xiao once again chose the first option with nary a second thought.

Thus the party remained a group of four, but the dynamics were somewhat altered.

To avoid being slowed down, they brought no servants—other than the four of them, they merely hired two coachmen and one guide to take them to Qiemo. This also suited the fake identity Cui Buqu had fashioned for himself as Master Ye, a man from a small family without much to flaunt. It would look strange if he were accompanied by a gaggle of maids.

After leaving Liugong City, they headed west in three carriages. Cui Buqu's health was still fragile, so they traveled slowly; by the time they'd emerged from the boundless golden desert, everyone had swallowed nearly half a month's worth of sand. Only then did they spy the dark silhouette of city walls in the distance.

"Is that Qiemo up ahead?" Cui Buqu coughed twice and lifted the carriage curtains to look outside. A pungent smell assaulted his nose—the burning scent of desert sands, scorched by blazing sun and whipped by stinging winds. He started to cough once more.

A hand reached over and drew the curtains shut.

"Your lordship's health is poor; don't expose yourself to the sands. Your wife will worry if you fall ill again."

The speaker's words were measured, her voice deep for a woman yet exceedingly gentle. Upon hearing it, anyone would yearn to glimpse her face.

Anyone, that was, but Cui Buqu. He failed to turn his head at the sound of her voice, and his coughing increased in violence.

Watching his plight, not only did the speaker not stop, her enthusiasm seemed to grow. "Oh my, look at you, my lord! Your wife said just a few words and you've worked yourself up again! Once we enter the city, let's find an inn to rest in. Your wife will help you expel all that unhealthful internal heat."

Cui Buqu slowly turned his head, his face a perfect blank. "Expel heat how?"

"That's... That's... Travel makes such things so inconvenient; your wife can see how you've been denying yourself! Once we're at the inn, I'll be able to serve you well." Cui Buqu stared at her, and she flushed a rosy pink. "Must your lordship make me say it so directly? I'm still a lady, you know. If others hear, they'll take me for a dissolute woman!"

Cui Buqu felt his head throb; he rubbed at his temples. "There are no others here. Can you please speak like a human?"

"How is your wife speaking if not like a human?" the woman said, aggrieved. "They say after three years of marriage, even the famous beauty Diaochan would look like a sow to her husband. To think your lordship was this kind of man!"

This woman was tall and slender; even sitting cross-legged, her presence made the carriage rather cramped. Her glossy raven hair was gathered in a loose bun at the nape of her neck, a recently popular style. A glimpse of red braided string shone through, imparting a brighter glow to her already fair skin. Though her features weren't as soft as those of Jiangnan women, she was no less lovely for it. As the saying went, beautiful skin concealed all flaws—here was a beauty who could dazzle at the first glance, so much so that one would forget any other blemishes.

Unfortunately, Cui Buqu didn't appreciate this beauty at all. If he could, he would have kicked her right out of the carriage.

Qiao Xian was a true master of disguise. The women of the Western Regions naturally had more prominent brows and taller and sturdier figures than women from the Central Plains. She had not only deepened Feng Xiao's facial features to give him such a look, she'd even concealed the telltale jut of his throat. A great many details others might easily notice had all been hidden by her handiwork. No one seeing Feng Xiao for the first time would think him a man disguised as a woman.

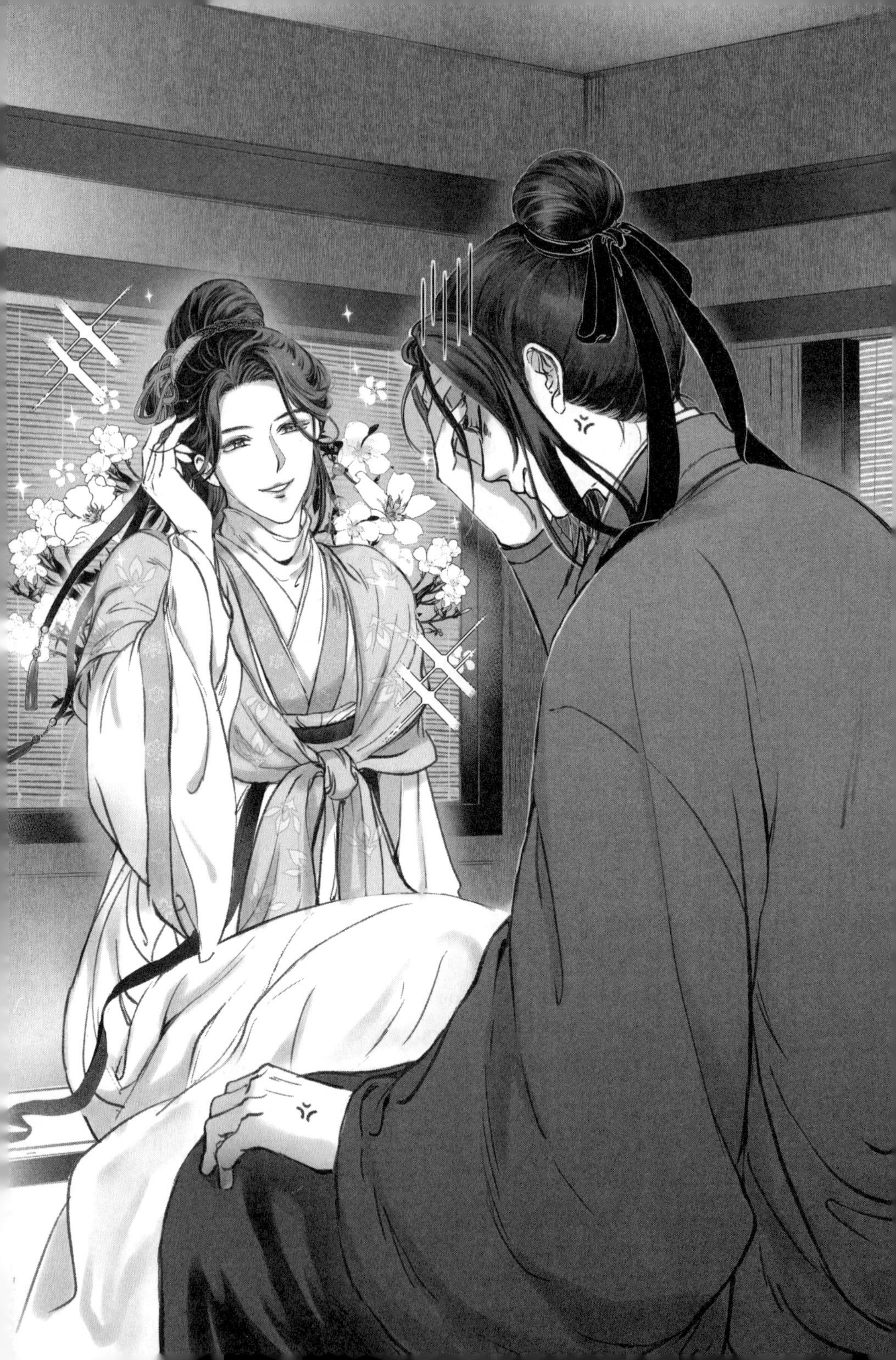

After Feng Xiao had agreed to the disguise, he demanded Cui Buqu take the role of his husband, Master Ye Yong. Thinking it would be good for a laugh, Cui Buqu agreed—but before they'd been on the road half a day, his heart was filled with regret.

Alas, regret was one ailment for which there was no cure. He had no choice but to endure. Now that Qiemo was in sight, his ears would finally experience some peace.

The city of Qiemo was a significant link between east and west, but it was far from the Central Plains. The Sui dynasty had been established for only three years, and in that time, most of the imperial court's energy had been directed toward the Khaganate and Southern Chen. They had no thought to spare for this small oasis town lying in uncertain territory. Even so, last year the emperor had decreed that Qiemo be made an official county under his rule. He'd had a county office set up and sent a magistrate and soldiers to guard the city in a display of the might of the imperial court. The act sent a clear message: though Great Sui had yet to take the territory firmly in hand, they hadn't relinquished it.

More than thirty years ago, when the Western Wei dynasty had conquered the Kingdom of Shanshan, the king of Shanshan led his people in an exodus and settled down in Qiemo. They had established their own influence here in the intervening years. Merchants traveling between the Central Plains and the Western Regions inevitably passed through Qiemo, and many stopped there to rest. Over time, this important waypoint had become an arena where three factions vied for power:

The first was Gao Yi, the magistrate appointed by the Sui dynasty.

The second was Xing Mao, a descendant of the king of Shanshan.

And the third was Duan Qihu, a wealthy merchant from the Western Regions.

It was obvious how the first two came to power. Gao Yi had been sent by the Sui dynasty to stake a claim on the city. Though he was only a county magistrate, he'd brought soldiers to back him. Next was Xing Mao: though their kingdom was no more, the king of Shanshan and his descendants had held sway over the city for three generations. Xing Mao was his eldest grandson, and it was said that the Shanshan diaspora within the city revered him as their king.

As for Duan Qihu, he'd gotten his start as a common bandit. This man had roamed the Western Regions in his youth, plundering settlements and striking fear into the hearts of decent folk. Merchants passing through the Western Regions had two options upon meeting him: pay up or lose their lives. Later, Duan Qihu retired from banditry and settled down in Qiemo. His reputation, however, remained—no one dared underestimate the notorious former bandit of the Western Regions. Duan Qihu dabbled in business both aboveboard and underground, and his influence within Qiemo was deep and unshakable.

Compared to the latter two, county magistrate Gao Yi was no doubt the weakest.

Or so things stood when Cui Buqu's group entered the city of Qiemo.

People of all ethnicities—riffraff and common folk from every trade—mixed in Qiemo's busy streets. Such a bustling populace, combined with the complex interplay between three powerful factions, meant tiny Qiemo was even livelier than Liugong City.

"Dage, let's find an inn first and get some rest," Qiao Xian urged Cui Buqu upon passing through the gates. "It's too late in the day to travel any further. We can stop here for a couple of days before setting off again."

She was currently disguised as Li Cong, a family friend of the Ye clan, taking his wife A-Lian to Kucha to conduct business. Qiao Xian too was naturally tall and slender. When dressed as a woman, she appeared untouchable—celestial even—but right then, she was transformed. No one knew what she'd done, but she'd managed to add bulk to her slim frame, and her facial features had undergone drastic change. Her skin was now as coarse as the average man's, and there were even short whiskers on her chin. If she was to tell anyone she was a woman, they likely wouldn't believe her.

Yet the true art of disguise lay not merely in changing one's appearance, but in changing one's voice and accent, mannerisms, and actions to become another person entirely. That level of transformation was beyond what even Cui Buqu could achieve, yet Qiao Xian had done it. Her current accent was that of a born and bred resident of Liugong City.

She waited for Cui Buqu's nod, then instructed their guide to recommend a local inn.

"It doesn't have to be the grandest, but it must be the most comfortable," she said. "My brother's health is poor; he needs good rest." Her voice was brash and booming, clashing completely with her previous chilly demeanor. Even Feng Xiao, who'd grown accustomed to hearing her speak this way over the course of their journey, shot her another glance.

Had she still been that aloof and icy beauty, she could have expected to draw attention or even harassment. Now, she had no such problem. If anyone here was to draw attention, it wouldn't be Qiao Xian, who'd practically switched faces entirely, or the matronly Jinlian. All eyes would be on the fair lady Feng Xiao.

The guide wasted no time leading them to an inn. "You Hans won't be comfortable at the inns run by Kucha or Shanshan people. This inn has been open five or six years; I've guided several groups who stayed here."

Jinlian had passed through Qiemo on her way from the Khaganate to Liugong City, but she'd had guards to take care of everything then and hadn't troubled herself with the details. This time she was with Cui Buqu, so again she didn't bother with them. She merely nodded, ready to follow Qiao Xian inside.

"Wait," Cui Buqu said suddenly.

The rest of the group stopped and looked at him.

"What's this?" Cui Buqu pointed toward the inn's entrance, where a wooden sign was nailed to the door pillar. The sign was the size of an infant's palm and carved with a crescent moon, upon the bottom point of which was perched a swan.

Few people noticed such a small sign when entering the inn, and even if they did, they didn't think much of it. Within the Central Plains, plenty of guest houses opened multiple branches and marked them with their personal emblem. They'd simply believe this moon was a similar trademark.

The guide smiled. "You're from the Central Plains; you must know many inns use their own symbols."

Cui Buqu's expression was indifferent. "We asked for a comfortable inn, not an inn that will bring us trouble. That swan—you brought us to one of Duan Qihu's inns.[1] Did his people bribe you?"

Foreign merchants were always susceptible to cons or other mischief, especially when traveling anywhere for the first time. Due to the complex politics of Qiemo, even booking an inn was tricky.

---

1 The "hu" (鹄) in Duan Qihu means swan.

Duan Qihu and Xing Mao had a pervasive influence that ran through the entire city. They controlled not only inns, but horse and donkey rentals, restaurants, and other necessities of travel. Jianghu wanderers had little to fear from such places, and various opportunists and criminals purposely chose to stay at Duan Qihu's inns—in this way, they could avoid the eyes of Sui officials as they trod in legal gray areas and peddled in various kinds of information.

But as for law-abiding merchants and common civilians, it would be best to avoid such establishments even if it meant staying at a more expensive inn. Cui Buqu's group had nothing to fear from this place, but they weren't looking for trouble—it was much better to keep a low profile. If they were to maintain their guise as honest citizens, there was no way they could stay in Duan Qihu's territory.

The guide hadn't expected Cui Buqu to be so knowledgeable. He laughed dryly. "Just trying to save you some money, my lord."

Qiao Xian stepped forward and clapped him on the shoulder. "Bring us to a safer inn."

The gesture was understated, but the instant Qiao Xian's hand landed, the guide felt a burst of excruciating agony. His face twisted, yet when he tried to cry out in pain, he discovered he couldn't make a sound. Only then did he realize how severely he'd misjudged these merchants. This group had seemed entirely ordinary and inconspicuous, but they were no easy marks.

"If you can't do it, we'll find someone else," said Qiao Xian.

The guide didn't dare equivocate; he nodded furiously, fighting back tears.

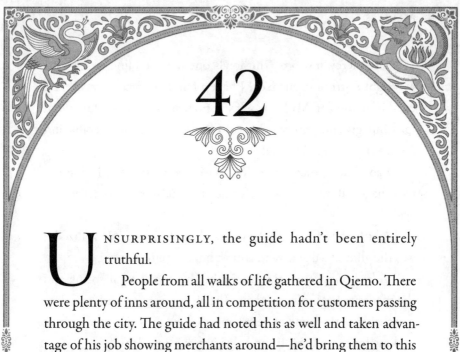

42

UNSURPRISINGLY, the guide hadn't been entirely truthful.

People from all walks of life gathered in Qiemo. There were plenty of inns around, all in competition for customers passing through the city. The guide had noted this as well and taken advantage of his job showing merchants around—he'd bring them to this particular inn in exchange for a small commission. Guest houses like this one, the Tianfu Inn, were shady establishments. It wasn't uncommon for valuables to go missing, and just making it out in one piece was considered lucky. Merchants who stayed there would write off these small losses as the price they paid for peace of mind. They didn't want trouble, so they didn't report anything—and even if they had, it wouldn't have made a difference. Magistrate Gao wouldn't overstep in Duan Qihu's territory.

As far as merchant convoys went, Cui Buqu's party wasn't particularly large, but their food, lodging, and clothes made it clear they didn't lack for money. They were fat lambs begging for the slaughter.

Perhaps they had kept *too* low a profile—their guide had misjudged them completely and fallen flat on his face.

By now, he'd been dragged into a dark alley. He took in Cui Buqu's words and Qiao Xian's shadowed, expressionless face. He assumed they were going to silence him and was flooded with terror.

"Have mercy, my lord! This lowly one was too blind to see what was right in front of my face! I have a family to feed; I was threatened into doing it. My lowly self was no match for them! I beg your lordship, give me another chance! I'll take you to a respectable inn. A perfectly respectable one!"

Qiao Xian's voice was cold. "Business is business; losing our patronage will make little difference to you. But try to deceive us again..."

Light flashed from her sleeve, dazzling the guide. He realized it was the glint of a dagger and almost burst into tears.

"I'll be honest," he said miserably. "It's the start of spring and the roads are beginning to thaw. The city is teeming with traveling merchants at this time of year—most of the inns are full. If you're looking for rooms, this is the only kind that's available..."

Qiao Xian frowned slightly and glanced toward Cui Buqu.

Influential local powers ran most of the inns here. The Zuoyue Bureau had a secret base of operations in Qiemo where they could send and receive information, but it wasn't somewhere they could stay.

At this point, the guide seemed to be struck by a flash of inspiration. "There's one inn that might still have room. But..."

"Spit it out!" Qiao Xian snapped.

"But it's cursed!" wailed the guide.

Feng Xiao spoke up in a sweet falsetto. "This Tianfu Inn is so chaotic! Look at all those people coming and going, so crowded and sweaty. I just know it'll stink to the high heavens in there. This wife can't abide it! My lord, you're a trusting man, but you've never been superstitious. Let's have a look, shall we?"

Cui Buqu looked at her askance, as if to say, *You're the one who wants to go. Don't drag me into it.*

Feng Xiao smiled back. There was nothing terrifying about that smile. Upon a closer look, one might even call it charming. But only those who'd never seen Feng Xiao's true self would think it so. Cui Buqu, Qiao Xian, and Jinlian looked away as one, turning their heads in perfect accord.

The guide, who knew nothing about Feng Xiao, was stunned. How fortunate this man from the Ye clan was to have married such a stunning beauty despite his sickly, lethargic demeanor. Though judging from his appearance, he'd have difficulty fathering a child.

After his previous mishap, the guide didn't dare put a toe out of line. He led them meekly along several streets until they arrived at a nondescript building marked with a sign reading *Yangji Inn*.

Qiemo was a remote city, home to a mélange of peoples. Even their businesses brushed shoulders. The Yangji Inn perched on the edge of a residential district opposite a row of small eateries frequented by men and women in Han dress as well as merchants in foreign garb. Evening approached; the eateries were bustling and the clamor of stallkeepers and customers rose and fell. On the residential side, children scurried home from playing as their mothers called them back for dinner. Some drew water, some returned from work, some waved and chatted with their neighbors. All these scenes blended, creating that legend upon the sands: the city of Qiemo.

Fugitives often fled here, and it wasn't hard to see why. Though the city hadn't the prosperity of the Central Plains, it had all the things one needed to make a living. The sky was high, and the emperor was far away. The city offered a freedom money couldn't buy. Here, even a murderer might not pay with their life. Qiemo was just the place for those without moral boundaries.

But there was something strange going on here. Surrounded by this rowdy atmosphere, the Yangji Inn was oddly quiet, and the hall on the first floor, where one would expect guests to mingle, remained unfilled.

When the porter saw them stop at the entrance, he came out with an enthusiastic greeting and led them inside. Qiao Xian grabbed the guide's arm and pulled him along.

"This way, please, honored guests. We still have several fine rooms available. How many do you need? It's early yet, but you must be tired from your journey. May I offer you some food and wine?" the porter asked.

Nodding, Qiao Xian followed him to book rooms and order their food.

The guide was terrified out of his wits. The moment he saw his tormentor Qiao Xian leave, he turned to flee. But as he lifted his foot, he heard a *whoosh*: his pantleg had been pinned to the floor by a chopstick. Half an inch to the left and it would've been buried in his leg instead.

He raised his eyes and found Jinlian, a woman he had considered utterly unremarkable until this moment, looking back.

"Where are you going?" she asked.

The guide broke out in a cold sweat. Even the women of this group were formidable! Why had they insisted on leaving Tianfu Inn when they were strong enough to terrorize everyone there?

"N-nowhere!" The guide twisted his mouth in a smile so wretched crying would have looked more cheerful. "This lowly one's leg fell asleep; I just wanted to move a little!"

"Why did you say this place is cursed?" asked Cui Buqu.

Trembling with fear, the guide extinguished any thoughts of escape. He told them everything from start to finish.

This inn was haunted.

People did come and go, usually only staying a night or two. These guests didn't care if it was haunted as long as they had someplace to rest.

But although the hall was almost full, it wasn't nearly as busy as other inns in the city at the moment—even the Tianfu Inn they'd left behind was livelier. Elsewhere, travelers gathered in throngs and packed the halls of the guest houses. This inn was a far cry from that.

Upon looking around, Cui Buqu noticed most of the people present were merchants staying at the inn for the first time, like themselves. Many peered about in open curiosity. Seasoned veterans who conducted business on this route obviously chose accommodations elsewhere.

According to their guide, the hauntings at the inn had begun a year ago, long enough that he couldn't remember all the details. But he clearly recalled the first incident, which had involved the well behind the inn.

A guest had gotten drunk that night and was nowhere to be found the next day. His companions searched for him to no avail. The court hadn't yet sent a magistrate to Qiemo, so they had no way to report the incident. They could only assume that in his drunken stupor, he'd slipped and drowned somewhere. The incident was left unresolved.

Afterward, guests began to hear faint cries for help in the middle of the night. Some, more courageous or nosier than others, followed the sounds to the dry well behind the inn. At last the innkeeper had no choice but to remove the stones covering the well. Lo and behold, at the bottom they found the sorry corpse of the missing guest.

From that moment on, rumors of the haunted inn spread throughout the city. Some said the man's companions had robbed and killed him, then thrown his body down the well. Unable to rest in peace, he'd become a ghost forever pleading for help. But that was only the beginning.

Half a month after the discovery of the first corpse, another guest brought back a prostitute for some late-night fun. Halfway through the deed, he slumped forward and died right on top of the poor girl.

Yet another person had come just for a meal. He went to a bathhouse afterward and somehow drowned in the shallow water.

The fourth unfortunate soul had simply drunk too much before croaking in an entertainment house elsewhere in the city.

At this last, Jinlian couldn't help but speak up. "The first two are fair enough, but the last two are rather a stretch!"

"How is it a stretch?" the guide said mysteriously. "The fourth man purchased his drinks here!"

Jinlian was speechless.

"Fights break out every day in this city," the guide continued. "Plenty of people lose their lives. But this inn really is cursed. They say every night after midnight the guests hear voices crying for justice for their tragic deaths. There's another rumor: any guest, no matter how uneventful their stay, will suffer financial loss after leaving. Those who get off lightly lose half their wealth, while others lose their entire fortune. What say your lordships? Does this not sound like a curse?"

Qiao Xian had finished arranging for meals and lodging, and returned just in time to hear these final remarks. "How do you know they lost their money? Did you follow them and witness it for yourself?"

"Everyone says so," the guide said matter-of-factly. "They can't all be wrong!"

Cui Buqu and Feng Xiao exchanged a glance. This sounded more like snowballing rumors than a genuine haunting.

But there was nothing more frightening to a merchant than losses, especially when they were traveling thousands of miles from the Central Plains to the west. A round trip spanned months, and if they traveled farther than that, the journey took longer still. Forget losing one's fortune—even a small loss would be heart-wrenching. Better to spend a night in the stables or lose some money at that Tianfu Inn than be cursed with bad luck.

The guide saw their skeptical expressions and said no more. *He* wouldn't be the one getting cursed—he'd made up his mind not to eat a bite or drink a drop at the Yangji Inn. Even while seated, he was on high alert.

Qiao Xian threw him his fee. With the job done, he didn't linger. The guide caught the money, then nodded, bowed, and fled.

❖

While they conversed, the porter brought over their meal.

The dishes were nothing compared to those from the capital; they even fell a little short of what Liugong City had to offer. But at the very least they were piping hot. Qiao Xiao picked up a steamed bun and was about to dig in when she caught sight of Feng Xiao's look of disgust as he stared at the congee.

"Do they not have clean bowls here?"

Qiao Xian couldn't resist mocking him. "You're going to put on airs even now?"

Feng Xiao ignored her. He tugged at Cui Buqu's sleeve and wheedled, "My lord, your wife wants a new bowl. Won't you purchase one for her?"

Cui Buqu raised his bowl expressionlessly and took a sip. "There aren't any. Eat or don't."

Feng Xiao's tone was aggrieved. "Is this about you wanting a concubine? I can see you're still upset over the matter. But I only protest out of concern for your lordship's health. Look at you, you're already so weak. You can't even satisfy me, yet you want another woman? What if you die an early death, what will your poor wife do then?"

His voice was perfectly pitched to carry to the guests at all the adjacent tables. As they glanced at this couple—one sick and ailing, the other glowing like fresh peach blossoms—comprehension dawned.

Everyone said women were wolves at thirty and tigers at forty. To think this woman still in her twenties was so ravenous!

Qiao Xian's teeth itched. She longed to roll up her sleeves and punch Feng Xiao in his lovely face. At a look from Cui Buqu, however, she silently let her hands fall. Punching one's sister-in-law in full view of the public was definitely unacceptable. They were only passing through this city; they shouldn't make a scene.

It was precisely for this reason that Feng Xiao grew bolder still. He pressed himself to Cui Buqu and rubbed against him, whispering loudly, "I know your lordship wants it, but your wife is having *that time of the month*. A few more days and I'll give you what you need, hm?"

Cui Buqu slammed his bowl down on the table. "Buy her a new bowl," he told Qiao Xian.

"A pair of chopsticks and a spoon too, please," chirped Feng Xiao. "No need to be overly picky when we're out and about. Poplar or bamboo will do just fine."

Qiao Xian couldn't bear to reply.

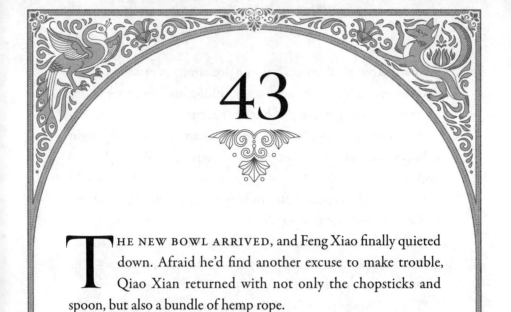

43

THE NEW BOWL ARRIVED, and Feng Xiao finally quieted down. Afraid he'd find another excuse to make trouble, Qiao Xian returned with not only the chopsticks and spoon, but also a bundle of hemp rope.

She threw the last item at Feng Xiao's feet.

"What's this?" asked Feng Xiao lazily. "To hang myself with? My apologies; the heavens would never permit the death of someone so peerlessly extraordinary as myself."

"Aren't you obsessed with cleanliness?" asked Qiao Xian coolly. "Inns like this don't change their bedding; everyone sleeps on the same sheets. You needn't share the bed with Ye-dage. If you tie this rope at each end of the room, surely you can balance on it to sleep. That's the cleanest option."

The four of them were traveling as two couples; naturally, Feng Xiao and Cui Buqu shared a room. What Qiao Xian didn't mention was that if Feng Xiao slept on the rope hammock, Cui Buqu could get some undisturbed rest.

Cui Buqu ducked his head and bit into a lamb pastry. Qiao Xian was too young yet if she thought petty tricks would work on that Feng bastard. If he could go a second without getting up to mischief, he wouldn't be Feng Xiao. Cui Buqu didn't know what the lamb had been spiced with, but the meat nestled within the flaky casing was tender and not at all gamey. The mingled aroma of meat and pastry flooded his mouth with each bite, soothing his heart after a long journey subsisting on nothing but dry rations.

Sure enough, Feng Xiao smiled at Qiao Xian. "You're right. I already asked earlier—if you pay a little extra, they'll provide clean bedding."

"You wasteful woman! Not only won't you save your husband money, you rush out to squander it!"

Feng Xiao had no interest in bickering with her. He turned and grabbed the corner of Cui Buqu's robes. "My lord, see here—" he whined, stretching the syllables.

"Pay it. Change them," said Cui Buqu decisively, preventing any further outbursts.

Qiao Xian pressed her lips together. She conceded this round.

⁂

After their meal, the masters and mistresses went up to their respective rooms, while their three coachmen stayed in the servant's quarters.

Both the Zuoyue and Jiejian Bureaus had wealth to spare; the tiny expenditure of an inn was nothing. But on this journey, they hoped to go unnoticed. If they paid for the three coachmen to have their own rooms, they could expect robbers to come knocking the next day.

The guest rooms here paled beside those of the capital, but they were spacious enough. The porter took their money and returned promptly with fresh bedding and pillows. The blanket had been freshly aired, and the smell of sunlight still lingered.

Cui Buqu was asleep the moment his head hit the pillow.

He hadn't the stamina of the other three, who all practiced martial arts. Even the coachmen, who were often out and about driving, were sturdier than he was. He fell ill often, with all the agony that entailed. If not for the fact that he'd been drinking medicine like water, he'd never have been able to hold on this long. He'd frequently been ill throughout the trip and spent most of his time in the carriage drifting in and out of consciousness. Yet his mind was terrifyingly sharp—seconds after waking, he could answer any question Qiao Xian posed to him.

Feng Xiao was constantly provoking Cui Buqu, trying to get under his skin and delighting in his setbacks. But he'd never laughed at his illnesses. He understood that Cui Buqu considered his ailments but superficial trappings of his mortal form and not a true weakness. In fact, Cui Buqu had used his physical condition many times to lull enemies into dropping their guard. Back at Qiushan Manor, when Feng Xiao had poisoned Cui Buqu with incense of helplessness, he too had fancied Cui Buqu in the palm of his hand. He'd grown complacent, and he knew it—though of course he would never admit such a thing.

The moment Cui Buqu fell asleep, he was dead to the world. When Qiao Xian knocked on the door some time later, she received no answer. Only when she entered to wake him did he crack open his eyes, his face still lined with fatigue.

"You only had a lamb pastry earlier. I was afraid it was too dry for you, so I brought some hot soup."

One sniff told Cui Buqu it was mutton-bone soup. The oily film on the surface had been skimmed away, leaving it clear, and it was sprinkled with slivers of green scallions.

Qiao Xian looked around. "Where's Feng Xiao?"

Cui Buqu took slow mouthfuls of soup. "The Zuoyue Bureau has a base of operations here. Naturally the Jiejian Bureau does too."

Feng Xiao had no Qiao Xian traveling with him. When it came to secret instructions or correspondence, he had to see to everything himself.

"What have you learned?" Cui Buqu asked.

"This inn has a poor reputation," she said. "But in my opinion, those deaths are coincidental. The curse is no more than the baseless conjecture of ignorant folk. Merchants are a superstitious lot, and the stories grow increasingly absurd and embellished with each retelling. It's more likely the guide was unwilling to bring us here because this is Xing Mao's territory. The descendant of the Shanshan king has always been at odds with Duan Qihu, so the guide purposely exaggerated to scare us."

"Is Xing Mao and Duan Qihu's relationship so hostile?"

"Originally, they were the two rival powers in Qiemo. They competed for territory, so they've never been friendly. However, things seem to have improved since the arrival of County Magistrate Gao Yi."

"Now there are three powers, all holding each other in check," said Cui Buqu.

"That's right," said Qiao Xian. "I heard Gao Yi held a banquet for this year's Lantern Festival and extended invitations to Duan Qihu and Xing Mao. Both attended. Everyone says the two have reconciled thanks to Gao Yi's mediation. Xing Mao's mother will celebrate her sixtieth birthday this month, and it ought to be a grand affair. The entire city is watching to see if he'll invite Duan Qihu."

"When is this birthday banquet?"

"Five days from now."

They were still speaking when Feng Xiao returned.

The curtain of night had descended, and the sounds of the city ebbed away. Yet it wasn't that Qiemo had fallen silent, only that the doors to the outside world had shut tight. In the neighborhoods around the inn, local folk blew out their candles and drew up their covers one by one, while across the way, others continued to dine and laugh in the eateries.

Feng Xiao sent a flirtatious glance toward Cui Buqu. "My lord, your wife has returned. Did you make yourself sick yearning for me?"

Cui Buqu set down his bowl. "I did. My organs are burning, my stomach is bloated, and my feelings of longing and desire are so strong they threaten to overflow."

"That bad?" Feng Xiao asked in faux shock.

"In short, I'm about to vomit."

Feng Xiao laughed. "Ququ, it's so much fun talking to you!"

Qiao Xian sneered but said nothing. She didn't need to— Feng Xiao knew she was silently cursing him but paid her no mind. She sat fuming with no way to vent her anger, yet refused to leave the room, glaring daggers at Feng Xiao.

In a competition for the thickest skin, Feng Xiao might not win, but he'd certainly place in the top three. What did he care for her glares? He took a seat and opened the paper packet he carried, and the aroma of roast chicken instantly filled the room.

Cui Buqu had been satisfied with his own meal, but the scent of the chicken made him greedy. He reached out without hesitation and tore off a drumstick.

Feng Xiao smiled. "I saw an old friend on the way back. Guess who?"

Cui Buqu chewed methodically. "Yuxiu."

Feng Xiao arched a brow in surprise. "However did you guess?"

"Do you think I'm a fortune teller? If you asked like that, it must be someone we both know, whom we saw not long ago. Yuxiu's background is questionable, and he works for the Prince of Jin. Yet rather than staying by his master's side like a proper adviser, he came all the way to Liugong City. The Jade of Heaven Lake can't have been his only goal; he must have other business. It's likely he also intended to head west, so one could expect him to turn up in Qiemo."

"But why didn't you guess Go Nyeong or Fo'er?"

"You defeated them in Liugong City," said Cui Buqu. "If they hadn't joined forces and ambushed you, they'd have perished at your hands. If you'd run into either of them, you'd have a different attitude."

It was obvious Feng Xiao was immensely interested in Yuxiu.

"Where do you think he's going this time?" Feng Xiao asked.

Cui Buqu thought a moment, then shook his head. "I can't guess."

"So there are times even you admit defeat," said Feng Xiao. "A rare sight."

Cui Buqu scoffed. "I'm no god. No matter how intelligent I am, my wisdom is that of a mortal. But I'll say he definitely isn't looking for Ishbara Khagan, or he'd have met with Fo'er in Liugong City."

"He's changed his appearance," said Feng Xiao. "When I saw him, he was wearing a wig. No more of that shiny bald head we saw last time. And he's staying at this inn, on the same floor as us even—only three rooms away."

Qiao Xian had stayed to listen when she heard Feng Xiao mention Yuxiu. Now she interrupted, "Could he have followed us here?"

The four of them were well disguised; even if they met Yuxiu face-to-face, they weren't worried about being recognized. But they were better safe than sorry.

"No," said Cui Buqu. "If he'd discovered us, he would have avoided this inn and stayed elsewhere."

It seemed Yuxiu was heading somewhere specific, either to see someone or do something. Qiao Xian's brow creased in thought. "Perhaps he's also going to meet Apa Khagan?"

But this, too, seemed unlikely. The Khaganate had many khagans, and Apa was of middling power among them. Yuxiu was a counselor to the Prince of Jin; what did he have to gain from Apa Khagan?

Cui Buqu laid down the drumstick, picked clean, and reached for a wing. "If we don't know, we don't know. Things will fall into place when the time comes. If Yuxiu takes the same road as us, we'll discover his aims sooner or later."

Feng Xiao smiled. "Since you've helped yourself, at least thank the one who bought the meal. Your lordship ate food meant for your wife. Should you not express your gratitude?"

"And how much of my money have you spent on this trip?" asked Cui Buqu. "A new bowl, spoon, chopsticks. I even paid for new bedding. I've only had a drumstick, yet you're demanding compensation? Cough up what you owe me first."

Having been justly called out, Feng Xiao smiled and said no more.

After finishing the chicken and bidding Qiao Xian goodnight, Cui Buqu washed his hands and got ready to go back to sleep.

Feng Xiao stared at him in disbelief. "You slept the entire day in the carriage, and you slept when I went out earlier. Now you're sleeping again?"

He was practically calling Cui Buqu a lazy pig.

Cui Buqu was phlegmatic. "My health is poor. Extra sleep is as good as taking supplements." Paying Feng Xiao no further heed, he pulled up the covers, turned on his side, and went to sleep.

In truth, though he'd seemed deep in slumber each day, the roads were bumpy. No matter how skilled the coachman, a carriage was not a bed; Cui Buqu hadn't been able to rest well. Now, his head hit the pillow and he was out cold a moment later, leaving Feng Xiao standing there in astonishment.

The room had only one bed. Feng Xiao refused to sleep on the rope, so his only option was to share with Cui Buqu. It shouldn't have been an issue: no matter how beautiful a woman Feng Xiao made, he was still a man. He wasn't at risk of being taken advantage of.

Yet Cui Buqu hadn't anticipated he'd have barely slept before a hand shoved him awake.

Dazed, he half-opened his eyes and heard Feng Xiao say, "Move over a little. I don't have any room."

It was true that the bed wasn't a large one. Cui Buqu shuffled over, only to see Feng Xiao place two pillows between them. "You sleep like a slob. Don't cross the line."

Cui Buqu couldn't resist mocking him. "Are you a woman?"

Feng Xiao quirked a brow. "You didn't even wash and change before getting in bed. If you go boil some water and wash, my venerable self will remove the pillows."

Bathing at this time of year was no simple task. One had to ask the inn staff to rekindle the furnace, boil the water, and carry it to one's room, pail by pail. At this time of night, most people were asleep. Who on earth would get up to boil some water?

Cui Buqu schooled himself to patience. He didn't move, his back to Feng Xiao. "Whatever you say."

He thought he'd finally get a good night's rest. But all too soon, he was shaken awake again.

"Don't snore. It's noisy."

Cui Buqu gritted his teeth. "I do not *snore*. My circulation is poor; my nose gets congested when I lie down, so my breathing is louder than normal. If you can't sleep, go on the roof and watch the moon! Deputy Chief Feng, I swear on all that's holy—I'll see that anyone who disturbs my rest suffers a fate worse than death. Are you sure you want to spend the rest of this journey fighting me?"

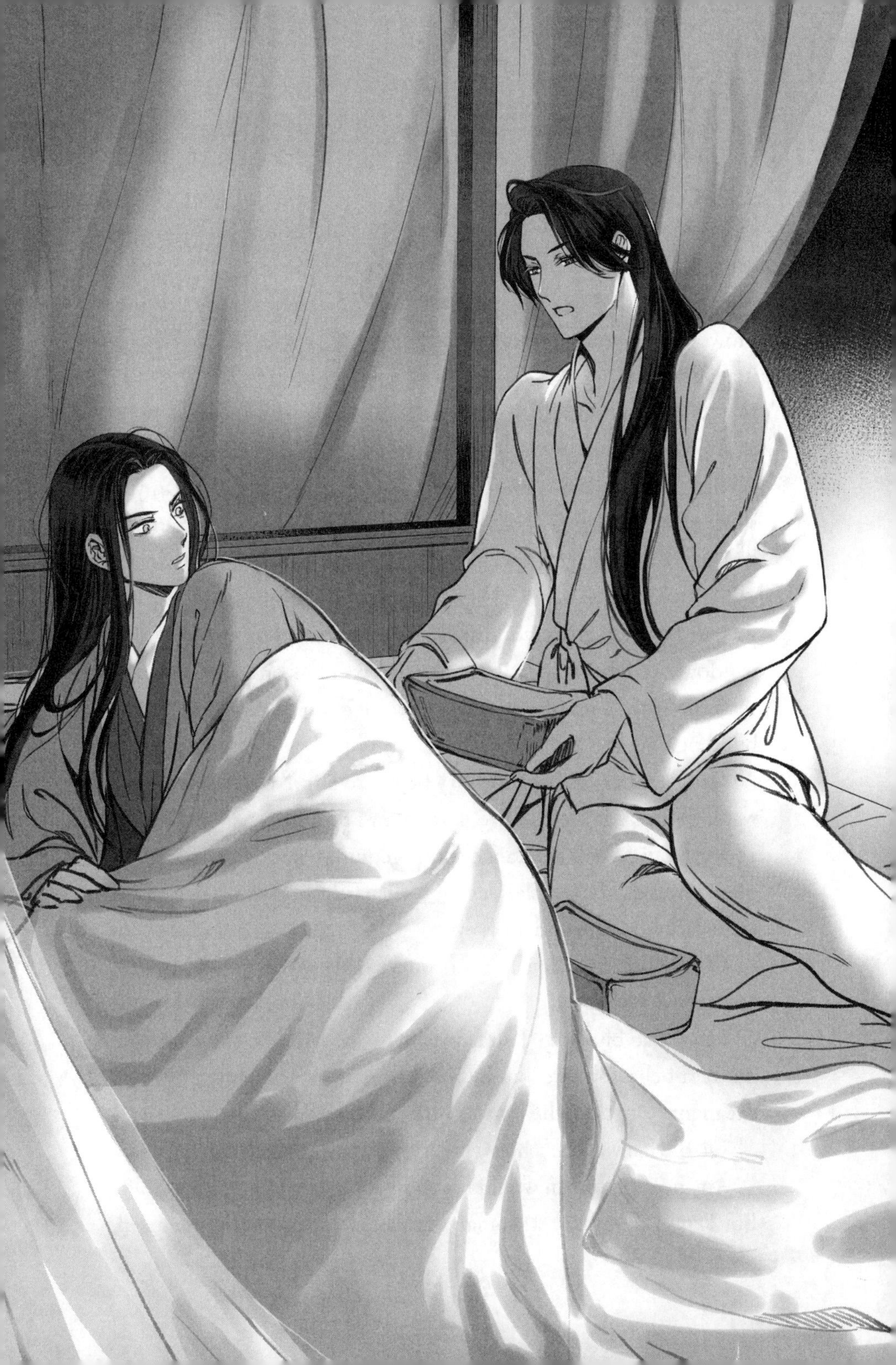

This man knew no martial arts, yet the bloodlust in his eyes was a match for any master.

Feng Xiao would never admit he was waking him partly out of mischief. He was the picture of innocence as he said, "I'm a light sleeper; the slightest noise wakes me. You really did disturb me. However, I'm a thoughtful and empathetic person—I won't hold it against you."

Cui Buqu huffed out a long breath, then lay down and went back to sleep.

But the world, it seemed, was out to get him tonight. Only a short time later, he was woken again. Before he could lose his temper, he heard Feng Xiao:

"There's a fire outside."

Cui Buqu smelled woodsmoke. When Feng Xiao opened the window, firelight flooded in. From their window on the third floor, they could see a massive blaze, so fierce it'd already consumed one building.

Gradually, the rest of the city began to stir. Neighbors carried water to help douse the fire, a task that took most of the night. Though Cui Buqu's assistance wasn't required, he'd been woken so often it was difficult to sleep again. When he rose the next day, there were dark smudges under his eyes.

Qiao Xian looked at him in concern. "Did you not sleep well, Ye-dage?"

Feng Xiao blushed. "I already told his lordship we should be on our best behavior here, but he never listens. He tormented me half the night! Oh, this wife is too embarrassed to say it!"

Qiao Xian was speechless. Her hand was itching again.

Any proper woman would never say such vulgar words in public. But Feng Xiao wasn't a woman, let alone a proper one—he cared nothing for a spotless reputation. Qiao Xian finally realized that riling Cui Buqu up was Feng Xiao's daily pastime, his great entertainment.

Yet Cui Buqu, who yesterday had seemed as if he couldn't stand Feng Xiao's antics, was unperturbed. He sneered coldly. "Just last night you ogled the hostler Zhang San, then made eyes at Li Si from the kitchens. And how many times did you cuckold me in Liugong City? I endured it in silence, but even here you refuse to stop! Why don't you head into the city and see who has a bed that needs filling! I'm sure there's plenty of fun to be had!"

In just a few sentences, he'd painted a lurid picture for the guests at the adjacent table. All turned to stare at Feng Xiao, some curious and others lascivious—perhaps they too could enjoy a clandestine encounter with this unbearably lonely woman tonight.

The corner of Qiao Xian's mouth jumped. These men were impossible. They'd all agreed to keep a low profile, yet this was drawing more attention. What married woman would so brazenly cheat on her husband? And what married man would shout it to the whole room?

"Let's switch tables," said Jinlian to Qiao Xian.

"Agreed." Qiao Xian said. The two of them rose to move.

At that moment, several constables entered the hall and looked around. "Is a man named Ye Yong staying here?"

The porter, who had bustled up to greet them, bowed. He was promising to check the register when Cui Buqu spoke up. "I'm Ye Yong. How can I help you?"

The constable in the lead glanced at him and waved the others forward. "Seize him."

"Wait." Feng Xiao stood and stepped in front of Cui Buqu. "Surely you can't arrest someone without a reason?"

The constable's voice was cold. "The reason is last night's fire. The guide Cheng Cheng perished in the flames. There's a report that *you* had a disagreement with him in the streets yesterday afternoon. Ye Yong, you're suspected of arson and murder!"

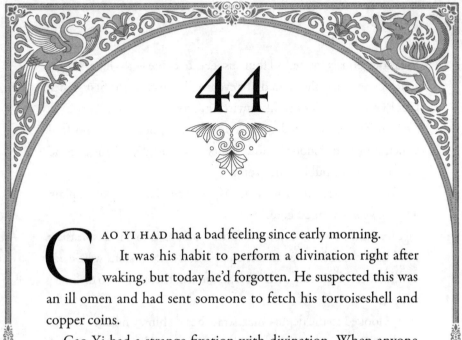

44

GAO YI HAD had a bad feeling since early morning.

It was his habit to perform a divination right after waking, but today he'd forgotten. He suspected this was an ill omen and had sent someone to fetch his tortoiseshell and copper coins.

Gao Yi had a strange fixation with divination. When anyone came to see him, he insisted on checking his fortune before admitting them. Even his wife was at the end of her rope. He might as well use divination to decide whether to lead with his right or left foot when walking, she'd jeered. Gao Yi had given her suggestion serious thought, but ultimately felt it too time-consuming.

He'd just sent someone for the copper coins when the constables he'd dispatched returned with four people.

Qiao Xian had wanted to answer the summons alone, but the constables had refused. They insisted on bringing the whole group, by force if necessary.

After Qiao Xian had crushed a cup to powder, however, the constables realized these people were no simple merchants. Qiemo was home to all kinds—good and evil, powerful and powerless—and there was no shortage of strange happenings and stranger people. Gao Yi was court-appointed, but he had little influence. His subordinates were wary of indiscriminately offending anyone and had thus courteously invited all four suspects to come with them. Forget shackles or ropes: they dared not even walk too close. At first glance, Cui Buqu's group looked like invited guests.

Gao Yi was addicted to his copper coins, but he was no fool. When he saw his subordinates' respectful attitude, he understood this must be a troublesome group.

Qiao Xian stepped forward. "Magistrate Gao, can you explain why we've been called here?"

She didn't bow or cup her hands, much to Gao Yi's displeasure. Looking behind her, he saw her companions' expressions were calm, confident, and entirely without fear. Indeed, these were no ordinary people.

He looked to the deputy magistrate beside him, who coughed belatedly. "This is our city's honorable magistrate. Why don't you bow?"

"We have our reasons, of course," Qiao Xian said evenly. "But first, let us discuss the death of Cheng Cheng."

The deputy magistrate glanced at Gao Yi. Seeing his superior wasn't about to upbraid them for their lack of manners, he had no choice but to do as she said. "Last night there was a fire in the city. Two people died. The first was Li Fei, the assistant broker of Rongxing Pawnshop, and the other was Cheng Cheng, who took odd jobs within the city. Someone claimed to have seen you arguing with Cheng Cheng yesterday and suggested you killed him because of a grudge. It is the magistrate's duty to call you in so we may ask for clarification."

In addition to Gao Yi and his deputy, another man sat silently at the side of the room. He was in his thirties or forties, with an arrogant demeanor and sumptuous dress to match. Presumably this was the witness who'd reported the argument.

"Cheng Cheng tried to con us yesterday," said Qiao Xian, "We taught him a lesson. When he realized his mistake, he begged for mercy.

The matter was resolved, and payment for his service in guiding us here rendered and received. There are no grudges between us. Not to mention, we never left the inn last night; we had no opportunity to commit either arson or murder. I ask the magistrate to judge fairly."

Before Gao Yi could speak, the splendidly attired man snorted. "Of course you absolve yourselves of responsibility in just a few words. But whether they're true or not must be determined after our lord magistrate's questioning!"

Jinlian may have been Apa Khagan's lesser khatun, but her status was by no means low. She had never suffered such contempt before and now scoffed. "If we say we didn't kill him, what is there to question? What do you plan to do? Torture us into confessing to a crime we didn't commit?"

Though her Chinese was excellent, her words were slightly accented. Gao Yi noticed at once. "Where do you hail from?"

The other man raised his voice over him. "It doesn't matter where they're from—a murderer must pay with their life! This is the law of heaven!"

Gao Yi frowned. "Am I the one presiding over this case, or are you? If you can't restrain yourself, you may return to your master and tell him to seek a promotion. Then he can conduct the interrogation himself!"

The man lowered his voice but insisted, "My lord trusts the magistrate. That's why we reported the incident to you!"

"If that's the case, let us detain them," Gao Yi said expressionlessly. "We will interrogate them when Duan Qihu's men arrive."

Within this short exchange, the two seemed to have decided their fate. Qiao Xian looked about to explode, but Feng Xiao was a step ahead.

"The nerve of you! Don't you know who my lord is?!"

His tone was haughty, no less so than that of the lavishly dressed man. But he'd taken the words right out of Cui Buqu's mouth, and Cui Buqu looked at him askance.

Feng Xiao raised his chin high. "My lord is the nephew of the king of Kucha, ordered by our liege to travel to the Central Plains on important business. Now that our business has concluded, we are returning to Kucha. Yet you've accused him unjustly and detained him without reason! If you can't offer a suitable explanation, you can be sure we'll take this to the king himself!"

Gao Yi's head had begun to throb. If only he'd remembered to do his divination this morning, he'd have refused to see Xing Mao's man, never mind Qiao Xian's group. He softened his expression, ready to placate them, but the other man refused to let it go. "What proof do you have of your identity?"

The group was composed of both men and women, and four was suspiciously few for a royal envoy. Though Kucha was a small country, it wasn't a poor one. This man had seen all sorts of people; he refused to believe them so easily.

Yet to his surprise, Cui Buqu produced a golden seal. Carved upon it, in both Kuchean and Han characters, was a clear statement of the identity of its holder: Kucha's Left Marquis of Wu, Shang Jing.

When someone like Cui Buqu did something, they did it thoroughly. A disguise was only the first step—he'd also prepared two sets of identities. If their journey went smoothly, they were ordinary civilians visiting their relatives in Kucha. But if they met with the unexpected, as they had now, they'd become nobles of Kucha who were traveling incognito.

Cui Buqu was sure Feng Xiao must have made similar arrangements. But as Feng Xiao had gotten the jump and deployed this scheme first, he had little choice but to go with the flow.

Gao Yi turned the heavy golden seal back and forth but could find no flaw. Audacious fraudsters did exist, but few were capable of creating a fake golden seal. Furthermore, there was little to gain from pretending to be the king of Kucha's nephew. This group had kept a low profile since entering Qiemo. Had they not been summoned here, their identities would have likely remained unknown.

The sumptuously dressed man still had his doubts. He reached out to examine the seal himself, but Qiao Xian grabbed his wrist.

"Who do you think you are? This is the official seal personally bestowed by the king of Kucha. It's not some trinket you can handle however you please! Don't think we'll forget how you slandered us today!"

"I am an assistant official under the king of Shanshan," the man argued. "I'd never make reckless accusations!"

"The nation of Shanshan has long been destroyed!" Qiao Xian scoffed. "What king of Shanshan?"

No ordinary civilian would speak of royalty in such a tone. Gao Yi was becoming convinced of their identities. He held up a hand and said to Cui Buqu, "Li-xiansheng isn't trying to make trouble. The truth is, besides Cheng Cheng, the second victim was a trusted subordinate of Duke Xing."

Rongxing Pawnshop was run by Xing Mao's people. Officially, the head broker was Xing Mao's youngest son, but he'd never managed the business. The real boss was the deputy broker, Li Fei. Under his management, this shop brought in considerable profit for Xing Mao each year. Li Fei had worked for Xing Mao a long time and was an especially trusted subordinate. Xing Mao was certain someone had deliberately assassinated him and had thus sent his people to Gao Yi.

Xing Mao and Duan Qihu's feud was well-known in the city. When anything happened to Xing Mao's people, many would instinctively believe Duan Qihu responsible. Cui Buqu's group was merely an unexpected third party dragged into the mess.

Gao Yi preferred to stay out of disputes between Xing Mao and Duan Qihu. His authority as county magistrate was middling at best, while the other two had operated in the city for decades. Their influence was immense. Every year Gao Yi accepted perks from both factions, which naturally meant he had to return the favor.

"We are in a hurry to return to Kucha," said Qiao Xian. "If our lord hadn't fallen so gravely ill, we would have been on our way yesterday."

Gao Yi examined Cui Buqu's complexion and noted all the signs of fatigue and illness. Now certain this man was indeed who he claimed, he stood and cupped his hands. "Murder is a serious matter, and I must execute my duty. Kucha and Great Sui have always shared a strong relationship; it is my hope that this incident will not change that. I ask Shang-langjun's forgiveness."

Xing Mao's man frowned. "Lord Magistrate, if no resolution is reached on this matter, what can I say to my lord? Please detain these people while I go back and consult with him."

"Why not hunt down Duan Qihu and settle scores with him? Why fixate on us?" Qiao Xian demanded.

The man had his own theories on the matter. "Duan Qihu was always going to be the most likely suspect, and he knows it. Hiring outsiders like you gives him more freedom to act. Once the deed is done, you simply leave the city. Then who would know?"

Qiao Xian laughed in anger. "If we wanted to murder Cheng Cheng, why would we argue with him in public and draw your suspicion?"

At this point, the man Duan Qihu sent finally arrived.

He too was a middle-aged man, but he had a gaunt and scarred face, a stark contrast to the lavish clothes and rotund figure of

Xing Mao's subordinate. Together, the pair formed an odd fat-and-skinny duo.

Enemy met enemy, with all the hostility one would expect. The moment the men laid eyes on each other, sarcastic remarks began to fly. Gao Yi's office was quickly transformed into a verbal arena.

Cui Buqu watched Gao Yi's brows knit with impatience but saw that the magistrate couldn't afford to lose his temper. In Qiemo's so-called triad of power, Gao Yi was the weakest. "If we must wait here, why don't we examine the corpses?" he said. "Perhaps we will find some clues that will clear our names."

Gao Yi couldn't bear listening to Xing Mao and Duan Qihu's men argue any longer. He agreed at once.

The fat one was immediately skeptical. "You're telling me the nephew of the king of Kucha knows his way around a coroner's table?"

Cui Buqu's expression didn't change. "You're too kind. My wife's father is indeed a coroner by trade, with generations of expertise behind him. She's learned a thing or two over the years. What better chance for a demonstration of her skills? We'll only know if there's anything to be gleaned after we try."

Feng Xiao choked. He'd set Cui Buqu up minutes ago, and here Cui Buqu was, ready with payback.

An autopsy meant touching the corpse, and that meant...

Feng Xiao turned faintly green. Had he known this was going to happen, he would have humbled himself and played the king of Kucha's niece instead.

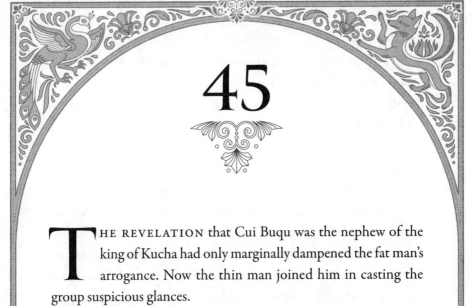

45

T HE REVELATION that Cui Buqu was the nephew of the king of Kucha had only marginally dampened the fat man's arrogance. Now the thin man joined him in casting the group suspicious glances.

This was Qiemo after all, far from the eyes of the emperor; they barely took Gao Yi's status as an official of Great Sui seriously. The king of Kucha wasn't about to send an army to collect his nephew. As they said, even a dragon couldn't kill a snake in its own garden. Cui Buqu was a mere nephew, but even if he were the king of Kucha himself, Duan Qihu and Xing Mao had hundreds of masterful ways to entrap him here forever.

The two corpses were at the morgue. Gao Yi refused to enter for fear of bad luck, so he had someone cart the corpses to the front courtyard instead.

It was a cool day, and though the bodies had been lying there since last night, there was no stench. Both men had burned to death, and their corpses were scorched black. It was hard to imagine any clues remained.

Let's see how you'll conduct an autopsy on this, the fat one's face seemed to say.

Cui Buqu walked once around the bodies, then waved Feng Xiao over. "A-Feng, isn't this what you're best at? Come take a look!"

Feng Xiao said nothing. The scent of char assailed his nose, and his mouth twitched. "My lord, your wife's lovely fingernails were freshly stained yesterday. Why don't you carry out the examination while I do the talking?"

Cui Buqu was bizarrely agreeable. His lips curved in a small smile. "Of course."

With no regard for the filth, he placed a hand on the first corpse and began to examine it, feeling upward from the stomach. The corpse's garments had been burned to flaking ash, and the pieces remained stuck to the skin. Touching it couldn't have been pleasant. The observers felt their hair stand on end; the fat-and-skinny duo covered their mouths and noses, and even Gao Yi had backed up to the doorway. Yet Cui Buqu remained unperturbed, as though what he touched was the jade-like skin of a beautiful woman and not a cracking corpse charred past the point of recognition.

Feng Xiao was an unrivaled martial artist, and when it came to intellect, he was first to rank himself among the sharpest minds. Still, that didn't mean he knew anything about autopsies. Since Cui Buqu had described his supposed generations of expertise, he had no choice but to play along. He watched Cui Buqu palpate the corpse and asked, "How's the torso?"

"His chest is uninjured. As for his back..."

Cui Buqu flipped the corpse over. With a *crack*, an arm fell to the floor.

Everyone stared.

"I didn't use much strength," Cui Buqu said innocently. "A-Feng, pass me his arm."

Qiao Xian quickly turned aside, lest Gao Yi and the others see the malicious glee dancing in her eyes.

Feng Xiao pressed a hand to his forehead. "Ah, I'm suddenly a bit dizzy. My lord, your wife just remembered: the doctor said our child is still small, so I oughtn't touch anything with too much negative yin energy. Of course we must listen to the doctor—your lordship wouldn't want his child to be born with any defects?"

Cui Buqu didn't answer. He glared at Feng Xiao's stomach, then looked away, face blank, and returned to examining the corpse. "The spine is uninjured." He turned the body over a few more times.

The fat one asked, "You still haven't found anything?"

The skinny one asked, "Aren't you just wasting our time?"

"There's definitely something odd about Li Fei's death," groused the fat man. "Magistrate, detain these four and interrogate them carefully. If you ask me, you should send someone to Kucha to inquire whether the king really has such a nephew. If not, they must be the culprits—someone secretly sent them to kill Li Fei!"

"What do you mean by *someone*?" The skinny man frowned. "Speak plainly, if you have the guts!"

"What? I didn't say any name!"

As the two prepared to rip into each other again, Gao Yi readied himself to mediate out of habit. Cui Buqu had shown the golden seal to prove his identity, but in all honesty, Gao Yi had no mind to meddle even if this "nephew" turned out to be a fraudster from the jianghu.

Ever since he'd arrived in Qiemo and discovered Duan Qihu and Xing Mao had already divided the city between them, Gao Yi had extinguished his once-fiery ambition of climbing the ranks. After enduring for so many years, he'd have accepted a mediocre position if it meant he could leave. Even a tiny county on the border would be better than staying in Qiemo. Though he received a considerable number of kickbacks from Duan Qihu and Xing Mao every year, he was caught between them like a rock and a hard place.

Cui Buqu's slow drawl came from beside him. "Neither of them has injuries on their chests or backs, however—they were both murdered before they were burned."

All three observers froze. The fat-and-skinny duo forgot their quarrel long enough for one of them to exclaim, "Ridiculous! On what do you base these sensational claims!"

"Look at his mouth," said Cui Buqu.

He pried open the mouth of one of the corpses. Too curious to resist, Gao Yi came forward to look. The fat-and-skinny duo, behind him, had no choice but to swallow their nausea and lean forward as well.

"If they'd burned to death, ash and dust would have entered their mouths and noses as they breathed. Their mouths are clean, which indicates they were burned after they were killed."

Until this moment, Gao Yi had wanted to wrap up the case without any fuss. When he heard they'd perished in the fire, he hadn't doubted the claim. But now he had to ask, "Can you tell how they died?"

Touching the back of the corpse's neck, Cui Buqu paused. "A-Feng, come take a look."

"My lord, you can tell me from there." Feng Xiao was certain Cui Buqu was setting him up. He refused to come a step closer even on pain of death.

Cui Buqu smiled at him. "Human life is precious. We can only avenge the lives of these deceased by uncovering the truth." He spoke gently, "A-Feng, I know you've been despondent since we lost our child. You feel the babe is still in your womb. But that's why we need to perform more good deeds, for the sake of our child. Isn't that so?"

Feng Xiao's mouth twitched. *Fine. You win this time, you lunatic.*

Cui Buqu arched a brow. *Who asked you to tell such brazen lies? I'm merely helping you polish them. Get over here before I show you my next trick; I assure you, you'll like it even less.*

The two locked eyes. Finally, Feng Xiao took a reluctant step forward. He stood beside Cui Buqu, suppressed his disgust, and groped along the back of the corpse's neck. "There's a crack along his cervical vertebrae. The killer was skilled; perhaps someone with extensive training. The bones are cracked but not displaced. Without a careful examination, it would never be discovered."

Gao Yi called the coroner over to perform his own examination. It was exactly as Cui Buqu and Feng Xiao had said.

"I knew someone murdered Li Fei!" the fat man shouted. "He spends all day managing the pawnshop and rarely goes anywhere else. Who could have such a strong personal grudge against him? Someone is trying to hinder my lord by picking off his subordinates!"

"If you have the balls then name names!" the skinny man shot back. "Enough with your vague insinuations!"

"Who's scared of naming names? Everyone in Qiemo knows Duan Qihu's Vajra finger technique can shatter metal and stone!"

"If my lord wanted to kill someone, would he dirty his own hands?" the skinny man sniped. "Is there a brain in that head of yours?!"

Gao Yi's temples throbbed from the noise. "Shut up, both of you!"

It seemed there was a limit to even this duo's impudence. They resentfully closed their mouths.

"The truth of this case is yet unclear," Gao Yi said. "There's no sense in arguing. I will send someone to conduct a full investigation and keep *both* of you informed of any results."

After a few more words of persuasion, he at last managed to send the two away.

Observing Gao Yi's relieved expression, the shadow of a smile crept over Cui Buqu's face. "Magistrate Gao should be the authority in this city. How have you ended up at the mercy of their whims?"

Gao Yi had an easy nature—he took no offense at the question and even cracked a wry smile. "Perhaps Duke Shang doesn't know. This city is controlled by Xing Mao and Duan Qihu, and has been for a long time. The court appointed me, but I lack the ability to overcome their influence."

"My uncle the king of Kucha sent me to travel the Central Plains. I journeyed through both Great Sui and Southern Chen, and found the north more prosperous and vibrant than the south. It's a matter of time before Great Sui unifies the Central Plains. When the day comes, how will Duan Qihu or Xing Mao resist the might of Great Sui's invincible army? Magistrate Gao should take heart."

The court has its hands full with the Göktürks. Where would they find the time for a small city like Qiemo? thought Gao Yi. But he was an official of Great Sui; he couldn't undermine his own nation before foreigners. He spoke some perfunctory words of agreement.

How could he know then that this sickly young man claiming to be the king of Kucha's nephew, along with his wife who squeaked all her words and acted like a madwoman, would accomplish what Gao Yi could not? With a wave of their hands, they would stabilize Qiemo, collapse three powers into one, and bring the city securely under Great Sui's rule. But Gao Yi knew nothing of these four's true identities, nor how terrifying they truly were.

"Duan Qihu started as a highwayman," Qiao Xian said. "How did he come to dominate Qiemo and amass so many followers?"

"I'm not sure myself," said Gao Yi. "They say he's charismatic and knows how to win people over. If he earned but a single copper coin, he'd split it among his men. That kind of attitude inspires loyalty.

He's a talented man, no less formidable than any hero. Not only do a third of the city's businesses belong to him, it's said his martial arts are first rank."

In contrast, Xing Mao sat on the legacy of the previous kings of Shanshan—he had more troops, more horses, more money, and more supplies, yet he could barely maintain their current stalemate. Clearly, he wasn't quite Duan Qihu's match.

But this murder case lacked any logic or motive. Other than the fractures in the corpses' spines, they had no other leads. With so little to go on, Gao Yi had no interest in pursuing the case against Cui Buqu's group. He only requested they stay in Qiemo so they could be summoned for questioning should need arise.

Feng Xiao asked Gao Yi for a basin of clean water and scrubbed his hands with soap a dozen times but still felt there was a smell. He left, set on finding a cosmetics shop to purchase perfume sachets he could rub on his hands.

Qiao Xian couldn't resist taking a shot at him: "Do you really fancy yourself a woman?"

"Are you insulting yourself?" asked Feng Xiao. "Or Jinlian?"

Qiao Xian rolled her eyes, and Jinlian joked, "I might be a woman, but I'm nowhere near as fussy as you."

"Between making myself happy and pretending to be happy for the benefit of others, I prefer the first," Feng Xiao said.

Cui Buqu had grown bored of the inn and itched for a stroll outside. He sent Qiao Xian and Jinlian ahead first and went with Feng Xiao to purchase the sachets.

To save a little time, Cui Buqu and Feng Xiao took a shortcut through a narrow alley, just wide enough for two people to walk abreast. This seemingly minor decision led to an unexpected encounter.

Up ahead, a white silhouette glided toward them with great haste, about to turn the corner into the alley.

Who else could it be but their old acquaintance, Yuxiu? But this time he wasn't alone—another figure walked beside him. They were about to come face-to-face. It was too late to retreat, and with Yuxiu's sharp eyesight, who knew what suspicious details he might spot in their disguises.

Feng Xiao did nothing by halves. Without a moment's hesitation, he wrenched his collar open and yanked Cui Buqu hard against him, panting delicately. "Don't be so impatient, my lord; we're in broad daylight! Your wife will be too embarrassed to look anyone in the eye after this!"

Cui Buqu was rendered utterly speechless.

46

IF CUI BUQU had reacted a little too slowly—or worse, not reacted at all—Yuxiu would surely have seen something wrong with this picture.

But the chief of the Zuoyue Bureau was the chief for a reason. Regardless of what curses he was hurling at Feng Xiao in his mind, the moment Feng Xiao pulled Cui Buqu's hand toward his body, Cui Buqu grabbed Feng Xiao's wrist and pinned it to the wall. His other hand came up to seize Feng Xiao's chin as he pretended to kiss him.

All the hair on Feng Xiao's body stood on end. Not due to Cui Buqu's bold actions, but the touch of his hands.

Cui Buqu had just examined a corpse—he'd even pried open the man's mouth. And afterward, he'd washed only once with soap. He felt as if those corpses were intimately caressing him through Cui Buqu's hand, and discomfort exploded through him.

Yet Cui Buqu seemed to think this still insufficient: he released Feng Xiao's wrist and brought his hand to the small of his back, palm trailing downward.

"That's—more—than—*enough*." Feng Xiao squeezed each word through gritted teeth.

"You didn't seem to think it was enough last time you tried to screw me over, hm?" Cui Buqu said with a smile.

Feng Xiao mouthed soundlessly, "Yuxiu is a clever man. If anything is off, he'll notice."

"That's why you must bear it," said Cui Buqu. "Don't give yourself away now."

They were pressed skin to skin, breaths mingling and noses brushing. To Yuxiu, it appeared he'd stumbled upon an indecent, thrill-seeking couple chasing pleasure in broad daylight. These deviants had no concept of propriety, neck and neck as they murmured into each other's ears.

It was rare to see such a dissolute woman in the capital. Were people really so open out in these border towns?

Yuxiu frowned slightly at their intertwined figures. Disgust flashed over his face, and he paused in his step. He turned from the alley and left without a backward glance.

Feng Xiao and Cui Buqu quickly made to retreat. Cui Buqu released Feng Xiao and took a couple of steps back. Feng Xiao raised his eyebrows.

Cui Buqu shrugged. "To avoid being shoved first. Remember, Deputy Chief Feng, I'm a scholar without even the strength to truss a chicken. I can't handle you flinging me into the wall the way you did before."

"Enough," snapped Feng Xiao. "Let's follow them, quick."

It was the middle of the day, and there were quite a few people about. But strangely, after Yuxiu and his companion left the mouth of the alley, they deliberately turned onto the road that was most crowded.

Feng Xiao grabbed Cui Buqu around the waist as he walked. To Cui Buqu, it felt as if there was a breeze beneath his feet—like he was gliding forward effortlessly. Though their pace was brisk through the crowd, they never bumped into anyone.

In the distance, they saw Yuxiu and his companion sit down at a roadside noodle stall. People milled about them, and they had no cover. But sitting in the open like this also made it easy for them to notice any suspicious characters approaching and was more convenient for conversation.

"We shouldn't get any closer." Feng Xiao said. He looked for a teahouse, and they entered and took a seat.

They were separated from Yuxiu by three or four stalls. It was a safe enough distance, but even Feng Xiao's excellent hearing couldn't catch what they were saying.

"Are Yuxiu's martial arts superior to yours?" Cui Buqu asked curiously.

"About the same." Feng Xiao pulled out a teacup and set it on the table, then ordered a pot of tea. Yet rather than drinking the tea, he began rinsing the cups: he poured tea into one cup, then rinsed another with it. He poured that tea out, refilled the cup, and started rinsing all over again. After repeating the process five times, he stopped, brows knit in disdain. "Right now, we're aware of Yuxiu, but Yuxiu isn't aware of us. This is an advantage. Before we figure out what he's doing here, we shouldn't let him catch us. Stop staring. A master's senses are sharp; he might notice."

Cui Buqu looked away. "I'm watching their mouths."

"Their mouths?" asked Feng Xiao. He instantly understood. "Lip reading?"

"Mm-hmm."

Feng Xiao would never admit Cui Buqu had managed to surprise him yet again. "Well? What did they say?"

"The other person's back is to me, and there are too many people in the way. I only caught two sentences of what Yuxiu said. The first was: 'Will Duan Qihu attend the banquet.' The second was: 'Do as we discussed.'"

Feng Xiao glanced in Yuxiu's direction and saw he was getting up to leave. The monk was quickly swallowed by the crowd, his destination unknown.

"What do you think?" asked Feng Xiao.

"First," Cui Buqu said, "I'm guessing Yuxiu and Duan Qihu know each other, but Duan Qihu doesn't know Yuxiu is here in Qiemo. Second, their plans will harm Duan Qihu in some way."

Feng Xiao pondered this. "Yuxiu is a mysterious character. How can the Prince of Jin have any connection with a bandit leader thousands of miles away?"

Cui Buqu correctly read this as an offer to exchange information. "The Zuoyue Bureau only knows that he was a disciple of Tiantai Sect in Jiangnan before he started working for the Prince of Jin. It should be impossible to achieve his level of martial arts at such a young age without devoting years to arduous training within his sect. On the other hand, Duan Qihu's activities have always been constrained to the western border; he's never been to Jiangnan. Logically, they shouldn't share any connection."

"One doesn't have to stay within their sect at all times, even if they're training arduously," said Feng Xiao. "Look at me. Someone born with outstanding talent who can achieve what others could merely dream, even at a young age. We exist too, you know."

"Hm?" Cui Buqu patted himself, then ducked his head and looked around, as if he'd dropped something. "Did you see it?"

"See what?"

"My respect for you. Where did it go?"

Feng Xiao was silent.

After drawing a little blood, Cui Buqu mood was buoyant. "Let's not delve into possible grudges between Yuxiu and Duan Qihu. Duan Qihu is surrounded by martial experts, and he himself is by all accounts a first-class master. Never mind sending an accomplice; even if Yuxiu went himself, he might not fell Duan Qihu in a single blow. So how is Yuxiu's ally supposed to get close to him?"

Feng Xiao stroked his chin. "Poison? Honeytrap? No, that can't be right. If it was that easy, Duan Qihu would be dead a few times over by now. There must be many who despise him. If Yuxiu isn't going personally, he needs a suitable opportunity—a time when Duan Qihu's guard is lowered, or when he has no choice but to lower it..."

He looked up at Cui Buqu in realization. The two of them stared at each other before exclaiming in unison, "The birthday banquet!"

At that moment, the man who'd been sitting with Yuxiu stood. He paid the bill, then left in the opposite direction as the monk.

There was no time to discuss. Cui Buqu and Feng Xiao threw down their money and sprang up to tail him.

"How are his martial arts?" Just as before, Feng Xiao half-carried Cui Buqu as they sped through the city. Cui Buqu noted that Feng Xiao kept noticeably closer to their mark this time, less cautious than he'd been with Yuxiu.

"Not bad. But not good enough to discover me," Feng Xiao said.

The other man walked slowly. He seemed to be in no hurry; as they watched, he stopped along the road and purchased two savory pastries and a long skewer of snacks before continuing on his way.

They soon realized the man's destination was an ordinary one. All around were the houses and courtyards of ordinary citizens. He turned to enter a yard with two children playing at the gate. On seeing him, they ran to welcome him with calls of "Daddy!" He handed out the snacks, then scooped a child into each arm, talking and laughing with them as he carried them inside.

Feng Xiao and Cui Buqu let the trail end there. They agreed to split up, each going their separate ways to the bases of the Jiejian and Zuoyue Bureaus to look into the man's background. Cui Buqu's men had lived in Qiemo five or six years and knew the city like the back of their hands; they could recite the history of anyone of even minor fame by heart. He merely needed to point them in the right direction and a report would quickly follow.

"My lord, the master of that house is a man named Peng Xiang. He's Xing Mao's third steward."

Cui Buqu's face was impassive as he listened. "Xing Mao seems to have a lot of stewards."

"It's just as you say," the Zuoyue agent agreed. "Xing Mao's family is powerful; the clan has considerable wealth and is successful in business. In addition to his family members, he has three stewards who help manage clan affairs. It's said the head steward is Xing Mao's closest confidant and a man of no little influence himself. Ordinary folk rarely glimpse him. The second steward manages Xing Mao's external affairs, while the third steward is responsible for more trivial matters of the household."

Upon hearing the last words, Cui Buqu started as if he'd realized the answer to some of his questions. "I heard Xing Mao's mother is celebrating her birthday in a few days. Then this third steward must be responsible for the banquet?"

"If nothing's changed, that should be correct."

Now this will be a sight to see, Cui Buqu thought. He bid the man farewell and hurried back to the inn.

Feng Xiao had returned a step ahead of him; when Cui Buqu arrived, he was relaxing in their room, drinking tea and eating snacks. The moment he heard the creak of the door, he smiled. "Looks like you found something."

"What are you so happy about?" Cui Buqu asked, suspicious. "Do you have a grudge against Duan Qihu? Are you so thrilled he's going to die?"

"I have no grudge against Duan Qihu, but it's true someone wants him dead. No, I'm happy because someone has kindly handed me a pillow right as I was about to doze off."

He produced an invitation and pushed it across the table toward Cui Buqu.

Cui Buqu picked it up. His brows shot up in surprise.

"You tell me," said Feng Xiao gleefully. "Should I not be happy?"

Cui Buqu nodded. "It's indeed convenient timing."

His fake identity as nephew of the king of Kucha had been revealed mere hours ago, yet a banquet invitation for Xing Mao's mother's sixtieth birthday had already arrived. Xing Mao was quick on the draw and a skilled diplomat to boot. Small wonder he'd dominated Qiemo for so many years.

Feng Xiao had clearly also discovered the identity of Yuxiu's accomplice. "Xing Mao's third steward is colluding with a counselor of the Prince of Jin, a disciple of the Tiantai Sect. How fascinating! I was wondering how to get my hands on an invitation, but it seems the king of Kucha's influence is not to be underestimated."

"My wife just lost our child, and her body took a severe toll. She should be lying in bed recuperating. Look how the autopsy frayed your nerves. You needn't attend the banquet; I'll take Qiao Xian."

"For my lord's sake, A-Feng would walk through fire and flood. A lost child is a trifle. Who knows what you may encounter at the banquet. How can I be at ease if I'm not by your side?"

In other words: *Don't even think about hoarding all the credit for yourself.*

Cui Buqu smiled. "You're a married woman. If you can't learn how to be an obedient wife, I'll have to set you aside."

"Even if I haven't given you a child yet, my lord's flesh and blood has lain within my belly. Is your lordship so callous?"

On the surface, they were talking nonsense, but Cui Buqu truly didn't want Feng Xiao to attend the banquet. Feng Xiao, however, insisted—and if Cui Buqu obstructed him, he'd undoubtedly find a way to spoil Cui Buqu's plans.

At the same time, Qiao Xian was on her way over to perform her routine check of Cui Buqu's pulse. She'd just reached the door when she heard Cui Buqu's voice inside: "The only thing you're good for is producing children. Don't think so highly of yourself!"

Qiao Xian stopped short. She stood in the doorway wearing a bewildered expression, wondering what she'd missed.

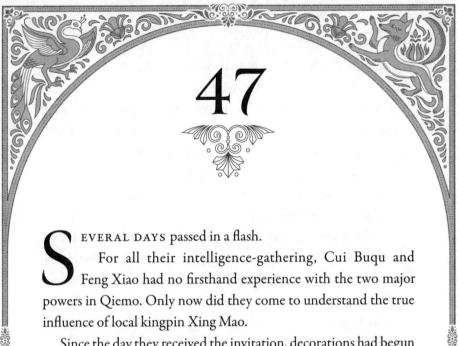

47

S EVERAL DAYS passed in a flash.

For all their intelligence-gathering, Cui Buqu and Feng Xiao had no firsthand experience with the two major powers in Qiemo. Only now did they come to understand the true influence of local kingpin Xing Mao.

Since the day they received the invitation, decorations had begun to fill the city. In the space of a few days, the streets of Qiemo were festooned with red lanterns and silk ribbon. Qiemo wasn't large, but such lavish festivities were something only the wealthiest of families could bear.

Powerful as a clan and successful in business—this wasn't sufficient to describe Xing Mao's influence. He was a descendant of the king of Shanshan himself. When their homeland was invaded, the king fled to Qiemo with the contents of the royal treasury and more than four thousand surviving households. Three generations later, Xing Mao's operations touched every corner of the city. It was said his businesses had branches as close as Liugong City and as far away as the capitals of Great Sui and Southern Chen.

The greater one's wealth, the more one needed to guard it. When Xing Mao was five years old, the king of Shanshan had invited many martial arts masters to teach his grandson. Unfortunately, Xing Mao was a mediocre student—even now, his skills were third-class at best.

But he didn't lack for bodyguards. Whenever he went out, it was with a mighty procession, ostentatious as any parade.

When Feng Xiao and Cui Buqu arrived at the gates of the Xing residence, they were met with an awful din. The street jostled with the carriages of guests. Guards stood in neat ranks not only before the entrance, but around the entire manor. As they approached the gates, Feng Xiao and Cui Buqu spied the third steward, flanked by two guards as he welcomed guests.

Cui Buqu smiled. "A sight not at all inferior to the crown prince and the Prince of Jin's royal tours. This is what happens when the emperor's influence is distant. Xing Mao no longer has a Kingdom of Shanshan, but he still fancies himself ruler of these lands."

Feng Xiao brought a thoughtful finger to his chin. "They say his subordinates and family call him *king* in his presence."

Carriages were parked all around them, many exquisitely appointed. They alone had come from the inn on foot, without any carriage or accompanying attendants. Most of the guests were prominent figures in the city or members of the jianghu with connections to Xing Mao. In comparison, Cui Buqu and Feng Xiao appeared downright shabby. They even had to carry their gift themselves.

Xing Mao had invited the nephew of the king of Kucha, so Cui Buqu had to attend. If Jinlian were to also attend, the only suitable disguise for her was a maid—but a single maid accompanying the king's nephew would also be conspicuous. Cui Buqu had ordered Qiao Xian to stay behind and protect her lest Fo'er threaten them again. But as a consequence, he and Feng Xiao looked all the more drab beside the other guests with their throngs of servants and guards.

They ignored the curious gazes that followed them on all sides—at that moment, their thick skins came in handy. As they took their places behind the other guests, completely at ease and without the slightest hint of embarrassment, the pair took the opportunity to observe the crowd with great interest.

Every guest had brought gifts, both large and small. Someone, eager to flaunt their wealth, had even brought a jade tree as tall as a man, hung with gold and silver. It drew countless exclamations of wonder. In contrast, Cui Buqu only carried a box the length of his arm.

The third steward was accustomed to seeing all sorts of precious gifts. When he saw the simple box, more like a complimentary gift a shop might offer when purchasing candied fruits than a lavish birthday present, he was momentarily stunned.

He looked at this guest's invitation again. Kucha produced large quantities of iron—it was rich in resources and far from destitute as a nation. Yet Cui Buqu and Feng Xiao's attire, while not cheap, was still a far cry from the luxurious fabrics one would expect.

The steward knew better than to comment, but the servant beside him couldn't curb his look of contempt as he received the box.

"What cheek!" Cui Buqu was displeased. "How dare you turn your nose up at our gift."

The attendant holding the box stared at him, baffled.

Cui Buqu's tone was haughty: "A-Feng, open the box and show them our gift."

In full view of the crowd, Feng Xiao, in a rare moment of obedience, took the box from the attendant. After untying the silk ribbon, he pulled out a plain-looking dagger.

"Watch," said Feng Xiao.

He drew the dagger from its sheath; its blade was glazed a dense frosty white, as if encased in ice and snow. The crowd watched as Feng Xiao lifted his hand and gave it a light flick. The attendant who'd taken the box was still waiting for something to happen when his clothes suddenly fell away, leaving him naked as the day he was born.

A woman's scream finally brought the attendant to his senses. Mortified, he turned beet red and dashed away to clothe himself.

Cui Buqu barked out a mocking laugh, then said loftily, "Duke Xing has seen all manner of treasures. What do you take us for? How could we bring some common gift? We would be no different from peasants or nobodies."

After witnessing the sharpness of the dagger, the crowd marveled—it seemed Kucha's reputation was well-deserved. No one dared look down on Cui Buqu.

The third steward, recalling his duty, quickly took the dagger with both hands and handed it to an attendant at his side with great care. He smiled. "I can only apologize for my subordinate's rudeness toward Shang-langjun. Your lordship, I beg you to forgive us, if only for the sake of my master's banquet today. Please come in! Your seats are prepared; this way please!"

All the guests before them had been led in by attendants. Only Cui Buqu and Feng Xiao were granted the third steward's personal attention.

The grandeur of the Xing residence went without saying. Thanks to the large number of attendees this year, it was impossible to fit all the guests inside the main hall. To accommodate everyone, they had spread the banquet over both the inside and outside. Only a small number of tables, meant for Xing Mao's most valued guests, were placed within the hall. The courtyard outside seated many more, and it was here that most of the guests were directed.

Even with the third steward guiding them, Cui Buqu and Feng Xiao didn't qualify for the interior seats. The steward led them to one of the tables in the courtyard closest to the entrance of the hall. It was probably an excellent seat. Cui Buqu knew initial arrangements would have placed them even further back—it was only thanks to their little altercation at the gate that the steward made this last-minute change.

He peered inside. In addition to the two seats for the hosts at the front, there were four more on either side. A total of eight distinguished guests. One of them must be Duan Qihu.

Cui Buqu made a face. "What's this? A relative of the Kuchean royal family doesn't merit a seat inside?"

The third steward's smile was fixed on his face. He cupped his hands politely. "I beg your lordship's understanding. Those eight seats are for my lord's dearest friends of many years. They are not assigned based on rank or status. The distinguished guests in the courtyard include such eminent personages as the leader of Qionghai Sect, juniors from the Wei family of Guanzhong, and the young master of the Xianlin Sect, among others. Their seats are all set far behind yours!"

Cui Buqu waved his hand with fake impatience. "Enough. The madam of the family is celebrating her sixtieth birthday; I have no interest in starting petty squabbles."

The third steward smiled wider. "Your lordship is truly a magnanimous man."

He still had many guests to receive, so with an apology, he left. Feng Xiao sat beside Cui Buqu, plucked a grape from the platter on the table, and tossed it in his mouth. He peered around curiously.

The guests took their seats one after the other. Four of the eight seats in the inner hall were filled. Feng Xiao didn't recognize any of the occupants, but he heard Cui Buqu say, "In the inner hall—that looks like Wei Huofang from the Wei family of Guanzhong. I don't recognize anyone else; they're probably not from the jianghu."

"Xing Mao will definitely place Duan Qihu's seat just below his own as a show of respect," said Feng Xiao. "We're too far away here. It's inconvenient if we need to make any move."

"We'll have to play it by ear then," said Cui Buqu. "By the way, where did you find such an incredibly sharp dagger?"

Feng Xiao finished his grapes, then skewered a piece of honey melon with a silver fork and popped it in his mouth. He smiled. "I infused it with my own internal energy. It's more than sharp—using it to split a mountain wouldn't be out of the question."

"But when you drew the dagger, weren't there wisps of white around it?" Cui Buqu asked suspiciously.

Feng Xiao chuckled. "I placed the dagger in the snow for a few days, then used my own internal energy to awaken the frost on it. Wouldn't that create your white vapor? I bought that thing at a weapons shop on the east side of Qiemo. A mere three hundred coppers and we get to sample these wonderful delicacies. Well worth the price if you ask me!"

Cui Buqu was speechless a moment. "Is the Jiejian Bureau so impoverished you can't even procure a decent gift?"

"I traveled thousands of miles to this border city for an investigation," Feng Xiao said with complete conviction. "You think that doesn't require money? Border cities are dry and dusty. Without my flower dew and smoothing oil, how could my hair and skin maintain their splendor? Your Qiao Xian is so stingy. Ask her to buy some hair oil and it's like I'm killing her. My venerable self has had no choice but to spend from my own pocket."

What could Cui Buqu say? If Feng Xiao had pretended to pout like a maiden, Cui Buqu could've at least fired back a sarcastic remark or two. But right then Feng Xiao wasn't putting on an act—he was utterly uncompromising, utterly imperious. Cui Buqu imagined Feng Xiao sitting in their room at the inn, feet planted wide like a mighty general, shaving his stubble and combing oil through his precious hair. He couldn't stop his mouth from twitching.

"Men need to groom themselves too, don't think they don't." Feng Xiao was warming to his lecture. "When someone's face is as peerless as mine, how can they honor the favor the heavens bestowed upon them if they don't cherish it? Your looks are a far sight below this venerable one, but you're still a handsome man. Alas, your body is sickly and will age faster than most. If you don't take care, I fear in another few years..." He chuckled.

Cui Buqu knew nothing good would follow, but he couldn't stop himself from asking, "In another few years, what?"

"I'll really be able to call you *Daddy*."

Cui Buqu stared at the platter of fruit for a good while. He was afraid he'd really lose it this time and grind Feng Xiao's face into the grapes.

A voice interrupted his dangerous thoughts.

"Pardon the intrusion. My name is Chen Ji. Would the lady and gentleman be so kind as to share their esteemed names?"

Cui Buqu raised his head.

The young man—Chen Ji—had taken a seat beside Feng Xiao. His words were clearly directed at "the lady." Cui Buqu was an afterthought.

"Ji...which Ji?" The punchable smirk Feng Xiao had worn while bickering with Cui Buqu had vanished, replaced with a shy smile. His gaze flitted slyly over Chen Ji, and he gracefully batted his long lashes.

Such tactics had no effect on Cui Buqu, but they clearly worked on men who didn't know Feng Xiao. At the very least, Chen Ji was immediately affected. His gaze seemed to sparkle as he looked at Feng Xiao.

"Ji, composed of the characters *Yu* and *Qi*. As when the sky clears after rain."

Chen Ji. Cui Buqu put the name with the person. A moment later, he'd recalled the man's background: the young master of the Xianlin Sect of Guanzhong.

The Xianlin Sect wasn't classed among such great sects as Xuandu Mountain or the Tiantai Sect, but it was still a name of some repute within the jianghu. Chen Ji's skills were average, and he was known to have an arrogant and willful personality. He was not unlike Lin Yong, the young master of Yandang Mountain Estate. Perhaps all wealthy children who'd been pampered from birth and never experienced any setbacks were similar.

Though Chen Ji's martial arts were nothing extraordinary, his father was the leader of the Xianlin Sect. Thus the Xing family had placed him in the seat next to Cui Buqu—a sensible choice.

Another glance at the inner hall revealed that the host and guests had all arrived. Duan Qihu and Gao Yi sat just below Xing Mao, on his left and right respectively. Next to Xing Mao was an older matron—presumably Xing Mao's mother, the guest of honor.

Cui Buqu had been contemplating how to get closer to Duan Qihu all this time. With the appearance of Chen Ji, a plan had suddenly presented itself.

Feng Xiao seemed to have read his mind. He flashed a smirk and winked at Cui Buqu, then shoved the fruit platter across the table.

This man thrived on chaos. Cui Buqu rolled his eyes. Then he picked up the fruit platter and threw it to the ground with a great *crash*.

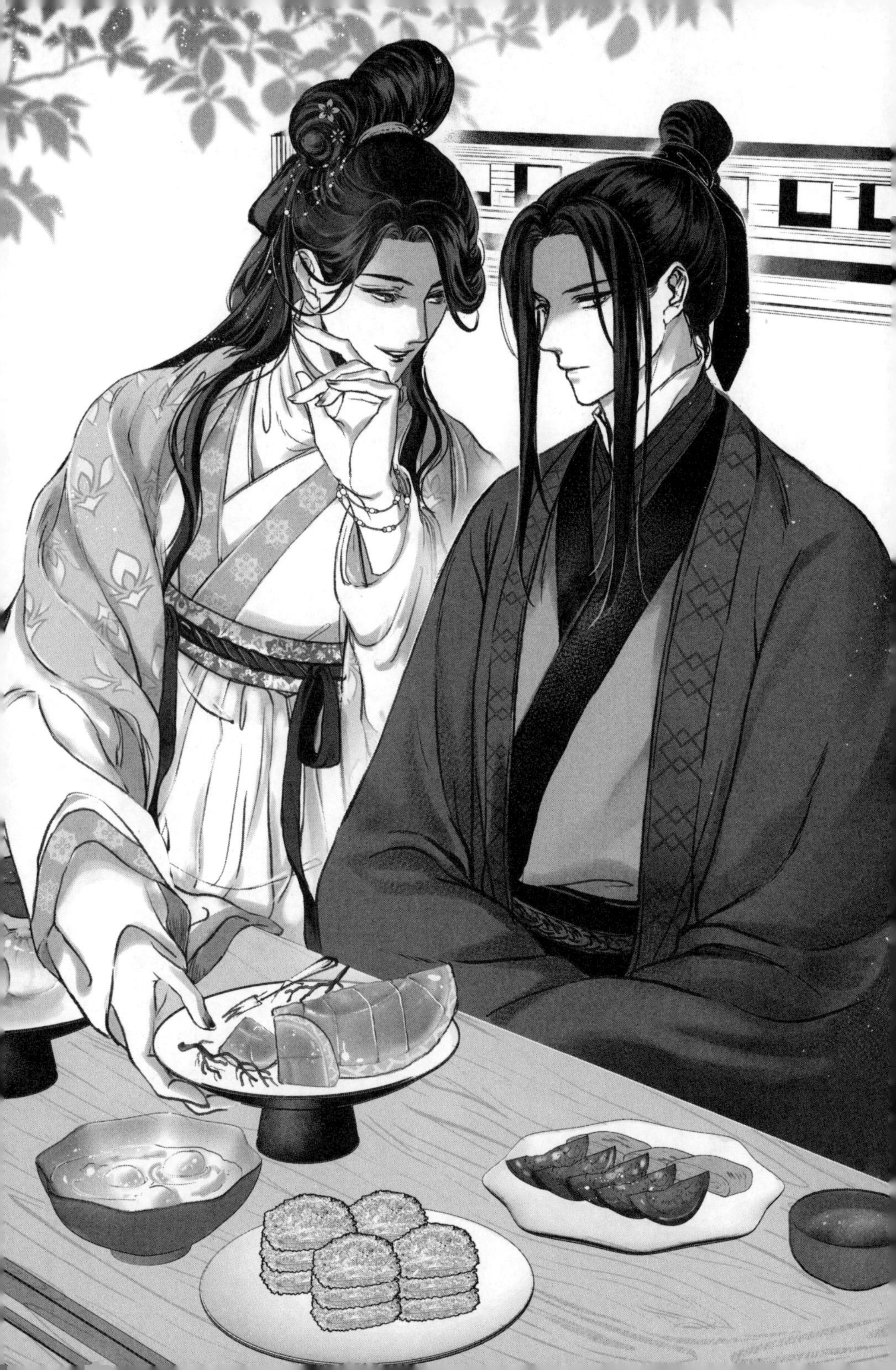

Instantly, the platter shattered to pieces, fruit rolling across the floor in all directions. Who could ignore such a commotion? The banquet went dead silent as everyone looked over—Xing Mao's group included.

48

B REAKING THE PLATTER was only the first step.

Cui Buqu leapt to his feet and pointed at Chen Ji. "Do you have any idea who I am?! I'm the nephew of the king of Kucha! How dare you disrespect my wife, lusting after her right before my eyes! Today is the birthday of Duke Xing's mother, to which I was honored to be invited. I sincerely desired to congratulate Patriarch Xing, but instead I've encountered a shameless scoundrel under his roof! If this were Kucha, I would have you flogged to death!"

He made the entire speech in one breath, leaving no one time to react. Chen Ji was momentarily stupefied. *All I did was ask for her name? I haven't even touched her! How am I disrespecting her?* He was no pushover, but Cui Buqu's attack was too sudden. Chen Ji had no ready retort.

Their host, however, wasn't about to let them disrupt his banquet. At a pointed glance from Xing Mao, the head steward hurried forward to smooth things over. "You're both my lord's guests today; there's no need to fight. Please think of my lord's reputation—"

"My uncle often said that Duke Xing lives in Qiemo, and that he is one of the most formidable men of his generation," Cui Buqu sneered. "To think even my uncle could so misjudge someone! I represent the king of Kucha, yet I'm not even seated in the hall, forced instead to endure the blazing sun. Who would attend a banquet like this? Farewell!"

The head steward held up a placating hand and smiled. "My lord misunderstands," he said. "These arrangements were made by us lowly servants. The inner hall is too narrow, and space is limited. There isn't enough room..."

Cui Buqu cast him a sidelong glance. "Isn't that just an excuse to snub people?" he asked disdainfully. "Why not knock down the wall and merge everything into one?"

As if it was that easy? Would the house even be a house any-more?! When Cui Buqu was trying to enrage someone, his manner grew so acrimonious as to be unbearable; the head steward felt an irresistible impulse to pound his face in. But he couldn't lose his temper now; he had to keep smiling. "The lord is right to criticize the arrangement; this lowly one didn't take this into consideration. I invite the honorable couple to sit in the main hall. I shall prepare two seats at once."

He waved his hand for an attendant, who immediately came to place the seats. The head steward ushered Cui Buqu and Feng Xiao inside.

Xing Mao rose and personally walked to the center of the hall to welcome them. "I offer both of you my sincere apologies for our lack of manners. Please, drink up!"

Cui Buqu's goal from the beginning had been to infiltrate the inner hall. Now, he looked toward Duan Qihu and said loudly, "I've heard there are two great men in the city of Qiemo. One is Duke Xing, the other Duke Duan. Since I was fortunate enough to come here, I cannot miss the opportunity to sit closer to Duke Duan. You needn't trouble yourself with changing the arrangements. Just place my seat and my wife's behind Duke Duan!"

Duan Qihu laughed heartily. "To think Shang-langjun regards me so highly. There's plenty of space beside me. Why not sit together?"

Cui Buqu was overjoyed. "I'd be only too glad to!"

Usually, each guest had their own seat and table; sharing a table was a display of closeness. Cui Buqu showed no courtesy whatsoever—he tossed aside the head steward and strode over to sit beside Duan Qihu.

Upon seeing that Xing Mao had no objection, the head steward could do nothing but curse silently as he set up another table for Feng Xiao next to Cui Buqu.

In one stroke, not only had Cui Buqu and Feng Xiao secured a seat close to Duan Qihu, they were but a few steps from Xing Mao.

All that was left was the unfortunate Chen Ji, who'd suffered Cui Buqu's wrath for no reason. By the time he came to his senses, Cui Buqu had attached himself to Duan Qihu. No matter how much he wanted to flip the table in rage, it was too late; he could only glare angrily at Cui Buqu's back. The head steward, still wary of these guests creating a scene, went over to console Chen Ji. Whatever he said, Chen Ji's anger was quickly replaced with joy. He paid Cui Buqu no further heed and gladly took his seat.

The disturbance was thus settled. The head steward breathed a sigh of relief and silently grumbled to himself. The third steward had arranged today's banquet—this kind of task should have fallen to him, yet he'd disappeared to who knew where.

"I traveled to Kucha a few years back and had the honor of meeting His Majesty. Tell me, how does he fare?" Duan Qihu asked.

"My uncle has no issues eating or sleeping. He can draw his bow and shoot eagles on his horse, and off it, he can fight wolves barehanded. He's always been strong as an ox, but two of his grandsons recently passed from illness. It broke his heart; he refused even his favorite dances and music. If not for that, he would have been the one to come to the Central Plains."

Since Cui Buqu was pretending to be the nephew of the king of Kucha, he'd done his homework in advance. Otherwise, he might have fooled Gao Yi, but he would never deceive wily old foxes like Xing Mao and Duan Qihu.

The king of Kucha really did have a nephew named Shang Jing. Because of his poor health, he'd removed to a villa outside the city at a young age and was rarely seen. For every dozen words Cui Buqu spoke, at least seven or eight were true. It was easy to trust him. Moreover, Duan Qihu and Xing Mao had both heard of the early deaths of the royal grandsons. After hearing Cui Buqu mention it too, they put aside any doubts about his identity.

Duan Qihu nodded and sighed. "Send the king my condolences and tell him this: please be at peace."

Xing Mao clapped his hands. The dishes, ready and waiting for his command, appeared in a steady stream. Jars of wine were brought up one by one, the seals cracked open before the guests. Their fragrance rose into the air—one sniff told Xing Mao's guests it was a good, aged vintage. Even those familiar with fine wines across the land couldn't help their mouths watering in anticipation.

Beautiful maids stepped up to pour wine for the guests and everyone raised their cups to congratulate the madam on her birthday. Xing Mao drank the toast and knelt before his mother, thanking her for raising him.

Duan Qihu had come in a show of goodwill today and afforded his host every courtesy. When a maid bent to pour his wine, he too raised his cup and said magnanimously, "May your fortune be as vast as the East Sea, your time as enduring as the Southern Mountains."

Just as he was about to tip his head back and drink, Cui Buqu cried, "Wait, Duke Duan!" He smiled. "Why is Duke Duan's wine jar different from mine? Is it because Duke Duan is a powerful man in Qiemo that the host's family offers him different treatment?"

It was possible to argue that Cui Buqu's outburst when he saw a man flirting with his wife outside was reasonable. But now he was making trouble for the sake of it. And when Cui Buqu exerted his troublemaking ability to the fullest, it was enough to drive anyone mad.

The head steward, for example, was beyond irritated with him. "Shang-langjun has misunderstood," he snapped. "There is deep significance to our wine jars. We have four kinds: plum blossom, orchid, bamboo, and chrysanthemum, which we store in our cellars in the spring, summer, autumn, and winter. Each of these wines has a distinct flavor, but they're equally precious and unique to our estate. Once you finish your jar, you may of course taste one of the others. There's no need to work yourself up over it!"

Professional nuisance Cui Buqu pretended not to see the irritated twist to the head steward's smile. He pointed to the cup in Duan Qihu's hand. "Duke Duan's wine must taste especially extraordinary. I wish to switch cups with Duke Duan!"

Duan Qihu laughed and handed over his cup. "Not a problem at all. I'll give you this cup, and someone can fetch me another!"

Xing Mao furrowed his brow, displeasure simmering in him. But in the end, he said nothing. Cui Buqu had dared to repeatedly disrupt his mother's birthday banquet, and Xing Mao had a hundred ways to make him regret it later.

But when Cui Buqu received Duan Qihu's cup, he didn't simply accept it. He handed it to the lovely maid who'd just poured for Duan Qihu.

"Here, you drink it!"

The maid froze, then quickly backed up a few steps and cast a pleading glance toward the steward, who had endured just about enough of this menace. He warned him, still smiling, "Shang-langjun, today is my lord's mother's birthday banquet. Please show some restraint."

Cui Buqu's brows rose in mock surprise. "How am I not restrained? Everyone knows Duke Duan and Duke Xing are rivals. Who's to say some scoundrel wouldn't try to sow discord by poisoning Duke Duan then framing the Xing family? I'm merely taking precautions that will clear Duke Xing of suspicion, aren't I?"

The steward had reached the end of his rope. He stepped forward and made to grab Cui Buqu's shoulder. "You little pest, you're not here to attend the banquet. You came to pick a fight!"

This man was Xing Mao's closest confidant in addition to being his highest-ranking and most trusted subordinate; he was a strong martial artist. His strike was as swift as lightning. Even if Cui Buqu had been trained in martial arts, he might not have been able to dodge—but of course, he didn't know any at all.

Yet before the steward could make him scream in pain and scare him out of spewing more nonsense, someone else gripped his hand, arresting his movements with the pinch of a mere forefinger and thumb.

The head steward swallowed down agony and looked over his shoulder. Feng Xiao smiled at him shyly. That smile sent a tremor through the head steward's body. He instantly lost any ability to retaliate.

Ignoring the head steward, Cui Buqu pushed the cup toward the maid. "Once you've drunk this cup of wine, I shan't bother you anymore, nor cause any further trouble for Duke Xing."

The maid looked at the ground, utterly still. By now, Duan Qihu too had noticed something was wrong.

Xing Mao was furious at the meddling Cui Buqu, but what enraged him more was losing face in front of Duan Qihu. The courtyard was festive yet, but guests in the inner hall had stopped drinking to look over at the commotion. The atmosphere had turned awkward. He barked out, "Since Shang-langjun says so, just drink it!"

Now that Xing Mao had spoken, the maid had no choice but to take the wine from Cui Buqu. But it seemed she'd been scared silly—her hand trembled as she held it, spilling wine everywhere.

Cui Buqu grabbed her wrist and pressed the cup to her mouth. "Don't be afraid," he said gently. "It's only a little wine. What are you so scared of? You act like it's poisoned."

Just as the wine was about to tip into her mouth, the maid broke free of Cui Buqu and turned to pounce on Duan Qihu. Light flashed—a dagger, hidden until now, leapt to her hand, the sharp point headed straight for Duan Qihu's chest.

Duan Qihu launched into the air like a great eagle spreading its wings in flight. Not only did he avoid the maid's fatal strike, he kicked her wrist as he landed, turning the dagger away. As she stumbled and fell forward over the low table, the dagger in her own hand pierced her chest and killed her on the spot.

Screams split the air. The once-lively banquet was transformed as everyone's faces paled with fear. The guests in the inner hall stood and backed away, one after another.

Xing Mao pointed at Cui Buqu and Feng Xiao as he raged, "Guards, seize them!"

Cui Buqu sneered. "What good is capturing me? Yesterday, I saw your third steward on the street, conspiring with someone to kill Duan Qihu. Why else would I make trouble at the banquet? And it's just as I feared!"

"Xing Mao." Duan Qihu's face was like a thundercloud. "I came here in good faith, yet you greeted me with a Hongmen banquet!"[2] The two guards he'd brought adopted protective stances, as though really afraid Xing Mao might attack at any moment.

"I knew nothing of this!" Xing Mao was furious. If Duan Qihu died here today, jumping into the Yellow River wouldn't be enough to wash himself clean of blame. Who but Xing Mao would want him dead? But if Xing Mao truly wanted to kill him, even sending a woman to seduce and poison him would be more effective than this crude method. Not to mention, today was his mother's birthday, and he was famously filial toward her. How could he kill a man in front of his own mother?

But things had already come to this point. No matter who wanted to kill Duan Qihu, if he died, his influence would be absorbed by Xing Mao. Without their patriarch, the Duan family would be an eagle with broken wings. In fact, perhaps he should finish what someone else had started...

As his thoughts turned, the darkness in his eyes deepened like a tempest brewing. Xing Mao's three stewards had been with him for many years and were familiar with their master's ways. Feng Xiao had obstructed the head steward, but the second steward was standing by. With a silent wave of his hand, the guards of the Xing residence gathered to surround the inner hall. The instant their master gave the command, they'd rush forward and slay Duan Qihu. No matter how skilled the former bandit was, he couldn't possibly escape this watertight blockade.

Shit, thought Duan Qihu.

---

2 A banquet with the aim of murdering the guest. Refers to a famous episode in 206 BC when future Han emperor Liu Bang escaped an attempted murder by his rival, Xiang Yu, during a sword dance at a feast held in his honor.

He'd attended today's banquet because he was sure Xing Mao would never act against him there. Who could have guessed he'd find himself in such dire straits? Whether or not Xing Mao was responsible for the poisoned wine no longer mattered. Duan Qihu, too, could see the murderous intent in Xing Mao's eyes.

Was he finally going to his grave, here and now?

Still in Feng Xiao's grasp, the head steward finally couldn't take the pain. He shrieked in agony.

Feng Xiao smiled. "It seems I've been too rough. But since you're the one who tried to attack my husband, I'm afraid you'll have to endure it!"

The head steward collapsed to the ground, motionless. Feng Xiao's figure flickered, and the second steward felt a wind rushing toward him. His heart thumped as he threw out a strike, meeting the enemy head-on. Their palms slammed against each other. The second steward tasted salty-sweetness surging up his throat—he coughed blood and collapsed backward.

In contrast, Feng Xiao was completely unscathed. He turned to Xing Mao. "You see? Even if all your men come at me together, I'll walk out of here without a scratch. Perhaps I'll even bring Duan Qihu with me."

When had such an unparalleled martial artist arrived in tiny Qiemo? The man who claimed to be the nephew of the king of Kucha was as weak as a kitten, yet his wife was hiding such incredible abilities.

Duan Qihu considered himself skilled, but saw immediately that he was outmatched. He knew of Fo'er, the foremost expert of the Göktürk Khaganate, yet thought even he might not have been able to defeat this woman.

Who *were* these people?

Xing Mao was enraged. "Who the hell are you?!"

"A beauty, naturally." Feng Xiao produced a handkerchief and wiped his hands, then twirled his fingers in a delicate flourish. The handkerchief fluttered through the air and landed precisely atop of the steward's head.

The man was speechless.

"Rather than worrying about us," Cui Buqu said indifferently, "perhaps you should be more concerned with the traitor in your household. Duan Qihu has two sons, and his eldest is grown. Should Duan Qihu perish here today, that son will inherit everything and avenge his father. The two of you will be at open war. Even if you win, it will be a costly victory. Remember the tale of the sandpiper and the clam. Who is the fisherman who'll profit from their squabbling and reap them both?"

This thought had occurred to Duan Qihu as well. While he was still suspicious of Xing Mao, he had some reservations.

Xing Mao's face flashed through a host of emotions, but when he finally spoke, it was decisive: "Bring me Peng Xiang, now! If he resists, do whatever you need to get him here! Only make sure he can still speak!"

The head steward's wrist had been crushed by Feng Xiao, but in the face of the storm tearing through the residence, his injury was nothing. He struggled painfully upright and dashed off to find the third steward.

The birthday banquet had become a battlefield. Xing Mao took a deep breath and quashed his frustration. He first ordered an attendant to escort his mother away to rest, then addressed the other guests: "This incident has been most unfortunate; everyone has had a shock. I owe you all my deepest apologies once the culprit is found. For now, please remain seated and enjoy the food and wine."

As if anyone was in the mood to eat. All they could do was sit and wait. There was no chance anyone would be allowed to leave the Xing residence before this matter was resolved.

Xing Mao was reluctant to believe his own steward had betrayed him, but all signs pointed to the man. The arrangements for the banquet had been entirely in the third steward's hands. He couldn't escape responsibility.

Yet, as it often happens, this situation was thornier than it first appeared.

A short time later, the head steward came dashing back. Although he'd run the whole way, his face was paler than before.

Xing Mao knew at once that something had again gone wrong. Sure enough, the head steward gasped out: "Peng Xiang, he... He hung himself to avoid punishment!"

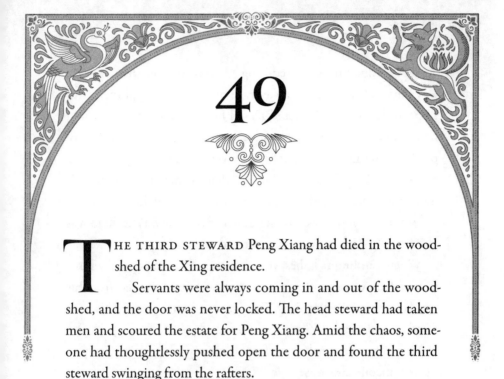

49

THE THIRD STEWARD Peng Xiang had died in the wood-shed of the Xing residence.

Servants were always coming in and out of the wood-shed, and the door was never locked. The head steward had taken men and scoured the estate for Peng Xiang. Amid the chaos, some-one had thoughtlessly pushed open the door and found the third steward swinging from the rafters.

No one wanted their dirty laundry aired, but the situation was already a mess. Duan Qihu said he wished to inspect the corpse and refused to back down. Xing Mao had no choice but to lead him there himself.

Of course, Cui Buqu and Feng Xiao followed.

No few guests also came to gawk, among them Magistrate Gao Yi and the man whose flirtations had been foiled by Cui Buqu, Chen Ji. He'd never seen anything so sensational before, and his eyes shone with the novel thrill of it.

If the third steward Peng Xiang was aware of his circumstances in the underworld, he was probably quite unhappy; fright remained etched on his face. Perhaps he'd regretted his suicide before his last breath but had been unable to break free and submitted unwillingly to his fate.

Yet Cui Buqu remembered Feng Xiao's words: the third steward was a martial artist, albeit an average one. If he really plotted with Yuxiu to kill Duan Qihu and feared he was exposed, why would he not choose to run away instead of hanging himself for fear of punishment? Even if he had been set on suicide, slitting his throat would have been simpler and more efficient than hanging himself, much more the kind of thing a martial artist would do.

While everyone was looking down at the body, Feng Xiao was also looking—but his eyes were pinned on Cui Buqu.

When Cui Buqu's lashes were downcast, his brows pinched in a frown, there was a gentleness to him. It was night and day from his usual demeanor. Feeling Feng Xiao's gaze on him, he turned his head, puzzled, as if to ask, *What do you want?*

"Whenever you make that face, I know you're getting ready to make someone's life miserable."

Those around them could see his lips moving but couldn't hear what he'd said. Feng Xiao had used a sound transmission technique to send those words straight to Cui Buqu's ears.

Cui Buqu smiled at him with teeth bared, then lowered his head to examine the corpse.

"There's something in his hand!" someone called out.

The head steward directed someone to pry the third steward's fingers open. Upon it were four words, written in blood:

Pay blood for blood.

They then looked at his other palm; again there were four words:

Heaven's law spares none.

"There's a wound on him!"

As they lifted the third steward's hand, his sleeve had slid down to reveal a cut along his forearm. The head steward frowned. The cut was shallow and not obviously poisoned, but he couldn't tell much more.

Could the third steward have made the cut himself before he died? Had he instructed the maid to poison Duan Qihu, then felt guilt when it failed and chosen suicide?

Duan Qihu's lip curled in a sneer. "Oh but Duke Xing has his ways! After failing to kill your target, you silenced your minion! You've destroyed the evidence! Now what recourse do I have?"

Xing Mao was incensed. "If I wanted to kill you, why would I jump through so many hoops? Nothing's stopping me from giving the order now—I guarantee you wouldn't walk out of here alive! Someone else is behind this, an instigator who intends to profit from our conflict!"

Gao Yi was silent.

If Duan Qihu and Xing Mao started killing each other, it was obvious who'd benefit the most—Gao Yi himself. With Duan Qihu and Xing Mao's influence collapsed, Qiemo would belong to him; he could become a county magistrate with real authority and manage the city properly. It wasn't that he didn't wish for this, but his faction was the weakest of the three. It was impossible.

"If Duke Xing agrees, I will send someone to fetch the coroner for an autopsy," Gao Yi offered.

"No need." Cui Buqu stood. "This man didn't hang himself. He was strung up after he died. That wound on his arm is posthumous, left by his killer."

Duan Qihu found it hard to believe the nephew of the king of Kucha knew anything about examining corpses, but he hadn't the wherewithal just now to question the man's identity. He frowned. "How do you know?"

"Look at his neck." Cui Buqu pointed at the third steward's throat. "When someone is hanged, their body is pulled downward. The ligature marks on the neck should be deep at the front but shallow on either side. The knot here in the noose will also leave bruises.

But see here—the marks on his neck are even all the way around. He was strangled to death with the rope first, then hung up."

Everyone looked closely; it was exactly as Cui Buqu had said. Yet this only invited more questions. If the third steward had been strangled, who within the Xing residence had killed him, and why?

The group looked to Xing Mao, who roared, "I too want to know the identity of the killer!"

"Duke Xing, calm yourself," Cui Buqu said coolly. "I don't believe you're responsible. With your abilities, you wouldn't need to go to so much trouble for so little gain. It's very likely the maid attempted to poison Duan-xiong under this steward's orders. But in that case, who in the Xing residence could have killed him? Therein lies the crux of the problem."

"The Xing residence is heavily guarded; I know all my subordinates inside out," Xing Mao snapped. "They'd never betray me."

Seeing Duan Qihu's mocking smile, he realized he'd gravely misspoken.

Hadn't his third steward already done so?

A traitor had revealed himself. And he might not be the only one.

Xing Mao remembered seeing Peng Xiang at the start of the banquet. He had been weaving through the crowd, making last-minute arrangements. Less than two hours later, he was dead.

Cui Buqu seemed to sense his thoughts. "This woodshed's not far from the kitchen. The cooks were no doubt busy preparing dishes for the banquet, with many people coming and going. If there was a loud noise in the woodshed, someone would have heard. But no one noticed a thing until the third steward was long dead."

"To kill him so quietly, the murderer must have been much stronger than the third steward," observed Feng Xiao.

"Correct."

Xing Mao frowned deeply. In all the Xing family, those who were strong enough to have killed the third steward were only the head steward, the second steward, and several skilled guards. But when the incident occurred, these guards had been at his side, and the head and second steward had been with him as well. If not these, then the murderer must be someone who had infiltrated the residence from outside.

"When I first arrived in Qiemo, I heard the Xing residence was large, but also secure and impenetrable. Anyone entering or leaving must identify themselves. Duke Xing can likely recite the names and backgrounds of all thirty guests who came today."

Xing Mao nodded. "Peng Xiang was in charge of the arrangements for the banquet, but not the estate's security. And I personally signed off on the guest list; he had no chance to tamper with it."

He looked to his head steward.

The man fell to his knees on the floor of the shed. "Master, please think! This lowly one would never collude with a traitor like Peng Xiang! Your second steward Lu Jiu was also present when we arranged for today's guard. We followed our estate's longstanding rules. All the security measures were overseen by both of us!"

Xing Mao too thought it unlikely all three of his stewards had betrayed him. He shot a glance at Cui Buqu, hoping for another hint. Somewhere along the way, this young man he'd just met had gained control of the entire situation. With just a few words, he pulled their thoughts along, leaving them powerless to resist.

"Bring me the guest list," said Cui Buqu. "Let no one leave the residence."

Even before his orders, the second steward had long shut the gates. The guests who hadn't come over to spectate remained awkwardly in their seats, waiting for Xing Mao to release them.

There were only thirty guests in total. With the exception of Gao Yi, Duan Qihu, Cui Buqu, and Feng Xiao, the rest were old acquaintances of Xing Mao. Even Chen Ji fell into that category, as his father was close friends with Xing Mao. When he'd received the invitation, he'd sent his son to congratulate the madam.

The head steward checked off each name on the list, one by one, until he discovered an issue: one person was missing.

Or rather, one person had entered the Xing residence and given a gift, but now was nowhere in sight.

"Where is Zhong Haomiao?!" the chief steward cried.

Who? Cui Buqu glanced at Xing Mao, who frowned.

"He's a disciple of Qiyue Monastery," he said. "My mother goes often to listen to their lectures and is familiar with the abbot there. When we sent an invitation, they replied that the abbot is in seclusion but that he'd send his eldest disciple to offer his congratulations."

The steward sent someone running to Qiyue Monastery at once for clarification.

While they waited, Xing Mao took Cui Buqu and the others into a side hall, along with the third steward's body. It made for a bizarre scene—a group of living people sitting around a corpse.

Gao Yi seemed to be ill at ease.

Feng Xiao, sitting beside him, whispered, "Is the magistrate feeling unwell?"

Gao Yi turned with a pained smile. "Before I left my house, I performed a divination and received the reading of 'calamitous luck.' I should never have attended the banquet today. The coins were right!"

"What does this plot have to do with you?"

"Nothing, of course. But what if they think I had a hand in it?"

Feng Xiao pressed his lips shut. Why had the court sent such a craven official? Tossing coins to decide whether to leave the house? Cowering like a mouse at each problem he encountered?

If instead Cui Buqu were magistrate of Qiemo—Feng Xiao scarcely needed to wonder. *Even if Cui Buqu spent two of every three days insensible with illness, he'd still turn Qiemo upside down. Not even dogs and chickens would find a moment of peace in the ensuing pandemonium. Xing Mao and Duan Qihu? They would be forced to stand aside. Only someone as brilliant as my venerable self could knock him down a peg.*

But no—there was also Yuxiu. That man was also terribly unpredictable.

As Feng Xiao pondered again over Yuxiu, the runner the head steward had dispatched returned not with a message, but with Zhong Haomiao himself.

His answer was quite unexpected.

Yesterday, a guest had arrived at Qiyue Monastery. This man had once shown great kindness to the abbot of Qiyue Monastery, and as he was of an age with Zhong Haomiao, the two got on instantly. When the guest heard Xing Mao's mother would be celebrating her sixtieth birthday today, he said he'd heard much of Xing Mao and would like a chance to see him. Zhong Haomiao had happily offered to bring him to the banquet.

Unfortunately, the abbot suddenly hit an impasse in his cultivation, requiring someone to stay and watch over him. Zhong Haomiao had handed the gift to his shidi[3] and instructed him to attend the banquet with their guest in his stead.

But according to the gatekeeper and the head steward, only one man had come with the invitation.

---

3 *Younger martial brother, used to refer to younger disciples of the same generation.*

Zhong Haomiao was apologetic. "It wasn't until your message that I discovered my shidi wanted to play in the city and so parted with our guest on the journey and asked him to go alone. But my friend is the disciple of a prestigious sect. He'd never commit such a heinous crime!"

"And who is this friend?" asked Gao Yi.

"Yan Xuexing. He's a disciple of the largest sect in Southern Chen, Linchuan Academy."

Everyone began pondering whether they'd heard this name—everyone but Feng Xiao and Cui Buqu, whose eyes were instead on the others' faces.

As they watched, Duan Qihu's expression shifted subtly.

The change was fleeting, but neither Feng Xiao nor Cui Buqu doubted what they'd seen. Feng Xiao prodded Cui Buqu's thigh, silently communicating his suspicions.

Cui Buqu moved his leg away.

But Feng Xiao was persistent. He prodded him again.

Annoyed, Cui Buqu grabbed Feng Xiao's meddlesome finger hard enough to break it. Feng Xiao flipped his wrist—in a flash, it was now Cui Buqu's hand trapped in his grip, unable to move.

"What are you doing?" This little scene happened to catch Chen Ji's eye. He was still brimming with dissatisfaction over the fight Cui Buqu had picked with him earlier, and now it spilled over. "Have you no reverence for the dead?! Are you lacking in manners or are you disrespecting Duke Xing?!"

"My sincerest apologies. My husband just can't control his wandering hands! It's this wife's fault for being too beautiful—oh, if only I didn't have this face capable of toppling nations!" Feng Xiao had never known how to spell the word *shame*.

Faced with numerous gazes all screaming, *To think this man spends his days drowning in pleasure despite a body that frail,* Cui Buqu extricated his hand from Feng Xiao's grip with no change in expression.

Wonderful.

He'd yet to settle old accounts, but new ones had just been added.

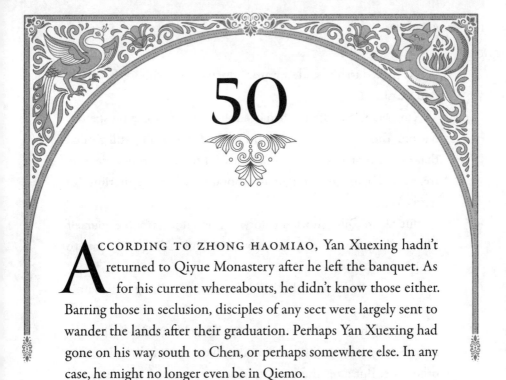

50

ACCORDING TO ZHONG HAOMIAO, Yan Xuexing hadn't returned to Qiyue Monastery after he left the banquet. As for his current whereabouts, he didn't know those either. Barring those in seclusion, disciples of any sect were largely sent to wander the lands after their graduation. Perhaps Yan Xuexing had gone on his way south to Chen, or perhaps somewhere else. In any case, he might no longer even be in Qiemo.

As he spoke, Zhong Haomiao became increasingly agitated. Yan Xuexing, he insisted, would never harm innocents. He was a member of a renowned sect who had saved his abbot's life. There had to be an explanation. Perhaps the man who'd come to the banquet hadn't been Yan Xuexing at all.

He could insist all he liked, but they had to find this Yan Xuexing—he was the key to getting answers to their questions.

Not only was a perfectly lovely banquet ruined, Xing Mao was now in a mountain of trouble. He sighed, frazzled, then cupped his hands toward Duan Qihu and Gao Yi. "I'm afraid I've made a fool of myself and allowed you to witness something disgraceful. Thanks to me, Duan-xiong received a terrible scare. I earnestly apologize. Once this matter is resolved, I'll offer you both a formal apology in your own homes. I beg your forgiveness."

He turned to his head steward. "Open the storehouse. Bring out two treasures."

Xing Mao's grandfather had been the ruler of a once-prosperous nation. Though his glory was diminished, his wealth still rivaled that of any monarch. In the storehouse of the Xing residence were treasures Duan Qihu might not obtain with three lifetimes of hard work.

But Duan Qihu snorted coldly. "Please, don't trouble yourself. I'll be taking my leave. I sincerely hope Duke Xing will come to explain himself soon!"

He turned and stalked toward the door, unwilling to remain a moment longer.

Duan Qihu had indeed believed Xing Mao initially had no intention of killing him; he wouldn't have attended the banquet otherwise. But after the maid's poisoning plot had been exposed, he'd seen the ruthlessness in Xing Mao's eyes—saw him itching to finish things then and there. In fairness, Duan Qihu might have done the same himself. If not for Feng Xiao's timely intervention, Duan Qihu's body would likely be cooling on the floor of the hall.

As he passed, he nodded slightly to Feng Xiao and Cui Buqu in gratitude. He had his own doubts about their identities—the idea that a nobleman from Kucha could conduct an impromptu autopsy was preposterous—but there was no point in pursuing it now. Still, Duan Qihu would certainly send a few people to investigate them thoroughly when things calmed down.

Just as he stepped over the threshold, a voice called out.

"Please wait, Duan-xiong," said Cui Buqu behind him.

Duan Qihu didn't so much as turn his head. He climbed up into his carriage without hesitation, only to be promptly treated to another taste of Feng Xiao's strength.

Feng Xiao seemed to drift over like a gentle breeze. Before the guards could blink, he'd grabbed Duan Qihu's arm.

Duan Qihu practiced the Vajra finger technique. He was a first-rate expert who'd defeated countless opponents in his early days. Though he'd let himself go a bit in the last few years, he hadn't forgotten how many wanted him dead, and never neglected his martial arts.

He instinctively moved to block, too late. Numbness spread through his arm, and he was forced to turn and face Cui Buqu.

Cui Buqu ignored Feng Xiao's raised eyebrows, which seemed to be saying: *There, that should be enough respect for you, shouldn't it?*

Cui Buqu spoke directly to Duan Qihu. "Did you know Yuxiu wants you dead?"

"Who's Yuxiu?" Duan Qihu frowned in confusion.

Cui Buqu had meant to catch Duan Qihu off guard. No matter how cunning one was, if they weren't expecting the question, their face would normally give something away. But Duan Qihu showed no reaction. He really didn't know Yuxiu.

Now that was strange—he didn't know Yuxiu, yet Yuxiu had asked the third steward to kill him.

Cui Buqu changed tack. "Is there some grudge between Duan-xiong and Yan Xuexing?"

"Over the past few decades, my activities have been confined to the border. Perhaps the Tianshan Sect might hold a grudge against me, but I don't know a single soul from Linchuan Academy. I'm grateful for your help today, but this incident took place at the Xing residence—you should be asking Xing Mao instead!"

He turned coolly and stepped into the carriage. This time, Feng Xiao didn't stop him; he and Cui Buqu watched the carriage roll away.

"If he doesn't know Yuxiu or Yan Xuexing, why did his face twitch earlier?" Feng Xiao was now fully invested. "Does he know who wants him dead?"

✦⚬⚬⚬✦

Xing Mao couldn't detain his guests forever. After Duan Qihu's departure, Gao Yi, Cui Buqu, and the other guests also departed one by one.

The lively and bustling banquet thus went out with a whimper.

Xing Mao was deeply vexed. He'd planned to use this occasion to make his mother happy while also reinforcing his prestige. Not only had he failed to achieve either goal, he'd been disgraced before all of Qiemo.

News of his third steward's death would spread rapidly through the city, and everyone would know his subordinates were disloyal. Soon they'd start saying he wanted to off Duan Qihu and Gao Yi and snatch Qiemo for himself. If that had really been Xing Mao's plan, it would be one thing. The problem was he hadn't planned any of it, yet he had no explanation to offer.

Duan Qihu would resent him for this. Perhaps he'd even start plotting his downfall.

"Master, a visitor has arrived." The head steward came forward and held out a note one-handed. Feng Xiao had broken his arm in their earlier tussle, but he had been too busy seeing off guests to tend to it properly and had only managed a hasty bandaging job.

"Turn him away!" Xing Mao waved a hand, distracted and restless. He didn't even glance at the note.

The head steward hesitantly spoke up again. "He said if you saw the note, you'd definitely see him."

Xing Mao snatched the note and opened it. His mouth fell open in shock.

"Master?"

Xing Mao folded the note firmly. "Show him in."

The visitor was quickly brought into the hall. This newcomer was a slender and graceful man; on entering, he removed his veiled hat in deference toward his host.

Xing Mao couldn't care less about the man's appearance. But at the sight of his face, he said, "You're not a Göktürk."

"I don't look like a Göktürk." The man's tone was gentle. "But that's not important. I imagine Duke Xing is in a foul mood. I'd hoped not to bother you..."

"Spare me your dithering!" Xing Mao interrupted.

The visitor smiled, paying no mind to Xing Mao's rudeness. His tone was amiable as he said, "I only wish to say that Duke Xing has missed an exceptional opportunity. Now that Duan Qihu doubts you, I fear if you don't make a move, he'll make one first."

"You think to provoke me? You're a hundred years too early. I won't cooperate with a Göktürk, and I don't need one to tell me what to do!"

The man smiled. "Duke Xing has overseen this city so assiduously for so long. Have you really never thought of restoring the glory of your ancestors? Does Duke Xing imagine the emperor of Sui will leave Qiemo untouched? The moment he gains the upper hand over the Göktürks, he will next recapture Qiemo. When the time comes, I fear Duke Xing will walk the same path as his grandfather and become a stray dog!"

Xing Mao's face contorted in fury. "Get the hell out!"

At Xing Mao's shout, guards rushed into the hall. But they had yet to lay hands on the visitor when a strong wind sent them flying.

Stunned, the head steward grabbed at the man with his uninjured hand. He moved with immense speed, too fast to see clearly.

But the man not only saw, he grasped the chief steward's wrist. Using only his thumb and forefinger, he snapped it with a crack.

Now both the chief steward's hands were useless.

Xing Mao's mouth snapped shut—no longer did he scream at the man to get out. For all he knew, his martial arts were comparable to Feng Xiao's. The entire Xing family combined might be no match for him.

Seeing that Xing Mao was finally listening attentively, the guest sighed and revealed a mocking smile that seemed to ask, *Regretting it now?*

"How much does Duke Xing know about the couple who claimed to be the nephew of the king of Kucha and his wife?"

Xing Mao frowned. "I *knew* they were suspicious! Could they be Duan Qihu's people?"

The visitor shook his head. "After Yang Jian ascended the throne, he established the Jiejian Bureau to neutralize his enemies and expand his intelligence network. In turn, Empress Dugu established the Zuoyue Bureau. They are two distinct organizations, but their roles are highly similar. Not only are they possessed of great authority, they also have the prerogative to act first and report later. They're sharp, cunning, and well-versed in the ways of deceit."

He continued, "As for that couple—one is the deputy chief of the Jiejian Bureau and the true power in the organization. The other is the head of the Zuoyue Bureau. Do you think they showed up here today just to partake of your fine wine?" He watched Xing Mao's eyes widen with astonishment.

Xing Mao didn't speak for a long while as he digested this information. "You're telling me the emperor of Sui sent them here?"

The visitor's lips curved. "He who strikes first strikes last. Duke Xing, perhaps now we can sit down for a nice chat."

❧⟨⟩❧

While Xing Mao was meeting with his mysterious visitor, Feng Xiao and Cui Buqu had regrouped at their room in the inn.

The banquet was planned to last until the evening, finishing with singing and dancing. Now, of course, the festivities had all been abandoned. It was afternoon when they returned, the sun bright and skies clear. A small vase of pale-yellow flowers sat on the windowsill, swaying in the breeze.

But they were in no mood to admire them—before them lay a complex case.

Lifting his brush, Cui Buqu wrote down a list of names. His hands were lovely as they moved across the paper, the characters beneath beautiful and fluid as flowing water.

Though Feng Xiao felt that the loveliness of Cui Buqu's hands couldn't compare to that of his own, he could still appreciate a change in scenery from time to time. He watched with rapt attention, a smile wreathing his face.

First, Cheng Cheng and Xing Mao's broker had perished in a fire at the pawnshop. Then they'd seen Yuxiu and the third steward talking in the streets. Finally, the assassination of Duan Qihu had failed, but the third steward had been found hanging in the woodshed.

When Cui Buqu finished, he circled Yuxiu's name.

"Let's assume Yuxiu has a grudge against Duan Qihu and wishes to incite the third steward to kill him, then frame Xing Mao for the deed. He has no need to kill Cheng Cheng and Li Fei."

Feng Xiao agreed. "I only fought Yuxiu briefly, but I could tell he's a proud person. Insignificant nobodies like Cheng Cheng and Li Fei are beneath him. Same with the third steward: if Yuxiu wanted him dead, he would simply kill him. Why waste all that time and energy to make it look like he'd hung himself? Why write those words on his palms? It's inefficient and unnecessary."

"Duan Qihu claims he doesn't know Yuxiu, and that's probably the truth. But then why was he surprised when he heard Yan Xuexing's name? Could he know Yan Xuexing instead?"

Feng Xiao shook his head. "Ququ, don't you know? There's a problem clever people often have."

"Go on," said Cui Buqu.

"They think too much," Feng Xiao said. "And they end up going in circles."

"That's two problems."

Feng Xiao pretended not to hear. "Have you thought of trying a different angle? These may be two separate cases. One: Yuxiu colluding with the third steward to murder Duan Qihu. Two: the deaths of Cheng Cheng, Li Fei, and the third steward."

"It's a good idea. But if you figured it out, does that mean you're not clever?"

Feng Xiao's smile was so radiant it put the vase of yellow flowers to shame. "It means I'm even cleverer than a clever person."

Cui Buqu had encountered many shameless men and women, but he'd never encountered someone who was both this shameless and had the nerve to spend the entire day flaunting it in front of him. He averted his eyes, lest he be tempted to slap that radiant smile off Feng Xiao's face. "Thanks to the death of the third steward, the antipathy between Duan Qihu and Xing Mao has deepened. They were already at odds; now a single spark will send everything up in flames."

"When you put it like that, I feel like you're up to something," said Feng Xiao.

"Aren't you?"

"Well, what's in it for me?"

Cui Buqu made a swift decision. He didn't hesitate—he didn't even blink as he said, "Daddy."

Ever since Feng Xiao had called Cui Buqu *Daddy* thrice, he seemed to have developed an obsession with the moniker. Every now and then, he tried to make Cui Buqu say it.

"...Your dad's dead. I don't want to be your daddy anymore."

Cui Buqu cocked his head and looked confused. "Then would you rather be my mother?"

Feng Xiao's mouth twitched. "I'm not keen on being your mother either. Tell me what you're planning first."

The corners of Cui Buqu's mouth turned up. "Go big or go home. How do you feel about unifying Qiemo and returning it to the oversight of the imperial court?"

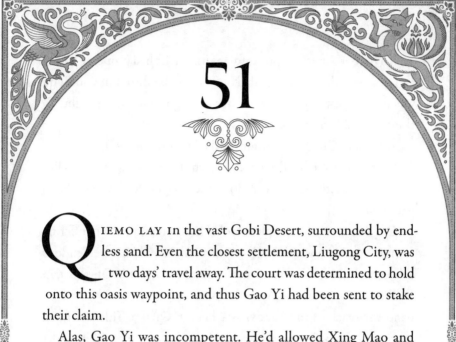

51

Qiemo lay in the vast Gobi Desert, surrounded by endless sand. Even the closest settlement, Liugong City, was
two days' travel away. The court was determined to hold
onto this oasis waypoint, and thus Gao Yi had been sent to stake
their claim.

Alas, Gao Yi was incompetent. He'd allowed Xing Mao and
Duan Qihu free run of the city for years without making a peep.
He cowered in his office like a tortoise, hoping their strife wouldn't
touch him.

Feng Xiao's group of four was only passing through on their
journey to distant Suyab, where they were to meet Apa Khagan and
convince him to cooperate with the Sui dynasty. But on arriving in
Qiemo, the chief of the Zuoyue Bureau, Daoist Master Cui, once
again couldn't suppress his restless itch to make trouble.

A small disturbance wasn't enough: if he were to do something,
it'd be earthshaking. He'd bag Qiemo in one fell swoop—a feat even
the court couldn't manage—and bring the whole county under
direct control of the Sui empire.

Even Feng Xiao, who feared neither heaven nor earth and was
only too happy to raise hell when he had nothing better to do,
was shaken by his audacity.

"I see your appetite knows no bounds!"

If a border general or powerful martial artist had proposed such a thing, it wouldn't have sounded quite so outlandish. But Cui Buqu was sickly; most days, he looked like he might not last the night. To think he still had such ambitions.

"Is Deputy Chief Feng afraid?" asked Cui Buqu coolly.

Feng Xiao smiled. "I've never known the meaning of *afraid*. But this isn't something you can do alone. Trying to drag me down with you?"

Cui Buqu gave him a queer look. "Drag you down? I'm offering to split a fortune with you. If we succeed, it will be a tremendous achievement. Aren't you always angling for merits? On this trip, we'll not only persuade Apa Khagan to become our ally, we'll expand the reach of the Sui dynasty here in Qiemo. This city has a magistrate from the imperial court, but it's never truly been under the oversight of a dynasty of the Central Plains. If we seize it for the throne for the first time, it will be a grander accomplishment than simply reclaiming lost territory."

Feng Xiao knew all this already. But with great reward came great risk. Xing Mao and Duan Qihu were no pushovers. They wouldn't release their territory and influence without a fight. "What's your plan?"

"The three factions have never coexisted peacefully," Cui Buqu explained. "The events of the banquet will linger as a thorn in their hearts. Even if Duan Qihu hasn't accused him outright, he must suspect Xing Mao ordered his poisoning and had the steward silenced when it failed."

"Duan Qihu's been a lawless force on the borderlands for a few decades now; it wouldn't be out of the question for him to take the initiative and end Xing Mao. But Xing Mao will also worry about that possibility. Perhaps he'll be the one to move first."

"Correct. This is our opportunity. We only need to persuade Gao Yi and wait until one side weakens the other. When they least expect it, we'll subdue them and absorb their forces. Once one's taken care of, the other won't pose a problem."

"Gao Yi is a toothless, bumbling old fool content with muddling his way through life. Why would he risk standing with you against Duan Qihu and Xing Mao?"

Cui Buqu smiled mysteriously. "Everyone has their weaknesses. I know how to deal with Gao Yi. But we can't rely solely on his men; they're not enough."

Feng Xiao paused. "It's getting late. We should bathe and go to bed!"

He stood and was about to walk out when a hand grabbed his sleeve. "The sun hasn't even set. What's the rush? Let's talk a little more."

Feng Xiao's expression was unreadable. "I fear if we continue you're going to suck me dry."

Cui Buqu's smile grew brighter. "There are troops stationed in Liugong City, but Gao Yi has no authority to mobilize them. I happen to know Deputy Chief Feng also holds the illustrious title of Zhenxi General and carries a military tally personally bestowed by the emperor. *You* can mobilize the army. Quality over quantity—how about a thousand elite soldiers? Surely that's no problem?"

"Were you already thinking about this when we were in Liugong City?"

"How could I be?" Cui Buqu blinked innocently. "I'm not a prophet. It's not as if I knew what would happen at the banquet."

Feng Xiao chuckled; he didn't believe a word this man said. "Give me your Zuoyue chief token, then. And you'll owe me a favor."

"I can't give you my token, but I can owe you a favor. If you like, we'll cooperate with the Jiejian Bureau on future cases. Don't forget, you'll also get a piece of the credit for this."

"Credit?" Feng Xiao snorted. "I have the authority to mobilize troops, but if this goes sideways, the blame will fall on me. If that's all you have to offer, I'm not convinced!"

With a sigh, Cui Buqu fished out an exquisitely crafted little seal from his sleeve. "My personal seal. I'll leave it in your hands for now. Once this is over, you'll return the seal to me. Will that do?"

Feng Xiao took the seal and turned it over. It was carved with four words: *Seal of Cui Buqu.*

"Your name is really Cui Buqu?" he asked, confused.

All this time, he'd assumed *Cui Buqu* was an alias—who had a name like *I won't go*? But if it appeared on his personal seal, it must be his actual name.

"Of course," said Cui Buqu. "I've been using it since I was ten."

"What about before you were ten?"

"I forget," he said, deflecting the question.

Feng Xiao smiled and tucked the seal into his sleeve. "Fine. Since you've shown me your sincerity, I'd be rude to refuse you. But even if I ride as swiftly as possible, it'll take two days to travel to Liugong City and two to travel back. If I go and Fo'er shows up during that time, I fear the three of you will be at his mercy."

This was indeed a problem. Cui Buqu smiled. "I have a solution."

"No can do," said Feng Xiao.

"I haven't even told you," said Cui Buqu. "How can you reject it?"

"You don't need to say it. I already know. You want to give Qiao Xian my tally so she can bring the troops from Liugong City."

"Qiao Xian is trustworthy."

"To you. Not to me."

The two of them locked eyes, silence stretching between them.

Feng Xiao's frank words didn't offend Cui Buqu. If he were offended so easily, he could never have crossed the threshold of the Zuoyue Bureau, let alone become its lord chief.

He and Feng Xiao were in the same boat now, but it was a temporary alliance. Even the emperor and empress, known for their matrimonial harmony, kept their guard up to some degree. If Empress Dugu really trusted that the emperor would never betray her, she wouldn't have created the Zuoyue Bureau. As for Feng Xiao and Cui Buqu, such wariness went without saying. Today the two of them got along swimmingly: Feng Xiao was even escorting Cui Buqu to treat with the Göktürks. But not long ago, they'd been cheerfully plotting against each other and trying to do each other in.

Feng Xiao refused to believe Cui Buqu had forgotten the incense incident so quickly.

Suddenly Cui Buqu laughed. "I'll be here with Deputy Chief Feng as a hostage. Surely you aren't worried Qiao Xian will run off with the tally?"

"You're ruthless toward others, but even more toward yourself. Never mind a tally: to gain my trust, you subjected yourself to incense of helplessness."

Cui Buqu rolled his eyes. "I only do what I'm confident will bring me success. I'm not a reckless lunatic. Tell the truth—have I upset your plans so often you've grown frightened?"

Feng Xiao's answer was blunt: "Yes."

Cui Buqu was silent.

"I'll hand the tally to one of my own agents," said Feng Xiao. "He will accompany Qiao Xian to Liugong City to summon the troops."

It was a concession.

"Deal," said Cui Buqu happily.

Feng Xiao was still skeptical that Cui Buqu could persuade Gao Yi. The man was timid as a mouse and content with the status quo. Unless something forced his hand, Gao Yi would never involve himself.

"How are you so confident you can persuade Gao Yi?"

Cui Buqu raised three fingers. "I have three plans for dealing with him, ranked from best to worst. Plans A, B, and C."

"Start with the worst one—Plan C."

"We march straight to his door, reveal our identities, then put a blade to his throat and force him to obey."

Feng Xiao shook his head. "You can't guarantee Xing Mao and Duan Qihu's situation will escalate to open conflict. Even if you threaten Gao Yi, it won't do any good. He has the least men out of the three of them. What's Plan B?"

"Use some incense of helplessness on Xing Mao and Duan Qihu. Make them come to us, begging and crying. We'll have subdued our enemies without a fight."

Feng Xiao scrutinized Cui Buqu with the same incredulity as if a flower had suddenly sprouted on his face. "Do you spend all your days thinking of ways to screw me over?"

"Is Deputy Chief Feng a fool? Do you spend all your days being screwed over by me?"

Feng Xiao snorted. "Do you think incense of helplessness is like fried flatbread from a stall? Costs mere coppers, and you order as much as you want? Its formula is exceedingly complicated; I only brought half a vial with me. Even the Jiejian Bureau might not have any more."

Left unsaid was that this half vial had already been used on Cui Buqu.

Cui Buqu shrugged. "Then there's only Plan A."

Feng Xiao waited. When Cui Buqu explained no further, he sighed regretfully.

Not because he thought Cui Buqu's plans were bad. Cui Buqu was too good at spotting even the tiniest changes in people. All their weaknesses became his to exploit in his bid to achieve his goals. It was truly a shame that a man like Cui Buqu couldn't practice martial arts. If he could, there'd be no one he couldn't handle and nothing he couldn't do. Feng Xiao sighed because he thought it was a pity—a pity for Cui Buqu.

Cui Buqu was a worthy rival. For some, the weaker their opponent, the better. But Feng Xiao was the opposite: the stronger his opponent, the more he relished the fight.

Only like this would life be entertaining.

This deep at night, there wasn't a sound to be heard.

Though merchants from across the land flocked to Qiemo and the city had no curfew, most retired early; even pleasure-seekers entertained themselves largely within the walls of brothels. Once the hour passed ten, the streets were deserted save for the night watchmen. Now and then a dog might bark in the distance as each house doused their fires and tucked themselves into bed, sinking into sweet slumber.

Feng Xiao, too, was asleep at this hour.

He was a brilliant martial artist, but he wasn't a god. He needed his rest as much as anyone. Yet tonight, he slept fitfully. Like many martial artists, his preternaturally sharp hearing picked up even the softest of sounds. And at that moment, a very distracting sound indeed was coming from outside the inn.

"Help me... Please help me... I'm begging you... Help me..."

It was a woman's voice, barely audible, brimming with hatred and resentment. To those who listened closely, it seemed to echo with endless grievances.

Though it was late spring, a chill clung to the nights. That voice made one's very bones tremble.

Who would cry for justice in the middle of the night?

And who would run to a well behind an inn, rather than shouting for it at the county office?

The answer was obvious: the cries came not from a living person, but from a ghost.

Feng Xiao sighed. He gave up on sleep and sat up. Whoever had disturbed his rest, he'd beat them until there wasn't enough left to make a second ghost.

But before that...

He patted the shoulder of the man beside him. "Wake up. There's a ghost outside."

If he couldn't sleep, no one else would either.

Cui Buqu rolled over, put his back to Feng Xiao, and tugged the blanket right up over his head.

Rousing Cui Buqu wasn't impossible, but Feng Xiao knew it would put him in a foul mood. And whenever Cui Buqu was in a foul mood, he started laying traps for Feng Xiao.

Feng Xiao wasn't afraid of traps. On the contrary, he quite enjoyed matching wits with Cui Buqu. But as he'd just won a round that day, obtaining not only Cui Buqu's personal seal but also a favor from the Zuoyue Bureau, he'd decided to quit while he was ahead and enjoy his victory for a few days at least.

He thought for a moment, then switched tactics.

Feng Xiao walked over to the clothes rack where his jacket hung and picked up the basin of water he'd used to wash his feet before bed. He crossed to the window, then flung the contents of the basin in the direction of the dry well. In a shrill falsetto, he exclaimed, "Who's that blubbering and howling in the middle of the night?! Disturbing a lady's good rest!"

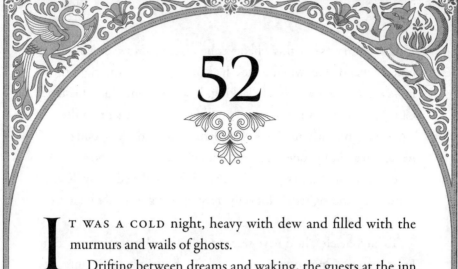

52

I T WAS A COLD night, heavy with dew and filled with the murmurs and wails of ghosts.

Drifting between dreams and waking, the guests at the inn heard a voice that sounded both very near and terribly distant. It blew in with the chill wind, sweeping into their rooms and under their blankets, funneling into their ears and shaking them out of slumber.

Then came Feng Xiao's shout. Even the ghost was shocked into silence, never mind the living.

Cui Buqu wasn't a corpse, and he shared a room with Feng Xiao. He, too, jerked awake. Due to his poor health, whenever he was woken abruptly his heart pounded like a drum. This time was no exception.

Feng Xiao looked over, his face the very picture of innocence. "Did I wake you? Sorry, I was yelling at someone outside. You should sleep a little longer."

He'd expected Cui Buqu to explode. But as the seconds ticked past, Cui Buqu remained on the bed, clutching his blanket in drowsy bewilderment. Had Cui Buqu been shocked silly by his shouting? Feng Xiao stepped over to the bed and took hold of Cui Buqu's chin, turning Cui Buqu's face toward him.

Cui Buqu was like this whenever he woke up. How long his daze lasted depended on whether he'd had enough sleep. And right then, it was clear sleep was sorely lacking. It was at times like this that Cui Buqu's guard was at its lowest and he became easier to bully.

Feeling mischievous, Feng Xiao patted his head. "My good child," he said in a kindly tone. "Time to get up and see some ghosts."

Finally Cui Buqu's gaze sharpened. He slapped Feng Xiao's hand away and sighed. "Not only must we see ghosts, we'll have to become them."

To anyone else, he'd have seemed to be speaking nonsense. But Feng Xiao not only took his meaning, he thought it deeply interesting. "Has someone come up with the same plan as you?"

Cui Buqu didn't answer. "Do you remember when we first checked in? The guide Cheng Cheng mentioned there was a ghost behind the inn, and that they'd found a body in the well."

"I looked into it. Apparently a couple of bones were found at the bottom. No one can say when they appeared, or who left them. They may have been tossed in after the victim's death, or the victim may have been thrown in and died down there. The incident was a long time ago, and no one stepped forward to identify the body, so the whole thing was clumsily covered up."

Cui Buqu rubbed his eyes as if he were trying to wipe away his fatigue.

"When Cheng Cheng mentioned the dry well that day, he looked terrified," Feng Xiao continued in meaningful tones. "But when others talked about it, they seemed more curious than afraid."

"The dry well, Cheng Cheng, Li Fei, the third steward, Duan Qihu," Cui Buqu said. "Could there be some link between all of them?"

"Li Fei and the third steward were Xing Mao's men. They shouldn't have any connection to Duan Qihu."

"But the third steward colluded with Yuxiu to poison Duan Qihu. Xing Mao definitely didn't order him to do so. It's possible the others share some connection we're not aware of."

Cui Buqu wasn't the only one awakened by Feng Xiao's cries. Several more guests stumbled groggily from their beds to complain. Who was shouting crude words outside, disturbing the whole inn? A few brave souls rose and threw on their clothes, thinking to go see what had happened at the well.

Through it all, the instigator sat at the table, sipping cold tea at his leisure. "Look at me. If I went to play a ghost now, would I be more convincing than the one we heard earlier?"

Feng Xiao had removed the disguise Qiao Xian had created for him. His uncombed hair hung loose over his shoulders, and he sat at the table in a single thin robe, not seeming to feel the cold. His handsome face glowed in the candlelight, practically flawless.

Cui Buqu watched him for a moment. "Put on a layer of pearl powder. Then you'll look the part."

"You're right," Feng Xiao said with a smile. "I'll get some from Qiao Xian."

With that, he really did stand and start to walk out. But as he reached the door, he remembered something and turned. "By the way, when I came back this evening, I noticed Yuxiu's room was empty. He's probably gone."

Cui Buqu frowned slightly.

A mysterious man; now even his whereabouts were unknown. If there existed anyone in this world Cui Buqu couldn't figure out, Yuxiu was undoubtedly one such man.

The Jade of Heaven Lake had been recovered and the case closed—Yuxiu had no call to remain in Liugong City. They had expected him to return to the capital and the Prince of Jin's side, but he hadn't done so. Instead, he'd gone west and incited the third steward to poison Duan Qihu.

But Duan Qihu didn't know Yuxiu. What grudge did Yuxiu have against him? What was his goal? Did the haunting of the inn involve him as well? And if not, who was responsible?

The tiny city of Qiemo held an incredible number of secrets. They had fermented in the dark for years, and now they were bubbling over. With Cui Buqu and Feng Xiao joining the fray, the city was sure to get even livelier.

Cui Buqu slowly pushed aside the covers and bent to pull on his boots.

A sudden gust of wind blew the window open with a *bang*, and the candle guttered and went out. Feeble moonlight fell across a stark-white face outside.

"Qu...qu..."

For a moment Cui Buqu didn't answer. Then he said impassively, "I told you to go scare Gao Yi, not me."

Duan Qihu sat before a jug of wine.

He'd once been a highwayman—in plain speech, a thief and a murderer. Those who lived in fertile lands enjoyed a life free of restraint: feasting and drinking, repaying kindness with kindness and grudge with grudge. That was the hallmark of a true man, they'd boast.

Duan Qihu, however, wasn't a drinker. In his view, alcohol corroded the mind and led people unwittingly to their deaths. He'd lost several companions to drink in his youth, and from that point on, he hadn't touched a drop. Yet today he was restless, so much so that he'd turned to a flask of wine to ease his worries.

He had started with nothing to his name and clawed his way to his position today. He'd lost much but also gained greatly, and made just as many friends as enemies. Many wished for his death, but Duan Qihu had never cared. He laughed at them in contempt—they were beneath his notice, not worth mentioning.

But today was different.

When his beloved concubine pushed the door open with a pot of sugar-braised pears, she found Duan Qihu staring solemnly at the table as if something extraordinary sat upon it.

"My lord..." Her syllables were drawn out, with a hint of sweet coquettishness. Normally, upon hearing her voice, Duan Qihu would have already stood with a smile on his face. But tonight he remained motionless.

Now faintly displeased, the concubine stepped forward and set down the pears, ready to drape herself over him. There was a soft *thud* as ceramic met wood. It wasn't loud, but Duan Qihu flinched as if startled. When he raised his head to see the face of his concubine mere inches away, he jerked back in his seat, his face twisting ferociously.

His concubine had never seen such an expression on him and gaped in shock. In the next moment, a sharp pain tore through her stomach and the scenery blurred as Duan Qihu kicked her toward the door, which slammed open as she crashed heavily to the ground. She spat a mouthful of blood, her face a mask of fear, before promptly fainting from the pain.

The servants guarding the door were stunned. Thinking there was some emergency inside, they rushed in and found Duan Qihu still sitting, face pale and chest heaving.

"My lord?"

"Go! It's nothing." Duan Qihu waved the servants off. "Have someone take her away."

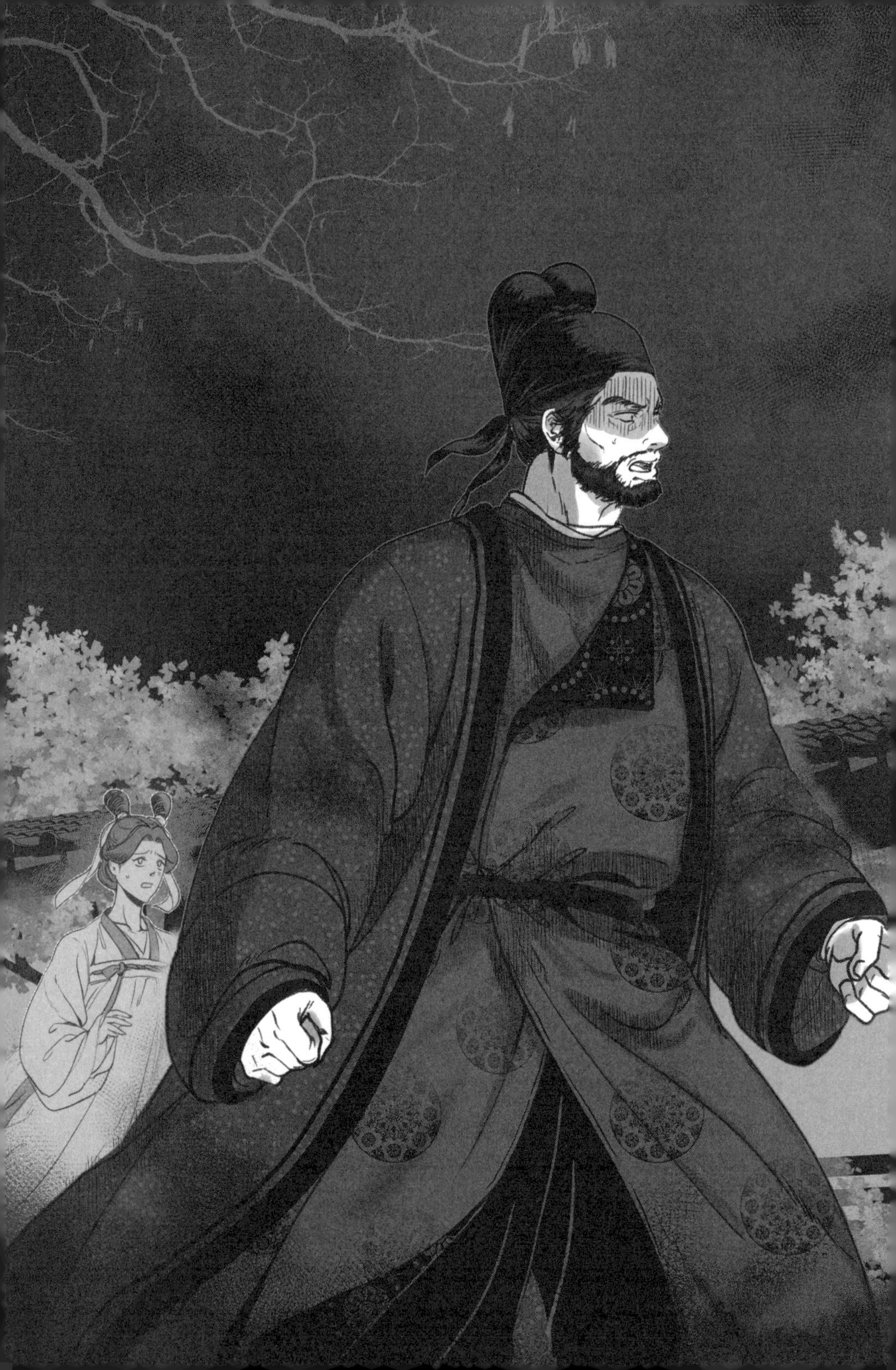

When his wife heard the news, she hurried over, thinking the concubine had done something to anger him. Duan Qihu particularly favored this concubine, to the extent of ignoring his wife. This had eaten at Lady Duan for a long time; though she looked worried now, she was secretly delighted. But Duan Qihu had no interest in women's squabbles. Lady Duan, too, he dismissed with a few words, nor did he call another concubine to serve him. He rose and went into the garden to relax.

The hour was late, and all was dark and silent, but the lanterns hanging in the garden illuminated the area brightly. This alone was evidence of the wealth and strength of the Duan family.

Duan Qihu walked for some time with his hands behind his back. Slowly he regained his calm, but his mood was terrible. What he hadn't told anyone was that in the moment he glimpsed his concubine, he'd seen another face.

Perhaps he was overtired, or perhaps it was the lingering influence of the incident at the banquet. Duan Qihu's brow furrowed again as he thought of the dead third steward, as well as the man mentioned by the Qiyue Monastery disciple: Yan Xuexing.

"Duan...Qihu..."

A mournful voice wailed beside his ear.

It sounded like a woman, gasping out her last words as someone tightened their hands around her neck—on the brink of death yet forcing her eyes open, blood trickling from the corners of her mouth and staining her teeth as she spat and hissed from the depths of hell.

"Who's there?! Fuck off! Don't skulk around like a ghost!" Duan Qihu roared.

Behind him, the two servants accompanying their master exchanged a glance.

They hadn't heard anything at all.

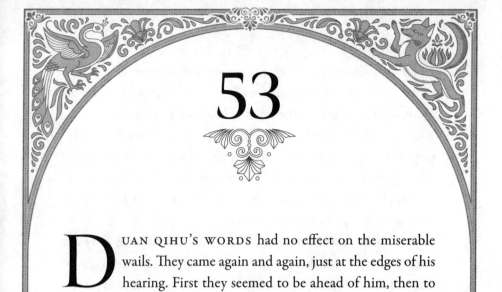

53

Duan Qihu's words had no effect on the miserable wails. They came again and again, just at the edges of his hearing. First they seemed to be ahead of him, then to his left, his right... But no matter which way he looked, Duan Qihu couldn't discover the source.

Eerier still was that he seemed to be the only one who could hear. The two servants behind him looked bewildered, unsure to whom he spoke.

Something was wrong.

Something was very wrong. Someone was playing tricks on him!

Breathing harshly, Duan Qihu fought to remain calm. His eardrums throbbed, and the flames of his rage threatened to burst even as he tamped them down. Yet not only did his emotions not settle, his eyes reddened as his panic grew.

"Which great master wishes to see me!" he roared. "Show yourself; why use such cowardly tactics? It's laughable!"

"Duan Qihu... Do you remember... You owe me a life..."

"I owe many lives! Not everyone is qualified to claim theirs!" Duan Qihu threw his head back in an icy laugh. His lavish city clothes couldn't disguise the bandit's swagger born of decades on the roads. The imperious nature that had made him famous was on full display.

The two servants locked eyes, their faces full of terror. Duan Qihu seemed to be talking to the air—an illusion only he could see and no one else. They suspected their master had been possessed.

Duan Qihu, however, knew this wasn't a case of possession. The culprit had to be a master martial artist masquerading as a ghost, using their internal energy to manipulate sound and confuse his senses. He closed his eyes and listened. Then he leapt into the air, soaring up into a nearby osmanthus tree.

Its branches bore no flowers at this time of year. Osmanthus trees weren't suited to the desert—but with enough money, even ghosts might do your bidding, never mind a humble tree. It grew in the Duan family garden just as it would in a misty Jiangnan courtyard. To sustain such a garden in a border city like Qiemo was a greater expense than the gardens of all Jiangnan's most lavish mansions.

The osmanthus tree swayed in the night breeze; in the twinkling of an eye, Duan Qihu landed atop it.

Had Feng Xiao been present, he'd have seen that Duan Qihu wasn't just an expert in finger techniques—his qinggong was also exemplary. A man almost seven feet tall perched atop a branch no thicker than a finger, yet the branch didn't snap or even shiver. This alone put him among the ranks of first-class experts. But as he raised his eyes and looked around, he saw nothing but flowers and trees, lush and evenly spaced. Other than the two servants running toward him, there was no one else.

"Duan Qihu... Twenty years... It's been twenty years."

He looked out over the garden; he refused to believe anyone could escape his sweeping gaze, no matter how well-hidden.

All was still.

The servants looked up from the base of the tree, unsure what to do. "My lord, should we call someone..."

Duan Qihu didn't answer. In the quarter hour he'd been standing atop the tree, the woman's voice in his ears had continued to repeat the same two words: *twenty years*.

Twenty years ago—

Twenty years ago, Duan Qihu had just joined a group of bandits and was still a nobody in the bandit stronghold. He longed to climb higher, to achieve great things, to be surrounded by soft women and chests overflowing with gold and silver, just like the bandit chieftain.

Whenever his band went down the mountain to plunder, he always rode at the forefront. Though he suffered many injuries, he also gained the respect of his superiors. Eventually he replaced the third chieftain and gradually climbed the ranks, transforming his mountain stronghold into the largest group of horse-mounted bandits in the region. He'd amassed power and wealth until he'd become the Duan Qihu of today.

No one could achieve fame and success without some blood on their hands. Duan Qihu was certain even those who sat at the pinnacle of imperial power were weighed down with blood debts—including the current emperors of Sui and Southern Chen. Who among them hadn't cut their way through human flesh as one might hack apart melons? How else could they have seized such incredible power?

Duan Qihu smiled coldly.

Twenty years ago, he'd already killed too many people. If there was such a thing as ghosts, they'd have to line up for their vengeance. A nameless little ghost who'd popped up out of nowhere would never get her chance.

He broke off a twig from the osmanthus tree and jumped down. His wrist twitched, and leaves from the twig shot out in all directions.

The two servants were unprepared—the tender leaves instantly pierced their throats, and they collapsed to the ground before they'd even had a chance to scream. Blood pooled beneath their bodies and the scent of blood rose into the air. The soft, sorrowful voice had fallen silent as well.

So it really was someone playing tricks, Duan Qihu thought to himself, face stony. He waved a hand, summoning another servant to drag the two corpses away.

Someone else would clean up the garden. When he returned tomorrow, not a single drop of blood would remain. It would be pristine and peaceful, as if no one had ever died there at all. Duan Qihu's mood lifted a little.

When Duan Qihu's wife heard he'd killed someone in the garden, she once again came to see him.

His wife had been with him since the beginning, and stuck by his side through thick and thin. Though Duan Qihu rarely spent the night with her these days, his respect was far greater for her than his concubine. When she arrived, he didn't drive her away.

They sat together for a moment. "Whatever's weighing on you, even if I can't help, I can still lend an ear. As inadequate as I may be, I will always be yours."

These words brought Duan Qihu no comfort. He furrowed his brow and asked, "Twenty years ago—do you remember anything significant that happened back then?"

Duan Qihu's wife thought it over. "At the end of that year, you returned to the mountain and said you'd bagged something big. You became the third chieftain soon after. Since then our lives have gotten better and better..."

His wife had never accompanied him on raids, so she only knew so much. But Duan Qihu, too, remembered that year as the one he'd become the third chieftain. It'd been an important turning point in his life, not one easily forgotten.

"That year, you returned from a long journey happier than usual. When I asked, all you said was you'd landed a huge prize this time; you wouldn't tell me anything more." She sighed. "I knew how you were making a living out there. I burn incense every day and pray to the bodhisattvas for your sake, so your past sins may be forgiven. If there should be any retribution, let it be borne by me, your wife..."

Duan Qihu had grown impatient and was about to stand and leave. But at the word *retribution*, his expression shifted. Lady Duan paid no heed. The older she got, the less she could resist chattering; she continued to prattle on.

"Enough!" Duan Qihu leapt to his feet. "It's late; you should rest. I'm going back!"

"Husband!" Lady Duan could only watch as he left with a flick of his sleeves. She didn't know what she'd said wrong—he'd been fine just a moment ago.

Duan Qihu returned to his room and sent everyone away. He lay in bed staring at the curtains over his head until drowsiness overcame him, and his eyelids grew heavy. But just as he was about to fall into a shallow slumber, the voice rang out again.

"Duan Qihu... You owe me a life..."

Duan Qihu's eyes snapped open, and he sprang upright. "I am the master of my life and my fate! Even the heavens can't snatch my life from me; you've got no chance! A soul like you should have gone to the underworld long ago. Choose wisely, or don't blame me for beating you until you scatter. You'll never be able to reincarnate even if you want to!"

He snarled through gritted teeth, eyes bloodshot as he glared outside. But the voice continued unabated, sounding both near and far away.

"Duan Qihu..."

"Pay blood...with blood..."

The wind carried the faint scent of copper.

"Duan Qihu..."

It was coming from the direction of the garden pond!

If Duan Qihu had been a man who sat around waiting to be killed, he would be dead eight or ten times over. He called for his two most trusted guards and rushed in the direction of the garden pond.

The closer they got, the stronger the stench of blood grew. One guard cried out, "My lord, look!"

Duan Qihu saw a corpse by the pond—one of the servants he'd killed earlier. "Didn't I tell them to clean this up!" he raged, thinking to find his slacking servants who had dumped the body here. But in the next moment a cold, slimy gaze seemed to fix on the back of his neck. His hair stood on end—*danger!*

He turned and struck out with a palm yet met only air.

"Duan...Qihu..."

An icy female voice sounded in his ear from right where the guards should have been standing.

Duan Qihu had walked down countless dark paths and braved innumerable storms. He was no stranger to struggling at the limits of life and death. But at that moment, he could no longer contain the terror in his heart. A savage expression came over his face and he roared, "Who the fuck are you! Show yourself!"

✤⟨⟩✤

In the Qiemo county office the next morning, Gao Yi's restless hands slipped as he reached for the tea the maid was offering, sending the cup shattering to the ground. Hot tea splashed onto his clothes and boots, scalding the back of his hand. He yelped and leapt a foot into the air.

The maid rushed to apologize, but Gao Yi waved her away, leaving sharp fragments littering the floor. He took out the tortoiseshell he used for divination with great care, but instead of his usual silent prayer, he sank into a stupor until a servant came to inform him guests had arrived.

"Send them away!" Gao Yi said impatiently. He was in no mood to receive anyone.

"But sir!" the servant exclaimed in disbelief. "The man is claiming to be the nephew of the king of Kucha. He said he saw something strange in the sky above the city last night, and that it was pointing to this building!"

Gao Yi's heart pounded. "Let him in!"

Within minutes, Cui Buqu and Feng Xiao stood inside the office.

"Magistrate," Cui Buqu said at once, "there's an impure aura between your brows—the area has turned black. I fear you've been tainted with some kind of negative energy!"

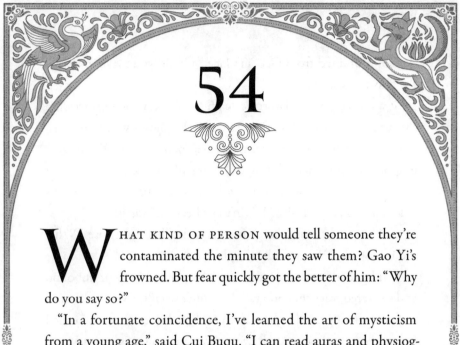

54

WHAT KIND OF PERSON would tell someone they're contaminated the minute they saw them? Gao Yi's frowned. But fear quickly got the better of him: "Why do you say so?"

"In a fortunate coincidence, I've learned the art of mysticism from a young age," said Cui Buqu. "I can read auras and physiognomy. The moment I entered, I saw a black aura curling around your forehead. I fear you may have encountered some dark influence yesterday."

Cui Buqu was being far too familiar. But after the scare Gao Yi had gotten last night, he both desperately needed someone to confide in and lacked the presence of mind to be suspicious. He hemmed and hawed, but ultimately couldn't resist asking, "Did you, too, encounter something strange last night?"

"I did." Cui Buqu nodded. "To tell the truth, it's for this very reason that we came to the magistrate so early this morning."

"Tell me, quickly!"

Cui Buqu sketched a rough summary of the ghostly wailing they'd heard the night before. Interestingly, his story made no mention of Feng Xiao's thunderous shouting, nor the basin of water he'd used to wash his feet.

Color drained from Gao Yi's face. "Could you make out what the ghost was saying?"

"It was crying about a horrific death—some kind of injustice. Did the magistrate hear it last night as well? The ghost's wailing?"

Now that he knew he wasn't alone, many of Gao Yi's doubts evaporated into relief. Although he was still unlucky, he was at least fortunate to have another witness backing him up. He lowered his voice and said cryptically, "I didn't just hear it. *I saw it!*"

Cui Buqu and Feng Xiao glanced at each other in surprise. "What did it look like? Was it really the ghost of a woman?"

"I didn't have a clear view. It was dressed in white, hair unbound and scattered, very thin and tall. I couldn't say if the voice was male or female. It appeared right next to my bed, but the instant I called for someone, it disappeared. Every time I lay down, its voice would ring in my ears, sounding both close and distant, crying about its death and begging me for vengeance."

Feng Xiao grabbed Cui Buqu's sleeve, eyes wide with alarm. "Husband, it didn't spare even the magistrate. Oh, perhaps we'll encounter the ghost again tonight. Husband, husband, should we change inns?"

"Now it makes sense," Cui Buqu said, solemn. "I performed a divination before we left, and the reading was 'calamitous.' It seems it was not merely an ill omen, but a harbinger of the thousand weeping ghosts."

Just the words made Gao Yi's skin crawl. "What are 'the thousand weeping ghosts'?"

"If a great injustice occurred twenty years or so ago, when there were no court officials in the city for the victims to appeal to, the resentment will have accumulated with the passage of years. The energy is concentrated around Duan Qihu, I could sense it. This is all because we went to the Xing family's banquet—we were contaminated by the heavy resentment around Duan Qihu. That's why it's become so easy to see negative forces like your aura, Lord Magistrate!"

In Gao Yi's opinion, this vengeful ghost was too inconsiderate. "Each debt has its debtor. If it wants revenge, it should seek out its nemesis. What's the point of disturbing *our* rest? It's simply not reasonable!"

Feng Xiao resumed his role as the straight man. "Husband, if you're right, does that mean things will get worse?"

"Undoubtedly," said Cui Buqu. "Each day the case is ignored is another day the resentment will deepen. Look at last night— it didn't merely appear at the magistrate's mansion. Even the inn we were staying at encountered the ghost. The luck of others in the city is bound to be affected if this continues. Once that happens, the thousand weeping ghosts will descend."

One of Cui Buqu's points concerned Gao Yi greatly. "What happens if one's luck is affected?"

"In mild cases, misfortune will follow you everywhere. In severe ones, you'll be plagued by evil spirits and become confused and disoriented. For merchants, their business will founder; for officials, their career will suffer setbacks."

Feng Xiao gasped. "Husband, won't we be struck by bad luck as well? We're merely passersby; whom have we provoked? Hurry, let us leave the city while we can. This isn't our home; we must leave them to suffer their own bad luck."

Gao Yi stared as Feng Xiao continued, "Husband, I'm so frightened. If this carries on, will there be a night I wake up and see a ghost sleeping beside me instead of your dear self?"

Cui Buqu shot him a furtive glare. *Enough; don't overdo it. Any more is overkill.*

Look how scared he is, said Feng Xiao's answering look. *So I've embellished a little; this way he'll be too spooked to sleep tonight.*

Gao Yi didn't notice their silent conversation; he was scared witless. Though he remained outwardly wary, in his heart he was largely convinced.

Someone like Duan Qihu, who'd pulled himself up by his bootstraps, might not have been so gullible. But Gao Yi had always believed in divination and the idea of good and ill omens. Half the city knew this incompetent magistrate would cower in his house the entire day if his coins showed bad fortune. This time, he'd seen a ghost with his own two eyes and hadn't gotten a wink of sleep because of it. Now that he'd been frightened again by Feng Xiao and Cui Buqu, his nerves were shot.

Judging they'd applied enough heat, Cui Buqu asked, "Has the magistrate considered investigating the case so the victim may rest in peace? The best course is to resolve the matter once and for all."

Gao Yi smiled bitterly. "You speak as if it's easy. Where would I start, and whom would I investigate? Surely you don't suggest I knock on Duan Qihu's door and ask him if he's ever killed anyone? The case is twenty years old at least. I've only been in Qiemo a few years. I don't even have a file on the case, let alone a corpse."

"The hauntings seem to have started at the inn's dry well. We might find something if we send someone down to search it. There are skilled coroners capable of extracting clues from bare bones. Lord Magistrate, this matter affects not only the luck of the city, but your own personal fortunes. You don't want to remain a county magistrate here for the rest of your life, do you?"

"What do you mean?" Gao Yi furrowed his brow.

"Take this opportunity to investigate Duan Qihu, then you can strike a blow against Xing Mao and eliminate both major factions of Qiemo in one fell swoop," Cui Buqu explained. "You can free yourself from being a puppet magistrate while recording a great achievement. You might even be promoted: an achievement of this magnitude could raise you to a marquis."

Gao Yi shook his head. He'd been here for several years, long enough to understand how deeply Duan Qihu and Xing Mao's factions were rooted. Unless the court sent an army to crush them, he'd never eliminate either of these men's influence.

"At yesterday's banquet, Xing Mao's subordinates were exposed trying to poison Duan Qihu. Xing Mao denied his involvement in the firmest terms. But do you think Duan Qihu believes him? Xing Mao certainly knows he doesn't. To protect himself, he'll make the first move to consolidate his power. Magistrate Gao, how do you know *you* won't be his next target?"

"Stop talking, stop talking, I can't do it..." Gao Yi fell silent as realization struck. When he spoke next, his face was dark with suspicion. "You're not the nephew of the king of Kucha. Who are you?"

Kucha had never involved itself in Qiemo's affairs. Why would the king's nephew encourage Gao Yi to overthrow Xing Mao and Duan Qihu?

"It's true, I am not from Kucha," Cui Buqu said coldly. "Gao Yi, your death is nigh. You still think you can stand to the side?" He took out a small, lacquered wood seal and threw it down before Gao Yi. "Look at this."

Gao Yi picked it up doubtfully. When he saw what it was, he started.

Officials who held multiple positions commonly commissioned two- or even three-sided seals for ease of use. The seal Cui Buqu had tossed before Gao Yi had more than six sides.

This seal was the genuine article. Cui Buqu didn't like to expose his position in the Zuoyue Bureau, but like Feng Xiao, he held a fair number of other titles. Altogether, it made an intimidating impression.

Two of the seal's sides were engraved with *Glorious Grand Master* and *Imperial Censor*. The former had no true authority—it was essentially an honorary title—but it was one the emperor granted to officials with great achievements. The latter title of imperial censor had been established only the previous year. Its rank wasn't high, so not many were familiar with it. But Gao Yi had heard from his friends in the capital that the role of this position was to impeach corrupt and tyrannical officials, as well as manage ceremonial affairs for the Three Departments and Six Ministries. Its power and authority were unprecedented. Though an imperial censor had to bow before many officials, the authority he wielded was enough to frighten anyone.

The title of glorious grand master was of the third rank, while the imperial censor was merely of the eighth. But an official's highest-ranking title was what mattered; when Gao Yi met Cui Buqu, he should be the one to bow.

But something was still off. This was a small border town. What privileged minister of the court would come here and subject themselves to the sand? Why would a third-rank official pop up in the middle of the desert?

"I'm investigating an important case and stopped here along the way. To remain discreet, I traveled under the guise of the king of Kucha's nephew. Gao Yi, after seeing this seal, do you still want to question me?"

Cui Buqu had already deceived Gao Yi once; naturally the magistrate was still on his guard. "Dare I ask Your Excellency what case you are investigating? What does it have to do with me?"

His message was clear: even if Cui Buqu was an imperial censor, he couldn't order Gao Yi around.

Cui Buqu looked at him coolly. "The imperial court had ordered me to Suyab in the Western Khaganate. Do you understand now?"

Gao Yi was not ignorant of the court's many disagreements with the Göktürks over the past two years. Any mission related to the Göktürks must be one of great importance. He felt a chill run through him as comprehension dawned.

Feng Xiao gave the table before him a tap, startling Gao Yi from his thoughts.

He didn't use much force—Gao Yi didn't hear a sound. But the entire table crumbled to sawdust, drifting to the ground and heaping upon the cattail mat. "Magistrate Gao," said Feng Xiao gently. "What do you think of my martial arts?"

Gao Yi swallowed hard and squeaked out, "Exceptional."

Feng Xiao smiled. "Who could possibly order a martial artist of my caliber around? Is there anywhere I can't go? Perhaps you think we're petty conmen. Wouldn't such a thing be unworthy of my talents? If Cui-langjun isn't who he claims, would I be at his beck and call?"

Cui Buqu's official's seal had gone a long way toward convincing Gao Yi. Under Feng Xiao's intimidation, he cast away the last of his doubts. Gao Yi stood and cupped his hands. "How should I address you, sir?"

"Cui, written with the characters *Shan* and *Zhui*. Cui Buqu."

"Cui-langjun," said Gao Yi. "You are a high-ranking official charged with heavy responsibilities. Perhaps it's not my place to ask, but your mission seems to have little to do with Duan Qihu's case."

"My business indeed has nothing to do with Qiemo. But I don't wish to come back on my return trip to find our court-appointed magistrate is dead and Qiemo has become the new Kingdom of Shanshan."

Gao Yi chuckled dryly, waving the remark off. "Don't say something so frightening."

"Fool! Do you know the Xing residence conceals more than five thousand sets of armor, and that aside from their estate, they have two granaries and treasuries hidden elsewhere in the city? These combined are more than enough to seize Qiemo."

Cui Buqu had wanted to slam his palms on the table to intimidate him further—but alas, it had been smashed to dust by Feng Xiao moments ago. He raised his voice instead, silently cursing Feng Xiao.

Gao Yi was skeptical. "How can you be sure?"

"The court has been establishing secret bases of operations within Qiemo to gather intelligence for years," Cui Buqu said coldly. "Though we've yet to pinpoint the location of the two granaries, we've confirmed the existence of the armor. Yet even now you deceive yourself into thinking Xing Mao won't mobilize troops. Or do you fancy that if he does, he'll let you go?"

If Xing Mao didn't wish to enter open hostilities with the Sui dynasty, he could simply bundle Gao Yi up and send him out of the city. Gao Yi might retain his life, but it'd be impossible for him to remain an official. The court would most likely indict him: losing one's nation's territory was a grave crime.

Gao Yi blanched.

He thought back to the fierce confrontation between Duan Qihu and Xing Mao at yesterday's banquet and the surging undercurrents beneath. He thought of the ill readings his divinations had yielded over the past few days. He even thought of his ghost-sighting the previous night, as well as the "thousand weeping ghosts" Cui Buqu

CHAPTER 54 🕴 147

had mentioned a moment ago. His thoughts tangled into a mess, and he was unable to make up his mind.

Cui Buqu had long known Gao Yi was a useless and talentless man. Any other day, he'd have pushed this man aside and simply rolled up his sleeves to do the job himself. But right then, their reinforcements had yet to arrive. The few people they had weren't enough. Ineffectual as he was, Gao Yi was a high-ranking official of the court, and behind him stood law and due process. His authority would make their task easier—as long as Gao Yi could be induced to cooperate.

"But...even if Xing Mao is hiding armor, it doesn't necessarily mean he's thinking about rising up, right? His ancestors were the kings of Shanshan; that armor is his inheritance. Besides, these borderlands are always in turmoil. We're also close to the Khaganate here; he might just want to protect himself..." Gao Yi had begun to come up with all kinds of excuses for Xing Mao.

"I've heard," replied Cui Buqu, "that after the third round of drinks at Xing Mao's banquets, there's often a performance of 'The Song of the Great Wind' by Emperor Gaozu of Han: 'The great wind rises, oh! The clouds are driven away. I return to my native land, oh! Now the world is beneath my sway.'"

"That song has spread everywhere and is sung among the people," Gao Yi replied feebly. "Xing Mao is familiar with Han culture—he's practically a Han himself. I'm sure he doesn't mean anything by it."

Cui Buqu sneered. "I've heard another story. The year Magistrate Gao arrived and took office, Xing Mao and Duan Qihu each sent you a messenger: one bearing a white fish and the other a precious blade."

The metaphor of "a white dragon in fish's clothes," used to describe nobility disguised as commoners, was a well-known one, tracing back Liu Xiang's *Garden of Stories* from the Han dynasty, which depicted Wu Zixu's admonition to the King of Wu during the Spring and Autumn Period. Xing Mao's message was plain. Meanwhile, the precious blade was Duan Qihu's threat, warning him that he shouldn't dream of meddling here. The mightiest dragons couldn't defeat a snake in its own territory; even if he were a Sui official, Duan Qihu would have no problem slitting his throat.

Gao Yi was well-versed in the classics; he'd understood at once what these objects implied. As for Duan Qihu's threat, it was arrogant, but there was no real need to be afraid. The man hadn't been proclaiming his ambitions to Gao Yi, only testing his reaction.

But Gao Yi was a coward. He'd reported Xing Mao's ambitions in a memorial, and that was the extent of it. The court had no energy to spare for the city, and thus he had comfortably whiled away his life in Qiemo. He'd never considered contending with Duan Qihu and Xing Mao to try and take back the city.

Xing Mao, on the other hand, learned much about Gao Yi's character from this incident. He grew ever more unrestrained and didn't take Gao Yi seriously at all.

If there was a ranking for the biggest slackers in the world, Gao Yi's name would undoubtedly appear. He might even make the top three. He was only lucky he wasn't Cui Buqu's subordinate—the lord chief would have had Qiao Xian toss him into a river as fish food long ago.

Gao Yi hadn't expected Cui Buqu would know these details. Embarrassed, he smiled bitterly and pleaded his case: "Cui-langjun is wise. It's not that I don't wish to help. Your lordship has been here for just a few days, but you must have seen it yourself. Xing Mao is powerful; Duan Qihu is imperious. Rather than putting ourselves in the middle, we should wait for them to clash, then reap the benefits!"

The idea in itself wasn't unreasonable, but Xing Mao and Duan Qihu were no fools. Would they really sit on their hands while Gao Yi profited from their conflict?

On top of being as timid as a mouse, Gao Yi was also stubborn and inflexible. Cui Buqu had no interest in continuing to convince him. "It's fine if you don't want to get involved," he said, rising. "I'll take charge, but it must be in your name."

Gao Yi opened his mouth to refuse and met Cui Buqu's frigid gaze. The words froze on his lips.

Feng Xiao was unruffled. "Gao Yi, if you're to drink, drink of the victory wine, not the poisoned cup. If we wished to harm you, we need only say the word. But we're all officials of the same court. We must have somewhat of an alliance, mustn't we? If nothing changes, you'll be haunted by vengeful ghosts day in and day out. Long before Xing Mao kills you, you'll exhaust your vital yang energy and perish."

For Gao Yi, being haunted by ghosts was a more terrifying prospect than getting offed by Xing Mao. He began to waver. Eventually he said, "I'm feeling unwell at the moment, so I'll be closing my door to guests. Cui-langjun's plans are his own."

In other words, he would give tacit approval to Cui Buqu's actions.

After they left the county office, Feng Xiao turned to Cui Buqu. "How did you know a ghost would get him to compromise?"

"When I was preparing to head to Liugong City two months ago, I had someone pull every file pertaining to the route between Liugong City and the Western Khaganate. That included one on the cowardly Qiemo County Magistrate who still believes in divination."

Feng Xiao gave Cui Buqu an appraising look. Two months ago, Cui Buqu had already investigated everything he thought he might need and memorized Gao Yi's proclivities and weaknesses. And as soon he set foot in Qiemo, he'd begun to think of ways to provoke Duan Qihu and Xing Mao.

"Your admiration is flattering but unnecessary. I simply thought several steps ahead of you." Cui Buqu's tone was light, his smile reserved.

Feng Xiao shook his head. "No, I was just thinking it's little wonder you're shorter than me and in such poor health. You spend all your energy plotting against others."

The corner of Cui Buqu's mouth quirked up. "It's true I'm in poor health. Maybe I can't bounce around aimlessly all day like you do, but are you positive you're taller than me? Aren't the soles of your shoes thicker than most?"

Feng Xiao's smile was enigmatic. "I know I'm taller than you," he said. "Because I'm longer."

Cui Buqu stared at Feng Xiao. For a few seconds, he said nothing.

Feng Xiao waved his handkerchief, putting on a bashful act. "Why is your lordship looking at me like that? Your wife is so scared, her little heart is pitter-pattering away!"

As he sat silent, Cui Buqu recalled: back when he'd fallen into Feng Xiao's hands and been poisoned with incense of helplessness, he'd spent day and night in a dazed slumber. The maids must have changed his clothes, and he was sure Feng Xiao had seen him then. This man's face was thicker than the Great Wall; he didn't know the meaning of the word shame.

Cui Buqu was beyond numb to it all. He kept his face blank and brushed right past the comment. "Tonight, let's make sure Magistrate Gao runs into the ghost again."

"Are you so sure Xing Mao will make his move?"

"If our surmise is correct, there are two factions who wish Duan Qihu dead." Cui Buqu spoke confidently. "One is the third steward and Yuxiu, and the other was responsible for the poisoned wine. The third steward may share an unknown connection with the poisoner. Xing Mao is also looking for his chance—so we'll fan the flames and make the threat of this 'thousand weeping ghosts' even more explosive. Xing Mao has waited so many years; he's long since grown impatient. He's certain to make his move!"

55

N O ONE COULD match Cui Buqu when it came to whipping up a storm.

From the moment they left the county office, rumors raced through Qiemo. *Magistrate Gao's residence heard a ghost crying in the middle of the night,* said some. Others whispered, *A strange case from twenty years ago has resurfaced.*

Much of the rumormongering was the work of spies placed by the Zuoyue and Jiejian Bureaus. Humans were naturally drawn to excitement—this kind of ghost story needed hardly any fuel to spread like wildfire.

News of the inn's haunting the previous night also spread. When Cui Buqu and Feng Xiao returned, they heard a guest in the hall on the first floor describing the experience in vivid detail to a friend.

"The well back there—can you see it? The moaning noises were coming from inside; I'm telling you, it was terrifying. I could hear it even with the blankets pulled over my head. Ah, it's too sad. Which family's lady met such a tragic end?"

"I don't know, but I looked in the well earlier. I couldn't even see the bottom—who knows if it's really dry. This inn really is cursed. How long has it been since the last haunting? But the county office is so far from here; how did the ghost get all the way to the magistrate's residence?"

"Doesn't that just prove how terrible the ghost's death was? The victim couldn't get justice, so they became a vengeful spirit growing more ferocious by the day. Magistrate Gao was sent here by the Sui court; he must have the emperor's aura about him. It makes sense for the woman's ghost to plead with him. Do you think Magistrate Gao will take up the case?"

"Ha! Forget it. Magistrate Gao hasn't done a damn thing since he arrived. You're not from around here, so you might not know. Recently, two vegetable-sellers got into a fight and one of them died. He didn't lift a finger then, so why would he do anything now?! Going to the king of Shanshan is probably a better idea. At least he'll do *something*."

Cui Buqu and Feng Xiao, sitting at the next table over, heard this last remark loud and clear.

The man was of course referring to Xing Mao. Though far from his homeland, he still saw himself as a king. His flatterers addressed him as such to keep him happy, and over time, the informal title had spread. Qiemo didn't belong to anyone; why shouldn't he set himself up as its king?

Feng Xiao and Cui Buqu had been responsible for the ghost that haunted Gao Yi last night, but they'd had nothing to do with the haunting at the inn. Clearly, Cui Buqu wasn't the only one trying to stir up trouble.

Cui Buqu didn't fear others causing trouble. He only feared the trouble was too little, that the chaos wasn't enough. "Gao Yi draws an imperial stipend, yet he's been slacking on the job. Perhaps we should lend him a hand."

Feng Xiao took his meaning at once. "You're afraid Xing Mao might move first?"

"That's right." Cui Buqu smiled faintly. "This is a matter of law. If there's an injustice to be redressed, Gao Yi should be the one to conduct the hearing."

He stood and crossed the hall to the innkeeper. After a brief conversation, he took out some money and asked him to send someone down the well to search for bones.

Over the years, rumors of the ghost in the well had led to a few busybodies trying to head down themselves. The innkeeper, however, was terrified they might really dig up something horrific and he would bear the blame. In any case, since there was no official present to investigate, he wanted as little trouble as possible. He'd asked someone to set a large stone over the well mouth long ago, sealing it shut to stop nosy guests from taking a peek.

Yet now Cui Buqu was here, handing him a hefty sum of money and claiming he'd been sent by Gao Yi. The innkeeper was quickly swayed and called someone to move the stone. Soon enough, the porter tied a rope around his waist and lowered himself down to search. Word spread swiftly through the inn, and a crowd gathered to watch the excitement.

With his skills, Feng Xiao could easily have completed the task without any ropes at all, and the search would have gone much faster. But the dry well had been abandoned for years. Even if no water remained, there were still spots of lichen and who knew what kinds of crawling creatures. Deputy Chief Feng refused.

He sat with his legs crossed, looking down from the inn's second-floor window with Cui Buqu. "Shall we make a bet?"

"On what? Whether they'll find bones in the well? No need to bet; you've already lost." Cui Buqu coughed twice. Cities on the border were all wind and sand, and the climate was dry. When Qiao Xian wasn't there to take care of him every step of the way, he paid little attention to his own body. After two days in the city, his cough had worsened again, and his throat was hoarse and dry.

"Why's that?" asked Feng Xiao.

Cui Buqu's face was blank. "Because after we arrived and heard those rumors from Cheng Cheng, I had someone throw a corpse down there. They'll definitely find it."

Whether the bones were old or new, the common folk wouldn't care. As long as there were bones in the well, the hauntings must be real, and this ancient case must truly conceal an enormous injustice. The victim had been unable to rest in peace and transformed into a ghost to seek vengeance and plead for their wrongs to be redressed. The story would spread further, the uproar grow and grow.

Gao Yi had been tossed a hot potato; he couldn't stay out of the matter now. Duan Qihu, once rumors of the haunting in his estate spread as well, would also end up on the rack.

If the original state of Qiemo had been a pot of warm water, Cui Buqu's arrival had tossed a bundle of firewood under the stove and lit a match. Now the water was at a violent boil.

Anyone could be a cunning fox. What was rare was the ability to see three steps ahead of the other foxes. Even Feng Xiao had to concede to Cui Buqu when it came to scheming.

Was there anything Cui Buqu couldn't predict? Feng Xiao wanted to ask but refrained. Instead he laughed.

Cui Buqu was baffled. "What are you laughing about?"

"Nothing," said Feng Xiao.

If something so unpredictable did exist—something Cui Buqu believed to be within his grasp, yet defied his predictions—wouldn't that be terribly interesting?

❀❃❀

While the curious ran to the inn to watch the show, Duan Qihu was at home sneering over a letter from Cui Buqu.

Or rather, a letter that had been sent on Cui Buqu's instructions, yet was in Gao Yi's name and stamped with Gao Yi's seal.

Gao Yi refused to step forward, but Cui Buqu had at least browbeaten him into writing a letter. The contents mentioned an old case from twenty years ago and invited Duan Qihu to visit and provide an explanation. There were no files, no statements from victims laying out their grievances. It was all just unfounded speculation.

Certain local rumors were circulating. Some said that, in Duan Qihu's youth, a young woman had hung herself after he'd betrayed her hopes. Others spoke of a blood debt he owed from his bandit days and warned the debtor had come to claim his life.

Duan Qihu didn't sleep the entire night.

Last night a voice was heard wailing at the inn, and Gao Yi had seen a ghost. Duan Qihu's own haunting had left him ill at ease—though the ghost hadn't appeared again in the latter half of the night, he'd still felt as if it was speaking beside his ear.

Duan Qihu was a martial artist, a strong and healthy man. A sleepless night was nothing to him. But right now his mood was horrible, which could mean only one thing: Duan Qihu had a guilty conscience.

"Will your lordship go see Gao Yi?" asked his steward. He'd overseen the Duan residence since its construction and was one of Duan Qihu's closest confidants.

"Of course I won't!" sneered Duan Qihu. "Gao Yi is a nobody. People call him 'magistrate' because Great Sui stands behind him, not because he's worthy of the title on his own."

Steward Lin nodded. He was staunchly loyal to Duan Qihu and never asked unnecessary questions. But he still had his responsibilities, so he ventured, "Shall we reply to the letter, or ignore it completely?"

"Send someone to tell him I'm bedridden with illness," said Duan Qihu. "Tell him I'll visit another day." He paused before asking, "Did you...hear or see anything last night?"

"This lowly one saw nothing," said the steward. "But I did hear the sound of weeping. Whoever made it must have been a top-notch martial arts master because this lowly one couldn't catch them."

Duan Qihu snorted. "Where did Xing Mao manage to find such a skilled expert..."

But as he spoke, he realized something was off. Even if Xing Mao found someone to impersonate a ghost, how could they know about an event that had happened twenty years ago? He thought of the deaths of the third steward, Cheng Cheng, Li Fei, and the others, and felt the muscles in his face tense.

"I heard Gao Yi and the Yangji Inn also heard a ghost last night," said Steward Lin.

"There aren't that many ghosts in the world," Duan Qihu scoffed. "This must be one of Xing Mao's schemes!"

At Steward Lin's look of confusion, he continued, "He's wanted to move against me for a long time, but never had the chance. His plot to poison me at the banquet failed, but he's sure to come up with another. He'll take advantage of the hauntings to stir up the imagination of the city, then send an assassin after me under the guise of a vengeful ghost and pretend he had nothing to do with it."

As master and servant were talking, a report arrived: a corpse had been found in the dry well behind the Yangji Inn. The victim had been dead for a long time—skin and flesh had crumbled to dust, leaving only stark white bones. Everyone in the surrounding neighborhoods had gone to watch the hubbub. Apparently the nephew of the king of Kucha, a guest at the inn, had requested the remains be delivered to the county office so Gao Yi might preside over the case.

Steward Lin frowned. "How should we handle this, my lord? Perhaps this lowly one should go make some inquiries with Gao Yi."

He could tell Duan Qihu was shaken. Something must have really happened twenty years ago that he didn't want to talk about. It wouldn't do for the steward to question him further; he could only help his master resolve the issue before them as best he could.

"No need." Duan Qihu spoke through gritted teeth. "Gao Yi is a coward, but Xing Mao will undoubtedly seize this chance to act. I've yet to repay him for last time, so why not pay it all in one go? Since he can no longer wait, we'll land the first strike! Wait until after midnight, then take our men to the Xing residence. You must fell Xing Mao in one blow!"

Steward Lin was stunned. "Shouldn't we take more time to plan?"

Duan Qihu buzzed with anxiety. He was overcome by an unfamiliar sense of powerlessness: the feeling of knowing precisely where the enemy was yet being unable to leap over and strike them dead.

"It's too late. Xing Mao has wanted sole dominion over Qiemo for a long time, and the first step is getting rid of me. But we are not unprepared. There are the fifty elite guards I've had you train the past few years—though none are exceptional, they're still first-class fighters. If we can catch Xing Mao flat-footed, even with the help of that fake ghost of his, he won't be a match for us."

Years of soft living had gradually worn away Duan Qihu's ambition and arrogance, but as he spoke now, he regained his confidence. "Once Xing Mao is dead, who in Qiemo can oppose me?"

It was thanks to his bold decisiveness that he'd climbed to his current position. Now, once again, Duan Qihu firmly believed he'd judged the situation correctly.

Steward Lin had no further objections but was still concerned for Duan Qihu's safety. "If I take all fifty men, who will protect your lordship?"

"Leave Bing and Ding behind. The rest will go with you." Duan Qihu's smile was cold. "There's no way Xing Mao can respond that fast. If anyone comes here, whether human or ghost, I'll make sure to show them a good time. I'm truly curious as to who could emerge unscathed against my Vajra finger technique!"

✦⟨⟨۞⟩⟩✦

In the Xing residence, Xing Mao's expression was like a fresh spring breeze, evidence of his good mood. "Duan Qihu is powerful, but he's grown old. A toothless tiger is nothing to fear." He looked at the man before him and his expression grew even fonder. "Besides, everyone has turned their backs on him. Even *you've* betrayed him. Is he still worthy of calling himself my rival?"

"It's just as Duke Xing says." The man cupped his hands respectfully.

"In the past, Lord Mengchang had an entourage of three thousand.[4] He treated all of them as family and showed great respect for the wise. Now I shall show you the same treatment. Duan Qihu believes himself above everyone; no one is worth his attention. Even an old man like yourself, who's followed him so many years, must refer to yourself as 'lowly' before him. How can a man like him be my equal in the city of Qiemo?"

---

4   A minister from the Warring States period famous for his large retinue.

Xing Mao stood and walked over, personally pulling the man to his feet. "Lin-xiansheng need not be so polite in front of me."

"I'm only too grateful for Duke Xing's regard," said the man, "but the fifty elite guards under Duan Qihu are all loyal to him and don't fear death. The group includes two of his most trusted subordinates, and I fear I have no authority over them."

Xing Mao showed him a small smile. "No matter. He's sent away all his best men, and the Duan residence has become an empty fortress. This is our chance to take it all in one fell swoop."

Another voice spoke: "After tonight, Qiemo will have to change its name to 'Xing.'"

The pronouncement came from the white-clad monk sitting below Xing Mao. He was respectful as he offered his congratulations, but his attitude was neither arrogant nor sycophantic, with no hint of flattery.

Xing Mao burst into laughter. "Then I shall thank Yu-xiansheng in advance for his fortuitous words!"

56

IT WAS A NIGHT without moon or stars.

Dark clouds smothered the sky yet refused to shed rain or snow. Even the wind seemed to have died, leaving only an unbearable, scorching heat that made sleep impossible.

And indeed, Duan Qihu was not asleep.

He'd sent his wife and children to the back courtyard early. Now he sat alone in the main hall as his subordinates surrounded the Duan residence. Although Duan Qihu's estate looked as quiet and peaceful as on any other evening, it was already under heavy guard.

Duan Qihu's crooked index finger tapped nonstop against the table.

He was waiting.

Waiting for news of Steward Lin's surprise attack with his fifty fearless guards.

Waiting for that audacious "vengeful ghost" to make its return.

In truth, no bitter grudge existed between Duan Qihu and Xing Mao. But one mountain could not hold two tigers; both knew Qiemo could accommodate one king only. They had gathered their strength, biding their time until they could land the fatal blow.

Now Duan Qihu couldn't wait any longer. The incident at the banquet had sparked a sense of crisis he'd never felt before.

Xing Mao must be eliminated. This couldn't drag on another day.

With restless thoughts came uneasy dreams. It was better to strike early than late—rather than waiting to be killed, he must land the first blow. Tonight, success or failure depended on this move.

He ordered someone to check the hourglass. Almost eleven. The ghost had appeared around this time yesterday. And tonight...

Duan Qihu laughed coldly. The Duan residence was brightly lit, guards stationed at every corner. He refused to believe he'd miss the ghost's entrance.

Yet at that moment, a frigid wind swirled in, carrying flowers and leaves into the hall. The guard at the door sneezed as its bone-piercing chill hit everyone full in the face. The lanterns flickered wildly and went out, plunging the room into darkness.

"*Ah—!*"

The scream came from the northwest corner of the Duan residence, the back courtyard where the women lived. And the voice was all too familiar—Duan Qihu's daughter, who'd only recently come of age. Duan Qihu leapt up and rushed in the direction of the cry.

As he passed, the lanterns above his head flickered out, one by one, as if planned.

"What was that!"

"There's someone over there!"

The voices of the guards rose and fell, but all they could hear was the whistling wind. The enemy was nowhere in sight. That ill wind blew from every direction, carrying a voice that spoke into Duan Qihu's ear.

Both near and far away.

"Duan Qihu... Pay blood for blood..."

Plenty recalled the rumors of the previous night's hauntings, and the stories they had heard in the city of the thousand weeping ghosts. Panic spread through the residence.

"A ghost!" someone shouted in the darkness. No one knew what he'd seen or encountered. Screams and cries echoed one after another.

But the guards of the Duan residence were well-trained; even in this atmosphere, they didn't run around blindly. Duan Qihu led his men toward the northwest corner and heard his daughter scream again.

His heart thudded in his chest as he rushed into the courtyard.

He saw his daughter lying on the ground, a bright slash of red across her neck. Her eyes were wide in a face twisted with terror, unable to rest in death.

The maids scattered and fled as screams echoed unceasingly in the courtyard. Duan Qihu's wife had also rushed over from the neighboring courtyard; when she saw her daughter, she fainted dead away.

Duan Qihu had never seen anyone killed by a ghost, but he knew the sword wound marring his daughter's neck was not the work of any spirit or demon.

"Come at me, if you have the guts! You think it's impressive killing unarmed women and children?!" He was like a wounded lion, roaring angrily into the void. "Xing Mao! I know it's you! Get the hell out here!"

A gale swept toward him bearing an unmistakable bloodlust. Duan Qihu dodged sideways and raised his arm; a flash of bright light shot straight at his enemy.

Many in Qiemo knew of his Vajra finger technique, said to be exceedingly powerful. Few were aware he also had a preternatural skill with hidden weapons—most who had witnessed it were in the underworld. He'd thought the speed of his strike fast enough to injure his opponent even if they dodged a fatal hit. But to his surprise, the black shadow he'd aimed at vanished midair, leaving the blade to bury itself in a nearby tree.

Could it really be a ghost?! But there was no such thing as ghosts!

Duan Qihu had no time to be startled; an intense agony tore through his back, and he was flung forward.

The guards rushed up, but none lasted beyond the first move. All were sent flying away. Some had their necks twisted and broken, perishing from a single strike. Others fell shrieking to the ground, gravely wounded. From start to finish, their assailant's goal remained Duan Qihu. The instant Duan Qihu stumbled to the ground, his attacker leapt over at a speed too fast to see.

A force capable of overturning mountains and seas pulsed in Duan Qihu's eardrums, as if he was battered by a merciless, roaring gale. By now, Duan Qihu understood this was no vengeful ghost, but a flesh-and-blood human—an expert among experts, with martial arts surpassing his own. Were he still in his prime, he might have escaped unscathed, but now...

His wife and children were here. He couldn't run. Even if he wanted to, it was impossible.

"A quick death is more kindness than you deserve. I want you to watch everyone close to you die, one by one." The words ended on the soft sound of a sigh, accompanied incongruously by a harsh and cutting palm blast.

There was no time to use the Vajra finger technique. Duan Qihu channeled all his internal energy into his palm, pitting his full strength against his opponent. "The one responsible for my deeds is me. Leave my wife and children out of it!" He gritted his teeth, straining to catch a glimpse of his opponent's face.

Pain spiked up his arm and blood spurted. Duan Qihu toppled backward. He panted heavily, still conscious, but the shockwave had damaged his meridians. He was already a toothless tiger. "You! Who the fuck are you! Did Xing Mao send you here!"

"My name is Yan Xuexing." The man before him was clad in black. He watched Duan Qihu, face indifferent.

"You? The disciple from Linchuan Academy?!" Duan Qihu suddenly remembered: "You were behind the poison at the banquet! Why are you doing this!"

He'd never seen this man before or ever offended Southern Chen's Linchuan Academy. They were like a well and a river, their waters never mingling.

Yan Xuexing bared his teeth in a cold smile. "It wasn't me who tried to poison you; blame yourself for having too many enemies. Countless people want you dead! As for Peng Xiang, I killed him because he deserved to die, just like you!"

"There's no grudge between me and Linchuan Academy, past or present!" Duan Qihu cried.

"This has nothing to do with Linchuan Academy. You need only remember me, Yan Xuexing."

What few experts remained among Duan residence guards were no match for Yan Xuexing and couldn't stop him. Linchuan Academy's high-ranking disciples deserved their reputation. This man's martial arts were beyond compare; no mere guard could oppose him. He caught the women and children in the courtyard one by one, throwing them to the ground and sealing their acupoints. Tears streamed down their faces, yet they couldn't make a sound.

Duan Qihu bitterly regretted sending the steward and his fifty elite guards away. With them, he'd at least have stood a fighting chance.

"Whom do you want to die first?" Yan Xuexing took slow steps toward the Duan family. "To men like you, women are no different from clothes. When one is gone, you can simply pick another. Let's kill your favorite concubine first."

Duan Qihu's chest throbbed with muted pain as he swallowed down blood. He looked at his daughter's corpse lying on the ground and roared, "Kill me if you must, but I deserve to know the reason! Why are you doing this?! You're helping Xing Mao act against me. Do you think he's any better? He'll abandon you as soon as he gets what he wants!"

Yan Xuexing shook his head. "I don't know any Xing Mao. No one can order me around."

"Yan-gongzi, since you've made up your mind, why bother talking to him? Just start killing them. He'll figure it out eventually." With an airy laugh, a woman in yellow appeared on the roof. Duan Qihu's eyes widened when he saw what she clutched in her hand.

It was a bead, carved from jade and hollowed out to enclose two more layers, so that the entire exquisite object formed three spheres, one nested inside the other. Rumor had it that this was a secret treasure from the imperial palace of the Western Jin dynasty. It'd drifted from person to person for centuries before it'd landed in Duan Qihu's hands—an item almost as precious as the Jade of Heaven Lake. Duan Qihu treasured it greatly and kept it hidden in a secret storehouse, only occasionally taking it out to toy with. Even his wife didn't know the location of his private cache, yet this stranger had discovered it.

The woman in yellow curled her fingers into a fist, and the priceless jade bead was crushed to fine powder. Dust trickled between her fingers and drifted away with the wind.

She smiled at the way Duan Qihu's eyes popped out. "Heartbroken?" she asked. "But these were all things you gained through robbery; they never belonged to you in the first place. It's been twenty years. *Do you still remember the blood debt you owe?*" The woman opened her mouth, and her voice changed—clearly, this was the ghost from the previous night.

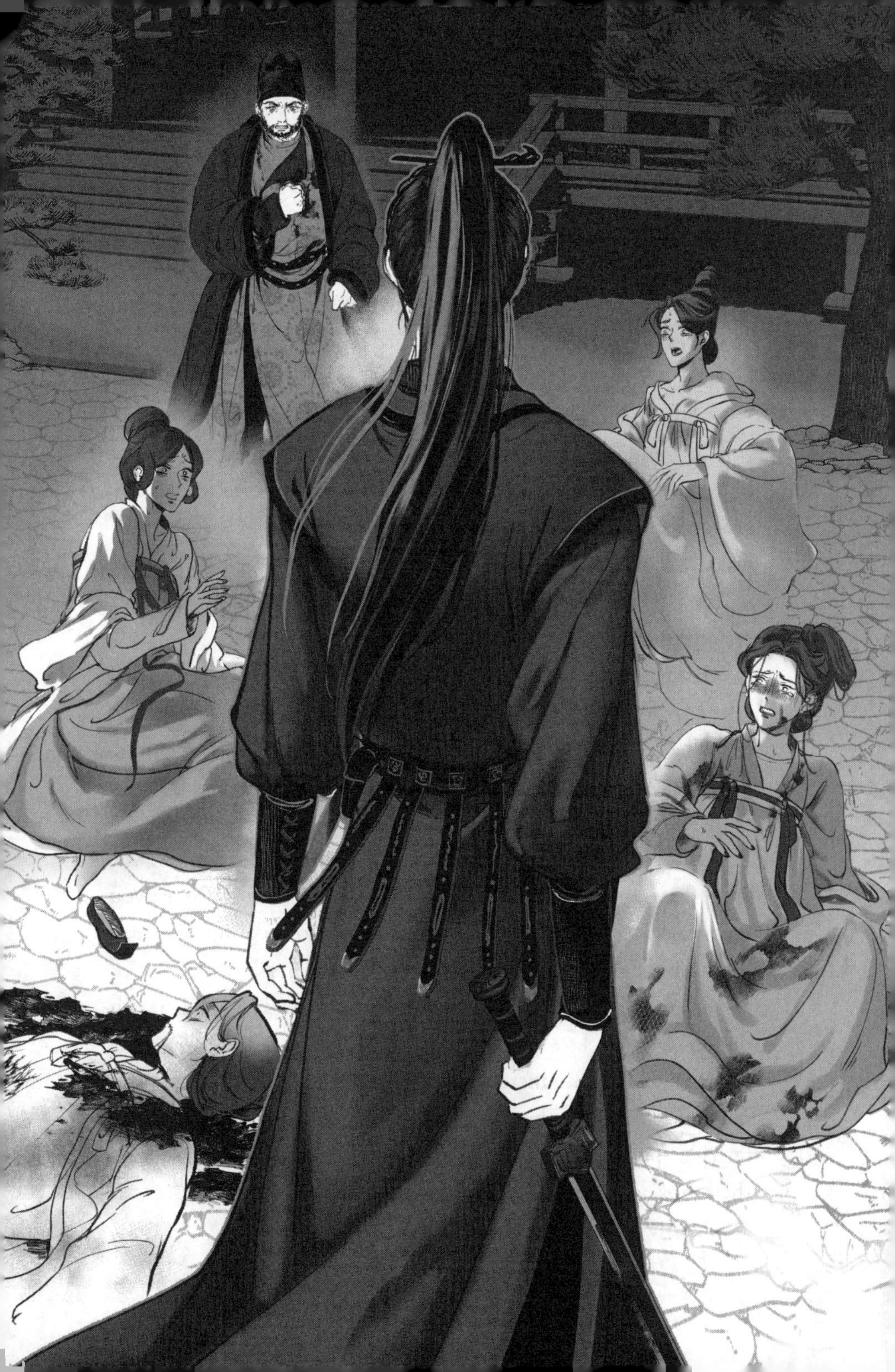

Duan Qihu understood at once: this woman could mimic all kinds of voices.

Yan Xuexing stopped in front of Duan Qihu's beloved concubine. The woman's face was a mask of fear, her complexion snow-white, yet she couldn't move an inch. She was a pitiable sight, but he showed no mercy—he reached out and wrapped his fingers around her neck, gripping it tightly.

Suddenly Yan Xuexing's expression shifted. He threw aside the woman and leapt backward. The yellow-clad woman sitting on the eaves, too, vanished, hiding herself in the shadows. Everyone else saw only a pale flash as a person appeared where Yan Xuexing had just stood.

Feng Xiao smiled. "It's my husband's fault for dallying—I've arrived too late and missed the beginning of the show."

He'd never been one to keep a low profile. Though he was still in women's clothes, his eyes were bright, and his wide sleeves flapped in the wind. His aura was oppressive, neither feminine nor masculine. Even Yan Xuexing took a few more steps back.

"Who are you?!"

"My friend, all debts have their debtors," Feng Xiao said pleasantly. "If you have a grudge against Duan Qihu, then kill him. Why are you dragging your feet? Ah, but since you waited to make your move, if you wish to kill him now, you'll have to ask me first."

Yan Xuexing didn't bother arguing; he attacked Feng Xiao without another word.

Both moved with incredible speed; in a blink, they'd exchanged ten or more blows. The bystanders glimpsed clothes whirling, the flurry of palms transforming, but it was impossible to see any of their moves clearly.

Cui Buqu had arrived as well.

He was no martial artist, so he couldn't drop from the sky as Feng Xiao had. He had to walk in on two legs like any ordinary person.

Yan Xuexing and the woman in yellow had kindly left the Duan residence guards strewn across the ground. There was no one to bar his entry, so he strode through the main gate with no trouble at all.

Catching sight of the woman in yellow, he said, "Maiden Bing Xian. It's been a while."

"Hello, Daoist Master Cui. Though it hasn't been that long." Bing Xian's lips curved in a smile. Neither showed any trace of embarrassment or awkwardness. They acted like old friends reuniting, familiar and natural.

"Since when has the Hehuan Sect started collaborating with Linchuan Academy? I had no idea."

"You've misunderstood, Daoist Master Cui," said Bing Xian. "Yan-gongzi has defected from his sect. This trip was purely for his personal revenge, but he intends to join Hehuan Sect. Naturally I must give our sect's new elite member a warm welcome and help him out a little."

"Personal revenge?"

Bing Xian smiled. "Would you like to hear a story?"

"Keep it short."

"Twenty years ago, a family of merchants passed through Qiemo on their way to Kucha. Along the way, they encountered bandits who took not only their goods but their lives. The bandits killed everyone in the convoy, not sparing the women and children of the family. Only a pair of siblings escaped the slaughter. But they weren't martial artists, and they couldn't get far. The young sister took her little brother and hid in a nearby hunter's cottage."

"You speak as if you witnessed it. Are you perhaps that sister?"

"No—but Yan-gongzi is the brother. As for the sister, she's long gone, raped to death by the bandits. When the hunter discovered the fleeing siblings, not only did he fail to show them kindness and hide them, he prevented them from escaping. The sister stirred his lust, so he held her down and raped her. When the group of bandits caught up, they joined in, taking the sister as spoils of war. An itinerant merchant also passed by. The group of bandits, high on their victory, asked the merchant to join them in violating the girl. At first the merchant didn't want to, but he was afraid the bandits might kill him if he refused. In the end, he couldn't resist his evil impulses, and he, too, became one of the sister's rapists. With the sister in their grasp, the group paid no heed to the younger brother, a child who couldn't run far by himself. But in a stroke of luck, the brother managed to escape. He hid in the dark and witnessed his sister's death from beginning to end."

Cui Buqu understood. "Duan Qihu was one of the bandits?"

Bing Xian smiled. "Not only was he one of the bandits, he was their leader and gave the order to rape the girl. So, what do you think? Does he deserve to die? Should he be killed now or later? Shouldn't we deny him a quick death?"

Duan Qihu heard these words too.

He'd long since remembered those events of twenty years ago, or he wouldn't have been so fearful when it was brought up. But he'd thought no one knew this story, and the other participants would never reveal their own crimes. Never had he expected the young brother would escape the jaws of death and return, much less that he'd become a disciple of Linchuan Academy and gain the skills he needed to seek revenge.

Cui Buqu nodded. "If it happened as you say, he deserves to die."

"I wasn't the only one who took part that day," Duan Qihu roared, "so why is it only me—"

His expression transformed into one of panic.

Li Fei, Cheng Cheng, Peng Xiang, and him. The itinerant merchant, the hunter, and the bandits.

They'd originally been strangers whose paths had only crossed thanks to that incident. Afterward, they'd parted and gone their separate ways. None had thought the encounter important. None had taken it to heart.

One by one, they'd all died.

Everyone who'd participated in that monstrous crime had perished one by one. Duan Qihu hadn't thought in this direction. But as he connected the dots point by point, he realized: not a single one of them had escaped.

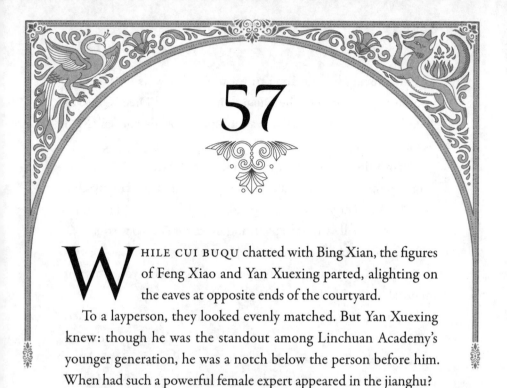

57

WHILE CUI BUQU chatted with Bing Xian, the figures of Feng Xiao and Yan Xuexing parted, alighting on the eaves at opposite ends of the courtyard.

To a layperson, they looked evenly matched. But Yan Xuexing knew: though he was the standout among Linchuan Academy's younger generation, he was a notch below the person before him. When had such a powerful female expert appeared in the jianghu?

"May I ask the lady's esteemed name?"

"My surname is Cui. I don't use my maiden name."

Cui Buqu was speechless. Bing Xian snickered.

"Which sect is Cui-niangzi from?" Yan Xuexing asked. "Who is your master?"

Feng Xiao smiled. "Why should I tell you?"

Yan Xuexing released a slow breath, as if trying to control his temper. He'd encountered more than one troublesome woman on this trip. Though things had improved in recent years, the world remained dominated by men, and so did the jianghu. Women wandered the jianghu, but very few were outstanding talents. Yet it seemed today they had planned their appearances so Yan Xuexing could meet them all.

For example, Bing Xian, and this Cui-niangzi before him now.

Yan Xuexing had no time to waste on this woman. His goal tonight was to torment the Duan family and kill Duan Qihu, to make Duan Qihu suffer as much as possible before dying. Feng Xiao stood in his way.

"Duan Qihu slaughtered my family; he defiled and killed my sister," he spat. "If I don't take revenge, I'd be unfit to call myself a man. If Cui-niangzi shares no friendship with Duan Qihu, please stand aside. I will owe you a debt, and make sure to repay you."

Feng Xiao arched one brow. "Repay me how?"

Yan Xuexing suppressed his anger. "As long as what you ask is not immoral, I will do all I can."

Duan Qihu had dominated Qiemo for decades, surrounded by the flattery and praise of others. Even Gao Yi, sent by the Sui dynasty itself, showed him the utmost courtesy. He'd never been so powerless as he was now, lying like meat on a chopping board.

In his bandit days, he hadn't feared death. He'd sustained plenty of grave injuries and spent days licking blood from his wounds, all to earn this wealthy, comfortable life. But the more he possessed, the more he desired to live. When he saw Feng Xiao apparently swayed by Yan Xuexing's words, he shouted, "Didn't you want to know my secrets? I'll tell you! So help me! I'll tell you all my secrets!"

"So you really do know Yuxiu?" asked Cui Buqu.

"I do!" he cried.

Cui Buqu snorted. "Duan Qihu, I may not know martial arts, but my skills are unmatched when it comes to reading people's words and expressions. You previously said you'd never heard of Yuxiu— that was the truth. Now you're claiming to know him. It seems to me you're trying to deceive us to save your own skin! Do you actually know anything that makes you worth saving?"

"I do!" roared Duan Qihu. "I know something! Have you heard of the Thirteen Floors of Yunhai?! I know their secrets, so save me! I'll tell you everything!"

"The Thirteen Floors of Yunhai?" Cui Buqu looked pensive. "It's true I'm curious about them—but not curious enough to save your life. Prove what you know is worth the exchange."

Duan Qihu's eyes were bloodshot. He was bent on preserving his life; he had no thought for anything else: "The Thirteen Floors of Yunhai isn't just an organization that trades money for lives! The 'thirteen floors' represent thirteen people and thirteen sections. I'm ranked twelfth among them, so I'm known as Shi'er-xiansheng! Is that valuable enough for you?!"

Cui Buqu frowned. He suddenly remembered something.

During the case of the murdered Khotanese envoy, one of the perpetrators, Su Xing, had confessed to being a disciple of the Buyeo Sect in Goguryeo. The person who'd sent him and Qin Miaoyu to the Central Plains was a high-ranking member of the Buyeo Sect they called "Yi-xiansheng"—One. The name was all they knew of him.

At the time, Cui Buqu and Feng Xiao had speculated that someone using "One" as an alias must be an extraordinary person with lofty aspirations. Since there was a One, why shouldn't there be a Two, Three, Four, or even Eleven and Twelve?

Could this Yi-xiansheng be related to the Thirteen Floors of Yunhai? If so, the scale and foresight of the organization was astonishing. Not only did they have roots in Goguryeo, they'd recruited Duan Qihu out in the western borderlands. Their influence was vast, from north to south and east to west, throughout Northern Sui and Southern Chen, even reaching into the major sects of the jianghu. It was likely they had even more allies Cui Buqu had yet to discover.

Cui Buqu's thoughts flashed like sparks; he instantly made the decision to save Duan Qihu's life.

They'd previously suspected Duan Qihu and Yuxiu had some grudge between them, and had hoped uncovering it would reveal the reason for Yuxiu's presence in Qiemo. They hadn't imagined they'd stumble over an astonishing secret about the Thirteen Floors of Yunhai.

Though Feng Xiao exchanged no word or glance with Cui Buqu, he'd come to the exact same conclusion. He shrugged at Yan Xuexing. "You heard him. He's offering to purchase his life with a secret, and it's one I'm quite interested to hear. Why don't you do me a favor and return in a few days to kill him?"

Yan Xuexing's reply was ground between his teeth. "Impossible. I've waited more than ten years for this day. Now that it's finally here, I won't just kill him. I'll kill every member of the Duan family in front of him, then carve him to pieces. I'll give him a taste of what it's like to watch your family die in front of you!"

Feng Xiao raised a brow. "A debt is a debt. But no matter how pompous Duan Qihu's wives and children are, they didn't kill your family. Don't the disciples of Linchuan Academy claim to be students of Confucius? They love talking about morality, benevolence, and righteousness—did your master condone this?"

"Morality, benevolence, and righteousness—can these bring my family back to life? Can they go back and stop those demons from violating my sister?" Yan Xuexing laughed, then scanned the quivering members of the Duan family with mocking eyes. "They've enjoyed the glory and wealth Duan Qihu brought them; it's only right they die with him too. If he were a man of courage and integrity, he would have exiled himself in atonement long ago. He'd have refused to spend wealth tainted with human blood! I killed his daughter with a single slash. I didn't recruit anyone to follow his example and humiliate his daughter in front of him. That alone was an enormous act of benevolence!"

Before he'd finished speaking, he sprang into action.

Yan Xuexing knew he wasn't Feng Xiao's equal. If he wanted to kill Duan Qihu, he needed an opportunity. He'd spoken partly to vent his misery, but more so to mask his intentions. With Feng Xiao here, Yan Xuexing's plan to torture and kill the Duan family wouldn't work. He chose to strike Duan Qihu with a single killing blow. Any hesitation would wreck his chances.

The night was dark, and in the dim light of the distant lanterns, Yan Xuexing looked like a lone and ethereal swan. He was so fast even Bing Xian could hardly see him, never mind Cui Buqu.

But no matter how fast he moved, his goal could only be Duan Qihu.

Feng Xiao also moved.

He took an ordinary step, his footwork unremarkable. Absent was his signature peacock-like style, where he aimed to intentionally dazzle onlookers. This move was completely straightforward: he dropped down from the eaves, sleeves raised like a legendary bird in flight, and landed right on top of Yan Xuexing.

The maneuver appeared basic, but Yan Xuexing felt an immense pressure bearing down on his head, like his entire body was about to be crushed. He blanched and quickly gave up offense for defense. Bending at the waist, he swept forward and slammed his palms into the ground, flying right back into Feng Xiao.

In a flash, they'd exchanged over a dozen blows. A confrontation between two such experts was a rare sight. In other circumstances, Cui Buqu might have sat down to savor the experience.

But Bing Xian couldn't simply watch Yan Xuexing fall in defeat;

she was trying to recruit him into the Hehuan Sect. She darted forward as well.

As soon as she joined the fray, the fight seemed to tilt in their favor—but only for a moment. In the face of greater adversity, Feng Xiao grew even stronger; he didn't lose the upper hand at all. Yan Xuexing saw that Feng Xiao had been holding back before, merely toying with him.

Duan Qihu was seriously injured, but he'd never relinquished his desire to escape. Seeing the three of them occupied fighting each other, he edged toward a dark corner. Yet he suddenly found someone standing in front of him.

Cui Buqu.

Duan Qihu thought very little of this man who knew no martial arts. But right then, he himself wasn't much better off. He lowered his voice. "I've hidden many treasures over the years. Let me go and I'll tell you where to find them!"

"I'm not interested in treasure," said Cui Buqu. "But if you tell me about the Thirteen Floors of Yunhai, I'll spare your life. My wife will also shield you from them; once this is over, you can escape."

Duan Qihu smiled bitterly. "Members of the Thirteen Floors of Yunhai must abide by its rules. We're forbidden from leaking even a single word. If I talk, death awaits me."

"But you talked just now," said Cui Buqu. He looked over at Feng Xiao and shouted, "Wife of mine, Duan Qihu refuses to cooperate. No need to exhaust yourself; let Yan Xuexing kill him!"

Feng Xiao was fighting two on one, yet he still had the breath to say, "Of course, dear. I always listen to my husband!"

"I'll talk!" Duan Qihu cried. "I'll talk! What do you want to know?"

"Do you know Yuxiu or not? Is Yuxiu a member of the Thirteen Floors of Yunhai?"

"I don't know him! I've never heard of such a person! The Thirteen Floors of Yunhai are composed of thirteen directors, each in charge of a section. Though I'm a director, I only know of the two before and after me. I don't know anything about the others!"

Out of a total of thirteen members, Duan Qihu was the twelfth, Shi'er-xiansheng. Before him must be the eleventh, Shiyi-xiansheng, and after him had to be the thirteenth, Shisan-xiansheng.

"Who are they?" asked Cui Buqu.

"Shiyi is a monk named Yuheng. Shisan is a woman named Feng Xiaolian!"

Setting aside whether this Yuheng the monk was actually Yuxiu, Cui Buqu was astonished to hear the second name. "Gao Wei's favored concubine, Feng Xiaolian?"

"That's right!" cried Duan Qihu.

Feng Xiaolian, a woman so beautiful her lord could charge a thousand gold pieces per glance? Anyone with the slightest understanding of world affairs knew the fame of this bewitching concubine. After the emperor of Sui usurped the Zhou dynasty, Feng Xiaolian was given to a Sui official as a reward. As far as Cui Buqu knew, she'd perished in some harem infighting. A peerless beauty of her generation had died too young, and many lovers of women had mourned her passing.

If this woman was really Shisan-xiansheng of the Thirteen Floors of Yunhai, she must have faked her own death.

58

DUAN QIHU had joined the Thirteen Floors of Yunhai completely by accident.

In those years, he'd recently turned over a new leaf, washing his hands of his marauding bandit lifestyle to settle down in Qiemo and make a proper living as a merchant.

Of course, *proper* wasn't entirely accurate. All his early wealth had been gotten unlawfully, and he'd amassed a group of loyal subordinates. He had no shortage of money or people. His transformation from bandit to powerful business mogul was unnaturally quick.

Upon his arrival in Qiemo, Cui Buqu had seen how Duan Qihu and Xing Mao had monopolized the business interests of the city. Even the inns were split between the two, half and half. If they declined to stay at one of Duan Qihu's inns, they'd have to go to one of Xing Mao's instead. There was little other choice.

But back when Duan Qihu had first established himself in Qiemo, it hadn't been so. In addition to Xing Mao, several other factions had held stakes in the city. The roots of Duan Qihu's influence were yet shallow—a foreign dragon couldn't defeat local snakes, and when it came to scheming, he wasn't necessarily their equal. Several other men of influence had joined forces and approached Xing Mao, proposing they work together to drive Duan Qihu out of Qiemo.

It was then that a man came knocking, claiming to be Yuheng, the eleventh director of the Thirteen Floors of Yunhai.

Duan Qihu had never heard of any such organization, but Yuheng got straight to the point: he'd help Duan Qihu eliminate the competition and establish himself in Qiemo—provided he joined the Thirteen Floors of Yunhai as their twelfth director.

At the time, Duan Qihu was being crushed by multiple factions. Despite his doubts, he was so frazzled and anxious he agreed to Yuheng's improbable offer.

But Yuheng kept his word. Not only did he assassinate several of Duan Qihu's enemies, thus resolving his immediate crisis, he also introduced Duan Qihu to silk and porcelain merchants in Jiangnan. Those connections allowed Duan Qihu to build relationships with merchants across the north and south, slowly growing his network. Within a few years, he'd risen to become Xing Mao's rival.

At the same time, he discovered the vast scope of the organization he'd joined. From north to south, across all classes of society, there seemed to be no one the Thirteen Floors couldn't reach. Duan Qihu was too seasoned to believe there was such a thing as a free lunch—he knew he'd inevitably have to pay for what he gained. But beyond making him the twelfth director and supporting his rise to power, the Thirteen Floors of Yunhai never asked him to do anything.

When Shisan-xiansheng, Feng Xiaolian, who was ranked last among the floors, appeared in Qiemo, Duan Qihu had encountered her by chance. After removing her makeup, the legendary concubine became just another fair-faced woman. Duan Qihu had always been a lecherous man, but he didn't dare harbor any untoward thoughts toward Feng Xiaolian. Though she was a rank beneath him, she was far from weak—as a martial artist, she was his equal.

If people of Duan Qihu and Feng Xiaolian's status ranked at the bottom of the Thirteen Floors, how strong and skilled were the people above them? Duan Qihu didn't want to dig any further. Knowing too much would only endanger him, so he chose ignorance.

Yet one day, Yuheng appeared again. He demanded Duan Qihu bring down Gao Yi and eliminate Xing Mao, taking control as the true ruler of Qiemo. The Thirteen Floors of Yunhai, he said, would lend Duan Qihu their full support. Money or manpower—if he required them, he need only say the word.

Duan Qihu, however, felt no enthusiasm for this scheme. His heart sank; he had accepted their help, and now it was time to pay his debt.

He was more than happy with the status quo. No longer did he have to live with his hands soaked in blood. He spent each day in great comfort, enjoying his reputation and his wealth. Those who had despised him for his background now had to hold their noses and try to please him.

As Duan Qihu aged, he'd grown fearful of death and change. He might have reluctantly agreed to kill Xing Mao, but behind Magistrate Gao Yi stood Great Sui. Duan Qihu wasn't so arrogant as to believe he could take on the entire Sui dynasty.

The Sui emperor was currently embroiled in a war with the Göktürks, which perhaps left them without attention to spare for Qiemo's petty politics. But the moment that ended, Duan Qihu refused to believe trifling Qiemo could stand up to Great Sui.

In Yuheng's instructions, Duan Qihu glimpsed a sliver of a grand and terrifying plan. He came to a realization: if the Thirteen Floors of Yunhai were a pool of water, it was one whose depths he couldn't fathom.

Thus he politely rebuffed Yuheng, promising to give it careful consideration. But in truth, he was drawing things out in the hope it'd come to nothing. Multiple visits from Yuheng had failed to persuade him. A desire to leave the Thirteen Floors of Yunhai grew instead. He'd accumulated enough money and power to spend the rest of his life in peace and comfort. There was no need to take any more risks.

Yuheng must have sensed his thoughts because he didn't come again. Duan Qihu had breathed a sigh of relief, yet he was still uneasy. The Thirteen Floors of Yunhai had invested so much in him. He doubted they would let him go without a fight.

With this in mind, he'd secretly trained a troop of loyal guards and surrounded himself in layer after layer of protections. He'd even dug out several secret underground rooms in his estate, just in case. But time passed and neither Yuheng nor the Thirteen Floors of Yunhai came knocking.

The moment he'd heard the ghost, Duan Qihu knew it was no vengeful spirit. It was someone masquerading as a dead woman to kill him. Perhaps this trick was devised by Xing Mao, or perhaps it was the Thirteen Floors of Yunhai—perhaps the two had even teamed up.

Duan Qihu had therefore rushed to strike first. But he hadn't expected either Yan Xuexing or Cui Buqu.

However one schemed and plotted, it was nothing in the face of fate.

After Duan Qihu had stammered out this story, he watched Cui Buqu pondering. The other three were still fighting; for the moment, there was no one watching him. He quickly rose and lurched toward the shadows.

Something whistled through the air behind him; he screamed and collapsed to the ground, an arrow protruding from his shoulder. More sharp arrows shot toward the three combatants.

Cui Buqu stood behind the colonnade, avoiding the rain of arrows, and looked up. Several figures had appeared on the rooftop, bows in hand and arrows nocked to stings. They took aim at the crowd in the courtyard.

In the wake of their next volley, Xing Mao coolly and confidently led a group through the gates. At his side was a monk clad in white.

This had to be Shiyi-xiansheng, Yuheng of the Thirteen Floors of Yunhai. He smiled at Duan Qihu and casually looked away, as if the master of this estate was no more than a stray cur. He indeed looked very much like the monk Yuxiu, but the moment he spoke, Cui Buqu knew this wasn't the same man.

"Haven't you heard the saying, 'the mantis stalks the cicada while the oriole waits behind'?"

Duan Qihu was the cicada and Yan Xuexing and Bing Xian the mantises. Cui Buqu and Feng Xiao had fancied themselves the orioles—unaware that Yuheng and Xing Mao would snatch the final victory.

This man's voice was nothing like Yuxiu's. When Cui Buqu and Feng Xiao had tailed him, they'd seen him talking to the third steward of the Xing residence, but they hadn't heard him speak. Yet Yuheng and Yuxiu were both white-clad monks with similar names. What was the relationship between them?

Cui Buqu frowned as he considered it. He wasn't a martial artist—other than Bing Xian, no one on the scene spared him a thought. That was perfect for him; he was happy to hide behind the colonnade and observe.

In addition to Yuheng, Xing Mao had several other martial experts around him. Each wore a different style of dress, unlike his subordinates. These must be free agents he'd recruited from the jianghu.

Everyone was hemmed in by the Xing family's guards, who surrounded the Duan residence and stood on the eaves.

On Duan Qihu's side, Steward Lin and the loyal soldiers he'd taken were nowhere to be found. Yan Xuexing had killed his remaining guards, and Xing Mao had probably cleaned up the rest on his way in.

There was no hope for him now.

"Don't be so happy just yet!" Duan Qihu's face was stained with blood, his hair disheveled as he stared unswervingly at Xing Mao. He had not a scrap of his former might as one of Qiemo's great overlords. He'd fought his nemesis for so long, and in all that time, neither had been able to gain the upper hand. Never had he expected the outcome of their battle would be determined today.

Xing Mao laughed heartily, completely at ease. "Good brother, are you thinking of your dozens of loyal guards? Why, they are waiting for you in the underworld!"

"Impossible!" said Duan Qihu.

"Speaking of which," Xing Mao continued, "you spared no effort training them. If not for Steward Lin's advance warning, I might have been in quite a spot. To think your loyal subordinate would betray you."

Duan Qihu let out a wail of despair. He coughed up a mouthful of blood, and his face flushed a deeper crimson. "Impossible! Impossible! Lin Feng would never betray me!"

Xing Mao clicked his tongue in dissatisfaction. He had no patience for more talk; he waved a hand. "Seize the Duan family! All of them!"

"Wait a minute!" Yan Xuexing said coldly. "The Duan family's lives are mine! Only I have the right to punish them!"

Xing Mao lifted a brow. "Are you also here to kill Duan Qihu? No problem at all. I'll chop off his head and you can have the body.

As for the women, children, and elderly, you may watch from there as I deal with them."

"No." Yan Xuexing rejected him firmly. "My grudge against him is deep; I must punish him personally!"

Xing Mao was growing restless. "Whoever is stronger has the final say!" He glanced at Yuheng.

The monk nodded and smiled. "Duan Qihu must die today."

Xing Mao took a step back and cupped his hands politely. "I leave this to you," he said to the group behind him.

The first to step forward was a scholar waving a fan. "Please allow this one to challenge you, distinguished disciple of Linchuan Academy!"

Before Xing Mao had arrived, Yan Xuexing and Feng Xiao were enemies. Now that he'd appeared, the situation had changed again.

Feng Xiao and Cui Buqu wanted to preserve Duan Qihu's life until they could make him spit up more secrets about the Thirteen Floors of Yunhai. Yan Xuexing sought Duan Qihu's death but didn't want him to perish in the hands of Xing Mao. Thus they reached a temporary truce. As the scholar attacked Yan Xuexing, Feng Xiao withdrew and watched from the side.

This scholar didn't look like much, but his skills were impressive. His iron-boned fan became an impenetrable barrier, cutting off Yan Xuexing's avenues of attack. But his internal cultivation was far below that of Yan Xuexing—though his moves were uncanny, he soon found himself unable to keep up. In the next moment, two others standing beside Xing Mao moved, one wielding a sword, the other a saber.

The sword was dark and plain, an unremarkable sight. In contrast, the saber shone with golden light. When it was unsheathed in the darkness, the watchers were almost blinded.

Feng Xiao was an excellent martial artist, but he rarely wandered the jianghu and knew nothing of his assailants' backgrounds. Fortunately there was a walking encyclopedia next to him, one who knew practically all there was to know about the wide world.

"The swordsman is Wang Hong, also known in the jianghu as the Nameless Sword. Though his sword is nameless, its wielder is quite well known. He specializes in unconventional tricks, and his master is a Miao man from the southwest, where they use poisonous gu insects. He uses them as well, to fell his opponents when their guards are down." Cui Buqu seemed to have intuited Feng Xiao's thoughts; his voice rang out right away.

Yan Xuexing cocked his head as a silent breeze brushed past his ear. Bing Xian flicked a finger; a black insect fell to the ground, her silver needle piercing its body.

Yan Xuexing glanced in Cui Buqu's direction. Had he not spoken, Yan Xuexing might have fallen for this trick.

"The man with the saber is Hu Yun, known for his wealth and virtue alike. He hails from a rich family in Shaanxi; food and clothing are never his worries. Gold is a soft metal, but he hired a skilled blacksmith to forge his golden saber. The gold was refined and mixed with iron before quenching. Ordinary swords are powerless before it, and his saber techniques are considered second-tier." Cui Buqu spoke quickly and calmly, outlining the key points of his history.

Listening, Hu Yun grew agitated. "You asshole, who are you calling second-tier?!"

Yan Xuexing's foot slammed into the saber wielder's gut and sent him flying; his golden saber landed with a *clang*.

The scholar chuckled. "Hu Yun, looks like your luck has run out!"

"The Fan-Wielding Scholar, Yue Xiafeng," Cui Buqu went on. "His weapon of choice is an iron-boned fan. He's a fearsome fighter at close range, but at a distance..."

Bing Xian's lips quirked in a knowing smile; she flicked her fingers again.

Yue Xiafeng had no choice but to abort his attack on Yan Xuexing to block her silver needles. Glimpsing an opening, Yan Xuexing slammed a palm into Yue Xiafeng's back, bringing up a mouthful of blood—a serious injury.

Bing Xian bowed to Cui Buqu. "Thank you kindly for your guidance, Daoist Master Cui."

"Maiden Bing Xian is the clever one," said Cui Buqu.

For some reason, Feng Xiao suddenly felt a twinge of displeasure.

He swept toward Xing Mao.

As Xing Mao stood shocked, the two experts remaining at his side sprang into action.

The first crooked his fingers slightly and grabbed at his face, while the other pinched his thumb and forefinger together as if plucking flowers. In truth he was holding a very fine thread, its edge sharper than most swords. With the aid of internal energy, this thread could slit an enemy's throat with a touch.

"Cloudcatcher Pei Yuan is a layman disciple from Shaolin Temple. His moves are heavy and powerful; he's known for his hard techniques that counter force with force. Defeat him with soft techniques that deflect his force and use it against him. Bai Bi, known as Moonwater Guanyin. A man with the delicate face of a woman, hence the sobriquet. But his silver-gold threads are practically mystical weapons. All those who've perished at his hands have underestimated him—"

Cui Buqu accurately pinpointed everyone's weaknesses. As he spoke, Feng Xiao raised his hands. Everywhere his true qi touched, Bai Bi's silken threads were sliced through.

Suddenly Cui Buqu fell quiet—a hand was clutching his throat.

Yuheng squeezed Cui Buqu's neck and smiled at Feng Xiao, who now had Xing Mao in his grasp. "Would you like to save a life, or take one?"

Pei Yuan and Bai Bi hadn't even seen Yuheng move; Feng Xiao had thrown them aside with their acupoints sealed.

Xing Mao's face was white with shock. He'd never imagined encountering variables like Feng Xiao and Cui Buqu as victory was within his reach. If not for them, Yan Xuexing and Bing Xian would have already been forced to withdraw. Anger exploded through him as he bellowed, "Yu-xiansheng, you can't abandon me!"

59

YUHENG'S GAZE flickered as he looked at Feng Xiao. "The mighty lord chief of the Zuoyue Bureau is in my hands. Let Xing Mao go, or I'll snap his neck. Then we'll see who suffers the greater loss!"

Feng Xiao arched a brow. "If you know his identity, you must know mine as well."

"The deputy chief of the Jiejian Bureau," Yuheng sneered. "Together with the Zuoyue Bureau, you form the left and right hands of the emperor of Great Sui. You've come to patrol and set up watchmen on his behalf in order to eliminate evil. What capable men you are!"

Finally Yan Xuexing and the rest discovered the true identities of this mysterious couple. Their eyes widened in astonishment.

"You're quite knowledgeable," said Feng Xiao. "And where did you hear this?"

"I have my sources. You two ought to learn—plenty of things in this world lie beyond your understanding," Yuheng said. "Not all will bow to your might. Qiemo is not Great Sui's territory. If you wish to come here and sow chaos, you must first show yourself to be worthy opponents!"

Over the course of this conversation, the martial artists Xing Mao had brought with him recovered. The archers stood steady, ready to shoot. The Duan family was surrounded by three rows of men. Although Feng Xiao was an exceptional martial artist and could have easily escaped unscathed, he couldn't do so while guaranteeing the safety of Cui Buqu and Duan Qihu.

Now that his identity had been exposed, Feng Xiao relaxed back into his natural voice. He remained carefree as ever, without any trace of anger or panic. "Since you know who we are, you should know the Jiejian and Zuoyue Bureaus have never been friends. I'm only cooperating with him because our goals temporarily align. Kill him, and I'll thank you for removing a roadblock for me. What a relief not to worry about battling my nemesis ever again!"

"You make it sound simple," Yuheng mocked. "If I kill him, how will you explain to your emperor when you return to the capital?" He tightened his grip on Cui Buqu's neck. The color of Cui Buqu's face wasn't visible in the darkness, but it must have been alarming.

"Wait!" Surprisingly, it was Bing Xian who spoke. "What do you want to set him free?"

"Make the deputy chief release Xing Mao first!"

"Whether or not he lets Xing Mao go isn't up to me," said Bing Xian. "But I do know the location of Duan Qihu's private storeroom. Why not exchange this for Daoist Master Cui's life? Duan Qihu has dominated Qiemo for years and accumulated wealth nearly equal to Xing Mao's. Surely this will do?"

Yuheng's lip curled. "How fortunate this invalid is—he's even got a lady to come to his rescue. Tell me, have you fallen for him?"

This question removed any doubts Feng Xiao might have had over whether Yuheng was the monk Yuxiu. A strategist capable of winning the trust of the Prince of Jin could never be so shallow. But if Yuheng wasn't Yuxiu, what explained the similarities between them? And how did Yuheng know their true identities?

Feng Xiao felt inexplicably restless. Yuheng was no more than a capering clown, but Feng Xiao's perfect control over the situation had been destroyed by the sudden intervention of Bing Xian.

"Daoist Master Cui just reminded me I still owe him a favor," Bing Xian said coolly. "Why shouldn't I repay him now?"

"Your offer is tempting. But if I want to find Duan Qihu's private storehouse, I can just ask him. I don't need you to tell me. However..." Yuheng's eyes raked up and down her figure. "You're not so bad yourself. If you'd like to take his place, I might give it some consideration."

"You've been running your mouth for a while now," Feng Xiao said, impatient. "Are you going to kill him or not?"

Bing Xian's brow furrowed slightly. Feng Xiao and Cui Buqu were traveling disguised as husband and wife; she'd assumed the two must be close. But it seemed that wasn't the case. Cui Buqu knew no martial arts. How did he feel, having followed Feng Xiao into danger only to be abandoned in his hour of need?

She couldn't help but glance over at him.

Cui Buqu had remained quiet throughout; his lashes downcast, as if it wasn't his fate the others were deciding. Even compared to martial experts, his reaction was unusually calm—so calm she itched to peer into his inner thoughts.

Bing Xian took a small step forward, then stopped, bewildered. She'd planned to stand on the sidelines and see what windfalls she could reap. Now she wanted to wade into trouble herself?

At the other end of the courtyard, Feng Xiao laughed and tightened his grip on Xing Mao. "If you won't make a move, I will!"

A dagger appeared in his free hand; he stabbed the blade straight into his captive's shoulder. Blood spattered, and Xing Mao screamed in agony.

"Yu-xiansheng, help me!"

Feng Xiao twisted the handle. Crimson soaked Xing Mao's robes as he wailed, eyes rolling back in his head, but Feng Xiao still wasn't satisfied. He yanked the dagger out and plunged it into Xing Mao's opposite shoulder.

Yuheng was stunned. He hadn't expected Feng Xiao to follow through, nor to be so cruel. The deputy chief of the Jiejian Bureau really was completely unconcerned about Cui Buqu's safety.

Should Yuheng do the same to Cui Buqu? But even if he killed him, Feng Xiao mightn't let Xing Mao go. Xing Mao already had one foot in the grave—if this continued, he might really die and no longer be of use.

Yuheng was disoriented; as he struggled to decide, his hand around Cui Buqu's throat unconsciously loosened.

No! *Something was wrong!*

From the depths of his mind came a spark of awareness, pulling him back from the brink of confusion. No one else around them had reacted to their confrontation—it was completely bizarre. And it wasn't only Yue Xiafeng and the other experts: Xing Mao's screams echoed unceasingly, oscillating between loud and soft. As for Feng Xiao, the smug curve at the corner of his mouth never changed.

It was an illusion—an incredibly brilliant one.

The Cui Buqu before him had been motionless, like a puppet. At that point, if he'd still failed to realize he'd fallen prey to an illusory technique, he wouldn't have deserved to call himself a martial artist.

Yuheng bit down hard on his tongue. Blood filled his mouth, but the pain brought clarity. The puppet-like figures around him returned to life. His hands were empty, and Cui Buqu was nowhere to be seen. In the same instant, someone rushed toward him, sleeves billowing like the wings of a great eagle as their internal energy surged over him in waves. Yuheng had no time to spare searching for Cui Buqu or Xing Mao.

When the fighting began, Duan Qihu had crawled behind the colonnade, hoping to sneak off quietly. The Duan family was still in the courtyard awaiting slaughter, yet at that moment, Duan Qihu could think only of saving his own skin.

Yan Xuexing had kept Duan Qihu in view the entire time, unwilling to let him go. Upon seeing Duan Qihu's attempt to flee, he made a grab for him.

Duan Qihu chuckled coldly. There was no fear in his eyes, only malicious mockery. As if he'd finally found his chance to escape, and Yan Xuexing was powerless to stop it.

Yan Xuexing was still trying to make sense of it when Duan Qihu disappeared.

Taken aback, Yan Xuexing dashed over, disregarding all else—yet as he took his next step forward, the ground beneath his feet vanished. Before he could make a sound, he was plummeting into darkness.

Bing Xian had taken advantage of Feng Xiao's illusion to pierce the hand of the confused Yuheng with one of her silver needles, breaking Cui Buqu free. "Are you all right, Daoist Master Cui?" She stepped up to support him.

Cui Buqu shook his head and looked around. "Where's Duan Qihu?"

"I saw him disappear behind a pillar just now," she said. "But I was worried about you, so I didn't follow him to look. Yan-gongzi has gone after him."

"We must find him!" If Yan Xuexing caught Duan Qihu first, he'd kill him. Cui Buqu would never get any of the answers he sought. He didn't want Duan Qihu to die just yet.

Meanwhile, Feng Xiao was facing not only Yuheng, but Yue Xiafeng and the others as well. Seeing Cui Buqu leave with Bing Xian, he couldn't help shouting, "Hey! I'm dealing with our enemies for your sake, and you run off with a new lover?"

Cui Buqu didn't turn. "Those who are capable should work harder. I've utmost confidence in you."

Xing Mao crawled upright. "No—none of you will escape. Archers, on my word!" he ground out through clenched teeth.

"Because the tiger has yet to show his claws, you've taken him for a sick cat?" Feng Xiao loosed a peal of laughter as his palm collided with Yuheng's. The monk flew backward, slamming heavily into a pillar.

Yue Xiafeng and Hu Yun's weapons cut toward Feng Xiao from both sides. Under the scouring true qi, Feng Xiao's delicate bun unraveled, and his long hair fluttered and danced in the wind. Though he was still dressed as a woman, his expression was unbridled, his movements bold, with a dashing elegance; it was impossible to mistake his gender. This was the true form of the deputy chief of the Jiejian Bureau. His previous frivolous manner was merely his way of relieving boredom. Any who underestimated him on its account would bring down their own destruction.

Just as Yuheng had.

Feng Xiao didn't dodge. Faced with this pincer attack, he shook out his sleeves and poured true qi through his meridians and into his palms, transforming it into an explosive palm technique. He grabbed both the iron-boned fan and Hu Yun's golden saber with bare hands.

A dull ringing sounded. Instead of feeling his sword bite into flesh, Hu Yun's wrist tingled, and the golden saber snapped cleanly in two. On the other side, Yue Xiafeng's fan had met the same fate.

Feng Xiao gave them no chance to react. He whirled and flung out his hands; the broken saber and fan turned sharply in midair, then swept back toward their masters. Yue Xiafeng and Hu Yun cried out in pain and crumpled to the ground.

A wise man understood when to retreat. Observing all this, the Nameless Sword Wang Hong took two quick steps back, turned, and fled.

Xing Mao's fury was turning into desperation. If not for Feng Xiao and Yan Xuexing, the Duan family would be in his grasp tonight. By dawn, there would be no one in Qiemo who could rival him. Yet somehow the situation had turned sour, his victory crumbling into defeat.

"Shoot! Kill them!" He no longer cared whether his guards' arrows might wound Yuheng and the others.

He yelled and yelled, but no arrows came.

Xing Mao looked up. The archers standing motionless on the eaves wore clothes he didn't recognize—they were no longer the men he'd brought from his manor.

"Your men have been defeated. Who are you calling for?"

A new figure strode through the gates—Qiao Xian, who'd taken the commander's tally to Liugong City and summoned an army.

Xing Mao had thought himself the oriole behind the mantis catching the cicada; it had never occurred to him that behind the oriole was a falcon.

Feng Xiao pursed his lips and shook out slightly numb hands. Acting so high and mighty while using his tally! The Zuoyue Bureau was certainly good at making the most of other people's privileges.

Unfortunately, Cui Buqu had missed the sight of his dashing figure as he fought four on one. Otherwise, Cui Buqu would've had to personally admit he owed Feng Xiao a great favor.

With this in mind, Feng Xiao looked around, only to discover that Cui Buqu and Bing Xian had vanished completely from sight.

60

EVEN WHILE ENJOYING their wealth and glory to the utmost, men like Duan Qihu always prepared for the unexpected. It would be stranger if he didn't have some kind of secret passage, bolt-hole, or other avenue of guaranteed escape should the need arise.

Still, Cui Buqu had expected the entrance of Duan Qihu's secret passage to be somewhere more typical—in his study, perhaps, or under his bed. Instead, it was triggered by a mechanism behind the railing in the rear courtyard.

This courtyard would usually be bustling with people and theoretically provide no concealment at all. But this most unlikely of places had now become Duan Qihu's final thread of hope. As Cui Buqu jumped down into the gap, he mused that this couldn't be the only entrance. Otherwise, if Duan Qihu met with danger in his study or bedroom, certain death awaited him.

The tunnel slanted down at a steep angle. Duan Qihu must have spared no expense with the excavation; the walls and floors were smooth, devoid of any rough stones that could cause injury. After sliding down steadily, the ground suddenly disappeared beneath Cui Buqu's feet, and he dropped into thin air. A gentle arm reached out to hold him up, preventing him from tumbling head over heels.

"Thank you very much," he said softly.

"No need for such courtesies, Daoist Master Cui." Though it was too dark to see, Bing Xian, like him, had been observing their surroundings. "Yan-gongzi and Duan Qihu fell down here too. They can't have gone far."

But all around was silence, with no whisper or scuffle of movement. Wherever Yan Xuexing and Duan Qihu were, they weren't nearby.

"Let's take a look," said Cui Buqu.

Bing Xian had no objections. "It's pitch-black in here; even I can't see where we're going. Please follow closely, Daoist Master Cui, or I won't be able to save you if anything happens."

"Let me walk in front."

The tunnel was wide at some points and narrow at others—but even in the widest spots, it couldn't accommodate two people walking side by side. There would be nowhere to hide if they ran into danger. But if Cui Buqu walked behind Bing Xian, he'd likely crash into her in the dark—and that would be terribly awkward.

Bing Xian smiled in the gloom.

She'd met no shortage of men who used any excuse to take advantage of a woman, and just as many hypocrites stuffed with false integrity. Yet Cui Buqu's actions spoke for themselves—he simply drew a line between them. Bing Xian admired him greatly for it.

"No need," she said, "It's better if the Daoist master stays behind me."

She stepped out with one hand on the wall for guidance, slowly moving forward. "There should be some candlesticks along the wall; let me see... Found them."

Bing Xian took a firestarter from her lapel and lit the wick. A small glow flared to life, and both breathed a sigh of relief. Darkness meant the unknown, and people always feared what they couldn't comprehend. If any traps or mechanisms awaited them, this small glimmer of light would make them that much easier to see.

Bing Xian took the candlestick off the wall, hoping to light the surrounding candles as well. But the wicks had all burned down; even the candle in her hands was reaching its limit, burned down to a nub. For the candles to be in this state, people must come here often.

They looked around. They'd fallen into a man-made stone chamber. Its four walls were flat and smooth, but besides them, there was nothing else—no beds, no seats, nor any desk with ink and paper.

Bing Xian frowned.

Perhaps people came here often, but what did they do? Did they sit on the floor, or stand around talking until it was time to leave? Yet the slope of the entrance had been almost sheer. Climbing out wouldn't be easy.

Cui Buqu crouched down and touched the ground, then sniffed his fingertips. "Blood. They were just here."

Bing Xian was secretly ashamed. She'd looked at the four walls but neglected the ground beneath her feet. She crouched as well and looked where Cui Buqu was pointing. Sure enough, there were faint traces of blood, evidence someone had been dragged through the room.

Cui Buqu asked Bing Xian for the candlestick, then lay flat on the ground to examine the traces. Eventually he pointed toward one corner of the room. "They went through there."

The bloodstains twisted and turned, and the sand and small stones on the ground shifted with them. The traces were faint in places and heavy in others—it was unlikely Duan Qihu was faking his injury. Perhaps he couldn't walk properly, and his feet had stumbled. When Yan Xuexing caught up to him, he'd apparently been dragged along the ground until the traces of both men disappeared together into this empty corner.

There had to be a mechanism hidden in the floor tiles or walls. Without a moment to waste, Cui Buqu and Bing Xian both started searching. Cui Buqu's efforts were fruitless, but Bing Xian soon exclaimed, "Ah?"

Cui Buqu had barely turned his head when the ground beneath his feet began to quake. Startled, Bing Xian clutched at the wall and turned to grab Cui Buqu, too late—Cui Buqu was already falling. Her hand brushed past his, grasping air.

In the next instant, Cui Buqu's back slammed into the ground. Agony exploded through him as a reeking wind hit him full in the face, accompanied by the bellow of a beast. Pain tightened his chest and a cough surged in his throat, but at the sound of that animal roar, he choked it back.

For Bing Xian or Feng Xiao, avoiding a ferocious beast posed no problem. But such a confrontation was far beyond Cui Buqu's abilities. There was no escape; all he could do was close his eyes. In all his countless calculations, he'd never anticipated that rather than succumbing to incense of helplessness or perishing at the hands of Yuxiu or Yuheng, he'd meet his end mauled to death by some nameless predator in an underground hideout.

Without warning, a hand came down on his shoulder and yanked him backward. Cui Buqu fell into someone's arms as they rolled to the side, narrowly avoiding the beast's claws.

The creature roared angrily at having missed and turned to make a second charge. Cui Buqu felt himself released, and there came a clang of a weapon as whoever had saved him faced the beast head-on.

In the darkness, human and beast fought in a tangle of limbs and claws. The beast had fancied Cui Buqu its dinner, yet someone had gotten in its way and was now wounding it all over. Impatient and hungry, it bellowed again and pounced at the newcomer, only for a sword glare to split its belly open. The creature collapsed to the floor with a dull thud.

A savage beast might be a terror to ordinary people, but it was no match for a skilled martial artist. And this person was more than skilled; they seemed to be an expert. Yet it wasn't Duan Qihu nor Yan Xuexing, and Feng Xiao didn't use a sword.

Who could it be?

Cui Buqu's thoughts felt sluggish; perhaps he was still disoriented from his fall. His mysterious savior spoke up:

"Are you all right?"

Cui Buqu coughed a few times, the familiar tang of blood stinging his throat. "Thank you very much, sir," he said hoarsely. "May I ask your name?"

"Xiao Lü."

Cui Buqu hesitated a moment. "Xiao. *Cao* radical?"

"Correct." Cui Buqu could hear a smile in his voice. "*Lu* as in 'stumbling forward.'"

Cui Buqu pressed a hand to his forehead and frowned, his mind still spinning. The name was familiar, but it was a moment before he recalled why. Sure enough, this was another famous name—in fact, an incredibly famous one.

What was so special about the Duan residence that it summoned such an assembly of heroes over the course of a single night?

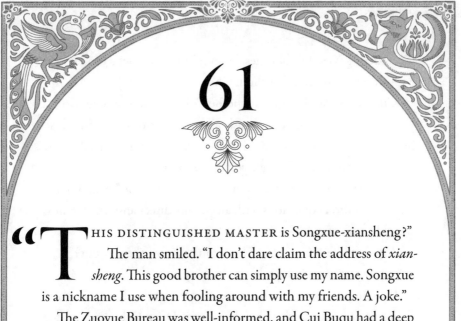

61

"THIS DISTINGUISHED MASTER is Songxue-xiansheng?"
The man smiled. "I don't dare claim the address of *xian-sheng*. This good brother can simply use my name. Songxue is a nickname I use when fooling around with my friends. A joke."

The Zuoyue Bureau was well-informed, and Cui Buqu had a deep knowledge of important names across the various royal courts and the jianghu. Still, he wasn't a god; it was impossible for him to recall every detail about someone the moment he heard their name.

Xiao Lü was an exception. This man was a low-ranking official from the Southern dynasty. Specifically, he was the lowest-ranking secretary in the Eastern Palace, an inconsequential position that wasn't even permitted to attend court. As far as his career was concerned, he was a complete and utter failure. This, however, was not the whole story. Xiao Lü was descended from a branch of the Xiao family in Southern Liang, and had studied under the renowned calligrapher Gu Yewang and the monk Zhiyong from a young age, excelling in both regular and cursive script. He was known for incorporating calligraphy into his swordplay, creating his own techniques, and was unrivaled with both the pen and the sword.

Yet when people discussed Xiao Lü, their conversations always included the words *what a pity*. What a pity the heavens envied talent.

Considering Xiao Lü's abilities, he shouldn't have met a dead end as a ninth-rank official in Southern Chen.

Cui Buqu couldn't guess whether Xiao Lü was an enemy or a friend. There was no time to ask all the questions he wanted, so he chose the most pressing: "Is Xiao-gongzi not an official in the Southern dynasty? Why have you come to Qiemo?"

"I resigned my position and came to save someone." Xiao Lü met Cui Buqu's direct questions with an equally direct answer. "Sir, how should I address you?"

"My surname is Cui. Does Xiao-gongzi know the way out?"

"I only just came in myself. I'm looking now."

Cui Buqu was becoming increasingly certain there was more than one entrance to this chamber. But if Duan Qihu had created this underground passage purely to aid his own escape, why employ such a complicated design?

They fell silent, and Cui Buqu coughed a few times. He endured the pain in his back as he and Xiao Lü split up to search for an exit.

"I had a look around before you fell down here," Xiao Lü said. "There're no levers of any sort on the ground; the tunnel can't go much deeper. If there's a way out, we'll find it on one of the walls."

As Cui Buqu murmured in acknowledgment, his palm brushed over a small gap. Feeling inside, his fingers met a loose brick. He pressed down; sure enough, there was a rumbling sound, and dim light seeped into the room. Behind him, a stone door ground open, accompanied by the feeble moans of women.

What are women doing in an underground passage?

The question rose simultaneously in both their minds. As the stone door opened fully, a peculiar scene was revealed. Cui Buqu was the type who wouldn't bat an eye if Mount Tai collapsed in front of him, yet even he stood dumbfounded.

Beyond the darkness of their surroundings lay a world of light. Hanging red veils of silk and satin gave off the aroma of sandalwood and apricot. The air was sweet and fragrant, as intoxicating as any earthly paradise.

Those wavering moans came from behind the veils.

Cui Buqu and Xiao Lü approached the doorway. That heady scent seemed to stir their minds, and both frowned and took a step back. Xiao Lü flicked his wrist, and the wind from his sword swept away the cloying fragrance.

As light spilled into the chamber, Cui Buqu finally saw that the beast they'd fought was a tiger. Two men were collapsed next to its corpse, sword wounds carved into their abdomens. Xiao Lü had probably slain them before Cui Buqu's arrival.

Other than the two men and the tiger, they found none of the traps they'd imagined. Several beds were scattered within the stone chamber on the other side of the doorway, each holding a woman wreathed in thin gauze. The women weren't naked, but what they wore left little to the imagination. Their cheeks were flushed and their eyes dazed as they ran hands over their bodies, movements and poses unconsciously seductive. Thin iron chains wound around their ankles and attached to the bedposts, imprisoning them within their scarlet curtains. Even without the iron bonds, they were drugged and trapped within a chamber guarded by a ferocious tiger. They had no chance of escape.

Xiao Lü's face was black with anger. He strode over to one of the beds. "Mei-niang!"

The woman looked at him with teary, hazy eyes; she didn't seem to have heard him.

Xiao Lü grabbed her wrist and inserted a thread of true qi into her arm, then kneaded a couple of acupoints across her face and head.

The woman trembled, her eyes slowly gaining focus. When she saw Xiao Lü, calling her name, she was stunned. She bucked on the bed as if to leap up, and her pale complexion turned green as fat tears rolled down her cheeks.

"Qi-ge?"

Now Cui Buqu understood. This wasn't merely Duan Qihu's escape route—it was also his pleasure den. The women he'd imprisoned here were likely from good families, tricked or kidnapped into captivity. He'd be too easily exposed if he kept them openly in his estate. Down here, they were hidden away from prying eyes, never to see the light of day. These women were powerless to resist—Duan Qihu could do anything he wanted in this chamber, satisfy any kind of secret or twisted fetish.

Since joining the Zuoyue Bureau, Cui Buqu had seen too much of the abundant filth of this world. The scene before him wasn't particularly surprising, but he hadn't expected Xiao Lü's loved one would be a victim as well. He walked a circuit around the room, kicking over the incense burners in each corner. That intoxicating fragrance instantly faded.

Mei-niang clung to Xiao Lü and wailed, as if pouring out a lifetime's worth of grievances. The other women, still under sway of the drug, lay insensible; even Mei-niang's weeping failed to wake them.

Cui Buqu frowned. "Xiao-gongzi..."

Xiao Lü smiled bitterly but took his meaning. He knocked the woman in his arms unconscious and laid her back down on the bed, then approached the others to wake them as he had Mei-niang.

"Wait, Xiao-gongzi," said Cui Buqu. "These women have been tortured; when they wake, they may react like your sister. It'll be difficult to bring them all out with us. Why not free them from their chains now, and after we find a way out, we'll send someone down to rescue them."

Xiao Lü nodded. "Cui-xiong has considered this thoroughly."

He did as Cui Buqu suggested, slicing through each of the chains binding the women. But they'd been under the influence of the drugs for too long; recovery would be slow. Even freed, they weren't going to suddenly spring up, cry, and run about. They remained on their beds, faces desperate as they twisted seductively against the bedding, bodies covered in bruises old and new—evidence of the torment they'd endured.

Lamenting now would do them no good. Cui Buqu wasn't a soft-hearted man, and Xiao Lü similarly wasted no time on useless expressions of sympathy. Together they began looking for an exit from the stone chamber.

After a few moments, Cui Buqu heard his companion sigh. The short huff of breath contained unconcealed anger and frustration, yet Xiao Lü suppressed his emotions, letting reason guide his actions.

This was the kind of man Cui Buqu admired—someone with an eye always on the bigger picture, never letting his own weaknesses drag him down.

"Take heart, Xiao-xiong. I've heard there are several skilled doctors in Qiemo. Take your sister once we leave." Xiao Lü had just saved him, after all. It would be rather too callous if he showed no concern.

Xiao Lü's smile was strained. "She's not my sister, but the daughter of my father's friend. When she was young, a fortune teller claimed she'd be robbed and killed, and to avoid this fate, she must leave home and seclude herself for a few years. Her family sent her to Mount Huang Sect to learn martial arts; we haven't seen each other for over a decade. Last year, her family's elders told me she'd gone missing on her way home from the sect, leaving no word or message. They feared she'd met with an accident and implored me to look for her. I followed all sorts of clues to find this place, but I didn't expect..."

For a woman from a decent family, an experience like this was a fate worse than death. Even in the less inhibited northern regions, it would be a stain on her life forever.

After searching the stone chamber at length, Xiao Lü and Cui Buqu had still found nothing like an exit. They had no choice but to return to the room from which they'd entered. The dead tiger and the two corpses were still strewn across the floor. As they passed over the threshold, the scent of blood and lingering incense interwove to create a subtle yet odious fragrance. Instead of arousing desire, it aroused nausea.

Xiao Lü searched the walls again but found no additional mechanisms. His brows knit faintly with anxiety, though not for his own sake—Mei-niang was still inside, in poor condition. The longer he tarried, the worse her situation would become.

"Here," said Cui Buqu. "A tile that's sunken in."

Xiao Lü's spirits lifted. He strode over and crouched to see what Cui Buqu had pointed out: one of the floor tiles near the corner of the wall was a hair lower than the ones next to it. Using all his strength, Xiao Lü pushed down.

"It's moving!" he cried.

Suddenly water poured down from above, soaking both their heads.

"Blast!" Cui Buqu suddenly understood why there were two guards. There were likely two mechanisms in this chamber that had to be activated at the same time. When Xiao Lü's side was activated alone, it didn't reveal the exit but triggered this trap.

The water showed no sign of stopping; it poured down endlessly, like they'd opened a hole at the bottom of a lake. The water level rose quickly; within seconds, it was at their calves. If this continued, forget rescuing the women—they'd both drown here today.

Cui Buqu and Xiao Lü exchanged a quick glance, forming a belated plan to save themselves. Cui Buqu quickly felt around for a second sunken tile. When he found it, he pressed down, while Xiao Lü simultaneously bore down on the first.

With a rumble of stone, the gap admitting the water gradually closed and was replaced by a brick that rose from the wall's surface.

Xiao Lü smiled wryly. "Is Duan Qihu trying to build an underground palace?"

"He couldn't have built all this by himself," said Cui Buqu. "Judging by the structure, it looks more like an ancient tomb. Duan Qihu must have emptied it, then put the mechanisms and stone chamber to his own purposes."

Xiao Lü pressed the protruding brick. Finally, a stone gate opened next to him—and beyond it, stairs leading up.

The true exit.

Both men breathed a sigh of relief. Cui Buqu walked in front, while Xiao Lü carried Mei-niang on his back and followed behind. As for the other women, they couldn't do anything for them at the moment. Cui Buqu and Xiao Lü would have to help them after they escaped themselves.

The stone staircase wasn't long; after half an hour of climbing, they reached the top. As light dazzled their eyes, they heard Duan Qihu scream.

Cui Buqu burst from the secret passage. He'd gone through too much trouble chasing Yan Xuexing, all to save Duan Qihu. If Yan Xuexing wanted to kill him, it would have to be after Cui Buqu got some answers about the Thirteen Floors of Yunhai. Feng Xiao might grab Yuheng, but he alone wasn't enough. They needed both men's testimonies to dig up the truth.

Yet he'd just glimpsed the black of the sky when he saw Yan Xuexing drive his sword into Duan Qihu's gut.

62

DUAN QIHU WAS HOLDING ON to life by a thread. His limbs had been hacked off, and only his head and torso remained. After that scream, he only had strength left to groan. He stared with round eyes, his breaths growing shallower with every exhale.

Yan Xuexing stood before him. Rather than stop Duan Qihu's bleeding, he'd subjected him to grievous torture and followed it with a stab to the gut. The moment Duan Qihu had abandoned his family to secure his own safety, Yan Xuexing knew threatening them was pointless. This man was selfish to the core: in the face of death, he cared only for himself. If Yan Xuexing wished him to suffer, physical torture was the only option.

Considering Duan Qihu's long list of crimes, Cui Buqu wouldn't have felt a scrap of sympathy if Yan Xuexing had dug out his eyes and cut off his nose in the process. But it was clear Duan Qihu was in no condition to reveal any more secrets about the Thirteen Floors of Yunhai.

Yan Xuexing sneered when he saw them. "Did you want to kill him too? Apologies; I got to him first."

He bent and tapped several of Duan Qihu's acupoints, staunching the bleeding, then channeled internal energy into his victim. It wasn't that his heart had suddenly softened; rather, Yan Xuexing ensured Duan Qihu would live a little longer so that he could torture him a little more.

He grabbed Duan Qihu by the back of his collar, ready to drag him off. But Cui Buqu had suffered quite the ordeal to get here and refused to leave empty-handed. He cried out, "Distinguished Master, please wait!"

Yan Xuexing continued to walk, as if he hadn't heard.

Xiao Lü pushed off the ground with a tap of his toes, his sword glare sweeping toward Yan Xuexing, incomparably fierce. Yan Xuexing hadn't thought much of this newcomer, yet now he realized the sword glare had sealed all possible exits. He had no choice but to toss Duan Qihu aside and meet the attack with all his strength.

Wrapped in a flurry of sword glares, the two exchanged several blows before breaking apart.

Yan Xuexing finally showed a hint of surprise. "Who are you?"

Xiao Lü dropped down from a tree, sleeves billowing as he fell. His long hair came loose from its topknot and fluttered around his shoulders. Though his hair was jet-black, the ends were a stark and snowy white. He wielded his sword in his left hand, but it wasn't because this was his natural inclination. Rather...

Cui Buqu recalled those popular evaluations of Xiao Lü as he swept his gaze over his right sleeve. Xiao Lü's wide sleeves engulfed his hands, but when the spring breeze brushed them, it revealed a secret: his right hand was withered and skeletal as a winter branch. It almost couldn't be called a hand at all.

Branches should have grown on trees, but this one had grown on a person. Xiao Lü had a handsome face, his demeanor no less elegant than Feng Xiao's. Yet a single disability rendered his flawless beauty irrevocably tarnished. His complexion was fair; beneath the sun,

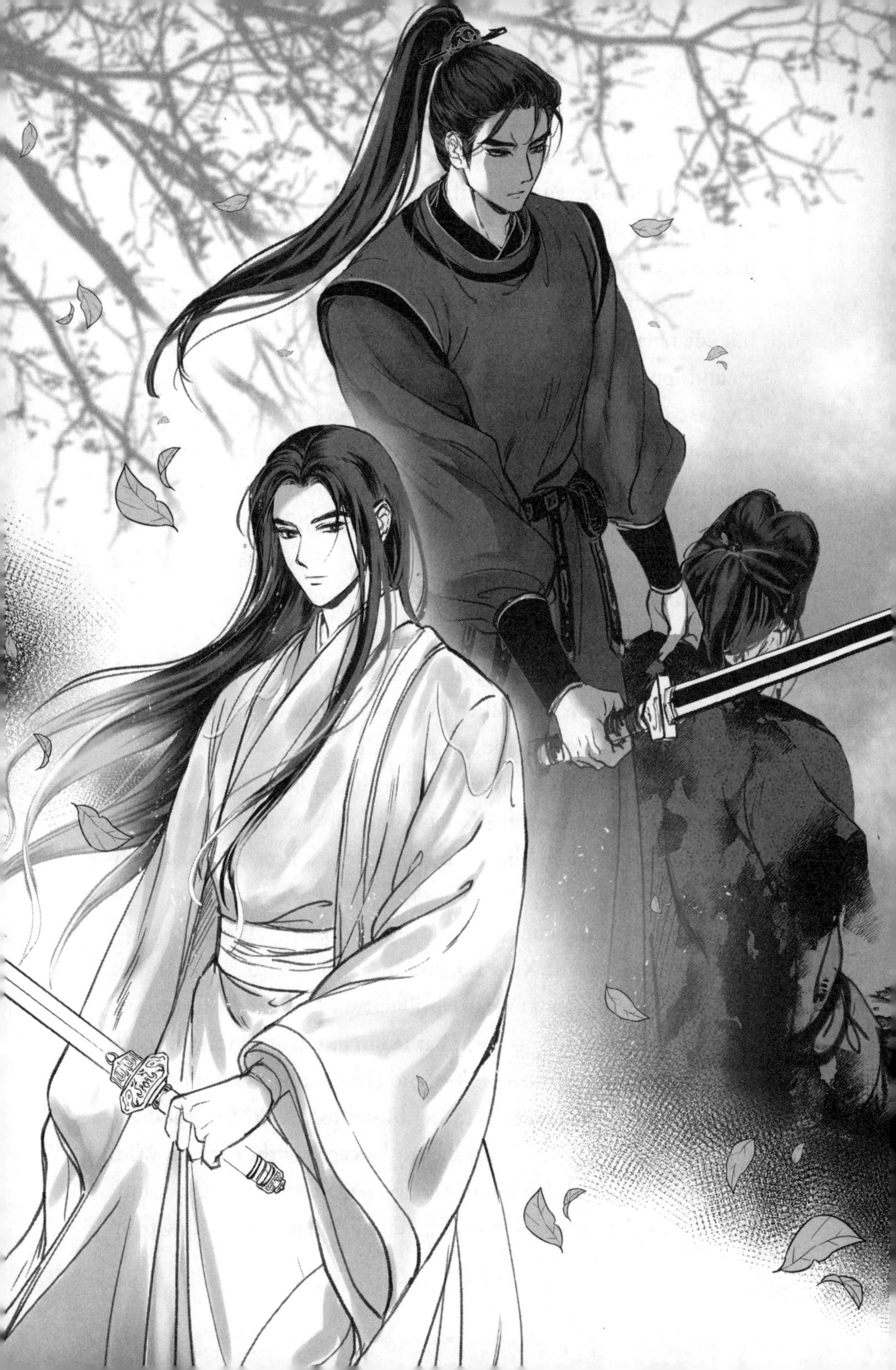

it shone with a faint luster. Even the hand with which he held his sword was slender and beautiful. But the more perfect his other qualities, the more hideous and frightening that withered hand appeared in contrast.

The Southern dynasty did employ exams when selecting officials, but what mattered most was family background, followed by character and appearance. Scholarly talents were last to be considered. Xiao Lü was a descendant of the ruling clan of a previous dynasty, and he had an ugly physical disability. The current emperor of Southern Chen had no love for promoting unconventional talents. No matter how brilliant he might be, advancement was difficult.

Thus, though people praised him greatly, they always added that final remark: *what a pity*. What a pity heaven marred what should have been a perfect jade with this tiny flaw.

Cui Buqu, too, had heard this tale; since he'd learned Xiao Lü's identity in the secret chamber, he wasn't surprised. But when Yan Xuexing saw, he couldn't hide his shock.

Xiao Lü seemed accustomed to this kind of look. He said calmly, "I also bear a grudge against Duan Qihu. My good brother, you've tortured him enough. I have a question to ask him, and past grievances to repay. Please give him to me."

Yan Xuexing's lip curled. "Ask that after you defeat me!"

He sprang toward Xiao Lü, and his sword cut through the air, overflowing with a radiance like brilliant starlight. As he'd just used it to torture Duan Qihu, it was bathed in blood and vibrating with a murderous aura, growing colder and ghastlier by the second.

Faced with this overwhelming bloodlust, Xiao Lü stood his ground. Instead of falling back, he crashed against the current. With a gentle shake of his left hand, his sword glare split into thousands of rays of light, enveloping his figure in brilliance. Watching from the sidelines, Cui Buqu couldn't tell which of the swift silhouettes within held the upper hand.

Cui Buqu turned from the fight and walked toward Duan Qihu. Deprived of his limbs, what was left of the man lay motionless on the ground. Only the slight rise and fall of his chest showed he was alive.

He was a former highwayman who'd led his band to pillage, burn, and kill in pursuit of wealth. Later, he'd washed his hands clean, transforming himself into a powerful mogul in Qiemo. In a sense, he was a self-made man. Even the Thirteen Floors of Yunhai had seen his influence and persuaded him to join. Unfortunately he'd balked at confronting an enemy as powerful as the Sui dynasty. Had he agreed to their proposal, Cui Buqu would likely have found him much harder to deal with.

Sensing Cui Buqu's approach, Duan Qihu opened swollen eyes brimming with shock and terror. One of the most formidable men of his generation had been reduced to a mess of flesh, yet he had no one to blame but himself. Cui Buqu had wanted to ask him a question, but he soon realized Duan Qihu was motionless, his eyes still half-open. Perhaps he'd thought Cui Buqu was Yan Xuexing returning—his footsteps had scared him to death.

In the end, Cui Buqu had no more answers than he'd had at the start; everything had been in vain. A rare gloom stole over him when he thought of his miscalculations. Resigned, he searched Duan Qihu's body and discovered a wrinkled letter.

Duan Qihu was covered in his own gore, and the letter was likewise streaked with bloodstains. Luckily Cui Buqu lacked Feng Xiao's obsession with cleanliness; he casually stuffed the paper into his lapels.

Across the courtyard, Xiao Lü and Yan Xuexing sprang apart. Yan Xuexing glanced coolly over. Upon seeing Duan Qihu dead, he turned and left without another word.

Xiao Lü came over and stared down at Duan Qihu's corpse. He sighed. "Poor Mei-niang and those other innocent women; they've suffered unspeakably. A monster like him could die a hundred times and it wouldn't pay for what they've been through."

"Xiao-xiong, the girl you saved was from Mount Huang Sect, south of the Yangtze River. How did she end up captive in a border town thousands of miles away?"

Xiao Lü's smile was rueful. "A great many dangers lurk in the jianghu; it has always been so. Mei-niang grew up sheltered within her sect; she never experienced the darkness outside. Plenty of villains exist who abduct people into slavery, and Mei-niang is beautiful and was traveling home alone. She thought her martial arts would protect her and became a natural target. When I first started searching, I traced her from Jiangnan, where she was abducted, all the way north. She even went through Daxing before she was taken west through the border pass. How much hardship did she endure? And her family..."

He sighed and said no more.

But Cui Buqu understood. Any notable family would worry about the damage Mei-niang's experience would do to their own reputation. And it wasn't only Mei-niang. Though all the women in the stone chamber's lives were saved, the fates that awaited them were murky.

"I need to escort Mei-niang home," said Xiao Lü. "Would Cui-xiandi[5] be willing to share his given name? If fate wills it, perhaps we'll meet again in the jianghu."

"My name is Buqu."

"Have you a courtesy name, or a sobriquet?"

"I do not," said Cui Buqu.

---

5   A respectful address for a younger man.

To address someone directly by their given name was rather impolite. For instance, Xiao Lü's sobriquet was Songxue, and thus many would respectfully address him as *Songxue-xiansheng*. Others, on more intimate terms, might instead address him according to his place in the family.

"Then what about your family, have you any siblings?"

"My parents died when I was young. I have no teacher, no father, and no brothers or sisters. I have no family, so I have no other name besides Buqu."

Xiao Lü cupped his hands in apology. "It seems I've asked a rude question." His withered right hand peeked out of his sleeve.

"Not at all; I surprised you."

Xiao Lü, when he saw the direction of Cui Buqu's gaze, casually lowered his right hand.

"I've been ill my entire life," Cui Buqu said calmly. "Some of the physicians who saw me said I wouldn't live to see nine, while others said I'd scarcely make it to six. Consultation after consultation concluded I would pass prematurely, but I have persisted until now. They say man plans and the heavens laugh, but we are the ones who determine our paths. People always forget that. It seems both Xiao-xiong and I are people who reject our fates."

Xiao Lü laughed heartily. "Well said, Buqu!"

There came a mocking click of the tongue, and a figure appeared just steps away from them.

"There I was out in front, exerting myself half to death, yet Daoist Master Cui was over here happily making friends. As expected, the moment you meet someone new, you throw aside your old companions!"

Xiao Lü was taken aback. Another martial artist of unfathomable skill had arrived.

63

A S USUAL, Feng Xiao arrived in style.

He didn't crawl out of the tunnel, filthy and disheveled, as Cui Buqu and Xiao Lü had done. He appeared out of thin air, sleeves spread like a crane alighting on the ground, and flashed an enchanting smile. He looked for all the world like an immortal, as pure and untouchable as a snow-cloaked tree in winter.

Qiao Xian's mastery of disguise was fully displayed in the way she'd changed Feng Xiao's face while preserving his extraordinary charm. Acquaintances would have had difficulty recognizing him, yet much of his original elegance remained—one that had nothing to do with gender.

Even Cui Buqu, who was by now used to seeing him, was a bit dazzled, to say nothing of Xiao Lü, who was meeting him for the first time.

"Is this lady from what the jianghu calls a garden of divine maidens?"

"No," said Cui Buqu. "A maiden like that might possess an even gentler beauty, but she'd never have such an imperious aura."

Before Feng Xiao could reply, Xiao Lü shook his head. He studied Feng Xiao a moment, then said, "You. You're a man in the guise of a woman, aren't you?"

Feng Xiao neither confirmed nor denied it. "My surname is *Feng*, as in phoenix. Call me Feng-er. Daoist Master Cui is someone with lofty standards; he pays no heed to ordinary men. For the two of you to have made friends so quickly, you must also be a dragon or phoenix among men."

Listening to Feng Xiao openly praise him while slyly mocking his supposed arrogance, Cui Buqu replied coldly, "Xiao-xiong saved my life. It's natural that I show him courtesy. If not for him, your Daoist Master Cui would be a lost ghost by now."

Feng Xiao smiled. "A-Cui, are you complaining that I'm late to the rescue? I sincerely apologize. You can hit me a few times when we get back if you need to vent."

Cui Buqu had been soaked to the skin in the secret hideout, and his clothes were sopping wet. The instant a breeze blew past, he let loose a flurry of sneezes. Eyeing the spotless Feng Xiao, he felt increasingly displeased. "This is Xiao-xiong, also known as Songxue-xiansheng, Xiao Lü, who uses calligraphy in his swordplay. He's a peerless martial artist, with skills not inferior to your own. The world is vast, yet you two were able to meet—why not treasure such an opportunity and spar?"

Cui Buqu's provocations were unnecessary; Feng Xiao had also recognized Xiao Lü as an excellent martial artist. Without warning, he threw out a palm strike. "Then I must ask Xiao-xiong for his guidance!"

Their palms met, the surge of internal strength breaking in waves around them. Cui Buqu was forced back several steps. With a loud *bang*, they flew apart midair, falling back to alight on the branches of the courtyard's trees.

Xiao Lü smiled. "Feng-xiong's skills are extraordinary. I fear I'm not your match—simply amazing!" He turned to Cui Buqu, "Mei-niang's parents are waiting for news of her back at home, and her sect has dispatched disciples to look for her; I can't afford to delay my return. I'll trouble Cui-xiandi to report the rest of those unfortunate women to the proper officials."

Cui Buqu nodded and cupped his hands. "You've a long journey ahead of you. Take care, Xiao-xiong."

Hoisting Mei-niang onto his back, Xiao Lü said, "If you find yourself in Chendu someday, I'll treat you to some good plum wine of my own vinting."

Cui Buqu stood beside Feng Xiao and watched Xiao Lü disappear into the distance. Only then did he realize someone else had yet to emerge. "Where's Bing Xian?"

Feng Xiao sighed. "I've just chased one off and now there's another. Daoist Master Cui, a girl named Bing Xian was willing to exchange Duan Qihu's wealth for your safety. Not an hour later, Xiao Lü sweeps in to rescue you. Thank heavens you're not a woman, or wouldn't you have to marry them all?"

"Thank heavens *you're* not a woman, or you'd be abandoned after every marriage. I'm afraid no one would keep you past the wedding." Cui Buqu held out a hand and said bluntly. "Hand it over."

"What?"

"Your coat."

"Why should I? You're asking me to strip out here in the open, yet you claim you don't lust after my beauty?"

"If I catch a cold, I'll need to spend time recovering." Cui Buqu looked back at him steadily. "At this pace, what year will it be when we reach Suyab? But if you don't mind, I don't either."

Feng Xiao pressed his lips shut. He reluctantly removed his coat and tossed it toward Cui Buqu, who wrapped himself in it immediately.

With the coat shielding him from the cold wind, Cui Buqu felt much better. He coughed a few times. "How did it go with Yuheng and the rest?"

Feng Xiao prodded Duan Qihu's corpse with a toe. "They're dealt with. Qiao Xian and Gao Yi are mopping up the mess. Did you get anything out of him?"

"By the time I came out, Yan Xuexing had already carved him into a human stick." Recounting it, Cui Buqu grew angry again. "I couldn't get anything out of him. Now we can only rely on Yuheng."

"That does make things difficult," murmured Feng Xiao.

Cui Buqu frowned. "Don't tell me Yuheng's dead too?"

"He's not, but the Thirteen Floors of Yunhai are secretive. They must have measures in place to prevent any director from exposing too much about the others. We didn't get any more from Duan Qihu. And if it's as I suspect, Yuheng will only know one more person, the director in front of him: Shi-xiansheng, tenth of the thirteenth floors."

"Actually, it's not a complete loss." Cui Buqu pulled out the letter. "I found this on Duan Qihu."

The moment Feng Xiao saw the blood, he refused to take a step closer. "Tell me what's written inside."

"I climbed Mount Jieshi in the east to behold the boundless turquoise sea."[6]

"Cao Cao's poem," said Feng Xiao.

"To your side I will return if safe; if dead, my love will never fade."

Feng Xiao's brows knit in puzzlement. "The two lines don't connect at all. Is it a riddle?"

Cui Buqu ignored him. "The third line: 'Before we could enjoy the wonders of spring, we glimpsed the approach of summer.' The fourth line: 'The river of stars runs clear and shallow.'"

What kind of nonsense is this? thought Feng Xiao.

---

6   From the poem "Behold the Turquoise Sea" by warlord and statesman Cao Cao, who rose to power during the Eastern Han dynasty.

"I have a few ideas, but I'll ponder it later," said Cui Buqu. "Right now I'll have to trouble you with something else."

"Whenever you speak to me this politely, it's bad news. I refuse."

Cui Buqu sneezed. "I'm going to faint."

That was all the warning he gave before slumping toward Feng Xiao. Feng Xiao instinctively reached out to catch him, but when his eyes landed on Cui Buqu's bloodstained clothes, he yanked his hand back.

Cui Buqu fell flat on the ground with a *thud*.

Feng Xiao coughed and looked around, as if waiting for some sucker to appear and help him carry Cui Buqu.

A woman's voice rang out with perfect timing: "Daoist Master Cui?"

Feng Xiao dragged Cui Buqu behind him without a second thought, lest he be eaten by this newly appeared demoness.

In the next moment, the "demoness" Feng Xiao feared revealed herself, dainty and graceful. It was Bing Xian, half-soaked from her stint underground. Her wet robes clung to the delicate curves of her figure, but her face was relaxed and carefree, without any hint of embarrassment.

Bing Xian took in Cui Buqu, lying prone on the ground. "Is Daoist Master Cui quite all right?" she asked in surprise, moving forward to help him up.

"He caught a chill and fainted. He'll be fine with a little medicine." Feng Xiao's former hesitation seemed to vanish as he lifted Cui Buqu onto his back. If Cui Buqu were spirited away by this demoness in yellow, the alliance with Apa Khagan would go up in smoke.

Jinlian Khatun's presence guaranteed they would reach the Western Khaganate. But persuading Apa Khagan to change his allegiance and throw in with the Sui dynasty wasn't something that could be accomplished solely with martial force or verbal intimidation.

Feng Xiao was certain Cui Buqu had some hitherto unrevealed trump card or key intelligence up his sleeve.

He sighed and hoisted Cui Buqu up a little higher.

"I have some small skill in medicine myself," said Bing Xian. "Perhaps I should take a look?"

"No need," said Feng Xiao. "He has someone to attend to him."

Bing Xian showed no embarrassment at being so bluntly rejected; instead, she smiled. "It's getting late; I should leave as well. Did you see where Yan-gongzi went?"

Feng Xiao pointed in a random direction. "That way."

"Thank you very much. Please give my regards to Daoist Master Cui and tell him I went after Yan-gongzi. If I meet him in the future, I'll ask after him then." Bing Xian drifted away.

"Go, go," said Feng Xiao.

Now that the last of the meddlers had gone, Feng Xiao adjusted Cui Buqu on his back up and made for the inn, muttering to himself as he walked. "Cui Buqu, Cui Buqu. Look, I've snatched you out of the hands of that man-eating demoness, then carried you back reeking of blood. It's fine if you don't know about this favor yet; once you wake up, I'll remind you every day. You'll repay me if it's the last thing you do."

❦

While Cui Buqu was lolling about unconscious, Qiemo underwent a series of earth-shattering changes.

The power balance between the three factions had been completely overturned. Not even Gao Yi, in all his wildest dreams, had ever imagined that the weakest point in the triad would suddenly emerge the clear winner.

The Duan family's influence collapsed with his death, and its members fled like rats from a sinking ship. Meanwhile, Xing Mao had been captured alive. Unlike Duan Qihu, the Xing clan had been operating in Qiemo for generations. They were deeply rooted; it was impossible to simply kill them and be done with it. They needed to be slowly interrogated, their influence addressed and depleted.

In the end, Cui Buqu and Feng Xiao had managed to bring an entire city into the fold of the Sui dynasty. It was a meritorious deed of expanding the empire's territory, a grand achievement. Even Feng Xiao himself was surprised at the outcome. When he'd first heard Cui Buqu's bold plan, his initial thought had been that the man had lost his mind.

Yet reality had proved Cui Buqu quite sane. Perhaps he knew no martial arts; perhaps he couldn't shoot enemies from horseback or weave his strategies behind the heavy curtains of the imperial court. Yet without a single soldier, he'd incited the Duan and Xing families to destroy each other while he sat to the side and reaped the benefits.

Still, it had to be said that coincidence had played a large part in his success. Yan Xuexing had sought vengeance, while the Thirteen Floors of Yunhai wished to kill Duan Qihu and silence him. Cui Buqu and Feng Xiao had merely fanned the flames in the right direction, exploiting the greed and suspicion that lurked in human hearts.

Though they'd dispatched a messenger to the capital at full speed, word would take some time to arrive. Any reaction from the court, including the doling out of rewards and punishments, would be slow. Over the course of one night, Gao Yi's fortunes had taken a complete turn; he was equal parts joyous and bewildered. He sought Feng Xiao's advice before giving any order, paying him multiple visits a day until Feng Xiao grew irritated at the sight of him.

When Cui Buqu finally woke, he found Feng Xiao sitting leisurely by the window, waving a fan and studying a document in his hand.

It had been impossible to conceal their identities after the uproar they'd caused. By now, half the city knew who they were. So many people had darkened their door that if Fo'er had been anywhere near Qiemo, he would have caught wind of the news long ago. Feng Xiao thus couldn't be bothered to maintain his disguise and had returned to his original appearance.

With his natural good looks, he'd have been a sight for sore eyes even if he'd been squatting down stuffing his face, never mind languidly fanning himself. One could almost ignore that there was still a portable stove smoking away in the corner and winter plums abloom outside the window.

Regardless of time or place, this man would never miss an opportunity to flaunt himself. He really was just like an oleander: even hidden in deep green foliage, he spared no effort to produce the most spectacular blossoms.

"My good Daoist Master Cui, you're finally awake." Feng Xiao raised two fingers. "There's good news and bad news. Which would you like to hear first?"

Cui Buqu said coldly, "First, I wish to eat and drink."

64

QIAO XIAN HAD already prepared a meal for Cui Buqu, ready to eat the moment he woke. Over years of taking care of him, her culinary skills had grown by leaps and bounds. Whenever they were away from home, if at all possible, she would cook his meals personally.

The sweet aftertaste of bamboo and partridge soup lingered on Cui Buqu's tongue. He could tell at once it was her handiwork.

"Before any news, I'd like to ask Deputy Chief Feng a question." Cui Buqu finished his soup and set down the bowl.

Feng Xiao made as if to stand. "Too late now. I would have told you earlier, but you didn't want to hear it. Now you wish to speak, but my venerable self does not wish to listen. Good day."

"Dare I ask why I woke up sore all over, most especially in my right shoulder? It feels as if I took a heavy fall."

"You're asking me?" said Feng Xiao innocently. "How should I know? You were crawling around in that secret chamber for ages. It's not surprising you're injured."

Cui Buqu brought a hand to his head, his expression stormy. "Then why is there an extra bump on my head?"

Feng Xiao clicked his tongue. "After you fainted, a certain villainous character came and tried to kidnap you. My venerable self chased them off and carried you back with painstaking effort, all while you were soaked in filthy water and Duan Qihu's blood. You're lucky I didn't complain. If you feel no gratitude, fine, but now you're interrogating me?"

Cui Buqu was puzzled. Both Duan Qihu's and Xing Mao's factions should have been taken care of by that point. "What villainous character?"

"Bing Xian," said Feng Xiao.

Cui Buqu stared at him.

Feng Xiao smiled. "What's with the look? Is Daoist Master Cui taken with her?"

"Yes, I am." Cui Buqu's voice was cold. "So can Deputy Chief Feng bring her back for me?"

"That might be difficult," said Feng Xiao, fanning himself. "Yan Xuexing is a powerful martial artist, and he's handsome too. I'm sorry to say you may not be a match for him. I suggest you give up on the girl. I'll introduce you to that plump maid of Gao Yi's."

"Enough. What have you learned from Yuheng?" Cui Buqu rubbed at the lump on his head. He estimated it'd take at least two days for the swelling to subside. Whether or not Feng Xiao was the culprit, he likely still deserved the blame.

Feng Xiao held up one finger. "Let's start with the bad news. Yuheng committed suicide."

Cui Buqu blinked. He'd freshly woken, and this news was like a bolt from the blue. The corner of his eye twitched, but he squashed down his fury. "Deputy Chief Feng, is this your first day on the job? We finally caught a key member of the Thirteen Floors of Yunhai— we could have pried all kinds of information from his mouth. Did it not occur to you to keep an eye on him?!"

Feng Xiao shrugged. "I understand his importance. But remember, this is Qiemo. It's not the Jiejian Bureau, nor is it your Zuoyue Bureau.

There are only the four of us on this trip. Other than locking him up, what else could I do? Surely I couldn't stay glued to him every second of the day?"

Cui Buqu knew Feng Xiao spoke the truth. The Zuoyue Bureau had the authority to detain people, though not to the same extent as the Ministry of Justice, which could lock prisoners away for as long as they pleased. Still, any case took time. A handful of days was enough to achieve many things—such as ensuring someone died under mysterious circumstances. There were countless ways to pull it off without leaving a trace.

He was silent a moment. "If he were going to kill himself, he would have done it the moment he was captured. There's no way it was suicide."

"You're right," said Feng Xiao. "But once he entered the prison, there were plenty of opportunities for someone to meddle. We might have been able to prevent one attempt, but not all of them. The people here in Qiemo are a mixed bag; plus, their security has always been lax. Gao Yi ordered Yuheng strictly supervised, but someone arrived claiming to be his friend and asked permission to visit. He offered the guard a hefty bribe to be allowed inside. After he left, Yuheng was found dead."

"We likely won't find any trace of that visitor either," mused Cui Buqu.

"Yes, he's long gone. Gao Yi was afraid I'd lay into him, so he had someone draw a portrait based on the guard's description of him and posted it all over the city. He's offering a reward for his arrest, but I doubt we'll see any result."

Cui Buqu's held his throbbing forehead. "I just woke up. Can't you say anything positive?"

Feng Xiao chuckled. "Didn't I say there was good news?"

"Oh," said Cui Buqu, then fell quiet.

"Aren't you going to ask what it is?"

"If I ask, Deputy Chief Feng will never tell me so easily. Perhaps he'll even demand something in exchange."

Things in Qiemo had settled for now, and despite the organization's ambitions, the Thirteen Floors of Yunhai behind Yuheng had little to do with the situation at hand. If Cui Buqu wished to pursue this lead, it had to be considered a separate case. He had a good grasp on Feng Xiao's character: he'd never tell Cui Buqu anything Yuheng had said for free.

Feng Xiao smiled. "How clever you are, Daoist Master Cui. So, have you decided what you'll offer in exchange?"

"I've heard Deputy Chief Feng is looking for a new zither," said Cui Buqu slowly. "You must be quite dissatisfied with your current one. Otherwise you would have brought it with you to Qiemo, correct?"

Few people in the jianghu used a zither as a weapon, but Feng Xiao was one of them. He not only used the music of his zither to disorient his opponents, he used the instrument itself as a blunt weapon at critical moments. The last time Cui Buqu had seen him smashing enemies with his zither, true qi channeled through it, the instrument had cracked. An ordinary zither couldn't withstand such abuse. Only one of special make could be used as a weapon.

"Even without a zither," said Feng Xiao arrogantly, "I can trounce any opponent."

"I know the whereabouts of Raoliang."

"The famous Raoliang of the Spring and Autumn period?"

"The very same."

Even among famous zithers, Raoliang was legendary. Rumor had it that someone once offered it to King Zhuang of Chu. The king of Chu became consumed with Raoliang's otherworldly sound and refused to attend court for seven straight days while he played the zither. At his queen's urging, he finally smashed it with an iron scepter.

Thus Raoliang's music had vanished from the world. When later generations told of it, they could only imagine the magnificence of the music that came from its strings.

"There was only one Raoliang," said Feng Xiao. "A second one doesn't exist."

"But it does," said Cui Buqu. "The zither was one of a paired set. The first was called Yuyin, the second Raoliang. Hua Yuan presented Raoliang to the King of Chu as a gift. Though Raoliang is no more, Yuyin still exists, hidden away to this day. I happen to know where it is. Raoliang was enough to drive the king of Chu to obsession; its music must have been extraordinary. A skilled martial artist wielding it would achieve double the results with half the effort. And there's more: from what I know, both Raoliang and Yuyin were crafted using rare stones from beyond the heavens. Even if you smash someone over the head with the thing, you needn't worry about breaking it."

"Where is it?" asked Feng Xiao.

"Tell me the good news."

Feng Xiao's mouth twitched. "Fine."

Cui Buqu gestured for him to speak. *You first.*

"Before Yuheng died," Feng Xiao began, "he told us everything he knew. But it wasn't much different from what Duan Qihu said. Each director only knows those before and after themselves. Feng Xiaolian is the thirteenth, Duan Qihu was the twelfth, and Yuheng was the eleventh. What we learned, however, is that the position above Yuheng is empty."

Cui Buqu frowned. "Was there no one suitable to take it?"

Feng Xiao nodded. "According to Yuheng, the Thirteen Floors of Yunhai search for talents from all across the land. They recruit them and rank each floor based on ability. Apparently, Duan Qihu was originally dissatisfied that he was only Shi'er-xiansheng—but once he heard the identity of the sixth director, he abandoned the idea of climbing the ranks."

"Who?"

"Far away in Goguryeo. The leader of Buyeo Sect, Go Un."

The same Go Un who'd sent Su Xing and Qin Miaoyu to lie low in the Central Plains for years, gathering intelligence and seeking opportunities to sow discord within the Central Plains. Su Xing had been the one to tell them that, in the beginning, their contact in the Central Plains had been a certain Yi-xiansheng.

Several disparate clues had unexpectedly fallen into place.

"Even Go Un only ranks sixth," Cui Buqu observed. "Then those above him must be quite terrifying."

Feng Xiao smiled and nodded.

"But if the Thirteen Floors of Yunhai are so secretive, how do they contact each other?" Cui Buqu asked.

"Messengers handle correspondence, but Yuheng couldn't identify them. Each time a messenger comes, their gender, appearance, and voice are all different."

"This doesn't make sense." Cui Buqu frowned in thought. "The Thirteen Floors of Yunhai recruit dragons and phoenixes to their cause. Yuheng was a powerful martial artist, but he was neither influential nor especially cunning. Why was his rank above Duan Qihu's?"

"He claimed to be no more than a small-time thug from Jiankang. A stranger took a liking to him, taught him martial arts and some basic social niceties, and had him ordained as a monk at Ronghua Temple in Southern Chen. He rose little by little to become the abbot, then joined the Thirteen Floors of Yunhai. It seems that was the stranger's goal from the start."

Something flickered in Cui Buqu's eyes. "Yuxiu?"

Feng Xiao shook his head. "I couldn't get an answer. If it really was him, he was careful. Yuheng wouldn't have known."

Yuxiu's background was mysterious, but he'd earned the trust of the Prince of Jin. If he really were Shi-xiansheng of the Thirteen Floors of Yunhai, one could imagine the storm that was brewing.

Cui Buqu remained silent and furrowed his brow.

By contrast, Feng Xiao appeared relaxed and peaceful. He sat with his legs crossed, one foot swaying. "A-Cui, there's a question I've wanted to ask for a while."

Cui Buqu didn't look up; he was still thinking. "Speak."

"Your health is poor, and you spend every day working yourself to the bone. When you wake up in the morning and comb your hair, do you find your hairline constantly receding?"

Shaken from his thoughts, Cui Buqu looked up, irritated. "I find nothing," he snapped. "I'm not Deputy Chief Feng, in love with his own reflection. If you lost a single hair, I'm sure you'd spend the entire day wailing and clutching your head, then find some flowering tree to bury the poor thing under!"

Feng Xiao burst into laughter. "Even when you're harsh, you do it so adorably!"

Cui Buqu stared at him coldly.

Wiping his eyes, Feng Xiao said, "Now, will you tell me where Yuyin is?"

"Anping. Cui family."

Anping, previously known as Boling. A group capable of keeping an ancient zither of such caliber in their collection? There could be no other.

The arch of a brow. "The Cui clan of Boling?"

"Correct," Cui Buqu said.

Feng Xiao was sharp; one wave of his fan and he'd connected the dots. "You're a Cui. Are you a member of the Cui clan of Boling?"

"I have neither father nor mother, courtesy name nor title, much less the airs of someone from a powerful family." Cui Buqu's tone was indifferent. "Do I look like a member of such a family to you?"

Feng Xiao nodded. "That's true." But before Cui Buqu could say anything further, he added, "In my opinion, a family of such mediocre talent as the Cui clan of Boling could never raise a man as capable as you."

65

C UI BUQU WAS LIKED by many but hated by more.
Although the Zuoyue Bureau wasn't widely known,
they enjoyed Empress Dugu's full support and thus
wielded great authority. Countless people had found themselves
in his hands, and even more cursed him behind his back. He had
a heart hard as steel; he never thought anything of it. Similarly,
Feng Xiao's flattery stirred no pleasure in him.

"Deputy Chief Feng, whenever you praise me, a certain phrase
comes to my mind."

"When it comes to the great men of the world, only Liu Bei and
Cao Cao qualify?"[7]

"The weasel paying the chicken a New Year's visit."[8]

Feng Xiao chuckled. "Then that makes me the weasel, and you
the chicken. Daoist Master Cui doesn't seem to me like a chicken
awaiting the slaughter. You're more like a cunning fox, seizing a win
at any cost."

"Is that so?" said Cui Buqu. "For myself, I find Deputy Chief Feng
quite like a weasel."

And a very flamboyant weasel at that.

---

7   Opposing generals from *Romance the Three Kingdoms*, a historical war epic considered one of
China's four great classic novels.
8   An idiom that refers to someone who comes with bad or insincere intentions.

Feng Xiao let such insinuations roll off his back; he'd never lost his temper in all their nonstop bickering. Instead, he tilted his handsome face toward Cui Buqu and said, affectionate, "We joined forces in Liugong City to solve the case of the Khotanese envoy, and now we've dealt with Duan Qihu and Xing Mao. Perhaps we're not bosom companions who'd lay down our lives for each other, but we can still share weal and woe. Why do you insist on pushing me away? You really are from the Cui clan of Boling, aren't you?"

Cui Buqu took out brush and paper and began to write. "Whether I am or not, what's it to you?" he asked without raising his head.

"Judging from your reaction, even if you *are*, you must have fallen out with them. Otherwise, why would you say you have neither father nor mother, courtesy name nor title?"

Cui Buqu raised an eyebrow, his brush never stopping. "So while I was talking to Xiao Lü yesterday, you were lurking about eavesdropping," he said with the shadow of a smile. "Is Deputy Chief Feng not ashamed of his ungentlemanly behavior?"

The corners of Feng Xiao's lips turned up. "Daoist Master Cui is always thinking how to screw me over. If I don't stay on my toes, I fear one day I'll be left without even a pair of pants to my name." He looked down at the paper Cui Buqu had pushed over to him. Upon it were written the four lines of the letter they'd found on the Duan Qihu. Feng Xiao nodded. "A perfect replica."

"Where's the letter?"

"I lost it."

Cui Buqu stared at him frostily.

"Please, it was stained with blood from a mangled corpse. Even you must find that filthy," Feng Xiao said self-righteously.

Cui Buqu heaved a sigh. Working with Feng Xiao had its advantages. When two men of intelligence conversed, much could be said in a few words. Feng Xiao was also an incredible martial artist; even the foremost expert of the Khaganate, Fo'er, was helpless against him.

But there were downsides as well. Feng Xiao wasn't Cui Buqu's subordinate; Cui Buqu couldn't order him around. The Jiejian Bureau was equal in status to the Zuoyue Bureau—though given Feng Xiao's temperament, the power of the emperor himself might mean nothing to him, let alone his sister agency. He was erratic and reckless, and Cui Buqu never knew when he might be thrown to the wolves. While working with him, Cui Buqu not only had to do his job, he had to match wits with Feng Xiao and remain constantly vigilant for tricks and traps. He was forced to split his focus. It was small wonder his old cough had resurfaced after a two-year absence.

Feng Xiao smiled. "Don't sigh like that; if Qiao Xian overhears, she'll think I'm pushing you around again. I've read the letter, and there's nothing mysterious about the paper itself. Anything useful is contained in those lines of poetry. Didn't you say you had some ideas? Let's hear them."

"Surely someone as clever as Deputy Chief Feng can solve it himself."

"All right, let's write down all our guesses so far and we'll trade notes. That's fair, isn't it?"

"Very well."

Each took a brush and paper and set to work.

After a moment, they showed each other what they'd written.

"The first line was, 'I climb Mount Jieshi in the east to behold the boundless turquoise sea.' I think it's referring to a place," said Feng Xiao. "Mount Jieshi, where Cao Cao wrote this poem, is in Beiping Commandery. But if it were that simple, anyone could guess. When you take just the first and last characters, however, you get Donghai Commandery."

Cui Buqu nodded. "Considering how cryptic the contents are, they must contain information about the Thirteen Floors of Yunhai. I've been thinking—the Thirteen Floors of Yunhai are watertight in their dealings; they refuse to disclose their own identities even to each other. Although this makes it easier to keep secrets, over time, their members are more likely to turn on the organization. Look at Duan Qihu: if he'd known anyone besides Yuheng and Feng Xiaolian, he might have taken the risk and fought for their sake. But he knew only two, one a monk and the other a woman. His doubts grew, and he balked at throwing in his lot with them."

"You're right. But the founder of the Thirteen Floors must have considered this too. To put those like Duan Qihu at ease, what they needed was a chance for everyone to meet. Unfortunately, it appears Duan Qihu perished before he could attend."

"The third line is a poem by Xie Lingyun," said Cui Buqu. "'Before we could enjoy the wonders of spring, we glimpsed the approach of summer. The changing seasons weigh my chest with sighs; hair hangs from my temples, streaked with white.' He wrote this in Nanting after he was demoted and sent to Yongjia County."

Feng Xiao quirked a brow. "There's plenty to dig into here. Yongjia, Nanting, even Xie Lingyun's ancestral home. Any of these could be our answer."

"Yet none of them are. The answer is summer."

"Why do you say so?" asked Feng Xiao.

Cui Buqu smiled. "Because of the next line: 'The river of stars runs clear and shallow.' This is an ancient poem from the Han dynasty, from the anthology of works Crown Prince Zhaoming collected. Here the poet paints a picture of the Milky Way to express their emotions:

'Distant lies the cowherd's star, luminous shines the weaver girl.

She lifts her pale and slender hand, shuttle clacking as she weaves.

Alas her work is never done; her tears pour down like rain.

The river of stars runs clear and shallow; what distance lies between them?

The width of just a single stream, yet their love will never reach.'"

Cui Buqu continued, "Then looking at the previous line again, 'Before we could enjoy the wonders of spring, summer—Zhuming—has already arrived.' *Zhuming* is another word for summer, just like *Jinsu* for autumn. When we combine the two, it points to the seventh day of the seventh month, the day of the cowherd and weaver girl's reunion."

When Cui Buqu spoke to Feng Xiao, it was normally with a sneer or a smile that failed to reach his eyes. It was rare for him to reveal an easy smile devoid of mockery, as he did now. For a moment, his brow was smooth and his eyes content. Feng Xiao suddenly realized Cui Buqu wasn't bad-looking at all. Despite his sickly complexion, his eyes were clear and bright. When he looked at others, they shone. He was intimidating when his expression was frosty—but when he smiled, it was like a spring mountain, flowers and trees in radiant bloom. No wonder Bing Xian was drawn to him.

"Daoist Master Cui should really smile more," said Feng Xiao with a smile of his own. "Who knows, perhaps I'll waver and find myself growing soft toward you."

"You should continue being hard on me," Cui Buqu said. "If there comes a day when Deputy Chief Feng is suddenly obedient, I'll suspect you're plotting something."

Feng Xiao sighed. "Why do I even try?"

Cui Buqu had no interest in bickering. "Enough," he said impatiently. "What do you think, Deputy Chief Feng?"

Look at him. His eyes might be alluring, but his temper's awful. He loses it at the slightest thing; small wonder his health never improves.

With that attitude, anyone who falls for this invalid will find them-
selves chased off within three days. Throughout this silent criticism,
his genial smile never wavered. "Oh, I agree completely with your
analysis."

Cui Buqu frowned. "Don't you have anything to add?"

"We have the date, but the location requires more discussion. My
guess is this second line—'To your side I will return if safe; if dead,
my love will never fade,'—must relate to the location, and whether
it's in Donghai Commandery. But I've got nothing at the moment."

Cui Buqu lowered his head, brow creasing. "With such a convo-
luted set of clues, even if Duan Qihu thought for an age, he would
never have come up with the answer. The Thirteen Floors of Yunhai
must have a key for decryption. Unfortunately, this is the only letter
we have; otherwise I could decrypt it by comparing them."

Here Feng Xiao and Cui Buqu differed. Cui Buqu was fond of
puzzles, but Feng Xiao never deigned to do anything difficult. If he
couldn't solve it in a moment, he'd set it aside and let it solve itself.
It wasn't as if the Thirteen Floors of Yunhai could run away. Sooner
or later, they'd slip up.

Seeing Cui Buqu still immersed in thought, Feng Xiao murmured
that he was going for a walk, then stood and left. Cui Buqu held his
forehead in silence, ruminating.

Feng Xiao met Jinlian in the hall.

Since they'd arrived in Qiemo, Apa Khagan's lesser khatun had
kept a low profile. She wasn't a patient person by nature, but she
understood Feng Xiao and Cui Buqu had their own business to
attend to and might not be able to protect her at all times. Wary
of an ambush from Fo'er, she'd hardly stepped from her room the
past ten or fifteen days, and only sent the maid they'd hired from
Liugong City out to inquire about the news.

Yet this had also given her an opportunity to watch from the sidelines and see what these two could achieve.

She hadn't expected them to turn the city upside down with a flip of their palms, fomenting a crisis that saw one giant of Qiemo dead while unseating the other. Ultimately, Xing Mao was a smarter man than Duan Qihu. As soon as he understood the hopelessness of his situation, he handed over his wealth in exchange for the lives of his family. The latest gossip reported that the emperor of Sui, in a display of generosity, had already issued a decree appointing Xing Mao the Marquis of Shanshan and granting him a residence in the capital. He was permitted to travel to the capital to greet the emperor, then expected to settle down there with his family.

Jinlian was secretly glad she'd chosen to work with Feng Xiao and Cui Buqu. If these two could destabilize the entire city of Qiemo, surely they could convince Apa Khagan to side with the Sui dynasty. With this, she grew a little more confident.

"Good day to Feng-langjun." Jinlian bowed to Feng Xiao.

She was still disguised as a woman from the Central Plains. Though her accent was a little stiff, she'd learned most of the required etiquette. Feng Xiao found her clever. While the majority of her countrymen's only concern was their nomadic and marauding lifestyles, she'd set her sights on the far-off Central Plains. She chose to pursue an alliance with the powerful Sui dynasty rather than be annexed and ruled by Ishbara.

"Is there anything I can do for Jin-niangzi?" Feng Xiao used the alias she'd assumed for their journey.

"How is Cui-xiansheng?" she asked. "The eight tribes will gather in Suyab very soon. I fear if we delay our departure even a few days, we may not make it in time."

"We can set out tomorrow."

"Wonderful," said Jinlian happily. "I left home so long ago; I can't wait to see the familiar grasslands. And when I return with the two of you, the khagan will surely be pleased."

After the incident with Duan Qihu, Jinlian's attitude toward them had undergone a shift. Where she'd once been distant and polite, she was now open and amiable. But Feng Xiao didn't mention it; he merely smiled. "We still have a generous gift for the khagan. Jin-niangzi will not walk away disappointed after this trip to Suyab."

The statement seemed chock full of implication. Excusing herself to pack her bags, she bade farewell to Feng Xiao and went back to ponder his words.

After a time, Feng Xiao returned to his own room. There was no doubt that Cui Buqu was brilliant; Feng Xiao wouldn't be surprised if he'd already unlocked all the mysteries within those poems. He'd thought to try a trick or two to drag some answers out of him, but when he pushed open the door, he was greeted by the sight of Cui Buqu with his head on the table, fast asleep.

When Feng Xiao had used incense of helplessness on him, long before he knew Cui Buqu's identity, he'd checked this man's pulse. Cui Buqu suffered from a lack of both qi and blood—he'd likely been frail from birth, a condition worsened by the circumstances of his upbringing. Feng Xiao didn't have to be a renowned doctor to tell he was unlikely to live long.

Cui Buqu had spent the past few days exhausting his brain with calculations, then dragged his body through that secret passage. He'd been at his limit for a while. Now he'd hardly woken up and he was back to taxing his mind with poetry. Of course he'd passed out.

The sunlight outside was just right. Warm spring rays spilled down over Cui Buqu's profile, limning it with a dazzling glow.

Feng Xiao stared. He couldn't help reaching toward Cui Buqu's face. His slender fingers brushed over Cui Buqu's cheek, never pausing for a second. They landed right on his nose and pinched.

Cui Buqu was sound asleep. Though he didn't wake, his discomfort was obvious. He frowned in his sleep, then opened his mouth to breathe.

Heh. Feng Xiao smiled mischievously. With his other hand, he covered Cui Buqu's mouth. *How will you breathe now, I wonder?*

"What are you doing?!" Qiao Xian's angry shout came from the doorway.

He'd been discovered so quickly. Feng Xiao clicked his tongue and regretfully let go.

Cui Buqu had slept through all Feng Xiao's mischief, but Qiao Xian's shout woke him. He rubbed his eyes and pushed himself up; one side of his face bore a red mark left by his arm where he'd slept on it. For a moment, he was completely absent the gravitas of the head of the Zuoyue Bureau.

He knew no martial arts whatsoever but made up for it with decisive and deadly tactics. Together with his exquisite mind, he rarely found himself at a disadvantage. Both Qiao Xian and Feng Xiao were well aware of this; they'd never dare underestimate him. But when they saw his bewilderment on being freshly woken, their hearts softened just a bit.

Feng Xiao glanced sidelong at Cui Buqu, and Qiao Xian quickly stepped forward, standing between Feng Xiao and Cui Buqu like a mother hen protecting her chick, as if Feng Xiao was a man-eating cannibal.

This Qiao woman really was an eyesore. Perhaps Feng Xiao should think of some way to mess with her too. Feng Xiao fluttered his fan, smiling at the thought.

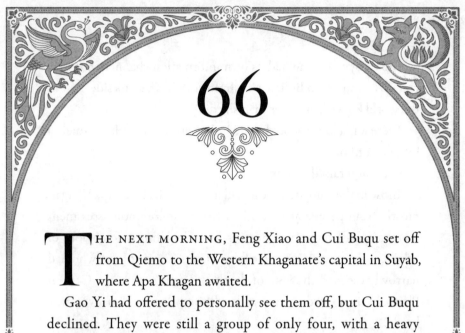

66

THE NEXT MORNING, Feng Xiao and Cui Buqu set off from Qiemo to the Western Khaganate's capital in Suyab, where Apa Khagan awaited.

Gao Yi had offered to personally see them off, but Cui Buqu declined. They were still a group of only four, with a heavy responsibility. Making a spectacle of their departure was inadvisable. The upheaval in Qiemo had exposed their identities; they'd gained a new enemy in the Thirteen Floors of Yunhai, and the issue of Fo'er remained unresolved. Their journey through the mountains would be long and arduous, and escorting Jinlian safely back to the Göktürk court, they expected, would be rife with challenges.

Yet it wasn't so. They departed Qiemo and arrived in Kucha, where they rested a few days before continuing toward Suyab near Mount Sanmi. As they reached the foot of the mountains, they could see the Göktürk wolf riders galloping in the distance—these were the lands of the capital. The entire journey had been uneventful, devoid of any danger.

Even Jinlian felt things were going rather too smoothly. She turned to Cui Buqu. "Has Fo'er given up on killing me?"

"Until we stand before Apa Khagan, it's too early to say. Tell me, what's Apa Khagan like?"

The Zuoyue Bureau had its own information channels, but they couldn't compare to Jinlian, who lived at Apa Khagan's side. Few in the world knew Apa better than she did.

There was a long silence before Jinlian answered: "He's actually a bit of a buffoon."

Cui Buqu raised a brow.

Those in the Zuoyue Bureau had heard much about Apa Khagan, mostly from people around him. The most common assessment was that Apa Khagan was mistrustful, calculating, and envious of others. Other testimony came from Han prisoners of war who had narrowly escaped the jaws of death and returned to the Central Plains. In their words, he was a bloodthirsty demon who loved only battle.

Jinlian had said nothing about Apa Khagan on their way here. But at Cui Buqu's prompting, she began to speak. "There are many Göktürk tribes, so there are likewise many khagans. Think of the Spring and Autumn or Warring States periods of your Central Plains—the nations are scattered and independent, and skirmishes between tribes are common. The khagan today might be replaced with a new one tomorrow, and no one would bat an eye. But with Ishbara's rise, he's demonstrated his intent to annex the surrounding tribes and unify the Göktürks. Apa Khagan, too, is aware of this. There are plenty of ways to kill without drawing a blade, and the people at Apa Khagan's side are constantly changing."

Cui Buqu nodded. He'd heard this as well.

Jinlian sighed. "The khagan has a wild imagination. Before I left for the Central Plains, he asked me to train a group of female body-guards for him. He said women are more loyal and reliable than men, so they could keep him safe in my absence."

Feng Xiao gave her a strange look. "Is your khagan a lustful man?"

"Everyone loves beauty, from kings to commoners. Why should the khagan be an exception?" she asked.

Though Jinlian Khatun retained her charm, her brow and eyes were marked by wind and frost. However greatly she was valued for her insight and assistance, she was ultimately still his concubine and worried his favor would fade along with her beauty. A good portion of this endeavor had likely been Jinlian's idea in the first place. She'd taken the initiative to court the Sui dynasty on Apa Khagan's behalf at great risk to her own safety. Training these female guards might secure his affection, and they would also serve as her eyes and ears.

With this, Cui Buqu had a rough picture: Apa Khagan was a man of middling talent with an appetite for beautiful women and deep suspicion toward others.

Both the Eastern and Western Khaganates were home to many tribes, each occupying their own territories. When Ishbara had emerged as a dominant force, Apa Khagan had never considered how to overcome him; instead, he'd waffled between Ishbara and the Sui dynasty. Even if he'd once harbored some small ambition, time had worn it away. Persuading a man like him to join the Sui dynasty shouldn't be difficult, provided he was too thoroughly cowed to consider betrayal. The meeting between the eight tribes would convene in just a few days. Cui Buqu would see they made good use of it.

He was still thinking when a group of the riders galloped over and intercepted them. The Göktürk soldier at their head seemed surprised to see Jinlian; he quickly dismounted to pay his respects with a bow.

Jinlian nodded back. She sat high atop her horse, lofty and arrogant, devoid of the warmth she'd shown Cui Buqu and Feng Xiao on their journey.

But after exchanging a few words with the patrol, Jinlian frowned in anger. She raised her voice with questions, and the Göktürks saluted and apologized, yet still surrounded Cui Buqu and the rest, drawing their long sabers. It certainly didn't look like they had come to welcome distinguished guests.

Cui Buqu translated for Feng Xiao and Qiao Xian: "They're arresting us. Jinlian said we're her honored guests from the Central Plains and asked them to report to the khagan. They said the khagan had issued an order: no Central Plainsmen may enter the encampment."

Jinlian's face was dark with fury. If the Sui envoy she'd toiled to bring all this way took offense at this treatment and became their enemies instead, not only would her long journey have been in vain, she'd have forfeited her honor and good word.

Neither Cui Buqu nor Feng Xiao were easygoing men. If the Göktürks slighted them, they might wreak untold havoc. Duan Qihu's fate was fresh in Jinlian's mind—she had no similar death wish.

She turned to Cui Buqu and Feng Xiao. "I must apologize sincerely to both of you; I had no idea the khagan would give such an order. Even on pain of death, I swear you'll suffer no humiliation. Please wait here. I'll speak to the khagan myself, then personally return to invite you in!"

"Before the khatun leaves, tell us: has the khagan always treated Central Plainsmen with such wariness?" Cui Buqu asked.

Jinlian shook her head. "I traveled to the Central Plains with the khagan's express approval. You saw the letter yourself; it was no forgery."

"In that case, something must have happened after you left to change the khagan's mind. Khatun, your sincerity is plain to us all. We will wait for you here."

Jinlian had feared his censure; now she breathed a sigh of relief. She quickly apologized once more and turned to scold the soldiers, to their evident displeasure. They eyed Cui Buqu and the others, then nodded reluctantly, apparently agreeing to leave them be. With Jinlian riding snugly in their midst, they returned to the khagan's court.

✦✦✦

An hour later, Cui Buqu, Feng Xiao, and Qiao Xian spied soldiers cantering toward them. Their faces were unfamiliar—this was a different group from before, and Jinlian was not among them.

"Was there a mutiny?" Feng Xiao mused. "Do you think the old khagan died and a new one took his place, so the alliance was voided and Jinlian lost her authority?"

"The Jiejian Bureau receives intelligence from every corner of the land. Does Deputy Chief Feng really need to ask me this question?"

Feng Xiao shrugged. "Hundreds of documents fly back and forth in the Jiejian Bureau every day. I'm not like Daoist Master Cui, who remembers anything he reads once. Things slip through the cracks. I had planned to return to the capital after dealing with the Khotanese envoy. How was I to know you'd abduct me instead?"

He deftly shifted the blame to Cui Buqu.

"Apa Khagan has two sons," said Cui Buqu. "His eldest, Yixun, was born to his first khatun. As for his second, Ade, his mother is unknown. She was likely from a humble background and passed away long ago. The Göktürks value strength above all; it's not uncommon for sons to usurp their fathers or a younger brother to depose the elder. But Apa Khagan is a cautious man. As far as I know, neither son holds much power. You see how he values Jinlian though she's borne him no sons—I find that very telling."

"So neither of his sons pose a threat," said Feng Xiao.

"I wouldn't say that. They say Apa dotes on his younger son and scorns his eldest. He believes his eldest cowardly, lacking the wolf-like nature of the Göktürks."

They fell silent as the Göktürk group reached them, splitting in two and encircling Cui Buqu's party. The leader barked out orders in Turkic, his expression ferocious.

Cui Buqu remained cool and indifferent as he replied in kind. After the brief exchange, Feng Xiao heard Cui Buqu's rapid whisper: "Defeat them but don't kill them. Grab the leader; we're charging straight into the capital!"

"Just the three of us? Are we not sheep wandering into a den of wolves?"

"With Deputy Chief Feng here, who else qualifies as a wolf?" Cui Buqu hissed.

Feng Xiao burst into laughter. "Now that's what I like to hear!"

The last word was scarcely out of his mouth before he appeared in front of a Göktürk soldier. Startled, the soldier yanked back on the reins, his horse's hooves rearing to trample Feng Xiao to death. As if Feng Xiao would give him the chance—his figure flickered, and the soldier screamed. In a blink, he'd tumbled from the saddle.

Qiao Xian waited until she saw him move to follow suit. She was no less valiant than he, but she also had to protect Cui Buqu.

These Göktürk soldiers might be strong enough to plunder ordinary folk of the Central Plains, but they were no match for Feng Xiao or Qiao Xian. Within minutes, the entire group was strewn across the ground, their leader dangling in Feng Xiao's grasp like a helpless chick.

"Now, let's go cause some mayhem!" Deputy Chief Feng was bubbling over with enthusiasm, as if a chaos-free world were his only fear.

Things should go much more smoothly with a few hostages in hand. And it happened that the leader of this group was no common soldier, but a yabghu, a position of similar status to a prime minister or general. Keeping a tight grip on their captive, the group proceeded toward the encampment to request a meeting with the khagan. Those who met them were shocked and enraged, but there was nothing they could do but rush ahead and report.

Not half an hour later they stood within the royal yurt, facing the illustrious Apa Khagan.

The khagan was between forty and fifty years of age, his beard full and his black hair streaked with white. Perhaps it was due to age that he hunched in his seat and had a habit of squinting when he looked at people.

Jinlian, who stood at his side, shone with a hundredfold more vigor and spirit. If *she'd* become khagan of the Western Khaganate instead, perhaps Cui Buqu's group wouldn't have encountered so many problems. But it was the way of the world that men came first. No matter how lofty Jinlian's aspirations, she could achieve them only through Apa.

"Central Plainsmen! Why do you hold my minister hostage?" Apa Khagan snarled, watching them through narrowed eyes.

Göktürk princes and officials filled the khagan's spacious yurt. Save for Jinlian, all glared balefully at the group in the center. Cui Buqu and Feng Xiao glimpsed an old acquaintance among them. Fo'er sat right beneath Apa Khagan, eyeing them expressionlessly.

A woman with Han features poured wine for the nobles in the yurt, her head and lashes lowered. She dared not risk a glance up.

"Ah—!"

A sudden cry of pain cut the tense atmosphere; the Han slave had been kicked in the stomach and sent flying. She groaned on the ground, then struggled, trembling, to stand, terrified of provoking the nobleman who'd kicked her again.

"Lowly bastards from the Central Plains. I'll crush you like ants!" growled the young Göktürk noble who'd kicked her. He glanced at Cui Buqu, his smile full of malice.

Jinlian hadn't been captured as they'd assumed. She'd changed into fresh robes, her dress stately and without flaw. But a hint of anxiety hovered around her eyes when she looked at them, as if she had much to say but couldn't speak.

Perhaps this will be a bit more challenging than expected, Cui Buqu thought.

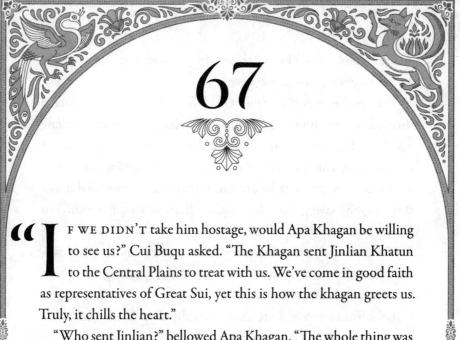

67

"**I**F WE DIDN'T take him hostage, would Apa Khagan be willing to see us?" Cui Buqu asked. "The Khagan sent Jinlian Khatun to the Central Plains to treat with us. We've come in good faith as representatives of Great Sui, yet this is how the khagan greets us. Truly, it chills the heart."

"Who sent Jinlian?" bellowed Apa Khagan. "The whole thing was her idea. If not for these guests with me who've come from so far, I'd punish her severely today!" His gaze seemed to drift toward Fo'er, who lowered his head and drank his tea.

When Cui Buqu saw this, everything became clear.

Something had happened before their arrival. Now they knew what—Fo'er had beat them here and bribed or intimidated Apa Khagan. The fearful khagan had capitulated, not daring to offend the foremost Göktürk martial artist. On seeing Cui Buqu's company and their apparent lack of manpower, he'd compared the two parties and picked the more advantageous side.

"The khagan fears offending Ishbara," said Cui Buqu coldly. "Does he not fear offending the Sui dynasty?"

"A mere three of you," another voice sneered, "and you think you speak for the Sui dynasty? If the people of the Central Plains are all so weak and useless, we have nothing to be afraid of. The lesser khatun has obviously been deceived by you—perhaps you seduced her into agreeing to lead you here."

The speaker was the young Göktürk nobleman who'd cursed them earlier. For him to be sitting in the khagan's yurt at his young age, he had to be someone extraordinary—the son of Apa Khagan, or a nephew. That he'd received no censure for kicking the female slave was a similar mark of his status. He'd clearly intended it as a threat; as the saying went, he'd made a show of killing the chicken to scare the monkey.

Unfortunately, Cui Buqu was no monkey, and neither was Feng Xiao. Before the young man had finished speaking, Feng Xiao was already rushing toward him.

Fo'er had been watching them carefully all this time; he didn't stand by. He dashed over to intercept Feng Xiao's attack.

The two of them were soon engaged in an all-out brawl within the yurt. True qi surged and swelled, overturning cups and plates. The bystanders paled in fright and retreated to the sides of the yurt, yet Apa Khagan gave no order to stop. It seemed he wished to see who was stronger before making his decision.

Feng Xiao shook his sleeves, and a table beside him was flung into the air, spinning toward that outspoken Göktürk nobleman. In a panic, the young man trod on his own robe and stumbled to the floor. Fo'er neither blinked nor turned as he sent a burst of true qi from his palm. The table cracked in two midair, saving the nobleman from grievous injury.

Fo'er had failed to defeat Feng Xiao in Liugong City, but he was still a powerful martial artist. Even if he fell short of Feng Xiao's skill, they were well matched. Too many parties had been involved at the time, forcing Fo'er to split his focus. Now he brought his full strength to bear, and his profound internal energy and imperious style consumed Feng Xiao's total attention.

The young man, seeing that he was no longer in danger from Feng Xiao, glanced toward Cui Buqu on the sidelines and sneered. He waved a hand for his men to seize both Cui Buqu and Qiao Xian.

He'd obviously never been to the Central Plains and didn't know an unwritten rule of its martial circles: when it came to women who wandered the jianghu, the more beautiful they appeared, the less one should provoke them.

The guards who had pounced toward Cui Buqu found themselves rolling on the floor: their reward for underestimating Qiao Xian. To subdue a mob, one must first capture its leader—she had learned this principle well from Cui Buqu and swept without hesitation toward the Göktürk noble. The noble saw a blur, then felt sharp pain in his arm as the world began to spin. The next thing he knew, his face was pressed to the ground.

A slender foot, more delicate than that of the average Göktürk woman, crushed him to the floor. In other circumstances, the young man might have grabbed at and caressed such a foot, but he didn't dare entertain the thought now. This foot was terrifyingly strong; he couldn't break free no matter how he struggled. If anything, it pressed down harder, mashing his face into the rug. Agonized tears seeped into the carpet as he cursed her up and down, but it was all false bravado. In this position, he wasn't intimidating in the least.

Qiao Xian didn't speak much Turkic, but she could hear the venom in his voice. She bent and yanked on his arms, making his face twist in pain as he pleaded with Apa Khagan for help. This man had belittled and mocked them, calling the Central Plainsmen lowly trash. Now he was howling on the ground, not unlike the female slave he had abused.

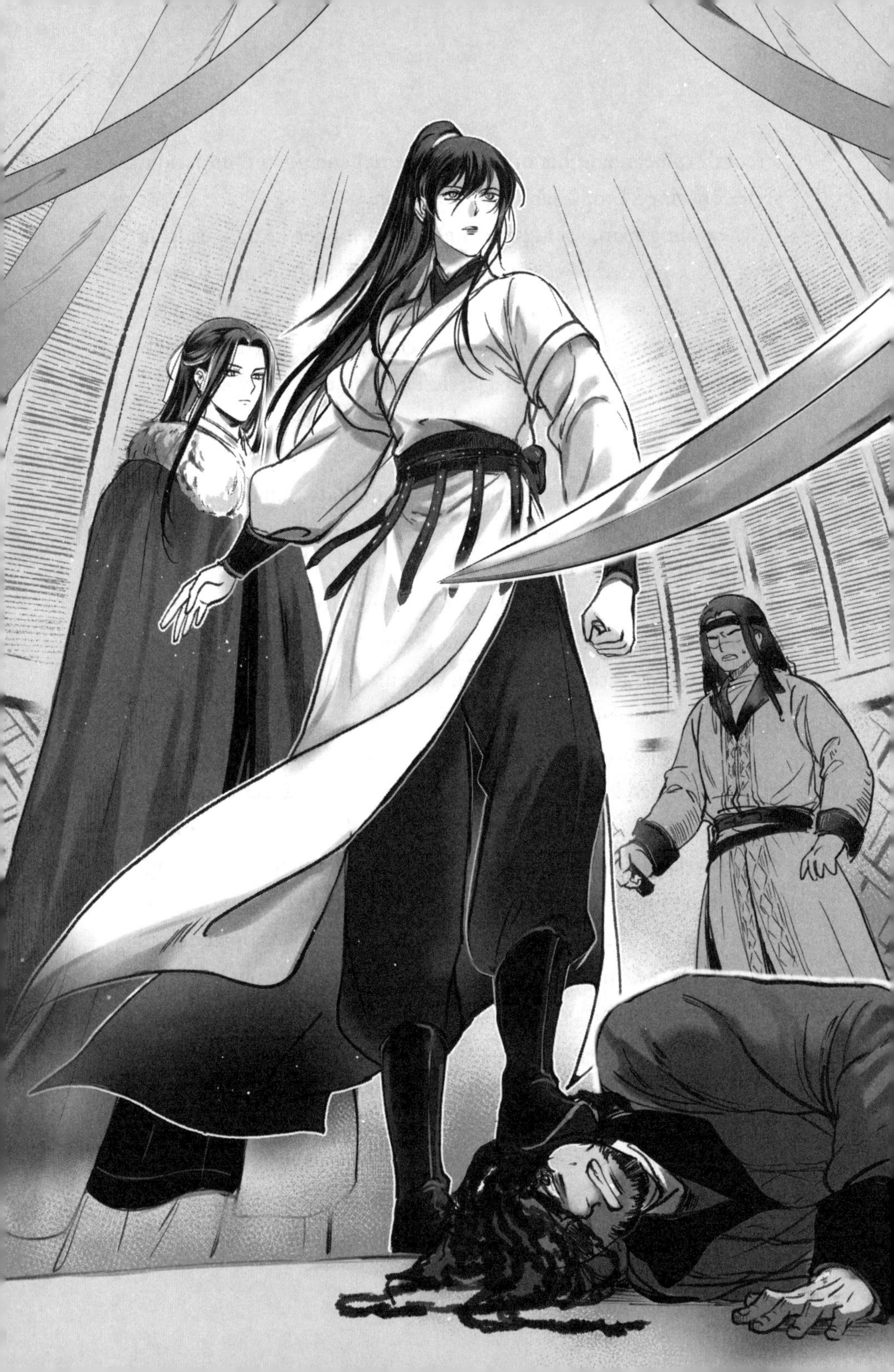

"Stop!" Apa Khagan finally roared.

Göktürk soldiers brandishing swords rushed into the royal yurt but dared not approach—Feng Xiao and Fo'er were still fighting.

"You claim to have come as guests," said Apa Khagan angrily. "Is this the behavior of guests?!"

"Aren't you Göktürks of the opinion that might makes right? We're simply following your example while in your lands," said Cui Buqu indifferently. "When you're ready to receive us, we can sit down for a proper discussion."

In the center of the yurt, the two martial arts masters never paused. Other than Apa Khagan and Jinlian—the khagan some distance away and surrounded by guards, the khatun still keeping her composure—the rest had either fled the royal yurt in fear or were cowering in a corner to avoid becoming a casualty themselves.

Only Cui Buqu remained in place, proud and unbending. Despite his sickly complexion, he showed no hint of weakness, standing as straight and tall as a young pine within this den of wolves.

Apa Khagan sputtered with fury and alarm, hesitating over whether to call for his guards to seize Cui Buqu. The man seemed to have glimpsed his thoughts, because he spoke first.

"My companions will have their hands around your neck before they can take a step forward. What do you think? Are your people faster, or mine? Would you like to make a bet? Your life against mine."

Apa Khagan had no interest in gambling his precious life. Realizing he had no chance of victory, he shouted, "Stop! Both of you are my honored guests; let there be no conflict between you. Tomorrow, there will be a contest at the Eight Tribes Conference. Our guests are welcome to decide the victor then!"

Feng Xiao and Fo'er sprang apart, landing on opposite sides as they stared at each other without expression.

Despite Fo'er's outward composure, his blood was pumping, and it took him a moment to smooth his harried breath. One sleeve had been torn, leaving a shallow wound. Feng Xiao's sleeve had also lost a corner, but he remained calm and relaxed. Other than a few new wrinkles creasing his clothes, he looked no different than before.

In this battle, it seemed Feng Xiao had come out on top.

"The khagan's son called us lowly bastards from the Central Plains. How did we return to being honored guests? I carry with me a document penned by the emperor of Great Sui himself, and we arrived in the name of peace between our nations. If the khagan allows his son to insult us without apology, he can't blame us for finding it unacceptable!" Cui Buqu's manner was haughty; he refused to give Apa Khagan any out. Instead, he kept pushing, demanding an apology from the young man presently under Qiao Xian's boot.

The moment he'd called for help, Cui Buqu had known he must be Apa Khagan's youngest son, Ade.

Apa Khagan was furious, but he couldn't leave his son to be humiliated. This group possessed incredible martial arts. He couldn't afford to be ruthless—even if he chose to fight, these Central Plainsmen would likely walk out unscathed.

"Ade, apologize to our honored guests. You were first at fault."

"I won't...ack!" Prince Ade's bluster was squashed as Qiao Xian ground his face into the rug. He was used to throwing his weight around; he treated even Jinlian like she was nothing. Though the khatun had remained quiet throughout, she couldn't help the gleeful *Serves him right* that came to mind.

Prince Ade had no choice but to apologize, albeit indignantly. When Qiao Xian finally lifted her foot, several guards stepped forward to help him up. Burning with shame, he sent a vicious glare toward Cui Buqu's group before storming out of the yurt.

Apa Khagan forced a smile. "The Shule tribe declined to send a representative to the Eight Tribes Conference, but now we have honored guests from the Central Plains to fill their place. It will surely be a conference to remember. This place is no longer fit to sit in; everyone, please go and rest. I will be honored to host you at our banquet later tonight."

At that moment, a servant entered and stooped to whisper something into Apa Khagan's ear. The khagan paled, then shot a glance at Fo'er.

"These guests from the Central Plains arrived unexpectedly. It seems we're short on accommodations, so our new guests must stay next to Fo'er-xiansheng. Does Fo'er-xiansheng have any objections?"

"Since the khagan made the arrangements," said Fo'er, "I naturally must accept."

❦

A short time later, they found themselves in a lavishly appointed yurt. It seemed Apa Khagan had no intention of slighting them—after such a shock, he was done stirring up trouble.

Still Qiao Xian worried that the Göktürks would ambush them during the night. Their hosts had the greater numbers; even if she went all out, she mightn't be able to guarantee Cui Buqu's safety.

Feng Xiao, on the other hand, seemed entirely at ease. He merely asked Qiao Xian to inquire whether there really was nowhere else to stay in the royal capital but here, right next to Fo'er's lodgings.

Qiao Xian returned with a plate of cut melon, supposedly a gift from the first prince. He'd also asked her to deliver a message: if the honored guests were uncomfortable where they were, he would be happy to host them.

The wealth of the Göktürks was modest compared to the aristocracy of the Central Plains, but it didn't stop their upper class from indulging themselves. Their group's yurt wasn't as expansive as the royal one, but it was still spacious. Thick wool rugs cushioned their feet, and beds had been placed along the sides. Colorful woolen tapestries hung on the walls, and the bronze tea service on the table was inlaid with gold and turquoise. It was clearly from the Western Regions, though whether it'd been purchased or stolen was impossible to tell.

Feng Xiao took a seat and reclined against a pillow as he listened to Qiao Xian recite the first prince's message. "Then there's no need to worry." Seeing her look of puzzlement, he sighed at Cui Buqu. "You called Pei Jingzhe stupid, but yours aren't much brighter."

"Instead of putting your energy toward healing your injuries, Deputy Chief Feng insists on idle chatter?" said Cui Buqu indifferently. "Do you believe yourself invincible?"

"To think you pay such close attention to me," said Feng Xiao with a smile. "You noticed."

Only then did Qiao Xian realize Feng Xiao was a little pale.

Feng Xiao untied his sash, exposing his shoulder. It bore a dark red mark; obviously Fo'er's handiwork.

Martial arts practitioners protected their bodies with true qi. Any injury that left a mark without an open wound came from internal damage.

"Fo'er managed to hurt you?" Qiao Xian asked in surprise. She'd sensed Fo'er had grown a little stronger since their last encounter, but as she hadn't fought him personally, she couldn't be certain. If he'd injured Feng Xiao, it appeared her instincts were correct.

Feng Xiao retained his blithe attitude. "I don't imagine he's much better off. He definitely had to swallow back some blood there.

He's putting on a brave face, but he'll have aggravated his internal injury. I'm sure he's also busy recuperating."

After saying his piece, he finally closed his eyes to tend to his injuries.

"So there *are* other suitable accommodations, yet Apa Khagan placed us next to Fo'er," said Cui Buqu. "He wishes to sit on the mountain and watch the tigers fight before deciding whom to ally with."

"The man's a scoundrel," Qiao Xian fumed. "Before, Jinlian... Actually, even though we were in a bind, Jinlian never spoke up for us. None of these Göktürks are trustworthy at all!"

"We still have opportunities," said Cui Buqu. "Tomorrow is the start of the Eight Tribes Conference. We must make an impressive showing. Not only to defeat Fo'er: every tribe must know the people of the Central Plains are not to be trifled with. The stronger we appear, the more respect we'll command."

Minutes later, Jinlian Khatun, that untrustworthy Göktürk, came knocking. Before they could say a word of greeting, she blurted: "You're really in trouble now!"

68

Q IAO XIAN'S FACE darkened. "Why does the khatun say so?"

Jinlian realized she'd misspoken. She rescued her calm and inclined her head in apology. "My agitation got the better of me. Please forgive me."

She even bowed like a woman from the Central Plains.

Cui Buqu waved an airy hand. "We're all in the same boat. Anything that harms us harms you, so you needn't be so polite, Khatun. First, tell us why the change in your khagan's attitude. Does Fo'er terrify him so much?"

"It's a long story," said Jinlian. "I told you the khagan asked me to train a group of women to serve as his guards. Those women weren't particularly strong, but they were more cautious than any man. And after they managed to help the khagan through a certain crisis, he trusted them deeply. But while I was in the Central Plains, one of the women tried to assassinate the khagan and almost succeeded. I'm told the assassin confessed that her father was a Han, while her mother was a Göktürk. Her father was killed by the khagan's men, so she loathed the Göktürks. She purposely infiltrated the guards and waited for an opportunity to kill him."

Jinlian paused, smiling bitterly. "The khagan killed the rest of the guards I trained in a fit of rage, and blame for the incident fell on me. Upon my return, I found myself detained. The greater khatun pleaded my case to stop the khagan from punishing me. This was why I was unable to return for you earlier."

"What does that have to do with us?" asked Qiao Xian coldly. Though they numbered only three, they were representatives of the Sui dynasty. As long as Apa Khagan was still of sound mind, he would never offend an envoy of Sui simply out of anger with Jinlian over the matter of some guards.

Jinlian sighed. "You've seen that the khagan has two sons, neither of them mine. The eldest was born to the greater khatun. I have a good relationship with her and her son, but the khagan prefers his youngest, Ade, the one who insulted you earlier. I wish to cooperate with the Sui dynasty, but Ade believes the Hans cannot be trusted. He shows me little respect; he's much closer to the conservative nobles of our tribe. I'm sure he took advantage of my absence to pour poison in the khagan's ear. As you Hans say, words can twist even metal. Perhaps the khagan brushed him off at first—but as time passed without me here, the khagan started to believe him. I could tell the khagan was more distant on my return."

Cui Buqu frowned. "Khatun, don't tell me you've been fighting alone all this time, without even an ally or subordinate willing to speak up for you to the khagan?"

"I share a friendship with the greater khatun and her son; as I said, I have her to thank for the khagan's temporary pardon. As for my subordinates, I had several who worked in and around the khagan's yurt or by his side. But when I returned, I found all of them had been removed for various offenses. There isn't a single one left."

Jinlian's mouth was set in a grim line. She was reluctant to reveal her vulnerabilities, but she understood that if she didn't speak now,

Cui Buqu's company would distrust her, and she'd lose any chance to redeem herself.

"Before I left, though the khagan favored Prince Ade, he listened to what I had to say. I never imagined Ade would gain so much ground so quickly; now the khagan listens to all his counsel. On top of that, Fo'er beat us here; he must have offered Apa something tempting for him to lean toward Ishbara."

Cui Buqu pondered this. "But earlier, Feng Xiao came out the victor in his scuffle with Fo'er, and Qiao Xian taught Ade a lesson of her own. If Apa Khagan is thinking clearly, he must know he needs to reweigh the pros and cons."

"The khagan believes the first prince and I are on your side. If I speak for you, it'll only serve to anger him further. But my subordinates will do all they can to provide you with assistance."

"Can you put us in contact with the greater khatun and her son?" asked Cui Buqu.

Jinlian understood at once. "Cui-xiansheng wishes to form an alliance with them? It won't work."

"Why not?"

"I've tried. Though the greater khatun spoke for me this time, she ignores external affairs and spends her days weaving her woolen rugs. Prince Yixun is timid, much like his mother. Ha, they don't act like Göktürks at all; they're more like southerners from the Central Plains."

She paused, realizing she'd put her foot in her mouth. Though the north and south stood divided, such derogatory words were obviously not fit for the ears of anyone from the Central Plains. "Perhaps that wasn't the best comparison," she added quickly.

None of the three minded. Jinlian was normally a calm and rational person. To vent like this, blurting things that wouldn't help resolve their problems, she must have been truly desperate.

"Then are you saying there's no chance to turn things around?" asked Cui Buqu.

"Not necessarily. You said it yourself—you caused a scene just now and enraged the khagan, but he also witnessed your strength and doesn't dare decide rashly. I heard that after you left, Fo'er tried to see him and was turned away at the door. Tomorrow we're meeting with the nations and tribes who are our allies among the Western Göktürks, but there will be contests of horsemanship and archery. The countries of the Western Regions love sport, not literature. If Feng-langjun prevails in the competition, I will try persuading the khagan again. He may change his mind."

"Don't you find it suspicious that one of your trained guards tried to assassinate the khagan?" asked Cui Buqu. "This incident happened just after you left the Khaganate, and when you returned, your people were dead. You've lost the eyes and ears you had around the khagan, along with his trust."

"I agree," said Jinlian. "And I suspect Ade is responsible. But there's no evidence, and the dead can't speak. I have no way to investigate."

"Apart from the greater khatun and her son, are there no other nobles who hold a high position yet are unwilling to participate in the conflict between you two? Any who would speak up before the khagan? The khagan's mother, perhaps, or any other elders."

"Yes!" said Jinlian. "Though it's not a family member. It's the Black Moon Shaman."

The Göktürks, of course, had their own gods. However backward or primitive their religious practices appeared to those from the Central Plains, the Göktürks themselves were pious, and their tribes had great shamans capable of communicating with the gods. The khagan would never share his authority, so these shamans took no part in decision-making unless the khagan specifically sought their opinion. Still, every Göktürk tribe, from large to small, had a shaman of this kind.

The Black Moon Shaman was aged and spent most of his time in seclusion. An audience with him was no easy feat, but Cui Buqu suggested Jinlian pay him a visit. Even if they were unable to win him over, they might still ask him to put in a few good words with the khagan. As for gifts, Jinlian had brought several treasures back from the Central Plains, all purchased from Linlang Pavilion. Though they were few, they were valuable, surely capable of swaying the Black Moon Shaman.

Time was short if they wanted to see him today; it'd soon be dark. Jinlian stood and bade them farewell, then left to seek the shaman.

The door had hardly swung shut behind her when someone arrived claiming to be the first prince's attendant, sent to ask how the honored guests were adjusting to their lodgings.

Cui Buqu called to the attendant to wait outside, then turned to Feng Xiao. "Quick, tear open my clothes, climb on top of me, and molest me."

Feng Xiao was dumbfounded. Had Cui Buqu gone mad? But his expression was entirely serene, as if Feng Xiao had hallucinated his last words. Before Feng Xiao could respond, Cui Buqu grew impatient and made the first move. He mussed his clothes and loosened his hair, then sprawled on the carpeted ground. He gave his neck a couple of hard pinches for good measure.

"Have they turned red?" he asked in a low voice.

Feng Xiao had begun to grasp Cui Buqu's plan. This was a risky situation, fraught with danger. Yet Feng Xiao wasn't nervous at all; he was greatly amused. That he was experiencing it with Cui Buqu only made it more entertaining.

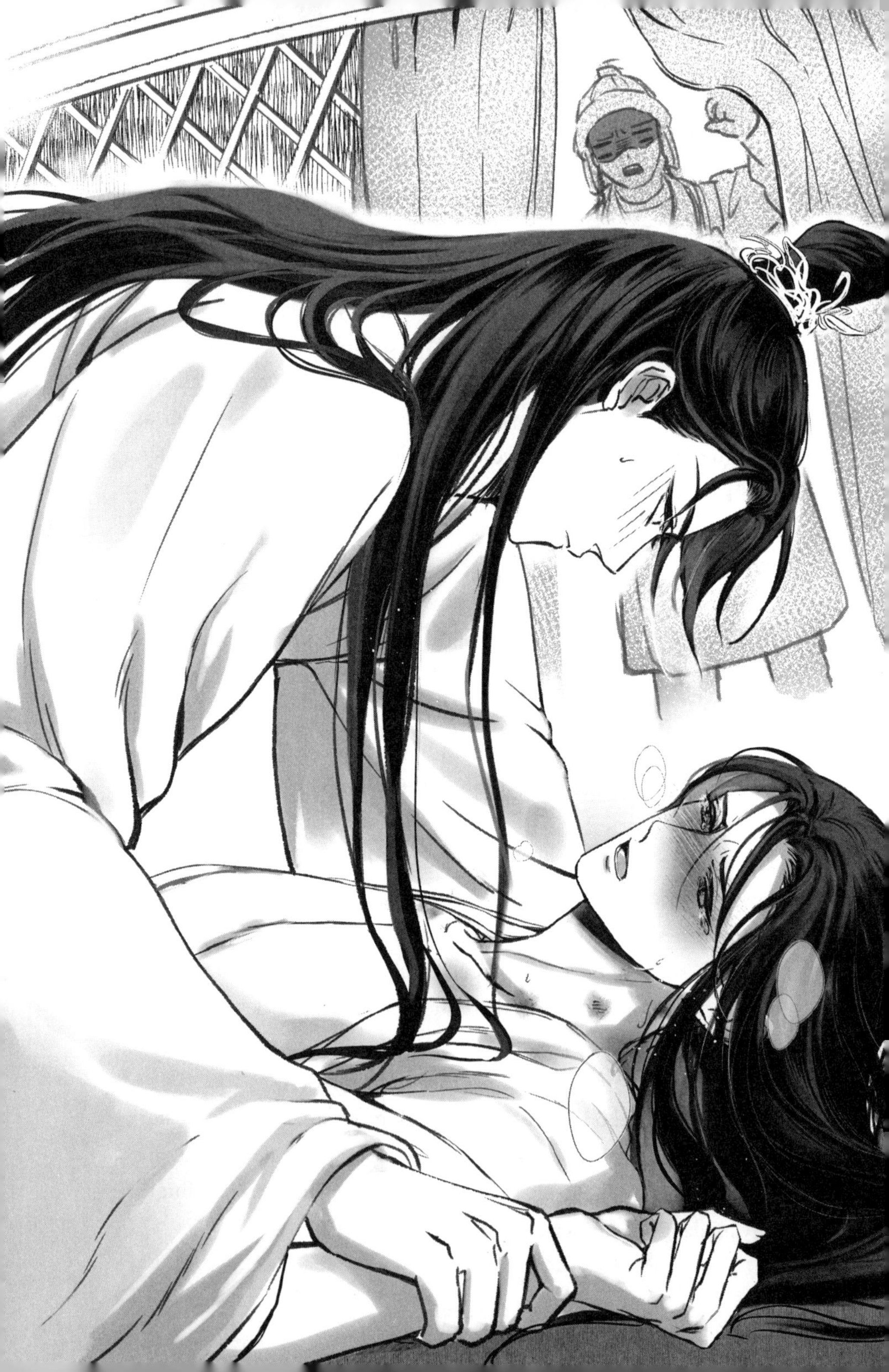

Without further ado, he climbed atop Cui Buqu and was immediately greeted with pained cries.

"No, no... Not here, ah!"

Cui Buqu's voice rose and fell, twisted and turned, slightly breathless and certain to cause misunderstandings. Feng Xiao's mouth twitched as he watched Cui Buqu throw himself into the performance.

Hearing the commotion, the man outside tossed open the door flap and rushed inside. He stared at Cui Buqu and Feng Xiao in shock.

Faking embarrassment and anger, Cui Buqu shoved Feng Xiao aside with one hand, stumbling upright and pointing at the attendant with his other. "You...get the hell out!" he yelled in Turkic.

69

THE ATTENDANT had merely been sent to deliver a message; he hadn't expected to stumble upon such a scene. He remained rooted to the spot, staring blankly. It wasn't until Cui Buqu shouted that he came to his senses. "Prin-Prince Yixun ordered me to bring you this fruit," he stammered. "Do the two honored guests require anything?"

Feng Xiao didn't look up; he waved him off the way one might swat a fly. "No. Leave it and go." He grabbed Cui Buqu's clothes, a ferocious smile spreading across his face. "I've been denying myself the entire journey. You won't get away today!"

Cui Buqu suspected Feng Xiao was using this farce to exact his revenge. While he didn't seem to be using much strength, Cui Buqu's arms were so sore where Feng Xiao held them they seemed about to fall off.

He gritted his teeth and whispered, "He doesn't understand Chinese!"

"Oh?" said Feng Xiao. "Then hurry up and say, 'no, no' in Turkic!"

Cui Buqu was speechless. He tried to kick Feng Xiao in the groin, but Feng Xiao caught his legs easily, holding them down and spreading them as he pressed their bodies together suggestively.

Feng Xiao blinked down at him. "How's this? Realistic enough for you?"

This was going above and beyond, transforming pretense into reality. Cui Buqu held his breath, bringing a flush to his wan and sickly face. In a voice that quavered slightly, he said in Turkic, "Please...please return to your prince and tell him I will personally bring him my thanks later tonight."

Perhaps the attendant understood or perhaps he didn't. Either way, he stammered a few disoriented words of assent before taking to his heels.

The instant he was gone, Cui Buqu shoved Feng Xiao off. "That will do."

"You got it the wrong way around," said Feng Xiao.

Cui Buqu quirked an inquisitive eyebrow.

"Compare our appearances and abilities. If I wished to force you, I have hundreds of ways to render you motionless in an instant; I'd have no trouble taking what I wanted. Such a dramatic, prolonged scene would only be possible in one instance: if *you* were the one molesting *me*, and I was the one feigning reluctance. Next time, you should be the one holding me down, and I'll be the one who shouts *no*."

Face devoid of expression, Cui Buqu said, "There will be no next time. The attendant will undoubtedly report what he saw to the first prince."

"You want him to mistake us for cut-sleeves. Why?"

Cui Buqu spoke each word deliberately: "Because the first prince is a cut-sleeve himself."

"Oh?" Feng Xiao's brows rose in surprise.

The khagan's yurt had been crowded, and Feng Xiao's attention had been on Fo'er and the other threats present. He'd pegged at least two besides Fo'er as first-tier martial artists. But Cui Buqu's focus had been elsewhere—he'd watched everyone's faces for the most minute reactions. Thanks to his eidetic memory, he could recall subtle movements even the person themselves might miss.

"From the moment we arrived, the first prince was completely taken by your looks. His eyes were glued to you the entire time, but the attendant behind him—the same one who just entered—kept looking between you and the first prince. I'd say he looked resentful."

The attendant was a Göktürk as well, a young and handsome one at that. By contrast, the first prince was in his thirties, with fine lines at the corners of his eyes, and hair and a beard that aged him further. His face had a look of deep unhappiness and early decline.

Not a man and a woman, but two men far apart in age. Had Cui Buqu not pointed it out, Feng Xiao would never have considered the possibility.

Still, it wasn't so strange if one gave it a moment's thought. Lechers had always existed. If some of them loved women, it stood to reason that others loved men. And there were certainly nobles and dignitaries all over the Central Plains, north and south, who didn't discriminate. The Göktürks were only human; it wasn't odd to find a cut-sleeve first prince.

"When the meeting adjourned, that attendant followed right behind the first prince. I'd noticed something between them earlier, so I was watching closely. When the attendant thought no one was looking, he secretly reached for the first prince's hand. The prince didn't shake him off either. After that, I was certain."

"Cut-sleeves aren't unusual, but in the land of the Göktürks, they value martial strength—not scholars with literary talent. The first prince is introverted and melancholic; he has no skill in governance, and his brother bests him in martial arts. If it gets out that he likes men as well, it's likely to be the end of him."

"Correct," said Cui Buqu. "In fact, perhaps this is the very reason Apa Khagan disdains his son."

Feng Xiao understood. "So you're saying the attendant will report us to the prince, and this will increase his goodwill toward us."

"It's true he's a Göktürk, and second only to the khagan in terms of position. But because of his proclivities, he's forced to hide; he can't commiserate with his equals. He's like a foreign species amid a pack of wolves; a life like this is hard on the heart. If he sees there are others like him—two of them, in fact—how do you imagine he'll feel?"

Feng Xiao smiled. "He'll be overjoyed and fancy us kindred spirits."

Cui Buqu's lips curled in a smile. "Now it'll be easier to approach the first prince. Later tonight, I'll find an opportunity to meet with him alone and tell him a few tales to win his trust. Maybe Yixun can't help us directly, but he can still provide us with many benefits. It's better to have as few enemies as possible."

Qiao Xian had earlier been sent to inquire for news. Soon enough, she returned with one of Jinlian's maids.

Jinlian's standing within the court was on shaky ground. She couldn't afford to draw any more suspicion by personally meeting with them and had therefore sent her trusted maid, an ordinary Göktürk woman with a tanned complexion named Muge.

Unfortunately, Muge's message was discouraging: the Black Moon Shaman was currently in seclusion. No one knew when he'd emerge.

The shaman was responsible for communing with the gods and entered seclusion whenever he received a divine edict. At that point, he'd meditate until he received enlightenment. Jinlian had no chance of seeing him until then.

But she had also learned of another matter: after Jinlian's guard's assassination attempt, Apa Khagan had fallen gravely ill, and the Black Moon Shaman had asked that the khagan be brought to him for treatment. The shaman had healed Apa Khagan, only to then fall ill himself. He'd announced to the public that he'd enter seclusion to recuperate. No one knew when he'd be well enough to return.

In antiquity, shamanism and medicine had been one and the same. Later, as the study of medicine flourished in the Central Plains, producing countless generations of renowned doctors, the two practices had diverged. The Hans came to view shamanistic techniques as witchcraft used to harm others. But in the Khaganate, a shaman with knowledge of medicine would double as both the tribe's religious leader and most qualified physician.

Feng Xiao sneered. "What luck we're having."

Jinlian had tumbled from power overnight, while Apa Khagan's attitude had flipped completely. Now they couldn't even visit the one person they wished to see. It seemed heaven itself was standing against the Sui dynasty, placing obstacles in their path over and over again.

"Tell her to draw me a map of the route between here and the house of the Black Moon Shaman," Feng Xiao said to Cui Buqu.

Cui Buqu hesitated. "You don't speak a word of Turkic. Even if you go, you'll have no way to communicate with him. You'll only alert our enemies of our plans."

"I just want to see if he's really recuperating in seclusion, or if he's only pretending. If he really wishes to oppose us, we should kill him and be done with it."

Feng Xiao, it seemed, had his own plans. Cui Buqu nodded and didn't interfere further. His throat had become dry, so he picked up a slice of the honey melon the first prince had sent.

A melon like honey, a hand like jade.

Everyone appreciated beauty. Even Feng Xiao, who proclaimed himself the most radiant in all the land, found his eyes lingering on Cui Buqu's hand. Before Cui Buqu could notice, Feng Xiao shifted his gaze to Muge and said carelessly, "Shall we playact in front of her too? That way, our relationship will be more convincing."

Cui Buqu glanced at him, baffled. "What do we gain from that? Jinlian isn't a cut-sleeve."

Feng Xiao smiled and fluttered his fan. "Then I'm relieved. Else I'd think Daoist Master Cui is truly yearning for me, ready to try his luck again the moment I drop my guard."

Cui Buqu blinked back at him.

Qiao Xian had no idea what they meant by this but jumped at once to the conclusion that Feng Xiao was harassing Cui Buqu again. Upon closer look, Cui Buqu's clothes and hair were mussed, and there were suspicious marks dotting his neck. She was immediately furious. "Lord Chief! Did this bastard lay his hands on you again?"

Feng Xiao laughed. "Did *I* lay hands on *him*? Your lord chief was the one who laid his hands on me!"

"The lord chief is a transcendent existence, without peer in the world," Qiao Xian said with disdain. "He might reject others, but he'd never be the one rejected... Why are you looking at me like that?"

Feng Xiao looked her up and down, then said curiously, "My good woman, you have eyes, so how are you so blind? Why do you think I was the one who harassed him? He's obviously the one with ulterior motives who tried to force me. Why else would he be in that state?"

Qiao Xian laughed coldly, ready to argue once more, when Cui Buqu interrupted them. "Someone's coming."

It was one of Apa Khagan's men, sent to invite Cui Buqu to the banquet that was about to begin.

Qiao Xian's knowledge wasn't only in medicine; she was also adept at testing for poison. Fo'er wouldn't attack Cui Buqu in the open, and with her at his side, he was safe from any other underhanded tactics. The two of them set off for the banquet, hoping to use the chance to approach the first prince.

As for Feng Xiao, he went alone to the Black Moon Shaman's residence under cover of night.

The bright moon hung in the brilliant starry sky. Distant mountains rose and fell, and the withered grass stretched endlessly toward the horizon. Up on the hillside, above shimmering water lapping at the riverbank, stood a lonely stone house. Swathed in the moonlight's gentle glow, it looked particularly desolate.

The Black Moon Shaman was revered among the Western Göktürks, and his residence overlooked the entire tribe, situated above even Apa Khagan's abode. The closer to the heavens, the better to communicate with the gods.

Feng Xiao left behind the joyous shouts and firelight of the banquet. In a few effortless bounds, he landed on the hillside near the stone house, where he stopped to observe.

The yurts of the capital clustered close to the river. This place was unlike the boundless yellow sands beyond the pass; it was lush with vegetation, a Jiangnan beyond the Great Wall and a paradise on earth. The Göktürks didn't build pavilions and towers like the people of the Central Plains. But the fragrant grasses and the trees bathed in warm sunlight, together with the mountains, the river, and the colorful yurts, provided a raw beauty all their own.

Feng Xiao was in no hurry.

He stood in place for a long while, sensing for danger. Once he was certain he was alone, he crept up to the stone house.

The Black Moon Shaman lived by himself, his dwelling set apart from the tribe. They'd heard he had two attendants, but Feng Xiao saw neither hide nor hair of them. Perhaps they'd taken advantage of the shaman's seclusion to slack off. Or perhaps they'd slipped down to the banquet, hoping to partake in the excitement. Apparently, both were still young.

Whatever the reason, they had left the Black Moon Shaman alone in that house.

Feng Xiao took his time, alert to any change in his surroundings. Martial experts of his caliber were sensitive to danger. If another elite martial artist lurked in the house, Feng Xiao would sense it. He'd much rather wait for his enemy to come out on their own.

But the stone house was tranquil. He could even hear the faint sound of snoring from within. It came in stops and starts as he listened, a sign that an elderly person in poor health lay sleeping within.

Feng Xiao gave the wooden door a gentle push. It swung inward, revealing a pitch-black interior. Moonlight spilled around Feng Xiao's figure in the doorway and illuminated all sorts of bottles and pots. A long curtain hung further in, where the moon couldn't reach. The sounds of snoring came from behind it.

A faint aroma wafted over; Feng Xiao took a sniff. He smelled medicine—lovage, musk, and ginger. It wasn't poison. If the shaman was ill, as he claimed, this made sense. Yet Feng Xiao felt that something was wrong.

The sound!

He realized: moments ago, outside the house, he'd been able to hear the sound of singing and dancing from the banquet in the distance. Now he couldn't hear a single thing.

A low laugh sounded at his side.

"You...finally came!"

The voice echoed in his ears; seemingly inches away yet drifting in from the distant horizon. Every word came from a different direction. In front, behind, to the left, to the right. It was everywhere—completely surrounding Feng Xiao.

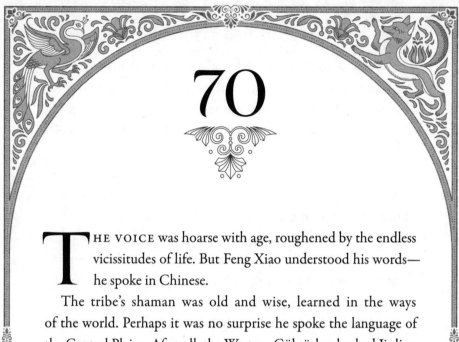

70

THE VOICE was hoarse with age, roughened by the endless vicissitudes of life. But Feng Xiao understood his words—he spoke in Chinese.

The tribe's shaman was old and wise, learned in the ways of the world. Perhaps it was no surprise he spoke the language of the Central Plains. After all, the Western Göktürks also had Jinlian, who even used their idioms and proverbs fluently. She was likely more literate in Chinese than the average commoner from the Central Plains.

The voice came from all directions, but Feng Xiao didn't move, listening carefully to discern his opponent's position. Yet he found he couldn't pinpoint the speaker's location at all—unless there was more than one person, spread out and speaking simultaneously. Did the Black Moon Shaman have accomplices?

Something seemed to have climbed onto his boot and was quickly crawling up his leg.

Feng Xiao didn't look down. He circulated his internal energy, and the thing flew off, but more surged toward him. A moment later they'd grabbed his legs, pinning him to the spot. A strong wind buffeted his face as murderous intent reared its head in the dark.

"Black Moon Shaman! I come as a friend, not an enemy. Why don't we sit down and talk?!"

So Feng Xiao said, but he didn't stop moving either. Legs pinned in place, he twisted his torso aside, narrowly dodging two blasts striking him from the front and back. He slammed both palms downward, and wind from his palms scoured the unknown reptiles. Wherever it touched they fell down dead, their corpses flying through the air and bouncing off Feng Xiao's clothes.

Feng Xiao, fastidious even in these circumstances, curled his lip. He'd be sure to repay the Black Moon Shaman for this.

But the Black Moon Shaman never answered, and the laughter stopped. If not for the words he'd spoken at the beginning, Feng Xiao would have thought him mute. It seemed he had no interest in working together.

Could it be that he was already Prince Ade's ally and an enemy of the Sui dynasty?

The creatures on the ground had been annihilated. Feng Xiao could move his feet again, but he soon realized he'd fallen into another quagmire. At some point, the light from the moon and stars had faded. The interior was an unrelieved black, and he couldn't see a thing.

All was deathly silent, as if the voice before had been naught but a hallucination. As he stared into the dark, a faint light flickered to life. It wavered in midair, blue and green interweaving, like a will-o'-the-wisp.

Luring him closer.

But what choice did he have? This house belonged to the Black Moon Shaman. There might be countless traps and mechanisms here he could deploy against Feng Xiao. Rather than remaining in enemy territory, it was better to seek a way out. Perhaps he could find a spot to break through.

In the dim light, the room appeared only a dozen strides across, but Feng Xiao spent a full fifteen minutes walking. The will-o'-the-wisp never changed, no closer or farther than before. Yet now there was a dense layer of fog around him, and he could no longer tell if he was within the house or without.

At last Feng Xiao understood. From the moment he'd climbed the hill and seen the stone house, he'd entered someone else's illusory array.

But this array was vast, its scale comparable to a mighty army laid out on the battlefield, defenses stretching on for thousands of miles. It exploited all the phenomena of the world to confuse and disorient its victims. From the sun and the moon, the starry skies, the mountains, the rivers and streams, down to each individual flower or blade of grass, even the stones upon the ground—all could be utilized within this array.

The deployer of such an array could enhance it with sound and smell. Just as when they'd spoken earlier: they'd aimed to distract Feng Xiao, pulling his focus into discerning their position and luring him deeper into the trap.

But Feng Xiao hadn't lost his composure. He laughed. "It seems the Black Moon Shaman anticipated my arrival and specially prepared this banquet for me. How much did they purchase you for, I wonder? It must be a hefty sum if you won't even listen to what I can offer before deciding you wish to kill me."

There was no answer. The will-o'-the-wisp swayed in the mist, beckoning those seeking its light, drawing them closer. But if they stepped forward, nine times out of ten it would be into the jaws of death.

There was a noise like the cracking of earth as something pushed out of the ground. Feng Xiao felt a cold touch at his ankle. He looked down and vaguely made out the white bones of a skeletal hand.

Without batting an eye, Feng Xiao raised his other boot and crushed the hand underfoot.

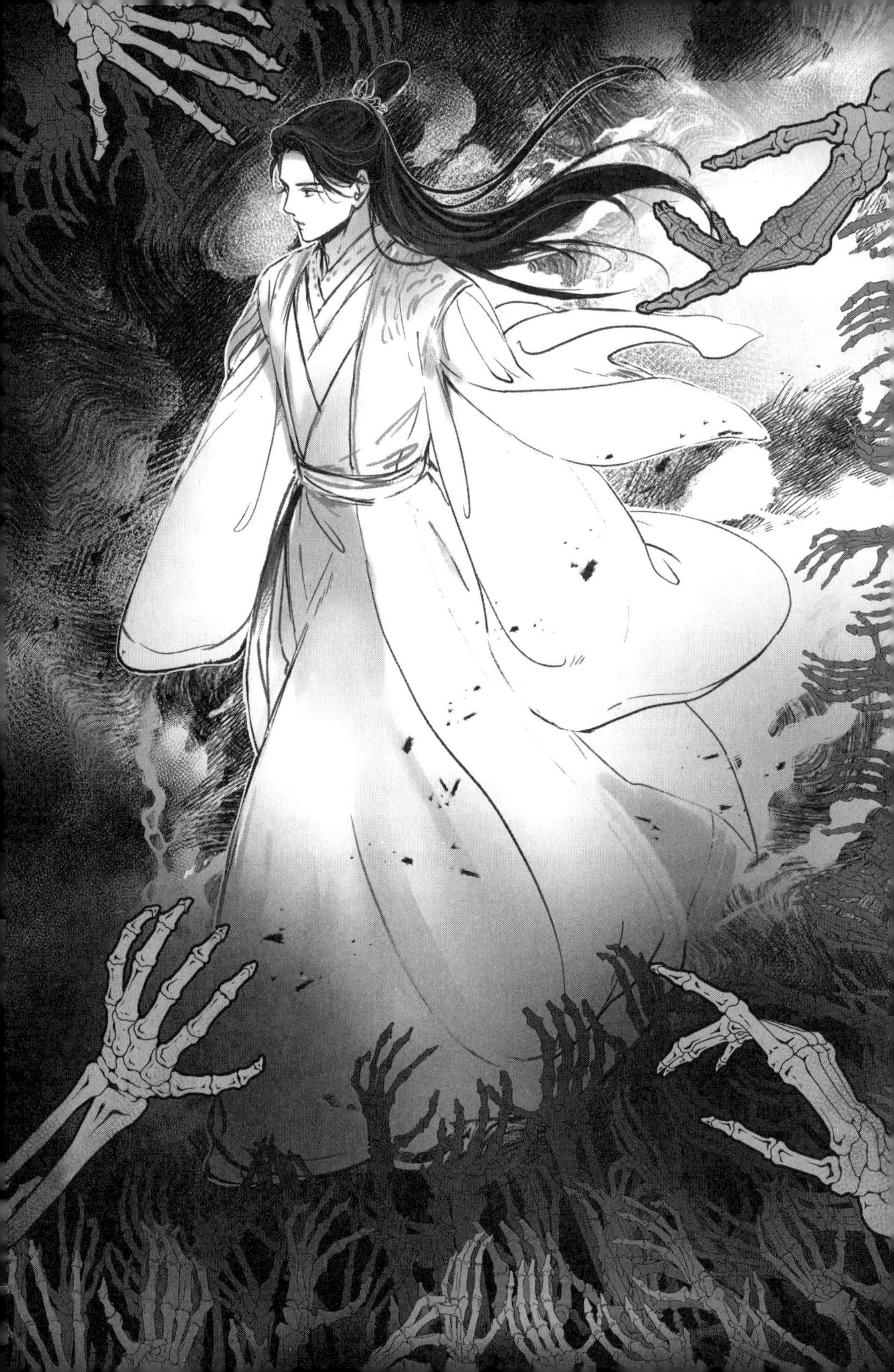

More ghostly hands stretched forth from the ground like demons bursting from the underworld, clamoring to drag the living down to join them. Thousands of withered, bony hands grabbed for Feng Xiao, yet he strode forward, shattering the bones to dust with his internal energy and eliciting the ululating wails of the dead.

Suddenly the sounds of weeping turned into a piercing scream that rushed toward his back. He flung out a palm behind him but met nothing. Ghostly howls rang out from all directions, shrill, mournful, and unbearable.

Feng Xiao frowned, hesitating over whether to cover his ears and save himself from the sounds of those torturous voices.

In that tiny pause, a ghostly figure drifted out of the mist whisper-silent. It was behind Feng Xiao in an instant, its palm thrusting forward, aiming right for the fatal acupoint in his back. Feng Xiao, trapped by the screams, remained motionless—unaware of the enemy about to strike.

✥⟨⟨⟩⟩✥

The royal yurt was filled with song and dance.

Here the khagan convened with his nobles and ministers for important meetings, received foreign guests, and threw banquets. The chaos of the day had been cleared away, and a great bonfire roared merrily in the center, a plump and tender lamb slowly turning over the flames. It was seasoned with various spices, and its tempting aroma filled the air as it dripped grease into the crackling fire, so fragrant the guests could practically taste it.

A Kuchean woman in a flowing skirt danced gracefully around the bonfire, accompanied by the music of harps and pipas. Her sashes fluttered, the trailing satin creating a scene so enchanting as to bewitch any watcher.

Cui Buqu swept a glance over the yurt. Most of the khagan's guests had already arrived. Some were watching the dance, while others whispered into their neighbors' ears. The atmosphere was lively and infectious, soaked in wine.

Fo'er sat across from Cui Buqu, beside the second prince Ade. The two were engaged in a lively discussion; they didn't even glance in his direction. In this relaxed environment, the previously reticent Prince Yixun seemed to take courage, opening his mouth to chat with Cui Buqu. "Does Cui-xiansheng not like the envoy of Ishbara Khagan?"

"We are envoys of the Sui dynasty. This man wishes to kill us and convince the khagan to side with Ishbara. Does the first prince believe I should like him?"

The prince chuckled dryly, as if he, too, felt he'd made a mistake with his conversation starter. He changed the subject. "Where is your deputy envoy tonight?"

"He's feeling unwell, so we left him to rest."

At that, a sly expression stole over the prince's face. He leaned closer and whispered, "Is it true that the two of you have *that* kind of relationship?"

Cui Buqu feigned ignorance. "I'm afraid I don't understand. The two of us have much in common, so we look after each other when we travel."

The first prince gave him another knowing look. This one seemed to say, *All right, no need to explain, I understand.* "He's indeed an outstanding individual. But Liegu told me he seems proud and overbearing. In broad daylight, he almost, er, had his way...with you."

Allowing the first prince to make such assumptions was just what Cui Buqu wanted. He smiled wryly. "Thank you for your concern, it's just..." He shook his head and sighed, neither confirmation nor denial, as if he couldn't say all he wanted to—leaving plenty of room for the first prince to imagine a long, complex, and messy relationship.

Sure enough, Yixun's eyes filled with sympathy. "Even I can see you're in poor health; are you unable to satisfy him? I have some virility-enhancing medicine at home. After the banquet, I'll have Liegu run some over to you."

The corners of Cui Buqu's lips twitched. He coughed twice, fighting back the urge to break character as he cupped his hands in gratitude. "Then I shall thank the prince in advance."

The first prince had been softspoken from birth, and due to his secret proclivities, he had few bosom friends in the Western Khaganate. Cui Buqu was an outsider, but that also meant the prince needn't worry about him spreading stories that could damage his reputation. And because they shared the same difficulties, the prince felt an instant connection to him.

They chatted a while, until Cui Buqu noticed the khagan's seat was still empty. "Is the khagan not coming tonight?"

Yixun looked embarrassed. "He'll be here, but a little late. Recently, a new concubine arrived from Kucha."

A cold snort came from beside them; Jinlian, lowering herself into the seat by Cui Buqu, had heard the first prince's words.

"So that's why I haven't seen this beautiful Kuchean dancer before. The new concubine must have brought her along," Jinlian scoffed.

"Not long after you left, Ade acquired several Kuchean women for my father," Yixun explained. "The one he took as his new concubine is even more beautiful than this dancer; Father was drawn to her right away. She's constantly at his side, and Ade is more favored than ever."

Jinlian frowned. "Why didn't I hear this when I came back?"

The prince smiled helplessly. "What could you have done even if you'd known? It's not as if you can go harass her. The new concubine slept in Father's yurt every night until his recent bout of illness. He set up a separate yurt for her after, but he still summons her every evening; she's his great favorite."

Now that there was a new flame, the old one had been abandoned. Jinlian had been beautiful in her youth. She no longer relied on her looks to secure Apa Khagan's devotion, yet when she thought back to those days, her heart knotted with indescribable emotions.

Cui Buqu, too, was lost in thought, though he didn't share her sorrow; he was working out how to turn the topic to the Black Moon Shaman and coax some information from the first prince. It was then that he saw an attendant rush inside and whisper into Prince Ade's ear. The prince slammed his hands down on the table and rose, his face black with rage. "Someone has disturbed the Black Moon Shaman!"

His gaze raked over the room as he roared, "The Black Moon Shaman is the sage of our tribe. Anyone who dares disturb him is the enemy of our Khaganate! Who did this?! Come forward and confess, and I may still plead your case before my father. If you remain silent, you must forgive me for inflicting the harshest tortures upon you when we catch you!"

The festive atmosphere was gone. All the guests exchanged glances, stunned.

Prince Ade's gaze landed on Cui Buqu. "What do you have to say, envoy of the Sui dynasty?"

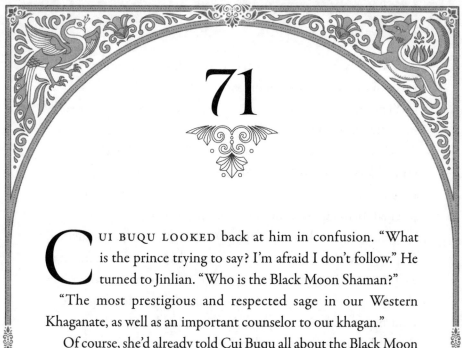

71

CUI BUQU LOOKED back at him in confusion. "What is the prince trying to say? I'm afraid I don't follow." He turned to Jinlian. "Who is the Black Moon Shaman?"

"The most prestigious and respected sage in our Western Khaganate, as well as an important counselor to our khagan."

Of course, she'd already told Cui Buqu all about the Black Moon Shaman, and was also beginning to wonder if Feng Xiao was behind this. But here in public, she gamely played along and answered Cui Buqu, donning a look of shock. She turned to question Ade: "Who dares disturb the Black Moon Shaman? I shall report it to the khagan this instant!"

Ade snorted. "I've sent my own people to inform him."

"What happened?" Yixun asked.

The attendant who entered with the report stepped forward. "A fire broke out near the stone house, and we heard sounds of fighting—if you step out, you can see it from here. The fire's been put out, but the villain who set it has yet to be caught. The shaman has been injured; a physician has gone to tend to him!"

"I'll go see him at once!" Yixun declared.

Ade held a hand out to stop him. "No need. The physician is with him; what more could you do? Such a thing is unprecedented. Tomorrow is the day of the Eight Tribes Conference. These outsiders arrived today, and this incident occurred this very evening! There's no need to search—the criminal is among us here!"

Yixun frowned. "Everyone here is an honored guest invited by our father himself!"

This second prince never held his elder brother in high regard. He immediately dismissed him. "Several people here were not invited." He glanced at Cui Buqu and Qiao Xian, then said darkly, "If I find you had a hand in this, you won't escape my wrath!"

Jinlian felt a spike of irritation. What did he mean, not invited? Cui Buqu had been invited by none other than herself. Ade might as well have said her word meant nothing. Though she'd found things changed on her return, she was still a concubine of the khagan. This went beyond a lack of respect; Ade regarded her as a thorn in his side and wished to rid himself of her.

She was considering what to do when a loud *bang* cut through her thoughts: Cui Buqu had slammed a hand on the table and risen to his feet.

"Though the khagan has yet to form an alliance with the Sui dynasty, he has welcomed us as honored guests. You've accused us without evidence, spitting in the face of Great Sui. Even if we should be convicted, the khagan must do it himself! I demand to see the khagan!"

Ade sneered. "If the khagan were here, he'd say the same as me!"

"Do you represent the khagan?" asked Cui Buqu, his tone cutting. "The khagan called us his honored guests just this afternoon. Are you saying his words hold no weight?!"

Ade too slapped the table and roared, "When did I say that?"

Cui Buqu raised his voice. "Your father yet lives! *He* is the ruler of the Western Khaganate, and you have an elder brother ahead of you. You have no claim to any authority here!"

Though the volume at which one spoke had little to do with the righteousness of one's arguments, when it came to men like Ade, the important thing was to grasp the momentum. Cui Buqu was a tall man. Though he was somewhat thin and frail, his stormy expression was fiercely intimidating. Ade flushed with rage and reared back, ready to strike him.

Qiao Xian and Jinlian would never allow such a thing; they sprang up and blocked Ade.

Watching, Prince Yixun prickled with envy. Not, of course, over the women who stepped forward to protect this man—he was envious that Cui Buqu, despite being a foreigner, had the courage to stand up to his arrogant younger brother inside the royal yurt, and the presence to hold his own.

Still, Prince Ade had no fear of this wan and sickly Sui envoy. If the Sui dynasty had sent him as their representative, that only demonstrated the Central Plains were stretched so thin they had to send a woman and an invalid to plead for them in foreign lands. Their Khaganate held the upper hand.

As for the beautiful woman at Cui Buqu's side, she'd managed to stomp him into the ground earlier today, so he conceded that she had some skill. Once he'd dealt with Cui Buqu, however, she would have no choice but to throw herself at his feet and beg for mercy.

He laughed savagely, summoning his guards with a wave. "When the khagan isn't here, I call the shots! Guards, seize the Sui envoys. The third one is missing—he must be the culprit behind the fire!"

"Wait!"

Before Jinlian could protest, Yixun had spoken up. "They are the guests of my father the khagan," he said, voice rising. "No matter what's happened, we must wait for Father's arrival to make any decision!"

Yet at that very moment, Apa Khagan's personal attendant slipped through the door. The khagan was feeling unwell, he said, and had retired early. He left the two princes to host the banquet; anything else could wait until the conference tomorrow.

Those who knew the khagan's habits glanced at each other, all thinking the same thing. *Unwell? As if.* He was obviously drowning himself in the pleasures of the flesh with his new woman.

Prince Yixun drew himself up. "In that case, we shall wait until my father the khagan arrives tomorrow before interrogating these envoys!"

"No!" cried Ade. "The Black Moon Shaman is the religious leader of our tribe; any aggression toward him *must* be punished. By tomorrow, the culprit will have slipped away. If he suffered fighting the shaman, he may be injured and unable to run tonight. I've sent out my guards, but who's to say he's not hiding in one of the yurts? Search every one and we'll find him!"

Yixun was furious. "All the envoys here are honored guests. How could you be so discourteous toward them!"

Kucha and Qocho, though ostensibly separate nations bordering the Western Khaganate, were effectively vassal states. Regardless of their displeasure at the second prince's orders, there wasn't much they could say; their silence was expected. It was the first prince's behavior that was surprising: at times like this he had always been practically mute, never uttering a word of protest.

Ade narrowed his eyes and stepped forward, looming over his elder brother. "Father is not here, so I'll give the orders!"

But Yixun didn't back down; in fact, he spoke up again. "You're not even a yabghu. Father's given you no position at all. I am the elder! If anyone has the final say here, it's me!"

Ade laughed in anger. "You're so set on protecting these Sui envoys? What kind of deal have you made with them?!"

"Silence!" A woman entered, hair tucked beneath a beaded head-dress. "You claim Yixun has no say? Then what about me? Surely I do!"

Though this was Cui Buqu's first time seeing her, it wasn't hard to guess her identity. The first prince who never dared speak up to his younger brother had opposed him for the first time tonight. Now the greater khatun, who rarely dipped into politics, had shown herself as well.

The Göktürk khatun held immense power. In the khagan's absence, she could command his authority in the tribe. Though she'd never made use of this privilege, that didn't mean it had lapsed.

Ade stared at this mother and her son. Two people who had never stepped out of the shadows before today were now barring his way, as if to intentionally provoke him. His anger turned into fury. "The Black Moon Shaman has been harassed and injured by foreigners! Who will take responsibility for this?! Does the khatun wish to shoulder the blame? Can you bear to?!"

"When the khagan is not here, the authority to make decisions is mine," the khatun said coolly. "Sit down."

It seemed the khatun's sudden appearance hadn't merely been to support her son. But if Ade conceded here, it would erode what small authority he held. "I refuse!" he said resolutely.

Cui Buqu stepped forward. "I have nothing to do with this attack on your shaman," he averred. "I'm willing to swear an oath to heaven before your Wolf God. If I speak any falsehood, may lightning strike me where I stand. May the avatars of the Wolf God tear me to pieces the moment I step from this yurt!"

Everyone gaped at the sheer ruthlessness of this oath. Even Ade was briefly stunned into silence. The Göktürks placed great impor-tance on oaths; such words weren't to be taken lightly.

Yet Cui Buqu didn't stop there. He fixed his gaze on Ade, eyes blazing. "Your Highness has been targeting us since the moment we arrived. You've already decided we're the culprits. Do you dare claim you have no ulterior motives? Animosity between the Sui dynasty and the Göktürk aristocracy is what Ishbara wishes to see. Is the second prince Ishbara's man?!"

Ade was furious. "Nonsense!" he roared.

"Then you swear as well!" Cui Buqu pressed him. "Swear that all you do is for the good of the tribe—that you have no ulterior motives!"

Before the eyes of all, Cui Buqu had turned the tables on the second prince and put him in a difficult position. Several of his close friends opened their mouths to speak, but Jinlian beat them to it: "I agree. Envoy Cui has sworn. The second prince should swear as well if his conscience is clear!"

A Göktürk attendant rushed in looking flustered. When he saw the standoff within the royal yurt, he stopped in his tracks.

Ade reacted as if a blade had been lifted from his neck; desperate to move the focus off himself, he shouted, "What's happened now?! Quickly, speak!"

The attendant knelt on the ground. "The Black Moon Shaman's injuries were severe," he said in a quavering voice. "He's...he's departed for the heavens!"

The assembly stared in shock. The shaman's injury had been presented as a minor incident. Yet in the blink of an eye, it'd become a murder? All color had drained from the khatun's face. Cui Buqu and Jinlian both frowned, and even Qiao Xian was speechless. Feng Xiao, she thought, had really overdone it this time.

Ade had frozen when he heard the news. Now he exploded. "These people killed the shaman; whoever defends them is their accomplice!"

"We are innocent!" exclaimed Cui Buqu. "Investigate us as you will! However, I have one request." He stared at the second prince. "If His Highness finds no evidence, he must make a public apology and treat us as his honored guests!"

Ade sneered. "And if I find that your companion killed our shaman, I will cut off your heads and hang them from the flagpoles, then toss your corpses into the wilderness to be gnawed by wolves!" He waved a hand and called for his men. "Search. I want that man found!"

Turning on his heel, he strode toward Cui Buqu's yurt with his men in tow.

Qiao Xian stepped up to Cui Buqu. "This second prince has had his sights set on us since the beginning," she whispered. "Could he have killed the shaman himself?"

Cui Buqu hummed noncommittally.

Behind them, the Göktürk guards had moved to surround their party, sealing off any escape—undoubtedly another order from the second prince.

The envoys of the other tribes didn't disperse, nor did the khatun and her son. The whole group followed Ade to the Sui envoys' yurt. Yet even with the camp in such an uproar, Apa Khagan didn't once come out for a look.

"Your khagan won't even bestir himself for the death of the Black Moon Shaman?" Cui Buqu asked Jinlian.

Jinlian laughed bitterly. "I had someone take me to see that Kuchean beauty earlier today. She's indeed an unequaled gem. No wonder the khagan is captivated by her!" She frowned at Ade's back, his fierce strides eating up the ground before him. "Do you really have nothing to do with this?" she whispered to Cui Buqu.

"Of course not." Cui Buqu answered her with a clear and limpid gaze. "I swore an oath, didn't I? Rather than doubting me, perhaps you should wonder about the second prince, who wouldn't even do that."

Jinlian's suspicions vanished. She apologized. "I was overly concerned about Xiansheng."

Listening to this exchange, Qiao Xian's mouth twitched, and she bit back a few words. She did speak some Turkic, though she wasn't as fluent as Cui Buqu. When Cui Buqu had sworn, he'd clearly said *I*, not *we*. The conditions of his oath didn't encompass any trouble Feng Xiao might have caused. But this wouldn't have occurred to the Göktürks; in their eyes, Feng Xiao and Cui Buqu were one entity.

Those who failed to pay close attention to Cui Buqu's words often found it came back to bite them. Feng Xiao understood this acutely; unfortunately, he wasn't present to remind Jinlian.

Ade led his men to search Cui Buqu's yurt; sure enough, they found no trace of Feng Xiao. Now certain that Feng Xiao was the culprit, he raised a clamor, calling for Cui Buqu and his company to be punished.

Jinlian once again stepped forward to oppose him. Feng Xiao hadn't been found, let alone caught red-handed. The prince's insistence on their guilt only proved he was champing at the bit to have them killed.

Since the start of the banquet, Fo'er had remained seated, not making a sound nor kicking them while they were down. Qiao Xian had almost suspected he'd swapped personalities. Now the foremost Göktürk expert suddenly emerged to watch the excitement.

More than the khatun and her son were witnessing this; in addition to Fo'er, envoys from the various tribes had all followed them. No matter how high-handed Ade might be, he couldn't convict Cui Buqu's group so hastily without drawing criticism. Tomorrow's Eight Tribes Conference was meant to consolidate the power of the

Western Khaganate. After a brief conference with his confidants, Ade forced himself to calm. He stood outside Cui Buqu's yurt with his hands on his hips, waiting for news as his men continued to search.

"Prince Ade, that man is a powerful martial artist. No weaker than I." Fo'er had finally spoken. He hadn't had a change of heart at all; he'd only been waiting for the opportune moment. "If he weren't injured, he'd have appeared by now. He won't make it far if he's wounded; he must have hidden himself. Perhaps you should check the storerooms and stables."

"Right!" Ade perked up. "Do as he says, quick. Go to my father's yurt as well and inquire, lest the criminal snuck in!"

By this point, Qiao Xian had guessed Feng Xiao had met with something unexpected on his visit to the Black Moon Shaman, resulting in the shaman's death and his own injury. Feng Xiao was a powerful martial artist; he was unlikely to be caught, but he couldn't remain hidden forever. The moment he turned up injured, he'd inevitably be accused of the shaman's murder. Ade and Fo'er were both eyeing them hungrily; there was no chance they'd let them go.

Their situation had become rather thorny. Qiao Xian glanced at Cui Buqu, but his face was placid, as if nothing was amiss. She couldn't remember ever seeing Cui Buqu panic. Qiao Xian felt a surge of admiration as she whispered, "Did you think of a countermeasure?"

Cui Buqu shook his head minutely.

Then how can you be so calm? Qiao Xian looked back at him, puzzled.

Grabbing her hand, Cui Buqu sketched a few words in her palm: *It's all an act.*

Qiao Xian thought it best to say no more.

Just as the second prince was growing impatient, one of the men he'd sent out finally returned: they'd located Feng Xiao.

Overjoyed, the prince shot a look at Cui Buqu that practically screamed *I'd like to see you wiggle out of this one.* He turned to the guards. "Where is he?! Take me there!"

Yet unexpectedly, the guard looked conflicted and began to stammer.

"Out with it!" snapped the second prince. "Unless you want to be considered an accomplice as well?"

Incredible. They hadn't even laid eyes on the man, yet they'd already decided his guilt. But at the news that Feng Xiao had been found, Cui Buqu relaxed. His lips curved in a faint smile.

Ade raised the horsewhip he carried, ready to strike the guard where he stood. The man shrank away, blurting, "He's in Your Highness's yurt!"

"What rubbish! How could he be in my yurt?!" The second prince's expression was thunderous.

"Aha, so it's the second prince who has colluded with the Sui envoys," said Cui Buqu leisurely. "Why not say so before? You were attacking your own ally all along."

"Ridiculous!" Ade's expression was grim as he strode toward his yurt. Flanked by his guards, he viciously threw open the door. His face, previously dark as pitch, turned green from his collar to the tips of his ears.

72

T HE SECOND PRINCE'S yurt wasn't as spacious as the
khagan's, but it was luxuriously furnished, cluttered with
everything from Jiangnan porcelain to wood carvings
from the north. Combined with the ever-present tapestries from
the Western Regions, it dazzled onlookers, extravagant to the
point of disorder. Yet what immediately drew the eye was the bed
covered in an impressive number of stitched-together arctic fox
pelts.

Two people were lying unconscious atop it—a man and a woman,
both in various states of undress.

Such a scene would set anyone's imagination running wild. Ade
hadn't ordered anyone to barricade the door, so all the crowd that
could fit had streamed in behind him. It was too late to chase them
out now.

"What's going on?" Jinlian exclaimed in surprise. It took her only
a moment to recognize the pair on the bed: the man was Feng Xiao,
and the woman was the second prince's favorite concubine.

The faint smell of blood hung in the air within the yurt. Upon
closer inspection, both Feng Xiao and the concubine were bound
with ropes and splattered with various bloodstains. A dagger was
tossed to the side, and the ropes had been loosened, but they showed
no sign of waking.

Ade was still reeling when Cui Buqu stepped forward. "What on earth has happened here?" he cried. "Why is my deputy envoy on the prince's bed?"

Fiery rage burst through the second prince. He rushed toward Feng Xiao on the bed, thinking to drag him up.

But before he could pounce, Feng Xiao's eyes finally fluttered open; he brought a hand up to knead at his temples with a pained expression. When he saw Ade's face mere inches from his own, he shouted in alarm and struck out with his fist.

Ade was only capable of pushing slaves around; he was no match for Feng Xiao. Feng Xiao used no internal energy, only his bare hands—yet within a few blows, the prince was beaten into a howling lump. The guards, who'd been blocked from the yurt thanks to Cui Buqu and the others standing in the entranceway, finally squeezed their way inside and pulled Feng Xiao and the second prince apart.

"How dare you strike me! I'll fucking kill you..." Ade spat a veritable flood of curses in Turkic.

The Göktürk guards rushed forward to seize Feng Xiao. They were overconfident; within seconds, they too were kicked to the ground to join the second prince.

At a gesture from Cui Buqu, Qiao Xian darted over to help as well.

"Everyone *stop*!" Jinlian shouted. She planted herself in the middle, blocking any more guards from coming forward.

"He slept with my woman," roared Ade. "How dare you get in our way! Have you sold your soul to these Central Plains bastards?!"

Jinlian doubted Feng Xiao would do something so crass. But with so many eyes bearing witness to their adultery, she could only guess that Feng Xiao intended to pick a fight with the second prince and had slept with his concubine to provoke him. "Feng-langjun. If your lordship desires women, I can find you as many as you want. Why would you offend the second prince?!"

"Nonsense!" Feng Xiao snarled in fury. "With my face, I could have any woman in the Central Plains! Have you any idea how many beauties would line up to spend a night with me? Yet none of them interest me in the slightest. Your second prince doesn't discriminate between men and women. He must have drugged me while my guard was down—he was hoping for a threesome! Have you ever heard of a man who sleeps with someone else's woman while bleeding all over himself?! I suggest you ask your prince about his shameful proclivities first!"

Few of the onlookers spoke Chinese, so Jinlian translated Feng Xiao's words. The listeners looked at Feng Xiao, then at the woman on the bed. It was true that Feng Xiao was extraordinarily handsome. Why would he need to steal the second prince's concubine? On the other hand, the second prince, like his father, was renowned for his lasciviousness. Dragging a pretty foreigner into his bed didn't seem outside the realm of possibility.

Upon seeing everyone's dubious expressions—including those of his own attendants—Ade almost coughed up a mouthful of blood. For heaven's sake. He was licentious, true, but he didn't bed men—let alone have any strange fetishes like making his partners bleed!

Yixun raised his voice. "Ade, even if you dislike these Central Plainsmen, they're honored guests recognized by our father the khagan. How could you treat a guest like this? Do you think nothing of the Eight Tribes Conference? The envoys from Kucha and Qocho are all here—can they expect similar treatment if they happen to catch your eye?!"

The envoys of the various tribes were all watching this spectacle. At this, the ones who considered themselves handsome all took a large step backward.

They were dependent on the Western Khaganate, it was true. The Sui dynasty was immensely powerful, a nation anyone would be wary of humiliating—yet the second prince had dared to ravish one of their envoys. There was no guarantee he'd restrain himself with anyone else.

His own brother had leveled such an accusation at him. Ade was about to pass out from rage. Breathing through his nose, he spat back at the first prince: "*You're* the one who likes men! Don't think that I'm the same as you! You think Father doesn't know? He's always known, that's why—"

"Ade!" This time it was the Göktürk khatun who stopped him. Her gentle face appeared shrouded in darkness, her aura suddenly fierce. "Look what you've done, yet you're still trying to shirk responsibility? Guards! Call the khagan!"

"What's all this noise? What is going on here?"

After the whole camp had been turned upside down, the main character finally lumbered his way over.

Apa Khagan held a young woman's hand as he walked. Even now, he refused to let his Kuchean concubine go; anyone could see how besotted he was.

Cui Buqu's gaze swept over her beaded headdress and Kuchean robes. She was indeed an incredible beauty, no less than Qiao Xian. But if Qiao Xian was aloof and untouchable, this woman possessed an arresting gentleness. The slightest smile at the corner of her mouth seemed to exude a charming air of decadence. No wonder Apa Khagan had been bewitched, even refusing to attend his own banquet.

As for the khagan himself, there was a spring in his step and a faint sheen of sweat on his forehead, as if he'd been pleasantly exerting himself only moments ago. Like father, like son indeed.

Apa Khagan paid no heed to the knowing looks. He cast around for his son. "Ade!"

"Father, it's all this man's fault!" The second prince jabbed a finger at Feng Xiao. He was apoplectic with fury: nine of ten words out of his mouth were curses. His explanation tumbled out in a heap, leaving Apa Khagan both bewildered and increasingly irritated.

"The shaman is dead, and you're worried about a woman?!" The khagan shook a finger at Ade, giving him a thorough scolding before turning to Yixun. "And you! You have time to watch? Where is the body of the Black Moon Shaman? I must see his esteemed self at once!"

"I've ordered some men to tend to his body, Khagan," said the greater khatun. "Let me go with you."

"Khagan!" Cui Buqu's brows were drawn low in a scowl. "I'm deeply sorry for the loss of your shaman, but I must have a word. The second prince has accused us of murder while taking liberties with my deputy in secret! I demand an explanation!"

"Once I have seen to the body of our shaman, I will of course give you a satisfactory answer." Apa Khagan raked his gaze over the assembly. "I hope this matter will not affect tomorrow's conference, nor the friendship we all share."

The envoys hastened to express that it wouldn't. With a final nod, Apa Khagan hurried off with his wife, concubines, and a group of close officials at his heels.

"Father!" Ade shouted, unwilling to let it go. But the khagan didn't turn or even slow his steps. It seemed he'd see no results tonight. He shot Feng Xiao a fierce glare and dropped a final curse, lest Feng Xiao think matters settled between them. At last, he dashed after his father.

Only Cui Buqu, Qiao Xian and Feng Xiao remained, along with Ade's lovely concubine, still unconscious on the bed. "Qiao Xian," Feng Xiao finally said. "Give my venerable self a hand."

Qiao Xian had assumed Feng Xiao faked the bloodstains all over his robes to rattle the second prince. But as she approached, the smell of blood grew noticeably thicker. She looked at him quizzically.

Cui Buqu seemed to have understood. "Help him back to our yurt first."

The three of them returned to their yurt, where Feng Xiao sat down on the soft bedding and began to undress. Before Qiao Xian could explode at him, he'd removed his shirt and turned to show his back. A bone-deep wound marred the skin near his shoulder blade, surrounded by dark fingerprints—evidence of internal injuries.

Cui Buqu sent Qiao Xian to find some salve and bandages for Feng Xiao's back. She bent to dress the wound, comprehension finally dawning. "So you purposely cut yourself and that woman earlier?"

Feng Xiao sat as she applied the salve, his body loose and relaxed, as if he felt no pain. "Of course I did. How else to disguise the smell of blood?"

"The second prince is quick to anger, but he's not a fool," said Cui Buqu. "It won't take him long to realize. Even if he doesn't, Fo'er will remind him."

Feng Xiao was a master martial artist. No matter what methods the second prince used, he shouldn't have been able to subdue him, let alone wound him. Yet Feng Xiao seemed unconcerned. "Let's get through tonight first."

Cui Buqu furrowed his brow. "Few can rival your skill, especially in a place this remote. Who here is capable of injuring you?"

"My opponent seemed to have anticipated my visit," said Feng Xiao. "They set up an illusory array around the stone house and lured me inside. Their martial arts weren't much inferior to mine. Combined with the territory advantage, I admit I fell into their trap."

Fortunately, he'd spotted Ade's subordinates during his escape and tailed them to his yurt. He'd knocked the poor girl out, then taken advantage of everyone's surprise to make a fool of the second prince.

"So you did kill the Black Moon Shaman?" asked Cui Buqu.

"That's the strange part," said Feng Xiao. "I did injure them, whoever they were, and it was more than a flesh wound—but they were a powerful martial artist; I couldn't have killed them. The fire only started after I left."

"Could someone stronger than you have arrived after you and killed the Black Moon Shaman?" Qiao Xian speculated.

"Looking at the entire Western Khaganate," said Feng Xiao, "the only one capable of such a thing is Fo'er."

He looked at Cui Buqu, who shook his head. "Fo'er was sitting with us at the table the whole banquet," he said. "He never left."

"Then it's even stranger," said Feng Xiao.

"There's one more possibility," said Cui Buqu.

Feng Xiao and Qiao Xian both looked at him.

Cui Buqu spoke slowly. "The Black Moon Shaman might have been dead before you arrived."

Feng Xiao sat up in surprise. The movement pulled at his injury, and he sucked in a breath.

"Whomever you fought is likely the Black Moon Shaman's murderer. If they'd managed to kill or trap you there, the Black Moon

Shaman's corpse would have sealed your guilt. But since you managed to flee, all they could do was burn the body and destroy the evidence."

Feng Xiao mulled this over. "But how did they know I'd come? I only thought of it myself at the last moment. Not even Jinlian knew."

"Their target might not have been you—you just happened to run into them. But why kill the Black Moon Shaman? That's what puzzles me. Could it be someone from the Western Khaganate? Or one of the envoys who came to attend the conference?"

"Perhaps it was a personal grudge against the man," Feng Xiao offered. "All kinds of people are here for the conference; it wouldn't be hard to blend into the crowd."

The plots of men would never overcome the will of the heavens. The world's most intelligent man couldn't have predicted the circumstances they found themselves in. Even Cui Buqu was flummoxed, unsure where to start.

Qiao Xian seemed to sense his worries and spoke up to comfort him. "I thought the first prince would cower on the sidelines, too afraid to speak. I never expected him to stand up to the second prince. Your lordship's move to befriend him was the correct one."

"Those brothers have a long-standing feud between them. Even the most timid man has his breaking point. The first prince has endured a long time; he's far past his limit. I just fanned the flames. But it appears the first prince does have some ability."

The greater khatun usually stayed quiet, yet she, too, had stood with her son in that critical moment. This wasn't the cowardly and incompetent character Jinlian had described. But these were the Western Khaganate's own internal politics. They might be exploited to encourage the Western Göktürks to lean toward the Sui dynasty, but they weren't much help in the current situation.

"Tomorrow is the Eight Tribes Conference," said Cui Buqu. "Our original plan was to have you steal the spotlight, but once the second prince comes to his senses, he'll do all he can to get in your way. Fo'er is also sure to exploit the situation to kill you, so..."

He looked at Feng Xiao but didn't continue.

Feng Xiao gazed back at him.

The chief of the Zuoyue Bureau, ever dispassionate in the face of mortal affairs, seemed to hesitate, as if unwilling to let Feng Xiao take such risks. He sat silent, his gaze clear and open. But that look alone was worth a thousand words.

For the first time, Feng Xiao's stony heart cracked open just a hair, softening the tiniest bit. "This injury is nothing," he told Cui Buqu. "Tomorrow, let them try if they dare."

Cui Buqu looked relieved. "Wonderful. Then we'll leave everything to Feng-xiong," he said, smiling faintly.

Feng Xiao was taken aback. Wasn't that a little too quick? Cui Buqu couldn't even try to talk him out of it for a few more seconds?

He had volunteered on his own, so why did he feel like a nice girl being forced into prostitution?! To hell with that clear and open gaze!

73

THE BLACK MOON SHAMAN'S passing was a great blow to the Western Khaganate, but even this couldn't keep the Eight Tribes Conference from proceeding.

The next morning, Cui Buqu and the rest had just finished washing and changing when Jinlian's maid, Muge, brought their breakfast. Once they'd eaten, she explained, she'd take them to the conference.

"Cui-xiansheng, my mistress says if you wish to see the shaman's body, she will arrange it," said Muge. "But you must be quick."

Last night, the second prince had accused Feng Xiao of murder, and not an hour later, Feng Xiao had appeared in his yurt. It wasn't difficult to connect the dots. Even if Jinlian had been considerably more slow-witted than she was, she would have realized this was fishy. Besides, she'd personally witnessed Feng Xiao's martial arts. Ade having successfully ambushed Feng Xiao was about as likely as the sun rising in the west. She still suspected Feng Xiao had something to do with the death of the Black Moon Shaman—though Cui Buqu had vociferously denied it, and it was true they had no motive.

Ade, on the other hand, was audacious and unscrupulous. It was absolutely possible he'd murdered the shaman himself and tried to pin the blame on Cui Buqu's group.

Jinlian had witnessed Cui Buqu's autopsy skills in Qiemo. She obviously hoped he could glean the cause of the Black Moon Shaman's death.

But Cui Buqu shook his head. "In order to destroy the evidence, the murderer burned the body. I fear they'll have ensured there's nothing left to find. Even if I go, it won't do us any good."

Muge only had a hazy understanding of his meaning, but she'd pass the message to Jinlian.

Cui Buqu and Feng Xiao partook of a Göktürk breakfast, though the meal wasn't anything spectacular. Stomachs filled, they followed Muge to the lake.

Translated into Chinese, its name was Verdant Lake, so called for the lush green grasses that surrounded it. It was midmorning when they arrived, followed closely by the second prince surrounded by his retinue of attendants.

Gone was his fuming rage of the previous night. He swept a cool glance over Cui Buqu and Feng Xiao, malice tugging up the corner of his mouth. He'd undoubtedly hatched some new and nefarious plot.

Fo'er's gaze, too, lingered on Feng Xiao for a moment before moving ponderously away.

"He knows I'm injured," said Feng Xiao.

A martial arts expert became a true master not merely through fighting prowess, but also razor-sharp perception and decisive judgment. When Feng Xiao boasted that he ranked within the top ten or even five as a fighter, his confidence came from his strength, not overblown arrogance. Fo'er had fought him twice and knew how formidable this man was. But the gap between them was small; Fo'er likely also ranked in the top ten.

Had Feng Xiao been uninjured, Fo'er would've had to consider carefully before launching an attack. But after last night's fiasco,

Fo'er was sure Feng Xiao had been hurt, and that the wound wasn't a minor one—otherwise, there'd have been no need to mask the smell of blood. Fo'er would do whatever he could to force Feng Xiao onto the field today.

This so-called conference wasn't the kind where everyone sat down for a friendly chat. The Göktürks were rough and straightforward: first they used martial arts to decide the pecking order. If one won, they were deemed worthy of respect, and all the discussions would go smoothly. But if one lost... If the Sui dynasty's envoys fell to a single strike, who would believe in the might of their emperor?

"He's guaranteed to request a one-on-one match with you," said Cui Buqu.

"So he can kill me in front of everyone," said Feng Xiao.

Cui Buqu nodded. Disposing of Feng Xiao was a sure way to intimidate everyone present.

A lazy smile spread over Feng Xiao's face. "Goodness, I'm so scared."

They spoke no more on it—Apa Khagan had arrived to begin the conference.

As attendants placed fine wines and exquisite delicacies before all the guests, Apa Khagan raised his glass, thanking the envoys for coming from afar. He raised a cup of wine to the Sui dynasty and another to Ishbara Khagan, honoring both Cui Buqu and Fo'er with a flood of courteous words.

When this Göktürk khagan wasn't losing himself in lustful pleasures, Cui Buqu mused, his mind was quite clear.

Ishbara practiced an aggressive brand of diplomacy: he'd sent Fo'er to intimidate Apa Khagan into allying with him, though he must also have offered tempting benefits. Fo'er had beaten them to Suyab by several days, which was why they had faced such a cold welcome.

But when Apa Khagan had seen the people of the Sui dynasty were not to be trifled with, he'd backtracked and treated them with courtesy. After the Black Moon Shaman's death last night, he hadn't accused them. Instead, he'd deescalated the situation, allowing Cui Buqu's party a peaceful night's rest.

As Cui Buqu's mind wandered, Apa Khagan continued addressing the envoys, his smile bright and amiable. It seemed he'd had a pleasant night—the Black Moon Shaman's murder had no effect on his enjoyment of his new concubine.

He clapped his hands, and several Göktürk warriors came forward brandishing curved sabers.

Unlike the graceful dance of the Kuchean girl the previous night, today's performance was a sword dance, a display of masculine vigor. This style had evolved on the battlefield where real blades and spears glinted with killing intent, and the dance was likewise full of murderous energy. The warriors moved in unison, leaping and somersaulting through the air. It was powerful in its simplicity, a spectacular sight.

But few people were in the mood to appreciate the dance—most were more concerned about the upcoming contest of strength. The envoys of the smaller Western Regions nations wondered how to stand out, while the lesser Göktürk tribes agonized over how to avoid annexation. The second prince contemplated how to make Cui Buqu and his companions suffer, while the first prince recalled his burst of courage last night, and how he'd opposed his younger brother. He stirred restlessly with excitement, hoping for the chance to give his arrogant sibling another kick. Through it all, Apa Khagan held his Kuchean beauty in his lap, laughing and whispering in her ear, watching the saber dance with no concern for anyone else's plans.

As for Fo'er, he eyed Feng Xiao from the other side of the dancing warriors, and his lips curved in a meaningful smile.

You can't hide your injury from me. We were evenly matched in the past, but you'll die here today.

When the sword dance was over and the warriors dispersed, Ade seized his opportunity. He rose and swept his gaze over the crowd, his expression haughty and satisfied. "Father, our conferences usually begin with the standard martial arts contest, but we have quite a few special guests this year. We should change the rules. Otherwise, it would be disrespectful to them."

Jinlian saw at once where he was going. "Khagan, the conference's martial competitions are an honored tradition here in Suyab. If anything, it would be disrespectful to alter them."

Apa Khagan raised a hand to silence her. "What kind of changes?" he asked with interest.

Ade shot Jinlian a gleeful look. "In the past, the competition started with a horseback archery contest, and the winner scored based on distance and accuracy. But Fo'er is the preeminent martial artist across both the Eastern and Western Khaganate. Such a contest is an insult to his skills. Instead, let's try this: have one person ride while holding an apple and the archer remain on the ground. The archer must maintain a distance of a hundred paces, and whoever hits the fruit will be the victor."

Murmurs of surprise rose from the crowd. The ancient practice of hitting a poplar leaf at a hundred paces was sufficient to deem one a master archer. Now the target would be in motion, and not even at a constant speed: someone had to carry it in their hand, jostled up and down as they rode. Missing the fruit was the least of their worries—what if the arrow hit the rider instead?

Ade was proposing using human targets.

He'd made up his mind last night; Neither Feng Xiao nor Cui Buqu would slip from his grasp. He wouldn't let the archers use some random slaves to carry fruit for them. "Both archers and target bearers must be of suitable status. They cannot be replaced with slaves and servants."

Fo'er clapped his hands. "A wonderful idea from the second prince. Allow me to do the opening honors!"

Before Apa Khagan or Cui Buqu could object, he instructed his deputy envoy to take the apple, mount a horse, and gallop ahead.

The horse cantered over a hundred paces away before wheeling around and galloping back. Only then did Fo'er raise his bow. He pulled the bowstring to full draw, infused the bow and arrow with internal energy, and let it fly.

Everyone squinted, watching the arrow streak toward its mark.

No ordinary marksman could hit such a target at this distance. They'd need to consider the trajectory of the arrow, and besides, Fo'er's bow had a maximum range of a hundred paces. But after the infusion of internal energy, the arrow didn't fall or even slow past a hundred paces. It flew straight until it pierced the apple in the deputy envoy's hand clean through.

Thunderous cheers exploded as the crowd burst into applause. Regardless of whether they were Ishbara's enemies or allies, Fo'er's shot was impeccable. Strength was worthy of respect.

Fo'er lowered his bow. He looked at Feng Xiao and smiled.

He had it all figured out. Of their party of three, Cui Buqu knew not a speck of martial arts, let alone archery. Qiao Xian was a respectable martial artist, but not necessarily a good marksman. This was a skill that required keen sight—if anyone could do it, armies wouldn't need dedicated archers. Even if Qiao Xian could draw a bow, there was no way she could hit a target as small as an apple from a hundred paces. And if their performance was in any way inferior to Fo'er's, they'd lose.

The loss of an archery contest seemed a small thing. But it was not only the Sui dynasty's reputation in the various nations of the Western Regions at stake—Cui Buqu risked losing Apa Khagan's respect when it came time to pick his allies. If they didn't want to lose, Feng Xiao had to compete. Yet that, too, was to Fo'er advantage. Feng Xiao was injured; drawing the bow would aggravate his wound. Even if Feng Xiao won the first match, he was sure to lose the second.

Fo'er smiled broadly. *What will you do? It's your loss either way.*

Cui Buqu knit his brows, as if he were also worried. He turned to murmur something to Feng Xiao, who looked dissatisfied. After a hushed debate, they both fell silent.

Fo'er watched their quiet dispute. A disagreement before the battle, hearts divided—it only increased their chance of losing.

The thought brought him immense pleasure.

Ade fanned the flames. "Are you afraid, envoys of the Sui dynasty? I can hardly blame you. You're no match for Fo'er, the strongest Göktürk martial artist. Admit defeat now and forget any alliance. I'll plead with my father to gift you some cattle and sheep so you won't embarrass yourselves too greatly when you return to the Central Plains."

Fo'er and Ade weren't allies—in truth, they shared no relationship whatsoever. Before today, Fo'er had found this second prince coarse and infuriating, inferior to Ishbara Khagan in every way. With such an heir, the Western Khaganate would never be powerful. But now they shared a common enemy. Fo'er didn't need to say a word for Ade to start hopping about of his own volition. Suddenly, Fo'er found this prince much less irritating.

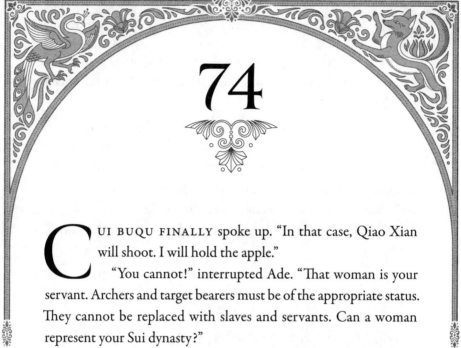

74

CUI BUQU FINALLY spoke up. "In that case, Qiao Xian will shoot. I will hold the apple."

"You cannot!" interrupted Ade. "That woman is your servant. Archers and target bearers must be of the appropriate status. They cannot be replaced with slaves and servants. Can a woman represent your Sui dynasty?"

"Qiao Xian is not my servant," said Cui Buqu coolly. "She holds a high position within the Zuoyue Bureau and is an official of the imperial court."

"The Eastern Khaganate sent their chief envoy to shoot while his deputy held the apple!" Ade changed tack. "That woman doesn't hold a rank equivalent to the Eastern Khaganate's deputy envoy. You may choose her, but her inferior status will be taken into account in the judging." He looked to Apa Khagan. "Father, what do you say?"

"This..." The khagan stroked his beard and hesitated but didn't disagree.

Ade was elated. "Do you insist on sending that woman to shoot?" he asked Cui Buqu.

Cui Buqu frowned and glanced toward Feng Xiao, who slowly stood up. "I'll do it."

The second prince looked like a cat that had gotten into the cream. His plan had succeeded.

Fo'er watched as Feng Xiao raised his bow and nocked the arrow. He waited until Cui Buqu was galloping toward him at full speed, then let fly.

The arrow whistled through the air and struck the apple.

The distance between Cui Buqu and Feng Xiao was almost exactly the same as Fo'er's shot. Jinlian fretted in silence, afraid Apa Khagan might show bias. But this time, the khagan was fair: "Both our honored guests are equally outstanding archers."

Ade hadn't expected Cui Buqu to comply so readily. He snorted coldly.

Yet Fo'er, though he made no move or sound, was deeply pleased. Regardless of where Feng Xiao's wound was located, Fo'er was certain that draw had aggravated it.

Feng Xiao lowered the bow and cupped his hands at Apa Khagan, then returned to his seat. His movements were free and graceful; there was no sign of discomfort. But Fo'er noticed a stiffness to his right shoulder when he turned, the motion the slightest bit unnatural.

Such details might escape others, but they didn't escape Fo'er, who'd watched him closely since the moment he stood.

By now the sun had climbed in the sky, and the foot of Mount Sanmi was broiling. Most of the assembled guests wore light and breezy attire, but peeking out of Feng Xiao's collar was a white cotton top, with a thick outer robe layered over. This wasn't because Feng Xiao feared the cold. His shoulder must be bandaged, and the additional layers were to conceal that his left and right shoulders weren't level.

So it was his right shoulder that was injured. Fo'er's lips curved.

Fo'er and Feng Xiao's spectacular showings had elicited thunderous applause from the remaining envoys, but with it came a creeping sense of inferiority. Those who still insisted on competing either fell short of the required distance, failed to hit the mark dead on, or missed completely. A few unfortunates managed to shoot the horse instead, almost crushing the rider.

After that, no one dared to try again, and the first contest of the conference ended in a draw. Yet having failed to embarrass the Central Plainsmen, the second prince was far from satisfied. He set out to make more trouble.

"Father, the first contest ended too quickly today. We can't let the same happen with the second!"

Apa Khagan nodded. "What do you propose?"

"The martial arts of the Sui envoy's maid left a deep impression on me yesterday," said Ade. At the words *deep impression*, he gritted his teeth. His smile turned savage. "My own subordinate Namudo wishes for a match, so he may learn from her skills."

The khagan looked toward Cui Buqu. "What say you, honored guests?"

"Who is Namudo?" asked Cui Buqu.

A middle-aged Göktürk man had stood silently behind the second prince. Now he took a step forward and saluted Cui Buqu in the Göktürk manner. Despite being Ade's man, he had none of his master's brash aura. Cui Buqu didn't need Feng Xiao to tell him this was a top-notch martial artist.

"Can you win?" Cui Buqu asked Qiao Xian in a whisper.

"I haven't seen him in action," said Qiao Xian. "He wasn't at the second prince's side yesterday. But look how calm he is—he must be strong. This subordinate is willing to try."

Cui Buqu read between the lines: had this man been present yesterday, Qiao Xian might not have been able to step on the second prince's head the way she had.

Many looked incredulous as they watched the delicate-looking Qiao Xian step gracefully out. Only a few had witnessed the scene in the royal yurt the day before, when Qiao Xian had crushed the second prince into the floor. How could this young, beautiful woman be a match for a Göktürk warrior like Namudo?

Before anyone could wonder further, Namudo threw the first punch.

A single glance revealed the power behind that blow—his was a style that valued sweeping movements and brute force.

Qiao Xian was slender, her footwork swift and agile, a complete contrast to Namudo. Yet she didn't shrink in the face of his heavy blows. Two silhouettes clashed, one gray and one white. The first was as fierce and vigorous as a tiger, his every punch capable of collapsing mountains and shattering earth as it whistled through the air. The second was weightless as a dragon cutting through water, her sword glare weaving through the wind from his fists, a wicked killing intent cloaked behind an ethereal exterior. If her opponent was even a little deceived, even slightly careless, they'd find themselves at her mercy.

Namudo should have looked down on an opponent like Qiao Xian, but he didn't. He brought his full focus to fighting her and ignored all else.

"How does he compare to Qiao Xian?" Cui Buqu asked.

"In time, he might become a second Fo'er," came Feng Xiao's answer.

Cui Buqu frowned.

To progress along the path of martial arts required hard work, but talent was also a significant factor. Feng Xiao's natural talent was extraordinary; Fo'er's, too, went without saying. No matter how hard they worked, someone without talent would never become a peerless expert, let alone a martial arts grandmaster.

If Feng Xiao said Namudo could grow to rival Fo'er, he had recognized Namudo's gifts. What was more, Namudo showed neither arrogance nor contempt when facing a woman like Qiao Xian. In this regard, he showed better judgment than Fo'er. Against this opponent, Qiao Xian would find it difficult to emerge victorious.

The world teemed with talented people. There was always a taller mountain, always a higher sky—always another better than oneself. Considering the size of the Khaganate, Fo'er couldn't be the only expert. While he'd monopolized their attention, Namudo had popped up.

"It will be hard for Qiao Xian to win," said Feng Xiao.

If Feng Xiao could see this, Fo'er could as well. He watched as one figure flipped and whirled upon the field, while the other stood stolid as a mountain. He smiled.

Ade, however, remained anxious. He was a mediocre fighter and couldn't tell who was the stronger of the two. Like many amateur spectators, he felt Namudo's slow, steady strikes were inferior to the quick and graceful flow of Qiao Xian's forms.

"What are you smiling for?!" The second prince snarled, glimpsing Fo'er's expression out of the corner of his eye.

Fo'er was unprovoked. He answered good-naturedly. "I'm merely happy for you, Second Prince."

Ade scowled. "What's there to be happy about?!"

"Namudo's victory is nigh."

"You mean Namudo can defeat that woman?" the prince asked, taken aback.

"The Central Plains woman has superior qinggong," said Fo'er, "but she will eventually exhaust her stamina. Namudo has abundant internal energy, and his fist techniques, though simple, are powerful.

There is a saying in the Central Plains: 'the truly artful are crude in appearance.'"

At that moment, Namudo struck Qiao Xian hard in the stomach. She froze and stumbled back a few steps, barely managing to recover her balance. Namudo seized his advantage and closed in, leaping up to kick the sword from her hand. He spun in the air, and his foot slammed into Qiao Xian's waist.

Qiao Xian blanched and struck out with a palm. Namudo had jumped back, but a line of bright crimson trickled from the corner of Qiao Xian's mouth: she'd suffered an internal injury.

"Stop!" Cui Buqu rose swiftly from his seat. "We concede! Stop the fight!"

Gratified, Ade urged Namudo, "Don't stop! Keep fighting!"

Namudo didn't move. "She's conceded the bout."

"Who is your master?!" Ade roared. "I want that woman dead!"

"Khagan!" Jinlian yelled, unable to watch any longer.

"Ade, sit down!" barked Apa Khagan.

"Father," Ade complained, "the Central Plains sent a woman as an envoy. This is an insult to us! On top of that, this woman laid her hands on me yesterday. Would publicly losing her life in a martial arts contest not be fair payback?!"

"This is the Eight Tribes Conference. It's not a venue for your personal revenge," said Apa Khagan coldly. "If I tell you to sit down, then sit!"

Qiao Xian slowly made her way back to Cui Buqu's side.

"How is it?" Cui Buqu asked in concern.

Qiao Xian shook her head—she was fine.

Within the jianghu, Qiao Xian was considered a second-tier martial artist. Losing to Namudo wasn't unexpected. Before she'd entered the arena, Feng Xiao, Cui Buqu, and even Qiao Xian herself had anticipated this outcome.

Cui Buqu's expression was one of faint anger and suppressed panic. It seemed to confirm all Fo'er's speculations about Feng Xiao. These three were cornered; they'd hoped to steal the spotlight today, yet instead they'd suffered defeat.

But the final blow had yet to be struck. It was time for Fo'er himself to step in.

Fo'er calmly got to his feet. He gazed at Feng Xiao from afar and raised his voice. "I wish to challenge Feng-langjun to a match."

He narrowed his eyes, scrutinizing Feng Xiao. Fo'er had failed to defeat him twice in their previous encounters. Today, before the eyes of the crowd, he would kill Feng Xiao openly and honorably, but not before making him accept Fo'er as his better.

So focused was Fo'er on Feng Xiao, he missed that Cui Buqu had spoken. But Feng Xiao heard him.

"I had Qiao Xian go to great pains to create this opportunity. Please don't waste it, Deputy Chief Feng."

Feng Xiao smiled. "Would you really be so harsh on an injured man?"

Cui Buqu said nothing more, but every line of his face, down to the set of his brows and the flutter of his lashes, said the same thing: *Yes, I would.*

75

CUI BUQU HAD a heart as hard as iron. Feng Xiao breathed a quiet sigh, face showing helplessness as he walked toward Fo'er.

He walked slowly—almost hesitantly. Fo'er didn't hurry him. He waited patiently until Feng Xiao was a few feet away.

"Are you well, Deputy Chief Feng?" he asked, all concern.

"I am."

Fo'er smiled a little at the sight of Feng Xiao's calm facade. "If Deputy Chief Feng is not at his best today, I'll let you make the first three moves."

"Sure!" said Feng Xiao.

Fo'er was speechless.

He hadn't expected Feng Xiao to agree so readily. He stared for a moment but received only an innocent smile in return. This man was the deputy chief of the Jiejian Bureau, a person of high rank and authority, and a martial arts grandmaster. Shouldn't he be brimming with youthful vigor and arrogance? Yet not only had Feng Xiao failed to haughtily refuse the handicap, he'd accepted it without the slightest hesitation.

Instantly, Fo'er regretted his offer. But the words were spoken; he couldn't take them back. All he could do was beckon toward Feng Xiao. "Then please go ahead."

Feng Xiao was entirely unapologetic. He sprang into the air like a crane spreading its wings, featherlight, and swept toward Fo'er at lightning speed—swift yet utterly soundless.

Fo'er's heart went cold; he instinctively moved to counterattack before he remembered his own promise. In a blink, he switched from offense to defense and dodged to the side.

But Feng Xiao clung to him like a shadow. Wherever Fo'er stepped, Feng Xiao followed, striking out with palms channeled full of internal energy.

The words he'd spoken bound him; Fo'er reined in his attacks and dodged Feng Xiao a second time. He was beginning to realize Feng Xiao didn't need these concessions at all. He'd only allowed Feng Xiao three moves, but to Fo'er, the assault felt unending. He thought quickly—he wasn't here to spar, and the onlookers likely couldn't tell how many moves Feng Xiao had made. Without warning, he switched from defense to offense, driving his palm toward Feng Xiao's right shoulder.

Feng Xiao danced aside. His figure was light and graceful as he drifted a foot into the air, blocking Fo'er's attack.

"You promised me three moves. How come you gave up after two?" He laughed.

"Deputy Chief Feng must have misremembered!" Fo'er sneered. He didn't slow his attacks in the slightest.

Fo'er's techniques had always had a bold style, but now there was an uncanny variability to them. He circled Feng Xiao, looking for an opening to deal him a fatal blow. But Feng Xiao was just as swift as he flashed left and right, his clothes swirling, leaving Fo'er no gap to find.

They'd yet to start fighting properly. When martial artists of their caliber went all-out, the sight was nothing like their current game of hide-and-seek. To onlookers, Feng Xiao's moves appeared downright cowardly, as if he was too afraid to face Fo'er straight on. Fo'er, on the contrary, took this as more evidence that Feng Xiao was injured and feared a direct confrontation. He could dodge all he liked and deplete his strength until it ran out. Fo'er was in no rush.

Yet on the sidelines, Ade was ill at ease.

After the disgrace he'd suffered last night, he hated Feng Xiao and his group to the bone. Had any of the Han slaves they kept on the grasslands humiliated him thusly, the second prince would have chopped off their heads and fed them to the wolves without a second thought. But he couldn't even beat Qiao Xian; confronting Feng Xiao was out of the question. Their status as envoys tied his hands for now, but his heart was filled with simmering rage.

Fo'er and Feng Xiao had tied in the archery contest, much to the second prince's consternation. He wished for nothing more than to see Fo'er send Feng Xiao to his grave with the single strike of a palm. With only two Sui envoys left—one an invalid, the other a woman— there would be nothing to worry about. The neighboring nations' image of the Sui dynasty would plummet, and Apa Khagan would side with Ishbara. No longer would he entertain an alliance with the Sui dynasty, and that harridan Jinlian wouldn't dare strut about. Once they all fell from grace, Ade would be free to kill them or skin them as he pleased.

He stared at the shifting silhouettes dancing on the battlefield, flames dancing in his eyes. His thoughts were like a blazing inferno, ready to burn all the despicable wretches of the Central Plains to ash.

Fo'er's third palm strike missed. He frowned. Over the last dozen exchanges, Feng Xiao had remained evasive, rarely counterattacking. Yet somehow, he had dodged or parried each one of Fo'er's moves at the last instant.

Why wasn't he striking back?

The longer it went on, the more Fo'er itched to force him to attack. The wind from his palm roared like mountain gales, sweeping toward its target and piercing Feng Xiao's cloak of true qi, leaving him with nowhere to hide—now he'd *have* to meet Fo'er head-on.

Their palms slammed into each other as two bursts of true qi collided with a deafening *bang*. The very ground seemed to heave as if two mountains crashed into each other and crumbled, stone shattering and sliding down steep slopes. Piercing agony spiked through Fo'er's palm as a sudden thought surfaced in his mind: all his conclusions were based on the premise that Feng Xiao was injured.

What if Feng Xiao wasn't injured at all?

Fo'er had fought Feng Xiao twice. He knew he'd come up short, but he'd subconsciously refused to accept it. He was the Khaganate's foremost martial expert. Across the vast reaches of the Central Plains, who could be his match? If Feng Xiao was injured, Fo'er would no longer be at a disadvantage. They'd be equal in strength.

Neither Feng Xiao's bizarre behavior last night nor his unnatural stance when drawing the bow had looked fake. Fo'er was confident in his victory.

The two separated midair, touching down on the ground.

Fo'er shook out his sleeve and something slipped down into his palm. A moment later, a tiny and exquisite vajra was clasped in his hand.

At first it was only the length of a finger. Yet with a gentle flick of Fo'er's wrist, the vajra extended until it was half the length of an arm. Secure in his grip, it swung toward Feng Xiao in an arc of golden light.

All sorts of strange weapons littered the world. Most preferred swords or sabers, but exceptions existed. Feng Xiao, for instance, preferred the zither. He could inflict damage with its music or use the instrument as a blunt weapon. But he didn't have a zither now. He didn't have any proper weapon at all. Faced with a vajra that was rushing toward his head like a meteor, he had two choices: avoid it, or face it head-on.

Fo'er was certain Feng Xiao would try to evade; thus before this move, he'd sealed all Feng Xiao's escape routes. Now that the vajra was impossible to avoid, Feng Xiao would have to give the battle his all.

Feng Xiao sucked in a breath, drawing up a lungful of true qi. He raised himself up as if preparing to catch the vajra with his bare hands.

How useless. Fo'er's mouth opened in a silent, sneering laugh. The fatal strike wouldn't come from the vajra, but from another place entirely.

As Feng Xiao caught the vajra in one hand, Fo'er's empty palm streaked toward a vital acupoint on Feng Xiao's chest. He channeled every ounce of his power into this blow. Even if Feng Xiao hadn't been wounded, he was distracted by the vajra—it was impossible for him to bring his full strength to bear against Fo'er's palm strike. And he was sure that Feng Xiao was hurt.

"Why are you so certain I'm injured?"

A voice as light as a feather drifted into Fo'er's ear.

Fo'er's vajra connected with empty air. His palm, too, felt like it had struck cotton, the weight of the blow completely absorbed.

"I've been waiting for you to use your full strength," continued Feng Xiao. "You're much more patient now than you were in Liugong City. However—"

The moment he'd missed, Fo'er had sensed something wrong and drawn back in retreat. But it was too late. Feng Xiao landed beside

Fo'er at a speed far beyond what he'd used to evade. One of his hands slammed into Fo'er's shoulder blade, while the other plunged a sword into Fo'er's back.

When two masters fought, neither could afford the slightest slip. Fo'er coughed up a mouthful of blood, but he didn't pause for a second. He lurched forward, trying to free himself from the blade piercing a key acupoint in his back.

He'd reacted swiftly, but Feng Xiao had seen through him. With an even greater speed, he turned his wrist and twisted the sword deeper. His other hand released Fo'er's shoulder, then tapped several acupoints along the back of his neck and head.

Fo'er's eyes went wide as he struggled to maintain consciousness. He wrenched his body around and grabbed at Feng Xiao, as if to take Feng Xiao down with him. But Feng Xiao's attack had succeeded; he had no reason to stay close. He flickered a few steps to the side, then slammed his palm into Fo'er's heart.

Fo'er spat another mouthful of blood.

He'd finally lost the strength to resist; his body crumpled to the ground. Yet his eyes remained open, fixed on Feng Xiao, his hatred undying.

Feng Xiao moved his arm experimentally. He'd paid a hefty price for catching his opponent's vajra. The impact had broken his arm and damaged his muscles and tendons, and he'd suffered some internal injuries.

It was a small price in exchange for Fo'er's life.

"You were right. I am injured." Feng Xiao squatted down beside Fo'er, who was breathing his last. "You probably didn't know: there's a secret technique known as meridian sealing. It temporarily seals your injured meridians in exchange for a boost in power. There are side effects, yes, but it allowed me to take your life. A worthy trade. Also…"

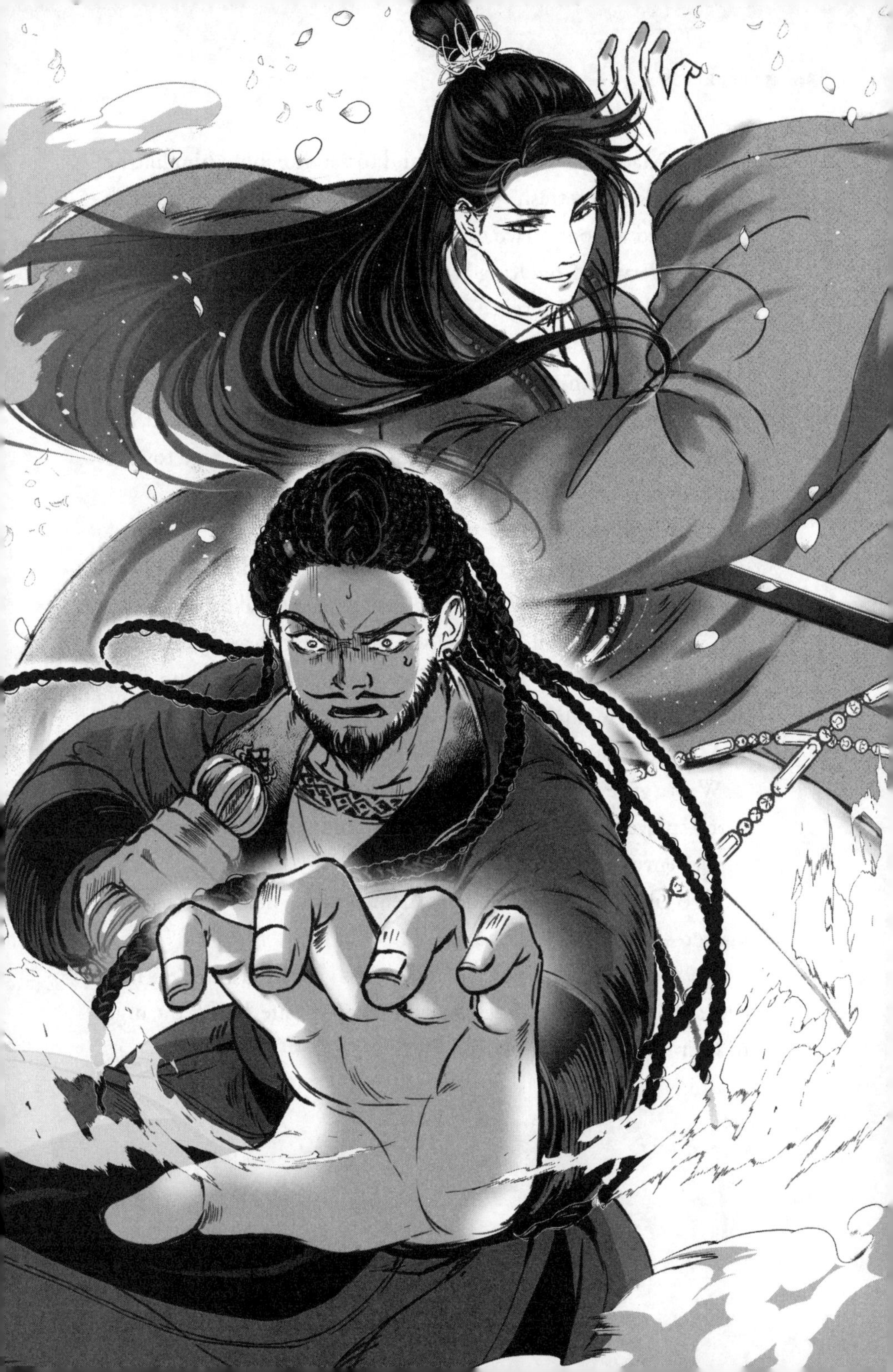

Feng Xiao picked up the vajra and tossed it behind him like he was throwing away trash. "Did you imagine you're the only one with a concealed weapon? Two can play at that game. When you arrive in the underworld, tell King Yama you don't want to run into me in your next life. Ah, I forgot. You Göktürks don't have a King Yama. Then go be a wandering ghost, O foremost expert of the Göktürks."

Fo'er opened his mouth as if to speak, but only fresh blood spilled out. Whatever last words he had remained unsaid. At last he fell still—in the end, he'd passed away from sheer rage toward Feng Xiao.

All around was stunned silence.

The greatest expert of the Göktürks had perished. Half an hour earlier, the crowd had been certain Feng Xiao would be the one to lose his dignity or his life. Prince Ade sat frozen with a grape halfway to his mouth. He stared at Feng Xiao, mouth agape and hand hanging in midair, looking for all the world like a shocked statue.

Feng Xiao turned to him and smiled.

With a great shout, Fo'er's deputy envoy rushed toward Feng Xiao. Blood sprayed into the air, hitting the ground at the same time as the deputy envoy's corpse.

Two envoys of Ishbara, one of them almost a martial arts grandmaster—both dead, just like that.

The second prince's hand trembled. His gaze fixed on Fo'er's face, eyes still wide in death. For the first time in his life, he felt the urge to shrink behind his father and hide.

76

THE CROWD STOOD frozen. Everyone, Apa Khagan included, stared blankly as Feng Xiao wiped the blood from his blade onto Fo'er's clothes, before slowly sheathing it at his waist and walking toward the second prince.

"Stay back! I'm warning you—another step and you're dead! *Guards!* Help me!" Ade shouted incoherently, uncaring of whether Feng Xiao understood.

Step by step, Feng Xiao stalked closer. Terror overcame the second prince; he threw away all other considerations and half-stumbled, half-crawled behind Apa Khagan, staring at Feng Xiao in alarm. Göktürk guards stepped forward with sabers in hand, warning Feng Xiao to stay back. He obediently stopped and raised a hand, uncurling his fingers to reveal a single grape.

"I only wanted to return this grape to you," Feng Xiao said innocently. "But if you don't want it, I'll deal with it as I please."

He pinched the grape between thumb and index finger, crushing it to a pulp. It fell to the ground, and the wind carried the refuse away.

The second prince trembled violently behind his father.

Apa Khagan rose to his feet, his face solemn. He brushed aside the hand the Kuchean beauty had placed on his lap, left the table spread with fine wine and delicacies, and approached Feng Xiao.

Ade, behind him, was left exposed. His eyes darted left and right in panic before colliding with the first prince's. Prince Yixun was unusually calm. Compared to the second prince's fidgeting, he seemed to have a steady aura of leadership. Ade realized his mistake and gritted his teeth in silence. He slunk back to his seat and sat as if nothing had happened.

The assembly watched as Apa Khagan approached Feng Xiao—but the scene they'd expected, the blame and interrogation, didn't occur. A smile spread across Apa Khagan's face. "I never thought I'd witness such a magnificent battle today," he told Feng Xiao. "In the words of we Göktürks, you are a warrior blessed by the Wolf God, worthy of respect!"

Cui Buqu stepped forward and whispered a translation to Feng Xiao in Chinese.

Apa Khagan's smile was warm, even solicitous—a complete about-face from his previous aloof demeanor. Fo'er had been stronger than anyone in the khagan's court, and thus Apa Khagan had treated him with great respect. Not only did Fo'er enjoy the backing of the powerful Eastern Khaganate, he was the Khaganate's preeminent martial artist—the Göktürks admired might and bowed to the strong.

But now Feng Xiao had slain Fo'er. There was no question of who was stronger. Any of the Göktürks could reach this simple conclusion, let alone Apa Khagan. His complete transformation wasn't surprising. Nor did the khatun, the first prince, or the other Göktürk officials see anything amiss. After all, if Feng Xiao could fell Fo'er easily, who could stop him if he wished to kill everyone present? Perhaps some worried Ishbara would retaliate, but for Apa Khagan, a good relationship with the Sui envoys was more pressing.

He had to pick a side, and now it seemed there was no more need to agonize.

Feng Xiao's smile was so radiant everyone was dazzled at the sight of it. "Thank you kindly for your praise, Khagan. However, this man was the foremost Göktürk martial artist, as well as a trusted subordinate of Ishbara Khagan. Are you not worried Ishbara will be furious and lead his troops in annexing your lands?"

Apa Khagan tore his eyes away from Fo'er's corpse and gazed at the smiling Feng Xiao. A chill raced up his spine, and he drew his cloak tighter around him. "It was my honor to witness a battle between masters. Swords and blades have no allegiance," he said with a wry twist of his mouth. "Ishbara Khagan will surely understand."

With that he waved a hand, calling for the bodies of Fo'er and his deputy to be removed. Two Göktürk attendants hurried forward to drag off the corpses. The Göktürks placed no value on returning the dead to their homeland; Ishbara Khagan wouldn't be interested in collecting the bodies. Even the number one Göktürk expert received such treatment in death. It was a miserable sight.

Cui Buqu and Feng Xiao, however, felt no sorrow. To be soft on an enemy was to be harsh on oneself.

Apa Khagan returned to his seat to resume the conference as if two men hadn't just died in front of him. The other envoys were only too happy to play along—they called out praise for Feng Xiao's excellent martial arts, naming him peerless and unparalleled, compliments pouring from their mouths as if they were terrified to stop.

The martial contests weren't over, but no one was foolish enough to challenge Feng Xiao again. Apa Khagan allowed Feng Xiao to rest and urged two Göktürks to enter a wrestling match on the field, much to the appreciation of the crowd.

Yixun made his way over to personally offer a toast. Apa Khagan smiled and watched without intervening, waving away the Kuchean beauty and summoning Jinlian to his side. Khagan and khatun spoke in low voices as he listened attentively to her account of the hardships she'd suffered on her journey to the Central Plains.

When the second prince timidly tugged at his father's sleeve, the khagan's face turned stormy. He turned to scold him, and the prince quickly retreated, looking wretched. It seemed he, too, faced a reckoning.

In a single moment, everything had changed.

Those who'd supported the Eastern Khaganate or been fearful of offending Fo'er now all stood to offer toasts to the Sui envoys. The ones who spoke some Chinese dropped a few witticisms, while those who didn't flocked over to flatter Cui Buqu in Turkic.

They had no notion of Feng Xiao's repute in the Central Plains; in fact, they'd never heard of him before today. But Fo'er was famous in the Western Regions; everyone knew his name. Personally witnessing the death of such a figure was a brutal shock. It was not only the people of the Central Plains who knew how to read the skies. It was human nature to seek benefit and minimize loss. The Sui dynasty loomed large over the land, and now Feng Xiao had killed Fo'er. The crowd removed the final feather, and the balance in their hearts tipped straight away. The once-swaying scale stabilized, and they came to their decision.

Apa Khagan had spoken just a few words, but everyone had seen him reprimand the second prince. He was sure to seek out Cui Buqu's party by tonight at latest. Although an alliance wasn't yet set in stone, it was increasingly likely. Cui Buqu finally breathed a sigh of relief.

"I've made great contributions this time, Daoist Master Cui. Don't you have anything to say?" asked Feng Xiao, the picture of composure at his side.

"Hm?" Cui Buqu looked at him, bewildered. "Do we not work for the glory of the court, and to relieve the emperor's mind of worries?"

Cui Buqu had already sent Qiao Xian back to her yurt to treat her injuries, or she'd certainly have been sneering at Feng Xiao by now.

"Ha, don't try that with me." The corners of Feng Xiao's mouth twitched. He recalled his first meeting with this man at Zixia Temple, his face devoid of emotion amid the curling incense smoke. Those worshippers had never imagined their Daoist Master Cui, so kind and gentle, so detached from secular affairs, was in fact a shameless ingrate with skin thicker than the Great Wall.

"I had to seal my meridians to kill Fo'er just now. My qi and blood are suffering backflow, and my true qi is circulating in reverse. I've exacerbated my injuries and extended my recovery to half a month. What complications I may suffer in the future are unknown—I've never used this method before." Feng Xiao didn't shout; he whispered rapidly into Cui Buqu's ear: "Without me here, even your silver tongue couldn't have softened up these barbarians, could it?"

There was the thinnest sliver of distance between them. Feng Xiao's breath fanned Cui Buqu's ear as he spoke, yet Cui Buqu remained as immobile as a mountain, as if to say, *Complain all you like; even the sky crashing down wouldn't move me.* Feng Xiao's gaze caught on that ear.

It was very fair.

It looked soft, too. *I wonder how pinching it would feel?*

He found his hands were faster than his brain: the instant he thought it, his fingertips were already squeezing Cui Buqu's earlobe.

Cui Buqu started. He's never expected Feng Xiao would do such a thing, and instinctively moved to shake him off. But Feng Xiao seemed to anticipate this too; his hand landed on Cui Buqu's back, preventing him from pulling away.

"Let go!" Cui Buqu's voice was icy enough to summon a hailstorm.

After rubbing his earlobe twice, Feng Xiao found it was as soft as he'd imagined. It was rather like an osmanthus cake, just without any osmanthus scent—though perhaps the smell of medicine from Cui Buqu's body could be considered a fragrance of its own. Satisfied, he released him.

Cui Buqu leveled him with a baffled look. "Has it been too long since Deputy Chief Feng enjoyed the company of a beautiful woman?" he asked coldly. "Allow me to inquire with the khagan. I trust the beauties of Suyab would be overjoyed to spend a night with you if that's what you want."

"I want to eat osmanthus cakes," replied Feng Xiao nonsensically.

Cui Buqu was beginning to suspect Fo'er had beaten Feng Xiao stupid. "Are you all right?"

Feng Xiao smiled in silence.

These two were members of the same party; if they acted more familiar than normal, no one thought much of it. But the first prince, who had made his way over hoping to befriend them and offer another toast, had a very different impression of this scene.

He sighed. "I envy you both, truly. You're in a foreign land, so you can do as you please!"

Recalling the nonsense he'd fed this prince yesterday, Cui Buqu laughed dryly and said no more.

Yet Feng Xiao seemed to have found Cui Buqu's weakness. If he let the opportunity slip, when would such a chance come again? He smoothly moved to pinch Cui Buqu's ear a second time. His fingers were incredibly quick; before Cui Buqu could react, Feng Xiao had already let go. He smiled at the first prince. "We appreciate your understanding."

The first prince gave him a knowing look. "I do understand, I really do!"

What do you think you understand? thought Cui Buqu, watching him walk off.

He jabbed an elbow into Feng Xiao's gut and felt him inhale sharply, then stood, thinking to stop the first prince but with no idea what to say.

Feng Xiao chuckled. "You dug this hole yourself, you know. Even if you cry, you have to jump into it."

Jinlian's standing had changed again.

Most obviously, Apa Khagan's attitude toward her was warm, just as it had been before her long journey—as if nothing had intervened. The Kuchean beauty was no more than a lovely trinket, and the only woman fit to stand beside the khagan was her once more.

The change had occurred the moment Feng Xiao killed Fo'er; Jinlian had no illusion about this. She didn't burn her bridges by ignoring Cui Buqu and his group. After speaking to Apa Khagan, she eagerly ran back to Cui Buqu's yurt and shared the news: after tonight's banquet, Apa Khagan would summon him to discuss an alliance with Sui.

"We killed Fo'er. Isn't he worried at all that Ishbara will respond?" Cui Buqu asked. On the other side of the yurt, Feng Xiao and Qiao Xian's eyes were closed in repose, undisturbed by their conversation.

Jinlian shook her head. "He must think he needn't fear Ishbara with the Sui dynasty's power behind him, no?"

Cui Buqu's expression turned pensive.

"Is something still bothering you?" Jinlian asked curiously. "Better to ally with the Sui dynasty than kneel to Ishbara. The Eastern Khaganate has the greater appetite; a wise man knows how to choose.

Now that you've made the decision a simple one, he should no longer hesitate."

What she said made sense. Cui Buqu didn't refute her or say what had bothered him. Yet it was precisely this inability to put his concerns into words that made him all the more uneasy.

✵✿✵

Night descended, and a banquet even grander than the previous night's was in full swing within the royal yurt.

Last night, the khagan had been entangled with a beautiful woman in his yurt and failed to attend—but tonight was different. When the khagan appeared, it was in lavish dress, with both khatuns and the first prince as well as a retinue of Göktürk officials and aristocrats. The air buzzed with pomp and excitement.

Only the second prince had yet to arrive.

But this wasn't strange either. He had tried every possible means of dragging Cui Buqu down, only for all to backfire. Prince Ade was a proud man; he was sure to be deeply unhappy, and it would surprise no one if he was late or absent entirely. Still, Apa Khagan was displeased and sent an attendant to urge the second prince along.

After three rounds of toasts, the guests were quite drunk. Wine lubricated thoughts and tongues, and the atmosphere grew increasingly casual. Feng Xiao was injured, so he had abstained, instead drinking a local refreshment made from crushed fruit, with a sour flavor that complemented the roasted lamb.

The banquet guests came over to toast them in turns; even Apa Khagan personally walked over with a cup of wine. It was difficult to refuse such boundless hospitality—though he was drinking a fruit cordial and not wine, Feng Xiao still had a bit too much and began to feel uncomfortable. He excused himself with a word to Cui Buqu, then stepped out to walk back to their yurt for a rest.

The breeze outside was cool and gentle. Warm firelight glowed in the distance, but around him all was black. A hand, smooth and tender, emerged from the darkness and soundlessly brushed his waist.

77

FENG XIAO STRUCK out like lightning and grabbed the stranger's wrist.

There was a gasp of surprise, and a soft body fell limply into his arms. A fragile hand, a pliant and delicate figure, a voice that dripped with seductive charm—it was enough to melt the hearts of the vast majority of men.

Feng Xiao was not the vast majority.

What was Apa Khagan's newest favorite doing out here in dark trying to seduce an envoy of the Sui dynasty? If word spread, they could look forward to navigating another series of stormy waves before they forged any alliance.

Feng Xiao released her wrist and took two steps back. Caught off guard, the beauty fell to the ground with a soft cry of pain.

"Who sent you?" Feng Xiao crouched and grabbed her chin. His hand was gentle, yet she was unable to break free.

"This concubine...admires the gentleman's grace." It seemed the Kuchean beauty could speak some Chinese, her slightly accented syllables lending her words a touch of the exotic.

"Are you not afraid of losing your head if the khagan discovers you?" asked Feng Xiao with obvious amusement.

The beauty had opened her mouth to speak when she found her acupoint had been struck, rendering her mute. Pain shot through her chin, so sharp her eyes brimmed charmingly with tears. How unfortunate that they were out of reach of the lamplight, and no one could witness her loveliness.

"Let me guess: someone told you to cling to me, then cry out and draw attention?"

Still mute, the beauty could only shake her head desperately as tears streamed down her soft cheeks. She wanted to protest that she really did fancy him, but Feng Xiao gave her no chance to do so. He grabbed a handful of her luxurious hair and dragged her straight to the royal yurt, showing not a shred of tenderness toward the fairer sex.

As they stepped into the light, Feng Xiao caught sight of a sudden uproar opposite the royal yurt. Firelight quickly gathered there, accompanied by shouts and screams. It took him seconds to realize the commotion was coming from the second prince's yurt. He watched as attendants fled from Ade's residence to the royal yurt, pale and stumbling in their panic. This was no small disturbance.

Feng Xiao gave the beauty a tap, and she crumpled limply to the ground.

Moments ago, the khagan's yurt had been a scene of singing and dancing. Jinlian had lost her glum aura of the past few days; her expression now was one of rare ease. She'd traveled thousands of miles to the Central Plains and braved every sort of hardship to bring the Sui envoys to her homeland. What she'd sought was not simply an elevation in her status but an increase in prestige and the accompanying right to speak. The greater khatun yet lived, and the first prince was her son—her position was stable and immovable. Jinlian's position was more precarious; all she could do was attempt to boost her importance by gathering power into her hands, with the hope of more in the future. It was for this she'd hitched her wagon to the star that was the Sui dynasty and Cui Buqu. She wasn't easily swayed from her course.

Fo'er was dead, but it would take time for the news to reach Ishbara. Even if Ishbara retaliated, the alliance would be a settled thing; his aggression wouldn't change the fundamentals. As for the second prince, after the latest incident, he wouldn't dare cause any trouble while Cui Buqu was still here...

A Göktürk guard burst into the yurt, interrupting her thoughts. He'd completely forgotten to announce his arrival. Everyone started, but no one scolded him—they stared at his sweat-smeared face as he shouted, "Khagan! The second prince is dead!"

Jinlian blanched.

Apa Khagan leapt up, ignoring the grape wine that spattered over his clothes. He shoved the maid attending him aside and strode vigorously out of the yurt.

Bewildered, the guests followed in his wake, all the way to Ade's yurt.

A physician from the royal yurt was already there, a Göktürk man with some knowledge of Central Plains medicine. He examined the motionless second prince, then shook his head—there was nothing he could do.

Apa Khagan raged. "He couldn't just die like that! Save him, quickly!"

He refused to believe his own son was dead. Even Yixun was stunned: his brother had been bouncing up and down mere hours ago, causing every kind of mischief.

The Göktürk physician knelt on the ground, trembling. "The second prince has no external injuries, yet there's no smell of alcohol either. Perhaps he consumed some poison..."

Though the Göktürk court lacked the sophisticated measures of the Central Plains' imperial palaces, it was still no easy feat to poison an aristocrat. If someone had poisoned the second prince, then Apa Khagan, too, was in danger.

Heartbroken over his son's death and fearing for his own life, the khagan furiously ordered the banquet suspended and all guests detained. While everyone stood shocked, the khagan's guards surrounded the prince's residence, preventing any entry or exit.

With Apa Khagan's baleful glare boring holes into him, the doctor steeled himself and called his apprentice over to continue examining Ade's body. As he worked, the prince's personal maid explained his whereabouts before his death.

Prince Ade had been humiliated today, and Fo'er was dead; he was in no mood to attend the evening banquet. Even so, he was unwilling to let his brother steal the spotlight. He'd dawdled in his yurt, snapping at the maids for poor service. After whipping them, he'd sent them all away. The maids had waited and waited, but when the banquet began, they couldn't tarry any longer. They risked another beating and headed back inside to fetch him.

The lights had all been extinguished. Half of them had been knocked over in the prince's rage; they'd heard him cursing and throwing objects as they waited outside. When they finally relit the lamps, they saw the second prince lying motionless on the ground.

It might have been reasonable to assume he'd fallen asleep from exhaustion after throwing his tantrum—but he'd never been in the habit of sleeping with his eyes open. The maids had rushed forward, only to find the prince was no longer breathing.

The crowd listened as the maid stammered through her report. Many, in their hearts, wondered if he mightn't have been so angry he died of it. But at that moment, the physician's apprentice shouted, "Here! There's something on the second prince's head!"

Apa Khagan strode forward and watched as the two men heaved the prince's corpse into a sitting position. He brushed aside his son's hair to expose the tip of an iron needle.

The needle had been inserted deep into the Baihui acupoint on the crown of the prince's skull—no amount of strength could yank it out. Clearly this was the cause of the second prince's death, but it wasn't something any ordinary person could pull off. Ade, while not a master, knew some martial arts, and there were additional guards outside the yurt. Yet someone had slipped inside with no one the wiser, killed the second prince without a sound, and vanished. They had to be an expert among experts.

Jinlian thought herself decently skilled, but killing Ade without alerting anyone was beyond her abilities. Across the entire Western Khaganate, there might be no one capable of such a feat. There was one person here today, however, who certainly was.

She shivered. A chill crept over her heart, spreading up her chest and throat, permeating her very breath. This smelled of a conspiracy.

Jinlian wasn't the only one with this thought. A Göktürk aristocrat exclaimed, "The Sui envoy! The envoy with incredible martial arts! He's disappeared!"

Jinlian glanced in Cui Buqu's direction. Sensing her gaze, he raised his eyes to meet it. Cui Buqu's face was half-cloaked in shadow, his expression impossible to make out.

Apa Khagan didn't look at Cui Buqu at all before shouting, "Find him! *Now!*"

"Looking for me?"

Feng Xiao pushed aside the crowd and stepped into view. He remained cool as ever, as if unaware of the many eyes upon him.

Apa Khagan's face darkened. "Where have you been?"

Even now he remembered Feng Xiao's martial arts skills and didn't rashly order for him to be arrested.

Feng Xiao listened as Cui Buqu translated the khagan's words into Chinese. "I excused myself early and went back to rest. I heard the commotion over here and came out to take a look."

He made no mention of the incident with the Kuchean beauty, which would only enrage Apa Khagan further. The young woman would deny it to the end; he'd only be digging his own grave.

"What do you have to say about Ade's death?" Apa Khagan asked coldly.

Feng Xiao shrugged. "I bear the second prince no grudge. His death is a tragedy. Besides that, what can I say?"

Apa Khagan turned to his servants: "Call Liu Sigu here."

Feng Xiao had no idea who this was. He stood calm and unmoving as the banquet guests around him were ushered away and replaced with a group of Göktürk warriors.

"Khagan," Jinlian pleaded, "the Sui dynasty is ready to form an alliance with us. What reason does he have to kill Ade? Someone has framed him—"

The khagan raised a hand to silence her.

The servants returned in short order with Liu Sigu. Apa Khagan again addressed Feng Xiao. "Do you know who he is?"

Feng Xiao shook his head.

"The Black Moon Shaman's apprentice. On the night of the shaman's death, he saw you sneak into his house with his own two eyes!" Apa Khagan sneered. "Know this, envoys of Sui. The shaman's death was suspicious. I've known of this since yesterday but was willing to overlook it for the sake of peace between our nations. No one said anything, and we were willing to believe you. But after Ade's death today, my eyes are opened! You came here to destroy my Western Khaganate! You killed Fo'er, spoiling our alliance with Ishbara. You left us without any other option, then killed the shaman and Ade. Whom will you murder next? Me?!"

The crowd gaped in shock. Even Jinlian looked back and forth between Cui Buqu and Feng Xiao, her expression one of alarm.

Cui Buqu's brow wrinkled slightly, but Feng Xiao remained calm. "I had nothing to do with the deaths of the second prince or your shaman. If I wished to destroy the Western Khaganate, I could kill you where you stand. Why practice such subterfuge and kill so many unrelated persons?"

"Who knows! I've long said the Hans can't be trusted!" yelled a voice from the crowd. Once the first stone was cast, an uproar quickly followed.

"That's right, the Hans are a malicious breed! They want nothing more than to see us Göktürks fight among ourselves!"

"They murdered the shaman and the second prince. Who's to say they haven't already made an attempt on the khagan's life, and he was fortunate enough to escape!"

"Kill them!"

"Kill the Hans!"

Jinlian's sweat had almost soaked through her clothes, the fabric sticking to her back. Apa Khagan's face was like a thundercloud as he glared at Feng Xiao. The first prince's mouth was agape; he'd yet to fully understand what was going on.

Not everyone present had been an ally of the second prince. But in the heat of the moment, the conservative factions reared their heads as one, urging the furious khagan to execute the two envoys.

Feng Xiao was a powerful martial artist; everyone here feared him. But he was a single man—there was only so much he could do against this many. Experts were thick on the ground in the khagan's court. Perhaps he could escape alone, but there was also Cui Buqu and Qiao Xian, and Qiao Xian was injured. The chances of all three of them leaving unharmed were vanishingly small.

But what choice did Feng Xiao have?

The Göktürk warriors approached step by step, surrounding them in a solid wall. The khagan had only to give the command, and countless sabers would slash down. In that moment, Cui Buqu, who didn't know a lick of martial arts, would become a burden to Feng Xiao regardless of his peerless intelligence.

The two gazed at each other from afar.

Feng Xiao couldn't see Cui Buqu's expression clearly, and Cui Buqu had no idea what Feng Xiao was thinking. He didn't know what Feng Xiao would choose—but he'd decided what he himself would do. He didn't speak loudly, but it was enough to cut through the din of voices.

"Wait," said Cui Buqu.

THE STORY CONTINUES IN
Peerless
VOLUME 3

APPENDIX

Character &
Name Guide

HISTORICAL PERIOD

Peerless is set in the first era of the Sui dynasty, Kaihuang. Emperor Wen of Sui (given name Yang Jian) established his dynasty in 581 AD after usurping the throne from the previous Zhou dynasty. Though Sui was a short-lived dynasty that eventually fell apart in the hands of his son, Emperor Yang, Emperor Wen is viewed as one of the most influential emperors of ancient China, both for his prosperous rule and for the reunification of the Central Plains after over two hundred years of war and turmoil.

CHARACTERS

FENG XIAO ("HIGH HEAVENS"): Deputy Chief of the Jiejian Bureau

CUI BUQU 崔不去 ("I WON'T GO"): Chief of the Zuoyue Bureau

JIEJIAN BUREAU

PEI JINGZHE 裴惊蛰: Feng Xiao's beleaguered assistant at the Jiejian Bureau.

ZUOYUE BUREAU

QIAO XIAN 乔仙: Member of the Zuoyue Bureau

ZHANGSUN BODHI 长孙菩提: Deputy Chief of the Zuoyue Bureau

HEHUAN SECT

BING XIAN 冰弦: A favored disciple of Hehuan Sect.

SUI IMPERIAL COURT

YANG JIAN 杨坚: Emperor Wen of Sui, the first emperor of the Sui dynasty.

DUGU QIELUO 独孤伽罗: Empress Wenxian

YUXIU 玉秀: A trusted consultant of Yang Guang, the Prince of Jin.

CITY OF QIEMO

DUAN QIHU 段栖鹄: A former bandit and one of the three great powers of Qiemo.

GAO YI 高懿: The country magistrate of Qiemo and one of the three great powers.

XING MAO 兴茂: A descendant of the destroyed Kingdom of Shanshan's royal family. One of Qiemo's three great powers.

GÖKTÜRK KHAGANATE

FO'ER 佛耳: The foremost martial artist of the Göktürk Khaganate, who pledges loyalty to Ishbara Khagan of the Eastern Göktürk Khaganate.

JINLIAN 金莲: Apa Khagan's lesser khatun, who arrived in Sui as an envoy, hoping for an alliance.

APA KHAGAN 阿波可汗: The ruler of the Western Göktürk Khaganate.

PRINCE ADE 阿德: The second prince of the Western Göktürk Khaganate, and the younger son of Apa Khagan.

PRINCE YIXUN 伊旬: The first prince of the Western Göktürk Khaganate, and the eldest son of Apa Khagan and the greater khatun.

GOGURYEO

GO NYEONG 高宁: A martial artist who shows up in search of the Jade of Heaven Lake.

NAMES, HONORIFICS, & TITLES

Diminutives, Nicknames, and Name Tags

A-: Friendly diminutive. Always a prefix. Usually for monosyllabic names, or one syllable out of a two-syllable name.

DA-: A character meaning "eldest." Can be used as a prefix.

-ER: Usually a character meaning "child." When added to a name as a suffix, it expresses affection. However, Feng Xiao's nickname, "Feng-er," uses a different character that means "second." Thus, in *Peerless*, "Feng-er" is an abbreviated way of saying "Deputy Bureau Chief Feng Xiao."

XIAO-: A character meaning "small" or "youngest." When added to a name as a prefix, it expresses affection.

Courtesy Addresses

GONGZI: A respectful address for young men, originally only for those from affluent households. Though appropriate in all formal occasions, it's often preferred when the addressee outranks the speaker.

LANG: A general term for "man." Can be used to politely address a man by pairing it with other characters that denote his place within a certain household. For example, "dalang," "erlang," and "sanlang" mean "eldest son," "second son," and "third son" respectively. "Langjun" is a polite address for any man, similar to "gentleman."

NIANG: A general term for "woman," which can be appended as a suffix. Follows the same pairing rules as "lang." "Niangzi" is a variant that can be used alone to address any woman, similar to "lady."

SHIDI: Younger martial brother, used to refer to younger disciples of the same generation.

XIANDI: A respectful address for a younger man.

XIANSHENG: A polite address for men, originally only for those of great learning or those who had made significant contributions to society. Sometimes seen as an equivalent to "Mr." in English.

XIONG: A word meaning "elder brother." It can be attached as a suffix to address an unrelated male peer.

APPENDIX

Glossary

GLOSSARY

CONCUBINES: In ancient China, it was common practice for a wealthy man to take women as concubines in addition to his wife. They were expected to live with him and bear him children. Generally speaking, a greater number of concubines correlated to higher social status, hence a wealthy merchant might have two or three concubines, while an emperor might have tens or even a hundred.

CUT-SLEEVE: A slang term for a gay man, which comes from a tale about Emperor Ai's love for, and relationship with, his male court official in the Han dynasty. The emperor was called to the morning assembly, but his lover was asleep on his robe. Rather than wake him, the emperor cut off his own sleeve.

INTERNAL CULTIVATION: Internal cultivation or neigong (内功) refers to the breathing, qi, and meditation practices a martial artist must undertake in order to properly harness and utilize their "outer cultivation" of combat techniques and footwork.

JIANGHU: A staple of wuxia, the jianghu (江湖 / "rivers and lakes") describes the greater underground society of martial artists and associates that spans the entire setting. Members of the jianghu self-govern and settle issues among themselves based on the tenets of strength and honor, though this may not stop them from exerting influence over conventional society too.

KING YAMA: King of Hell or the supreme judge of the underworld. His role in the underworld is to pass judgment on the dead, sending souls on to their next life depending on the karma they accrued from their last one.

NINE-RANK SYSTEM: During the Sui dynasty, officials were divided into ranks that denoted their status within the court. First rank was highest, ninth rank the lowest. Courtesy demanded that lower-rank officials show appropriate respect to those ranked above them.

QINGGONG: A real-life training discipline. In wuxia, the feats of qinggong (轻功 / "lightness technique") are highly exaggerated, allowing practitioners to glide through the air, run straight up walls and over water, jump through trees, or travel dozens of steps in an instant.

SWORD GLARE: Jianguang (剑光 / "sword light"), an energy attack released from a sword's edge, often seen in wuxia and xianxia stories.

TRADITIONAL CHINESE MEDICINE: Traditional medical practices in China are commonly based around the idea that qi, or vital energy, circulates in the body through channels called meridians similarly to how blood flows through the circulatory system. Acupuncture points, or acupoints, are special nodes, most of which lie along the meridians. Stimulating them by massage, acupuncture, or other methods is believed to affect the flow of qi and can be used for healing—or in wuxia, to render someone unconscious.

Another central concept in traditional Chinese medicine is that disease arises from an imbalance of elements in the body caused by disharmony in internal functions. For example, an excess of internal heat can cause symptoms such as fever, thirst, insomnia, and redness of the face. Excess internal heat can be treated with the consumption of foods with cooling properties, such as lotus tea.

TRUE QI: True qi (真气) is a more precise term for "qi," one's lifeforce and the energy in all living things. True qi is refined in the lower dantian (丹田 / "elixir field") within the abdomen, which also holds the foundations of a person's martial arts, especially their internal cultivation.

In wuxia, a practitioner with superb internal cultivation can perform superhuman feats with their true qi. On top of what is covered under internal cultivation above, martial artists can channel true qi into swords to generate sword qi, imbue simple movements and objects with destructive energy, project their voices across great distances, heal lesser injuries, or enhance the five senses.

YIN ENERGY AND YANG ENERGY: Yin and yang is a concept in Chinese philosophy that describes the complementary interdependence of opposite and contrary forces. It can be applied to all forms of change and difference. Yang represents the sun, masculinity, and the living, while yin represents the shadows, femininity, and the dead, including spirits and ghosts. In fiction, imbalances between yin and yang energy may do serious harm to the body or act as the driving force for malevolent spirits seeking to replenish whichever energy they lack.

ZITHER: Also called a guqin, or qin, a zither is a stringed instrument, played by plucking with the fingers. It is fairly large and is meant to be laid flat on a surface or on one's lap while playing.

ABOUT THE AUTHOR
MENG XI SHI

Meng Xi Shi is a renowned web author whose works of fiction combine detailed research with witty writing, winning the hearts of readers around the world. Her works are published in China by Jingjiang Literature City. She goes by "Meng Xi Shi Ya" on Weibo.

Yan Wushi, leader of the demonic Huanyue sect, is a master cultivator, a brilliant strategist, and an incurable cynic. In his philosophy, every human heart is ruled by cruelty and selfishness. Anyone who believes otherwise is either a liar or a fool.

Enter the humble Shen Qiao, leader of the Daoist sect at Xuandu Mountain. He is both gracious and charitable, and exactly the type of do-gooder that Yan Wushi despises.

When Shen Qiao suffers a shocking loss in a duel and is left for dead, Yan Wushi happens upon him and concocts a plan to teach him about the wretchedness of humanity. He'll take Shen Qiao under his wing, test the limits of his faith, and lure him into demonic cultivation. After all, it is easy to remain righteous atop a mountain peak that touches the heavens. But a thousand autumns toiling on the blood-soaked earth will break any man.

*Available Now in Print and Digital
from Seven Seas Entertainment!*

FROM THE *USA TODAY* BESTSELLING AUTHOR
MENG XI SHI

Thousand Autumns

QIAN QIU